BY THE DARK
OF HER EYES

BY THE DARK OF HER EYES

by
Cameron MacElvee

2016

Credits
Editor: Ruth Sternglantz
Production Design: Susan Ramundo
Cover Design By Jeanine Henning

Acknowledgments

I want to express my appreciation to Bold Strokes Books and Len Barot for providing writers like me an opportunity to tell our stories and reach a wider audience. I was blessed to have the opportunity to work with Ruth Sternglantz, my editor, who provided me not only mentoring in the art and craft of storytelling, but also a keen eye in revising and editing. Thanks also to Jeanine Henning who far exceeded my expectations and created a remarkable cover that blows my mind each time I look at it. To the rest of the team and staff at Bold Strokes, each of you has been welcoming and supportive from day one. Thank you for your kindness.

I want to thank Judy Worman at The Professor's Pen for cleaning up the initial rough draft and helping me prepare it for submission. I also want to acknowledge Erin Vinton at Symmetry Language Services who edited the Spanish and confirmed the cultural nuances of the characters and their worldview. I must also recognize and thank Professor Laura Ruiz-Scott, my colleague at Scottsdale Community College, who worked with me on the initial Spanish phrasing. Others of my SCC colleagues supported and guided me in my process as well. I thank professors Jared Aragona, Darrell Copp, Sandra Desjardins, Julie Knapp, Ann McCage, Rhonda McDonnell, Susan Moore, and Suzette Schlapkohl for their encouragement and faith in the story and its themes.

I was fortunate to make the acquaintance and friendship of Jacky Abromitis at LesFan. She encouraged me to write creative fiction and provided me a platform to reach readers worldwide. Many of those readers have become dear and important people in my life and have cheered me along the way. My heartfelt thanks goes to my friends Nadine Ausbie, Mary Basso, Lai Leng Boon, Bess Carrick, Sue Edwards, Bella and Karla Hauersperger, Michelle Karel-Ward, Bonny McKnight, Teri Palinkas, Tirza Rusland, and Doris Stubblefield. I know several more loyal readers followed this story; more than I can name. Still, I want you all to know the book you're now holding in your hands is a result of your encouragements.

In addition, I am deeply grateful to Lodeerca whose wit and wisdom inspires and uplifts me. You are a rare gift, my friend. Thank you for believing. Also, to Lynette Crockett, my best friend for over three decades and who has never allowed me to give up or give in, thank you for encouraging me to write from the heart.

And finally, the greater part of my gratitude rightfully goes to my partner, Taime Bengochea, and our daughter, Eleanor Rose. You two have borne the burden of my physical and sometimes emotional absence while I shut myself away to write this story. Thank you for your patience, your care, and your love. This book is for you, first and foremost.

Dedication

In memory of Helen Kathleen Rose O'Hara.

May you rest in the hollow of her mantle and in the crossing of her arms until we are together again.

PROLOGUE

Grapefruit in various stages of rot covered the ground. They caused his boots to slide as he ran and sent him to his knees. The sweet smell of decaying fruit mixed with the scent of damp earth and desert air, and he gagged each time he fell facedown into the putrid mess. But he got up each time and continued to plunge through the forest of citrus trees while branches tore at his clothes and he waved his pistol above his head. He dodged among trees, leapt over gnarled roots, and crawled through irrigation channels. All the while he sobbed, muttered curses, and glanced back from where he'd come.

But she hadn't followed him.

The farther he ventured into the grove, however, the rotting fruit on the ground only grew thicker, for there'd been no one to pick the harvest that season or the last. When he fell again, dropping his pistol then fumbling to retrieve it, he finally gave up running and hugged his knees and wept. A full moon shone high in the sky, but he was entombed and hidden among the trees. He might be safe from her. Perhaps she'd yet to find a way to venture past the house.

As he began to regain his composure, a campfire sparked to life in front of him. The family gathered in a semicircle with their faces hidden in the shadows, only their soiled clothes and bodies visible.

He howled and waved his pistol. "Fuck you! Fuck all you goddamn spics to hell."

An old woman in a faded red skirt stepped away from the family toward him. The mantle of her black shawl around her head hid her face.

He stared at her and swallowed. "This is my land, my trees, my fruit."

She pulled a ripe grapefruit from a low-hanging branch and held it out to him. "Sí, jefe. The fruit, she is all yours." She split it open between her arthritic hands and held out the two pieces. They dripped with blood and maggots. "But vengeance, señor, is ours. Nuestra venganza."

As the others began to chant, "Venganza, venganza, venganza," the old woman's shawl fell away and revealed the face of Death.

He tore at his ears, screamed, and brought his pistol under his chin. For one beat he glared into her empty eye sockets before grimacing and pulling the trigger.

❖

At the upstairs window, she looked across the dark grove. The flame from the oil lamp she held in her hand sputtered, casting the shadow of her long black hair against the gravel drive below. She'd seen the campfire in the distance, heard the gunshot, and watched as the firelight winked out once again. Trapped here in the house, she couldn't reach her family, but at least he was dead. It was a start. Perhaps now the others would listen to her and help her find her son and end this nightmare. And if they would not listen, she would make them pay as well.

She would have her revenge.

Chapter One

Numbers in black-and-white print lay aligned in a list next to a shaded pie chart showing the various investments and their proportions to the total amount. It was an amount Brenna couldn't comprehend, all those zeros, abstract and empty. She was wealthy, incredibly and obscenely wealthy, but there was no joy for her in this revelation.

"I had no idea Edward had invested this much." She looked at the paperwork on the desk.

"Take some comfort in the fact he'd always intended to provide for you and Michael," said Stan Thomas, the family lawyer.

She pushed the documents away. "Yes, for Michael."

"And you."

She squirmed, knowing she didn't deserve her late husband's accumulated wealth. She glanced at Thomas and saw the pity in his eyes, the uncomfortable smile. She understood how hard it was for people to know what to say to her even these many months after Edward's and Michael's deaths. And as she diverted her eyes from his sympathetic gaze, she squirmed again knowing if he knew the truth, he'd think much less of her.

Thomas shifted in his chair. "Brenna, as Edward Wilson's wife and widow, you're entitled to his estate. He has no other living relatives. The house, the bank accounts, the investments, and the real estate belong to you now. Realize what this means to you."

She ground her teeth together, forcing the shame, bubbling beneath her grief, to retreat.

"Understand with this amount of wealth, you're free to start over," he said. "You can sell the house, move out of Davenport, and travel the world. In fact, if you monitor the investments correctly, you won't have a worry for the rest of your life."

She considered this. "You're right. I've been thinking about getting out of town. I haven't been anywhere since high school when I went on my senior trip to Chicago. Leaving Davenport may be what I need." She smiled, but she knew she was faking it. It was the same phony smile she'd learned to don in the last six months, two weeks, and three days. The smile put people at ease, made them think she was working through her grief, made them leave her alone. But more important, it covered the shame and rage that twisted inside her.

"I'm glad you're thinking of moving on," he said. "I know these last months have been hell on you."

She gritted her teeth once more. She hated when people pretended to understand.

Thomas pulled a portfolio from the pile of documents on his desk. "This lists all his investments, his stocks and bonds, the certificates of deposit as well as the real estate. Here's the card of his investment advisor. I'd suggest you give him the go-ahead to manage all of the accounts for you and determine the particulars for a monthly income."

Brenna brought the portfolio into her lap and began flipping through the various sections. When she turned to the real estate portion, she studied each of the cover sheets for the properties Edward had purchased.

"He had property in Arkansas? I guess because of his parents," she said. "And Florida. He'd wanted to retire there, I know." She stopped at a page. "What's this? Poulsen Citrus Grove? Way out in Arizona?"

"If I recall, he'd invested in some acreage out there. The speculation was the housing market would recover sooner than later, and he'd hoped to sell the land to one of the large new-home contractors for three times the amount he'd invested."

"No kidding." She paged through that section of the portfolio scanning the photos, maps, and zoning diagrams. "Edward hated the desert heat. I wonder if he even bothered to visit or invested blindly."

"Yes, he went to Arizona. In fact, at least three times I'm aware of. A few months before the accident, he'd talked to me about finding a way to dump that particular property. I guess there've been some issues with the original owners. I'm not sure of the particulars."

She came to a picture of a two-story house with a large covered porch. "There's a home on the property?"

"Apparently, but I doubt it's been occupied for some time."

"Why's that?" She examined the picture. The house, stucco and frame, resembled many of the farmhouses which dotted the Iowa countryside. It was quaint and traditional, and the second-story windows along with the covered porch reminded her of her grandparents' home she'd visited as a little girl. Something about it, the two blank windows over the large porch, like a face, a sad and lonely face. The house looked inviting in a strange sort of way.

Thomas came around to look over her shoulder, turned to the introductory page for the property, and slipped out a business card from the clear-plastic divider. "Here's the broker Edward was working with. Give her a call, she can give you more information on the property."

Brenna took the card. "I wouldn't mind taking a look at the house in person."

"All the way to Arizona? I guess it's a lot warmer than Davenport this time of year. It may do you some good to leave the cold and be in the sunshine for a while." He patted her shoulder.

Brenna slipped the business card back into the portfolio and said, "I could use some sunshine."

❖

She sat on the bed in her sister's guest room, where she'd been living for the last six and a half months. Next to her, a filled suitcase lay open, waiting for the last item, which she held in her hands. It was a wooden music box with a decoupage image of a smiling sun, and it played the tune "You Are My Sunshine." She'd given it to her son, Michael, when he'd been a baby, and she'd wound it often to play it while he'd fallen asleep in her arms. When he'd wake in the middle of the night from a scary dream, she'd hold him and play it again, soothing him with the comforting melody. But since his death, she'd kept the box by her bedside in her sister's home, never once opening it and listening to the song. She hadn't had the courage yet. She ran her thumb over the image of the sun, touched the copper dial, which wound the instrument, and finally stuffed it in the middle of her suitcase alongside a framed photo of her husband and little boy. She was about to close it and head downstairs when her sister knocked and entered the room.

"Bill brought in the mail. You have a card from Debra. Look, postmarked all the way from Nairobi. Pretty stamp." Jessica held out the envelope.

"You emailed her, didn't you? Told her about what happened?" Brenna asked.

"No, Brenna, I didn't. But I'm sure someone from church did." Jessica glanced at the suitcase. "You've packed a lot in your van for only a few weeks. And now this suitcase? I don't understand. Can't you fly to Arizona and rent a car? It looks as though you're moving there, for heaven's sake."

Brenna swallowed to keep her voice from coming out short and hateful. "I told you, Jess. I'm going to look into remodeling the house. The broker Edward worked with told me it's quite old, built in 1910. It would make a nice historical restoration."

"You aren't planning on staying in Arizona to see about restoring the place," Jessica said.

Brenna set her jaw and glared at her.

"And how long will that take?"

Brenna didn't answer.

"But you don't know anyone out there. You'll be alone. All alone."

Brenna swallowed again and tapped her unopened mail against her thigh. "I am alone." And it was a true statement, she knew.

Jessica covered her mouth while she shook her head. When she spoke, her voice faltered. "Sister, you've never been alone."

Brenna looked away.

"Seeing you like this tears me up inside, Brenna. You need to talk to me. Why won't you talk to me?" Jessica began to cry.

But Brenna wouldn't look at her. She doubted Jessica could handle the truth.

"When you were little," Jessica said, "and Mom and Dad died, and you came to live with me, I tried my best to—"

"*Stop.*" Brenna pummeled the side of the bed with her fist.

Jessica took a step back.

In a softer voice, still strained, Brenna said, "I'll be down in a moment to say good-bye to you and the boys."

She watched Jessica leave the room while inside she reeled with both guilt and anger. She loved her sister, was thankful when they'd lost their parents seventeen years ago, Jessica and her new husband had taken her in. She knew she'd been an imposition on them. But in the last months, Jessica had become suffocating and cloying. She asked too many questions, pried into her every move. Brenna couldn't contain her irritation with her any longer, and she knew it was best she was leaving for a while.

As she debated whether she should go apologize, she fingered the scar at the base of her neck that ran up the back of her head into her hairline. It was prickling, itching, and as she touched it, she thought it felt hot. She knew it was from stress, from the constant suppression of her grief and anger, which she felt she had to maintain for her family's benefit. She wouldn't let her two nephews or her sister and brother-in-law see her fall to pieces as she'd done in the weeks after the accident. But more important, she couldn't let them glimpse her inner turmoil, at the guilt she felt for Edward's and Michael's deaths. She was certain her sister would start to figure things out and realize what had happened, perhaps even discover the truth.

Brenna examined the envelope and recognized Debra's handwriting, and she wondered why Debra had bothered writing her at all. Hadn't she claimed she'd broken her heart? Nearly ruined her marriage? She scoffed. She knew she'd ruined most everything in her life anyway. Debra was simply one more unfortunate casualty.

After tearing open the envelope, she pulled out a standard sympathy card. Inside, below the printed sentiment, Debra had written, *I'm sorry for your loss. Know Allen and I will pray for you. Debra.*

Brenna turned the card over. There was no other message. She ripped it in half and tossed it in the bin by the bed. There was no point in treasuring a keepsake of a failed relationship.

Downstairs, she said good-bye to her sister and brother-in-law as well as her two nephews, who hugged her and wept. She realized for them, both still young boys, her departure was confusing. They'd struggled to come to terms with their uncle Eddie's and cousin Mikey's deaths, and now they were losing their aunt to the other side of the country.

She hurried to her packed minivan and waved out the window as she drove off. By the time she hit the Iowa-Missouri state line, she took a breath of relief. She'd managed to drive hours without the compulsion to swerve her van into an oncoming semitruck and end it all. This was some improvement, she thought. And she realized she was actually looking forward to the sunshine in the Southwest desert. She knew it would never heal the loss of her little sunshine, her son Michael, but to be out of the gray and bleak Midwestern winter would be some relief. Perhaps just enough to give her the will to face another day without him.

❖

"Ms. Leighton, your ten o'clock, Mrs. Wilson, is here," the receptionist spoke into the phone. She smiled at Brenna.

Brenna thought it was a sad smile, one that showed pity. She gathered Cassandra Leighton, Edward's property broker in Arizona, had informed her secretary that Mr. Wilson's widow would be dropping by that morning.

"You can go right in, ma'am," the secretary said.

Brenna hesitated and fidgeted with her purse. She'd felt self-conscious about her casual dress the moment she'd stepped into the large and richly furnished office in downtown Phoenix. She knew she looked awful. She'd seen her image in the mirror. Her appearance was cliché, down to the dark circles under her eyes and her limp blond hair, which she hadn't bothered to color or style since the accident. She looked every bit the grieving widow and tragic mother. All but her jawline, which often remained rigid as her teeth ground together, not to prevent herself from breaking down and weeping, as most anyone would expect from her, but rather to keep herself from screaming.

Now as she opened the door to the broker's private office, she felt even more underdressed and uncomfortable when she saw how stylish and sophisticated the woman inside appeared.

"Brenna, it's good to meet you in person." Cassandra Leighton extended her hand.

"Thank you, Cassie, for agreeing to see me," Brenna said. She couldn't prevent herself from staring at the woman. She was a blonde, like herself, but Cassie expressed a polished beauty dressed in her expensive business suit. Her hair was impeccable, her nails manicured, and her jewelry perfectly accented her attire. She was beautiful and classy, just the type of woman Brenna always found herself timid around.

"You don't look any worse for wear after your long drive. Are you comfortable at the Scottsdale Hilton?" Cassie motioned for her to have a seat.

"I am. Thank you for recommending it. I'd have ended up at some roadside dive with my luck." Brenna settled into the leather chair, scanned the office, and noticed the many photos, plaques, and awards covering the walls. It was clear Cassie was successful in her line of work.

"Not a problem," Cassie said. "I want you to be comfortable while you visit us here in sunny Arizona. Let me get you some coffee." She buzzed her secretary, and in a few moments, the two were sipping their drinks and discussing Arizona's weather and the economy.

"I never thought of the desert as having much to offer," Brenna said, "but the golf courses, farms, and housing developments are amazing. And the citrus groves, they're everywhere."

"Citrus, cotton, copper, cattle, and climate—the five *C*s Arizona's known for," Cassie said. "Sadly, most of the citrus economy has shifted away from us to California and Florida, even Chile. That's the reason many of the old citrus dynasties have been sold off and parceled out for housing developments and golf courses."

"And that's what happened with this Poulsen land?"

By now any misgivings Brenna had about her own casual dress had fallen away as she'd continued to talk with Cassie. She decided she liked Cassie's face, thought it sweet and open. In fact, there was something familiar about Cassie, something Brenna couldn't describe right then, but it put her at ease nevertheless.

"The Poulsen grove was never known to be one of the bigger producers," Cassie said. "If I remember correctly, they grew grapefruit, but from what I recall hearing, the family was always undergoing some sort of labor dispute or the trees weren't producing. The harvest shut down about twenty years ago, and they've never sold to developers."

"And the trees? They're all dead?"

"Yes, the grove has gone fallow."

"And Edward, what was he hoping to do with the land?"

"The property lies a good twenty miles outside the city limits, on county land, and little development has sprung up around it," Cassie said. "I'm sure Edward thought, as many of us did, there'd be expansion out that way when the economy turned around."

"I see." Brenna crossed and uncrossed her legs while she sipped her coffee. She'd yet to divulge to Cassie she intended to refurbish the house which stood on the property. Even considered living in it. "So what's the legal battle my lawyer referred to?"

Cassie opened a file and flipped through some papers. "The family didn't want a portion of the property, including the house, sold off in the purchase. I think if I remember..." She flipped again through the paperwork, went to a file cabinet, and pulled out a larger file. She unfolded a document on her desk, an aerial view of the property overlaid with a topographical grid. "You can see here, the house and this area over here were portioned off from the original sale. But logistics made it difficult for the land to be surveyed and mapped for individual plots. It devalued the property around it. And the family had this large slab, a tennis court, I think it was meant to be, poured right here." She pointed to the spot. "There had been some plan about eventually building a large home for one of the grandsons. Anyway, Edward and I were fighting to have those two areas included in the purchase. About three months before he passed, I was able to get the go-ahead on the house and the land around it, but not this area, not the area with the concrete slab that sits on the back acreage."

Brenna examined the map. She could see the top view of the house and next to it a smaller building. She saw another small building near the slab. "What are these structures?"

Cassie consulted a legend and some documents in the file and pointed to the map. "That's a detached single-car garage and that's the pump house. It covers the irrigation mechanism for the grove."

Brenna continued to study the map. "So all those trees, like you said, are dead?"

Cassie chuckled. "Without irrigation, not much can survive our desert environment. But there may be a few that've hung on with our little rainfall. I think I saw a few with fruit when I visited the property with Edward last year. Why do you ask?"

"Only curious. It seems a pity to let all those trees die, all that citrus go to waste."

"Yes, it does." Cassie cocked her head. "Are you thinking of trying to revive the grove? Going into the fruit-stand business?" She chuckled again, but furrowed her brow all the same.

"No, I was thinking of restoring the house, living in it for a while."

"Living in it?"

"Yes."

Cassie folded the map and sat again. She took a sip of coffee and said, "That's not possible."

"What do you mean? Why not?" Brenna asked, surprised by Cassie's sudden change in tone and posture.

"Listen, Brenna." Cassie rubbed her forehead. "I don't think that's a good idea. That house hasn't been lived in for the last five years, and previous to that the family had a caretaker living there. It's been boarded up and empty all this time. It needs to be bulldozed along with the other buildings and dead trees."

"But it's a sweet little house. Reminds me of my grandparents' place in the country. I'd love to restore it."

"You don't want to do that. It's too far from town and besides it's old. I mean really old." Cassie checked something in the file. "As I told you on the phone a few weeks ago, it was built in 1910. It's ancient. You don't want to live there."

"But I do, Cassie. As soon as I saw the photos in Stan Thomas's office, I knew this house was what I needed."

"What you needed?"

Brenna clamped her mouth shut and grimaced. Cassie didn't need to know how close she'd come to being done, to checking out for good. She rubbed her shoulder, tense from the long drive, and said, "Before I became pregnant with Michael, Edward let me take classes at the community college. I earned a degree in interior design. I've never gotten a chance to do anything with it. But now, I can put into practice everything I learned. The house is over a century old, a perfect candidate for restoration. I could list it as a historical building."

"It's hardly on the historical circuit being so far out there."

"You don't understand, Cassie, I need the distraction." It was true. She did need something to grab hold of, to keep herself from sinking any lower.

"I'm sorry, Brenna, but I wouldn't be comfortable with you working out there by yourself, let alone living there."

Brenna stopped herself from screaming an obscenity. She bit her tongue and forced her fake smile. "Thank you for your concern, but it is my property."

Cassie opened and closed her mouth. After a long pause, she said, "It is your property. Forgive me. I was only thinking of your welfare." She went to the window, her back to Brenna. "If you insist on making that property your residence, even for a short time, I feel obligated to disclose some history about the place."

"Like what?" Brenna watched Cassie's back. "Is it something bad?"

"It depends on how much credence you give an urban legend." Cassie turned around. "There's a story about the property, but then lots of old places have stories."

"You mean like a ghost story?"

"Yes."

"I don't believe in ghosts."

"Don't you at least want to know the story?" Cassie asked, sitting again. "Aren't you curious?"

"Did you tell Edward the story?" Brenna could feel herself becoming annoyed. Perhaps Cassie was making this up to dissuade her.

"No, I didn't. There was no reason to do so. He was going to sell the land, not live on it."

Brenna tightened her jaw. "Okay, what's the story?"

Cassie refilled her coffee cup and sat back as if she were about to relate some long epic tale. "There's a legend about Hadley Poulsen. He was the first to live there, built the house, and homesteaded the place before Arizona became a state. Anyway the story goes, one night he went crazy, no one knows for what reason, and shot his wife, cut up her body, and buried it in the grove."

Brenna listened stone-faced, tightening her jaw even more, aggravated with Cassie for trying to spook her.

"When the sheriff's posse came to arrest him," Cassie continued, "they dug up her body, well, her body parts. They found every piece but her head. However, Poulsen wasn't prosecuted, didn't even spend a night in jail. The sheriff was his cousin, you see."

"How long ago was this?"

"This would've been over eighty years ago."

"Is that all there is to the story? It doesn't sound like much of a ghost story." Brenna could hear the irritation in her voice.

"Well, the legend says because her murder was never avenged, at night her spirit wanders the grove looking for her head."

Brenna scoffed. "A headless woman wanders my property at night?"

"That's the tale."

"That's ridiculous, is what it is." Brenna folded her arms across her chest.

Cassie leaned forward and touched her knee. "I know it's a silly legend, Brenna, and I'm not trying to insult your intelligence."

"Uh-huh." Brenna pursed her lips and raised one eyebrow.

"But the thing is there's something off about that land. I've heard the story all my life, and when I was in high school, my friends and I used to go out there and party. You know, as part of a dare, drinking beer around a campfire, smoking cigarettes. We heard strange noises, saw strange things even then."

Brenna pulled the map closer and opened it once more. She supposed any place with a hundred-year-old history was bound to have legends attached to it. But she wasn't superstitious and neither did she believe in ghosts. Besides she hadn't driven clear across the country to be turned away.

"Cassie, I know you don't want me to stay out there by myself. But understand, I'm a grown woman, and I'm not going to be frightened off by some lurid tale told by teenagers and old men."

"Will you at least let me find you a rental in Scottsdale to stay in while you work on the place?"

Brenna looked at the map once more, traced her finger over the outline of the house. She was aware Cassie was watching her and probably thinking she'd lost her mind. Finally, she spoke. "I've lost everything that ever mattered to me, Cassie. Everything in the world. I know it doesn't make sense to you, but I need this house. I need the isolation, the quiet from the sirens." She closed her eyes. "I still hear the sirens, and I'd give anything to stop them screaming in my head. Please understand." She opened her eyes to see Cassie watching her.

"All right. It is your property, as you say." Cassie reached once more and touched her knee, giving it a firm squeeze before dabbing her eyes and smiling.

Like the secretary's smile, Brenna thought, Cassie's was a sad smile, one of sympathy, and it made her cringe. She knew in her heart that she didn't deserve any kindness.

At her desk, Cassie pulled out a notepad and began to write. "I'll go ahead and see about having the utilities turned on. It won't be for a few weeks, so don't plan on going out there until at least the end of the month. And I better have one of my guys do an inspection, make sure there's no problem with the gas line or the electric panel. The place wasn't even wired up, I think, until the 1940s."

"Thank you." Brenna managed her first genuine smile in a long time.

"I wouldn't be surprised if once you see the condition of the house, you'll change your mind." Cassie waved her hand over the map. "And for the rest of the property? Are you planning on keeping it or do you want it surveyed, graded, and segmented for sale?"

"I hadn't considered that." Brenna leaned over the map. "I'd like to keep the land the house is on with maybe an acre or two around it. I'd like to see if I could nurse a few of the trees back to life as well. For the rest, I'll probably have it prepared for sale. But I don't know anything about that. I guess I'll leave it to you, if you don't mind."

"Of course." Cassie dug through her desk drawer. "The first thing we need is to have it properly surveyed, as I said. Edward had been debating whether to go ahead with the trouble of having it surveyed or to simply sell it off, but if we get it plotted and mapped out, particularly for mini-mansion lots, you'll have a much better chance of luring in a housing investor." She looked up from her notes. "Also, the road that leads in from the highway needs to be graded right away before you even think about driving it regularly."

"You have a contractor you can recommend?"

"I do. In fact, I've worked with this one particular company for years on similar projects. I'm good friends with the owner. I'll call tomorrow and set a time to go over the contract and to meet at the property in a few weeks." Cassie handed her a business card. "Here, this is the company. I know we'll get a good rate, and the crews are professional."

Brenna read the card: *Santana and Sons, Professional Survey and Grading Contractors, Commercial and Residential, Licensed and Bonded, Alex Santana, Owner*. She glimpsed at Cassie who'd begun smiling with a look she couldn't read. It was as if she had a secret she couldn't wait to share.

"Is there something else?" Brenna asked.

"Nothing much." Cassie continued to smile. "I only wanted to say that I admire you, Brenna. After what you've been through and then driving clear across the country, well, I hope you'll find what you're looking for out there among those grapefruit trees. I really do."

Brenna glanced at the business card again and noted the company logo was a simple line drawing of a sun coming over mountains. "I hope I do, too," she said, and she slipped the card into her purse.

Chapter Two

For the next few weeks, Cassie treated Brenna to a number of lunches and dinners at upscale local eateries. Cassie also exposed her to the posh and swank shopping district known as Old Town Scottsdale. Together they perused galleries and boutiques and admired the custom jewelry shops full of handcrafted silver and gold. Brenna had never thought much about art or jewelry, and she balked at most of the prices while wondering if people actually purchased those items. Who could afford such luxuries? Then she reminded herself she had the means to purchase any number of pieces if she wanted. She'd inherited a fortune, a fortune she didn't deserve.

But these guilt-ridden thoughts were easy for her to keep at bay as her friendship with Cassie grew. Brenna was becoming enamored with the woman, not in the obsessive way she'd yearned for Debra, but in a close friendship sort of way. She'd not had many friends as a child. Her parents' unexpected deaths while she was young had left her withdrawn and socially awkward. But now with Cassie, Brenna discovered someone with whom she felt comfortable, with whom she could share a laugh. And besides, Cassie talked about herself rather than questioning her constantly, as Jessica liked to do. She told Brenna about her career in real estate, her childhood and teenage years growing up in Tempe, and her partner, Kelly, a golf pro at the exclusive Phoenician Resort. Brenna wondered how Cassie's partner had time to deal in high-end commercial real estate and be a golf pro at the same time. She noticed Cassie was careful not to ask too many questions about Edward and Michael. In fact, Cassie avoided the subject of Edward altogether, something Brenna was thankful for.

Her time with Cassie was offset, however, with time spent alone in her luxury hotel room. She occupied herself with looking up information on home improvement stores and warehouses. She dutifully called Jessica once a day and checked email on her laptop. She read about the native culture and scanned travel magazines to make note of the local attractions she wanted to see while she stayed in the Phoenix Metro area. On those evenings when she didn't have dinner with Cassie, she'd order room service, including a bottle of wine. She knew mixing the wine with the sleep aid her doctors in Davenport had prescribed was dangerous. Her heart could stop while she slept. But it would be a blessing, she thought, a quick death for sure.

The night before she was to go meet Cassie at the property, she sat on the hotel bed and swirled the wine in her glass while she mused on thoughts of self-harm. Those thoughts had haunted her for months, and anytime she began to formulate a more detailed plan, she felt the sensation of choking and coughed, sometimes so violently she retched up mucus streaked with blood. This night was no different. She coughed and cleared her throat while downing another glass of wine until her head was so foggy all she could do was sit on the bed and hold her son's music box and weep. She wept for Edward as well although she'd not been in love with him. But her guilty feelings over him paled in comparison to her absolute despair over losing her sweet boy. Conceiving Michael had been difficult. In fact, she'd had a miscarriage before becoming pregnant with him. She'd put so much of herself and her dreams into the life of her son, and in one swift moment, he was torn from her. In some hidden corner of her mind, she suspected she'd deserved to lose him.

Through her tears, she stroked the music box, running her thumb over the image of the smiling sun beaming down on sunflowers. She began to slur the lyrics to the iconic song. But as it always did, her voice broke, and she began to weep harder. Her physical body might have been in the Valley of the Sun, as the Phoenix Metro area was known, but her spirit was broken and hidden in the shadows of her shame.

❖

The sign on the chain-link fence read: *Poulsen Citrus Grove*. Brenna pulled her minivan to the side of the highway, a short distance from the gate blocking the entrance to the property. The area was overgrown with weeds and tall grass, and up to the property fence were twisted, dead grapefruit trees in neat rows, one after the other. She tugged on the gate's padlock and looked down the gravel and dirt road leading to the house. She could barely make out the second story of the structure. She glanced up and down the highway and across the road to a cotton field. In the distance she could make out another home. But Cassie was right, the property was isolated. In the few moments she'd been waiting, only two vehicles had driven by. Other than the distant neighbor, the closest civilization was the gas station miles back where this highway met the main freeway.

As she waited, she surveyed the land around her. She spotted an oddly shaped mountain, red in color and looming out of the unspoiled desert. She smiled, thinking it resembled a large red breast with a prominent hardened nipple. She began to pace along the roadside and drew in a breath, taking in the scents of mesquite and sage. She understood now why so many retired folks from the Midwest wintered in this state. It was temperate, full of sunshine and wide-open land. She checked the time on her phone. Another ten minutes had passed, and Cassie should be meeting her any moment. Just then a sports car pulled alongside her.

"Found it okay, I see." Cassie climbed out.

"Well, again, you gave great directions," Brenna said. "It's peaceful out here."

Cassie fiddled with a key ring, which held a dozen keys. "Yes, it is, but it can be a bit spooky at night. There aren't any streetlights, you know." She found the right key and undid the lock. "There we go."

She pushed one side of the gate away from her as far as it would swing, and Brenna pushed the other side in a similar manner. They looked down the rough road leading to the house. It hadn't been graded in a long time. Deep gutters and potholes pitted the narrow lane, and evidence of water runoff made the road uneven.

"Last season's monsoons," Cassie said. "These dirt roads get the worst of the runoff, especially out here." She considered both vehicles. "I think you have more clearance than I do. I'll leave my car here, and we'll take your van in. But go slowly. I don't want you tearing out your undercarriage."

Brenna agreed, and back in her van, she maneuvered around the largest potholes.

"Good thing the crew can start on Monday," Cassie said just as the house came in view. "You're not going to want to drive your van over this often."

Brenna pulled into the gravel drive in front of the porch, looked through her windshield at the structure, and killed the engine. "It's small. For some reason from the pictures, I thought it was larger."

Once they were out of the van, Brenna began looking around. Off to the side of the house, the garage stood just as she'd seen in the aerial photo. An abandoned bucket and ladder leaned against the building, and the small windows running along the top of the double doors were dirty and yellow, a few broken. The remnant of paint, once a brilliant sky blue on the frame siding and a clean white on the eaves and trim, was peeling and dulled from the intense desert sun. The house, painted with the same theme, was in no better condition. At the garage, Brenna pulled on the handles of the double doors, but grunted when they didn't give way.

"Is there a key?" She turned to see Cassie staring at the second-story windows. She followed Cassie's gaze, but both windows were boarded up from the inside, some of the individual panes broken out. "Cassie?"

Cassie shook herself. "I don't know." She studied her key ring as she came toward the garage.

When they examined the doors more closely, they saw no indication of a keyhole, a lock, or a latch.

"Maybe it's latched from the inside." Brenna tried tugging and pushing on the doors again.

"Maybe. But how did whoever locked it get out?" Cassie asked. "We may have to have it pried open. You can get one of the crew next week to use a crowbar on it."

Brenna walked back toward the house and tested her weight on the porch steps. The wooden planks squeaked as she stepped. Under the covered awning to one side of the front door and below the picture window, also boarded up, were a bench and an old coffee can of sand, containing cigarette butts. Empty soda cans, beer bottles, and candy wrappers littered the area.

"High school kids," Cassie said.

"Looking for Hadley Poulsen's headless wife, are they?" Brenna giggled when Cassie harrumphed.

Around the side of the house, she found the remains of a vegetable garden, a weathered clothesline, and a wheelbarrow turned on end, rusted and decaying.

"Did you say someone lived here five years ago?" Brenna gazed out at the citrus grove, dark and lifeless.

"Yes, a caretaker. He was a Poulsen goon, I'm sure." Cassie searched for the key to open the weather-beaten front door.

"Goon? Why do you say that?"

Finally, Cassie located the right key and pulled open the flimsy screen, but before she unlocked the main door, she said, "I'm guessing you don't know much about the politics of this state, but the Poulsens are old money, old power. They hold a lot of sway in Arizona. It's almost impossible to conduct any kind of business without running into one of their grandsons or cousins or goons."

"Are you telling me they're like the Mob?"

"Something like that." Cassie swung open the door to the house, and the two peered inside. With the windows all boarded up, little light made its way inside from the open door.

"Let me get my flashlight," Brenna said. She returned from her van with a light and beamed it inside. The entryway was empty with thick dust on the hardwood floors. She took a step forward, but Cassie grabbed her arm.

"You're sure about this?"

"It's an adventure, come on, Cassie. It'll be fun." Brenna stepped inside and flashed her light around. She stood in one large room, which served as a living and dining area and blended into a small kitchen. Opposite the front door was a narrow staircase, and next to the staircase, just off the kitchen, was an open door leading to another room. Brenna headed in that direction. "Small kitchen," she remarked as she passed the area.

Cassie glanced around in the dim light, staying close to Brenna. "This is creepy," she said. "Let's pry one of these boards loose and let in more light." She pulled Brenna over to the kitchen window, and they tugged away a plank from the jamb. When a beam of sunlight pierced through the dim interior, it revealed boot prints on the dusty floor. Cassie squealed and attempted to flee.

"I think it's from your guy, Cassie." Brenna laughed at Cassie's startled expression. "Remember? You sent him over a few weeks ago."

Cassie smiled, but it looked more like a grimace to Brenna.

"So now that you've seen it, you're not staying here tonight, right?" Cassie followed her into the room off the kitchen. "You're going to stay at the hotel until you get the place cleaned."

The room the two had entered was the downstairs bedroom, and at one end of it was a short hallway leading to a bathroom and then to a back door, opening to the rear of the house.

"I don't know. You said the utilities are on. Let me try the water." Brenna slipped into the bathroom and turned the knob on the sink. Water sprayed and a dark sludge began to pour from the spout. After a few moments, it still hadn't turned clear.

"You're going to need to run the lines and clear them." Cassie made a face of disgust. "And I'd buy bottled water, too. Don't drink this stuff."

"Not a problem. I have a case of water in the back of the van." Brenna started toward the staircase.

"You're going up there?" Cassie asked.

The staircase was steep and dark, and the top of the landing was hidden from view.

Brenna turned to her. "The ghost haunts the grove, not the house, right?"

"Um, well…"

Brenna snickered. "Come on, let's check it out."

Cassie scoffed as she hurried behind her. "You can make fun all you like, Brenna. Besides, what if she spends the day in the house and the night in the grove? Have you thought of that? Huh?"

"Cassie, you're being silly." Brenna searched for a switch, which she found and flipped on. "Ah, look, the lightbulb your friend left in the hallway fixture."

The light revealed plastered walls, peeling and discolored where old water damage had stained and leached through the paint.

"I'll need a roofer to come check for leaks. Let's hope mildew hasn't grown under the paint." Brenna ran her hand over the stain while she observed Cassie glancing around and down the stairs. "Cassie?" She walked close to her. "You are scared, aren't you? You're not just joking."

Cassie licked her lips and held her arms around herself. "Brenna, now that I'm out here, I must insist you stay in town at the hotel. I'm not sure this house is safe to occupy."

"It'll be fine. The water's on and I have electricity. And you said he checked the gas and lit the pilot light. So come on, I want to check out the rest."

Brenna pulled Cassie by the arm and turned to one of the two doors of the upstairs rooms. She pushed the first door and it swung open. She flashed her light inside and saw it was just as empty and dusty as the downstairs. "Help me pull a plank away and get some light in here."

The wood, as before, gave way, and a beam of sunlight pierced through the dirty and broken windowpanes. Brenna looked down at her van and out across the citrus trees. She could make out the pump house she'd seen in the photograph in Cassie's office, and by the disruption in the pattern of the trees, she gathered that was where the concrete slab lay.

"You're going to want to put cardboard in these panes or all your heat will be lost," Cassie said.

"I'll call next week and see about having the windows replaced." Brenna stood back and guesstimated the width and height of the window. She turned toward the hallway. "Let's see the other room." She tried the door handle on the second room and pushed with her shoulder against the door. "Huh, this one seems locked." She examined the door with her flashlight. "Is there a key for this room?"

While Cassie tried the keys, Brenna beamed the flashlight on the door handle. Cassie finally found the right key and gave the handle a turn. The door swung open, and Brenna flashed her light into the room. But this one wasn't empty. Instead it was filled with stacks of loose papers, boxes, and a desk.

"What's all this?" Brenna wove her way to the window. "Give me a hand."

They pulled loose a plank, and just as in the previous room, sunlight poured into the area, but this room's walls had been papered in an old-fashioned velvety print, yellow and embossed.

"Icky." Brenna ran her hand over the paper and noticed it left a powdery trace on her fingers. She wiped her hand on her jeans and began to examine the boxes overflowing with files. There were photographs, too, stacked on top of each other and scattered on the desk. "I wonder what this is all about." She picked up an old photo off the desk. As she did so, she spotting something else. "Look at this lamp." She lifted an old oil lamp. It was grimy, sooty, and empty of fuel. "And it still has a wick."

"I bet that's an antique, and this desk looks old, too," Cassie said.

"Maybe I'll get some oil for it. There's a hardware store on the other side of the freeway where we turned off." Brenna returned the lamp to the desk and began leafing through the stacks of papers. "What do you think these papers are about?"

"I don't know. Maybe the caretaker left them. I'm not sure." Cassie began to examine the clutter as well. She held a faded document. "Some of these receipts and documents are dated back over eighty years."

Brenna opened the desk drawers, finding them empty, and now she tried to open the largest drawer, but it was stuck.

Just then they heard a car door close, and Cassie peeked out the window. "Great, she's here." She headed toward the hall. "Come on, I'll introduce you to the owner of Santana and Sons. I think you'll like her."

"Her? Okay, just a second and I'll join you." Brenna tugged with a little more determination on the desk's largest drawer. But it was no use. The drawer wouldn't budge. She glanced out the window to the gravel drive. She was intrigued by the idea of a woman owning her own construction business. Then, as she was about to turn to go downstairs, she saw the woman emerge from the pickup truck.

First two worn work boots and then legs in blue jeans emerged, followed by a shapely woman with wavy brown hair pulled back in a ponytail. She was dressed in an Eisenhower-style jacket, unzipped, revealing a tight knit shirt underneath. Brenna watched the woman smile, pull off her sunglasses, and reach out to Cassie. Even from the window, Brenna could see the woman's large brown eyes. She watched the two embrace, but before the hug ended, Cassie and the woman kissed on the lips.

"Huh. Okay." Brenna cocked her head then hurried downstairs to join them.

When she left the room, a cold chill swept through it, and the antique lamp sputtered and sparked. A flame flickered, lighting the old wick and spreading a weak light across the room before the flame died once again. Although it was a warm sixty-five degrees on that November morning, a frost had formed on one of the dirty windowpanes and a handprint appeared, as someone, something leaned against the window to watch the three women in the driveway below.

Chapter Three

B renna paused in the shadow of the front door and observed the woman and Cassie talking. She thought the stranger was attractive with her tanned skin, dark hair, and bright smile. While she continued to observe, Brenna saw her reach inside the front pocket of her jeans, pulling back her short jacket to reveal a wide leather belt with a clip of keys on a loop. Brenna found her fascinating, a familiar sensation, but one she'd not felt since Debra. Then as she walked out onto the porch, Cassie motioned her over.

"Alex Santana, Brenna Wilson. Brenna, Alex." Cassie pointed to each as a way of introduction

Brenna extended her hand. "Hello."

"A pleasure." Alex took her hand in a firm grip. "I understand from Cassie you're thinking of renovating this old place."

Brenna blinked. She'd never known a woman with such long eyelashes. "That's the plan." She glanced at the side of Alex's truck and recognized the logo of the sun and mountains she'd seen on the business card.

"Ambitious plan." Alex smiled.

Brenna blinked again. Alex's teeth were milky white, perfectly shaped. She glanced at the truck once more. "You're the Santana of Santana and Sons?" She felt her neck grow warm and her face tingle at her own awkwardness.

Cassie and Alex looked at each other and snickered.

"No, not the original Santana," Alex said. "That would be my father. He started the business forty years ago. I inherited it when he retired."

Brenna detected a mild accent as she spoke. Alex clipped her words, and Brenna realized that was her way of minimizing her inflections.

"So it's you and your sons then?" Brenna wanted to smack her own face. It was an asinine question, she knew. Clearly Alex wasn't old enough to have working age sons.

Again Alex and Cassie shared a glance and a smile.

"No sons for me," Alex said. "My father started the business before I was born, and I think it was wishful thinking on his part he'd someday have sons. But here you have it. He ended up with a daughter instead." Alex smiled again, revealing deep laugh lines on either side of her full lips. "We've never bothered to change the name since the business is so well-known in the Valley."

Brenna blinked a few times more. She thought she might be hallucinating; the morning sunlight seemed to be pouring, not from the sky, but from this woman's radiant face. She felt something shift inside her head, the pressure around her jaw and throat ease.

"I see." She wondered why both women watched her with odd grins. She sputtered as she spoke again. "So, yeah…" She cleared her throat. "So Cassie said you may be able to get the road graded and cleared starting next week."

"I'll get a crew on it first thing Monday morning." Alex scanned Brenna's minivan. "Yes, you'll rip out your underside if you're not careful."

Brenna looked back at her van. She and Edward had purchased it more than a year ago. Michael had taken up soccer and T-ball, and she'd become the stereotypical soccer mom, driving other women's children to practices and games since most of them had careers or jobs outside the home.

"I'm thinking of trading it in for a Jeep anyway," she blurted out. She'd been unaware of that desire until now.

Alex pulled her wallet from her jacket's inner pocket and fished out a business card. "Go see my cousin Victor at San Tan Jeep and Chrysler. Tell him I sent you, and he'll give you a good deal." She took a step closer and grew serious.

Brenna held her breath, uncertain what was happening as Alex seemed to be just inches from her, looking as if she was about to hug her.

"Cassie told me you lost your family in April," Alex said. "I'm sorry to hear that. And she also told me you don't know anyone out here, so"—she pulled another business card from her wallet and a pen from her pocket and scribbled something on the back—"take my card. The front number rings the main office, but I've put my personal cell on the back if you can't reach me otherwise."

Brenna gazed into Alex's eyes and reached for the card. When she tried to speak, her voice caught in her throat. She coughed and covered her mouth. "Um, thanks, that's kind of you to offer your number." She began twirling a lock of hair, something she hadn't done in a long time. It was a habit from childhood, something she did when she was feeling uncertain. Again, she saw Cassie and Alex exchange glances.

"Hey, Alex," Cassie said, "could you take a look at the garage doors? We can't get them open, and there's no keyhole or lock we can see."

Brenna let go of her breath, grateful Alex's attention was diverted from her as she walked toward the garage. And as she did, Brenna watched her and admired the way her jeans hugged her hips and curves. She twirled a lock of hair with more vigor.

Alex pulled and pushed on the double doors. She examined the bottom of each door and stood on tiptoe to run her hand along the top lip of the frame. She rattled and yanked one more time and even put her shoulder against one of the doors and shoved. Nothing happened.

"They're warped from the rain and heat, I'd guess," Alex said. "You'll need to pry them open, if you don't mind damaging the wood." She ran her hand along the seam where the two doors met. "What's this?" She leaned close. "It looks as if someone's nailed the doors shut. Look here, they've countersunk the nail heads and even bothered to paint over them. Strange."

"Why would they do that?" Cassie asked.

"Who knows?" Alex shrugged and came back over. "Did you plan on parking inside?" she asked Brenna.

But Brenna was concentrating on Alex's boots.

"Brenna?"

"What?" Brenna startled and looked up.

"If you want, I can work on it Monday, maybe work the hinges loose. Do you want to park inside?" Alex asked.

Brenna stared at Alex's lips. The little smile lines on either side fascinated her.

"Brenna?" Alex moved her head to the side and made eye contact.

"Huh?" Brenna shook herself. "Sure. What did you say?" She felt her ears burning and almost groaned out loud. She hated when she became tongue-tied like this around women. Beautiful women, strong women, women to whom she couldn't help but be drawn.

Cassie snickered and put her arm around Brenna's shoulders and patted. "She's got a lot to think about, Alex. Maybe the garage can wait."

"Yes, it can wait," Alex said. "But I'm sending in my guys when we do get those doors open. You know there're snakes and scorpions inside, not to mention black widow spiders." She made spidery movements with her fingers and did a fake shiver before chuckling.

"Snakes?" Brenna squeaked. She felt the heat drain from her face.

"*Alex*," Cassie said.

Alex glanced first at Cassie and back at Brenna. "Don't worry. If there're snakes, my guys will clear them out, and they'll clear out the scorpions and spiders, too. Trust me we have all kinds of experience working in the desert. Snakes, tarantulas, rabid coyotes, and—"

"Alex." Cassie stopped her and turned to Brenna. "She's exaggerating, sweetie. I'm sure it'll be fine."

Brenna swallowed and licked her lips.

"I was only going to add, and the ghosts of Apache warriors and conquistadors, Cassie. No need to bite my head off." Alex laughed.

Cassie shot her another look.

At this, Alex muted her laugh and took hold of Brenna's upper arm, lowering her voice. "Don't worry, Brenna. You have my word. I'll make sure all the creepy crawlies are rounded up and returned to the open desert."

Brenna nodded, calmed by her touch.

"I didn't mean to frighten you. I'm sorry," Alex said.

"Okay, thank you." Brenna liked the way Alex looked at her, and for a moment she was able to return her gaze. But she caught Cassie out of her side vision and glanced to see her smiling that same secretive smile she'd given her in the office weeks ago.

"I should go run the water lines." Brenna held out her hand. It was shaking. "Nice to meet you, Alex. I'm glad to have you working on me for my property. I mean..." She groaned. "I mean, for me on my property." She bit her lip and pulled her hand away.

"You go on, Brenna," Cassie said. "Alex and I will look over the contract."

"Great. Okay." Brenna hurried to the front door, but stopped when she heard Alex call after her.

"I'll check on you next week, if you're around," Alex said. "And don't worry, my crews are clean. We'll haul in our own john and won't leave any trash behind. They're also expected to be respectful to the client, so no need to worry about them catcalling or harassing you in any way. They'll have me to answer to if they do."

"Okay. Right. Okay." Brenna struggled to form a coherent reply, gave up, and darted into the house, where she stood inside and worked to catch her breath.

It was a silly feeling, she knew. Silly, but exhilarating. She'd been sure she'd never feel this way again, not after losing Michael. But as she held her hand to her heart and felt the rapid beating, she realized the feeling was there and couldn't be denied. Leaning against the door, but out of view, she watched Cassie and Alex talking. She could hear their voices, but couldn't make out what they were saying. Then she saw Alex run her hand down Cassie's shoulder and rest it on her lower back. It was an affectionate gesture, and Brenna grunted with disappointment. But her observations were interrupted when she heard movement behind her. She turned, curious only, and faced the darkened stairway. Was something moving at the top of the stairs? She took a few steps closer and strained her eyes. She turned on the flashlight she'd been holding and moved the beam of light upward, a step at a time, certain she'd heard something almost like footsteps. A hand closed on her shoulder.

"Contract looks in order," Cassie said.

Brenna jumped. "Damn, Cassie, you startled me!"

"Startled you?" Cassie looked over at the stairway and back at Brenna. "Are you okay? You've gone pale."

"I'm good. The dust, I think I'm having an allergic reaction to the dust."

"Okay, well the crews will be here Monday morning, and we'll get this thing moving along."

"Great."

"You sure you're okay?" Cassie asked again.

"Yes, I'm sure. I'm going to check the water in the kitchen." Brenna pushed past her and in moments was occupied with the kitchen faucet while Cassie inspected the dials on the old stove. As the water sprayed, Brenna leaned against the countertop. She was aware Cassie was studying her. "Alex seems nice." She tried to sound nonchalant.

"She is."

Brenna looked sideways at her. She wondered about their relationship. "You two seem close."

"She's one of my dearest friends. I've known her since high school." Cassie checked the kitchen cupboards.

"She's incredibly pretty. It's hard to think of someone that attractive being in construction. She looks like she could be a model."

Cassie chuckled. "I've always hated her for her complexion. She spends all that time out in the sun and never wrinkles."

"Yes, she has beautiful skin." Brenna cringed. Had she admitted that out loud?

"I have to tell you," Cassie said, "she's one of the most dependable and faithful friends I've ever had. Maybe the most ethical person I know. And she has the goofiest sense of humor in the world. You never know what sort of practical joke she'll pull. Sometimes I want to strangle her, and other times she makes me laugh so hard I wet myself."

"I sort of picked up on that." Brenna thought about the way Alex had joked about snakes and spiders.

"Listen, Brenna, you should call her if you need anything. I mean, you have my number, too, but Alex wouldn't have given you her number if she didn't want you to use it."

"I'll keep that in mind, thanks." Brenna turned off the water, convinced it was running clear enough. "Both you and Alex are such nice people. I appreciate all your help." She handed the flashlight to Cassie. "Would you check for the key that unlocks the back door? I'm going to bring in a few boxes from the van."

Cassie took the flashlight. "Okay, but don't be long. I don't like being inside here by myself."

Brenna went out front and started moving boxes from her van inside. As she worked, she thought about Alex and Cassie, wondered if they were simply close friends or a couple as she suspected. On her third trip back to her vehicle, she lifted a box from the back and happened to glance at the two windows on the second floor. That was strange, she thought. Cassie must've gone back upstairs into the room with the desk and boxes—she was standing at the window watching her. But wait, Cassie was a blonde. The person at the window was—

"What are you looking at?" Cassie came around the side of the van.

Brenna jumped once again. "Cassie, I swear you keep sneaking up on me." She rubbed her eyes and looked again. She must've been mistaken. It couldn't have been Cassie. She could've sworn she'd seen a woman with long black hair watching her from the window.

"Why are you so jumpy all of a sudden?" Cassie asked.

Brenna shook her head and giggled. Her nerves were all scattered, she realized. But she wasn't sure if it was because of her unexpected attraction to Alex or Cassie's ridiculous story. She wagged her finger in Cassie's direction. "Your stupid ghost story has got me all worked up."

"But you said you don't believe in ghosts."

"I don't." Brenna glanced at the window once again. She knew she was being silly, but something felt off, something she couldn't explain. "I think I'll stay another couple nights at the hotel. I need to pick up a sleeping bag and air mattress anyway."

Cassie let out a dramatic sigh of relief. "Thank goodness. Now we'll both get some sleep tonight."

After locking up and getting back into the van, Brenna turned her vehicle around to head back toward the entry road as Cassie began to chatter about the restaurant she wanted to take her to Saturday afternoon for lunch. Brenna nodded while she navigated the road, but she wasn't listening. Instead, she watched in her rearview mirror as the house retreated in the background. She wondered what she'd heard—or thought she'd heard—at the top of the stairs, what she'd seen, or thought she'd seen in the window. However, by the time she'd said good-bye to Cassie, driven down the highway, and turned onto the freeway heading back to hotel, she'd managed to convince herself her unexpected excitement over meeting the beautiful Alex Santana had knocked her off her guard, had momentarily made her forget her rational mind. And Cassie's absurd story had simply wrestled with her imagination. She didn't believe in ghosts, she told herself once again. In truth, she believed in very little anymore.

Chapter Four

Brenna brooded for the rest of the weekend, despite the fact she'd spent most of Saturday with Cassie having lunch and shopping. By the end of that afternoon, she was certain Cassie and Alex were a couple—Cassie talked about her nearly the whole time. Brenna felt resentful. She wanted that sort of relationship. She'd not had it with Edward and was denied it with Debra. So the talk of Alex, as charming as Brenna found her, did little to lift her mood. By Sunday evening, she was despondent, and as she talked on the phone with Jessica, she couldn't hide the feeling in her voice. Jessica pleaded with her, but to no avail.

"You need to come home, Brenna. Please, honey. Hire someone to oversee the preparation of the property. You don't need to be there for that," Jessica said on the phone.

However, Brenna insisted she needed to accomplish something from start to finish on her own. So, in order to relieve Jessica of worry, she compromised, promising she'd return to Davenport for Thanksgiving, stay through Christmas, and then return to Arizona to finish with the property. Of course she had no intention of doing any such thing. This would be the first holiday season without Michael. She only wanted to ignore the upcoming dates, let them pass without acknowledgment. Perhaps next year it would be easier. Perhaps.

By Monday morning, she'd recovered a bit and refocused on the Poulsen place and the challenge of restoring it. She stopped at a hardware store and picked up cleaning supplies including a bottle of lamp oil and a new cotton wick. She liked the old oil lamp in the upstairs room and thought that maybe the little flame would soothe her while she worked in the evenings. She arrived at the property later that afternoon. As she pulled her van over to the side of the road, she could see pickup trucks parked along the perimeter fence and men in orange construction vests and hard hats looking over paperwork. She parked behind one of the trucks while she considered turning around and coming back in several days after the crew had finished with the road. But a man glanced up from his paperwork and walked toward her.

"Can I help you?" He removed his hard hat.

He was an attractive man in his late twenties with cropped black hair and a well-manicured moustache and goatee. Brenna thought it looked like something the devil would wear, but the man's warm eyes along with his thick black eyelashes ruined the impression.

"Hi, I'm Brenna Wilson." She stopped herself. "I mean, Taylor, Brenna Taylor." She'd been considering reverting to her maiden name and was getting comfortable trying it out. "This is my property, and I was wondering if I could get down the road to the house."

He looked at her van. "I don't think so, Mrs. Taylor. We got a front loader on the road, and you don't got the clearance to drive the ditch. You need to get to the house today?" He talked with a slight accent.

"I guess not. But I have all these supplies loaded in back, and I was hoping to get started on cleaning."

"If you want, we can put your stuff in my truck"—he pointed to his vehicle—"and I'll haul it in for you. You want to do that?" He smiled, revealing dimples in both cheeks, which further destroyed any hopes he might've had to look like the devil with his smartly trimmed goatee.

"You know, that'd be great," she said. But she had to know. "Is Alex Santana on the property today?"

"She showed up an hour ago, out in the trees getting an idea for the equipment we'll need to bring 'em down. You need to talk to her?"

"No, I was only curious."

"Let me pull my truck over." He held out his hand. "I'm Johnny. I'm the foreman on this job."

"Thanks, Johnny. I'm Brenna." She took his hand. As she did, his shirtsleeve pulled up to reveal a web of tattoos on his forearm. She also saw tattoos along his knuckles and the side of his neck. She'd never seen someone so tattooed. She pulled her hand away, feeling apprehensive, thinking he looked hard around the edges and intimidating, even with his cute dimples.

It took the two of them a few minutes to transfer all the cleaning supplies and other items from her van to the back of his truck. Afterward, she climbed into the passenger seat while he hopped in behind the wheel and smiled at her once more, his dimples winking alongside his beard.

"I'll give you a hand and carry these things inside," he said. "Then if you want, I'll drive you out to the trees to see the boss."

"No, I can unload it. You don't need to do that, and…you call her the boss?"

Johnny grinned. "The boss, la jefa. She's the lady, you know? Most of us do it out of respect, and to tease her a little, but she don't mind." He stroked his goatee and waited for one of the crew to flag him down the road.

"Have you worked long for Alex?"

"About seven years," he said. "She's let me be foreman on some jobs for about the last two. How about you? You been in the Valley long?"

"No, I only arrived in Arizona a few weeks ago."

"So you just bought this old place? What made you decide on it?" He drove around the bend toward the house.

"My husband bought the property." Brenna leaned forward as they came within sight of the house and peered at the upstairs window, the one where she'd imagined someone a few days ago. But the window was empty. The house looked as tired and as sad as she'd remembered it.

"Your husband. I see." Johnny glanced at her as he came to a stop. "He coming out here later?"

She cringed. Clearly Alex hadn't shared her situation with the crew. "No, my husband passed away a few months ago. I'm here alone."

"Dios mío," he exclaimed. When he looked at her, his expression was tinged with pity. "Hey, I'm sorry. I didn't know."

"Thank you, it's fine." She hated these awkward moments when people offered her pity. If they only knew, she thought.

Standing on the porch now, she fiddled with the key. Both the screen and door probably needed to be replaced, she noted absently. Johnny carried two of the lamps she'd purchased and peered over her shoulder.

"You know the story about this place?" he asked.

"Cassie told me all about it." She held the door for him.

"You know Cassie? Great lady. She the one sold this to you?"

"To my husband, but I'm working with her to prepare the property for sale to a housing developer."

"And what you gonna do with this house?"

"Restore it. Have it listed as a historical site."

After all the supplies were in the middle of the living area, Brenna thanked him and shook his hand once again. He held her hand longer than necessary, and it made her bristle with discomfort.

"I know a little about this and that. You need something, you let me know. I'm happy to help," he said.

"You're very kind, thank you."

He shoved his hands in his pockets and looked around, up the stairs. "It's small. How many rooms upstairs?"

"Only two and they're small as well."

"Right."

"Well, thanks again."

"You putting those lamps in the rooms? I'll carry them upstairs if you want."

Although she felt hesitant to be alone with him, she agreed it would be helpful and led the way to the upper level. She had him put one of the floor lamps in the empty room, plug it in, and make sure it worked, and then she led him to the other room with the desk and boxes. When she entered, she felt an instant chill and visibly shivered.

"You gonna want to put something in those broken panes. It's cold in this room. Where you want this lamp?" He held it up.

"Right there next to the desk will do." She flipped through a few scattered documents.

Johnny set up the lamp, plugged it in, turned it on, and switched it off again. He commented on the ugly yellow wallpaper, then noticed the stack of photographs and began examining them. "This one looks like it was taken from this room almost." He held a grainy black-and-white photo and pressed it against one of the few unbroken windowpanes.

Brenna joined him and bent to peer out the window. She recognized the way the horizon at the top of the trees in the photo lined up perfectly with the mountain range in the distance.

"Those are the Superstition Mountains," Johnny said. "Looks like someone took the picture from this room. And see these?" He pointed to some small white structures in the photo, five of them in a row. "That concrete slab is right where those houses used to be."

"Those were houses?"

"Just four walls and a roof. No plumbing or electricity. Workers could sleep inside and get out of the heat or rain. You can still see some like 'em on the road to Tucson, just outside Marana."

"Houses for the workers?" Brenna thought the structures looked primitive.

"Sure, migrant farm workers and their families moving from harvest to harvest. Owners would throw these up for 'em. But some were greedy bastards and charged the workers rent, taking it out of their wages."

"That's terrible." Brenna glanced again at the photo and out where the tennis court now stood.

"It doesn't happen so much now. Thanks to César Chávez. You know, Alex's father worked with him and the UFW. That's how he met her mother. You should have her tell you about it sometime. Rubén, her father, he's a great man."

"I've heard of César Chávez, but what's the UFW?"

"United Farm Workers." Johnny turned when tires ground to a stop on the gravel below. Alex's truck had just pulled up. "I'll let her know you're here." He set down the photos and left the room.

Brenna stood at the window and watched Alex climb out of her truck just as she'd done last Friday morning. Johnny walked out on the porch to meet her, and their Spanish conversation wafted up through the broken panes. She guessed he was telling Alex he'd helped with her supplies. After a moment, the two headed inside, and Brenna heard them talking as they climbed the stairs. She waited at the window until they appeared in the doorway.

"Brenna, I didn't realize you were coming out to the property today." Alex smiled.

It was a bright smile, and for Brenna, it warmed the chilly room.

"I wanted to start cleaning and Johnny helped me haul my supplies inside." She couldn't stop herself from staring.

Alex exchanged a glance with Johnny, who held the old photos.

"These are what I was telling you about," he said.

Alex stepped to the window and held up the various photographs, examining each while Brenna idly tugged on a strand of hair. She focused on the way the sun from the window fell on Alex and reflected in her brown eyes.

"These are cool," Alex said. "Look how small the trees were back then. And you're right, it looks like they were taken from this room." Alex turned to her. "You okay?"

Brenna had been gazing at her and lowered her eyes once Alex addressed her. "Yes, I'm...yeah...okay. I'm fine, thanks." She cleared her throat and chided herself for being tongue-tied. She began to ramble then, making small talk to cover her nervousness. "Maybe I'll have those pictures blown up and framed. They'd look good on the walls. Part of the history, you know, having it all restored and renovated. This would make a nice bed-and-breakfast, don't you think, if it had more than one bathroom? But I guess I could rent it out as a single unit. Do you think people would want to stay out here? The mountains are lovely. People from back East might like it."

Alex frowned then smiled and exchanged another look with Johnny who shrugged. She turned back to Brenna. "Yes, having the photos framed would be nice," she said. Then she faced Johnny once more. "Get down to RJ Rentals and make sure they schedule us for three weeks with two compacts and a truck. Tell them we'll need the heavy excavator, too, and to put us on the schedule. I want the equipment delivered next week before Thanksgiving."

"We gonna start leveling the trees those three days?" Johnny asked.

"Depends on how quickly we get it mapped and surveyed," Alex said, and the two began discussing other points of business.

Brenna knew they were busy, so she started toward the door. But Alex turned just as she was about to step out into the hallway.

"Brenna, you want to take a drive out there and see the property before we start stripping it?" Alex asked.

"Sure, I guess."

"Johnny, when I'm done with Mrs. Wilson, I'll drop her back out by the highway, by her van and—"

"Taylor," Brenna interrupted.

Alex turned her head.

"I'm going back to my maiden name."

"Okay." Alex turned back to Johnny. "I have to drive out to Queen Creek and check on Robin's progress. Then I'll swing back by here. Tell the crew, pizza and beer at five."

"Actually," Brenna said, "I'm planning on cleaning for the rest of the afternoon, so you can drop me off here. I can walk back to my van."

"You need to get it cleaned today?" Alex asked.

"I want to get it ready for furniture," Brenna said. "I'm going to need a bed, for one thing."

"A bed?" Alex frowned. "Why?"

Brenna wondered why Alex and Johnny were looking at her strangely. "To sleep in of course. I need a refrigerator, too. When will the entry road be done? I need to schedule deliveries."

Alex raised her eyebrows. "You're planning on sleeping in this house? I thought you'd be staying in town and only coming out to work on it."

"Of course I'm going to sleep here," Brenna said. "Cassie had all the utilities turned on, and once I get a bed and a refrigerator, I'll be set."

Alex shook her head. "But you're miles from the closest neighbor and—"

"I'm perfectly capable of taking care of myself." Brenna covered her mouth. She'd surprised herself with the curtness in her voice.

Johnny clicked his tongue and slunk toward the doorway. Alex stood with her hands on her hips and turned her head as she stared at Brenna with fixed eyes. An uncomfortable pause ensued, a heavy silence.

"I never said you weren't capable," Alex said finally.

Brenna felt her face grow hot with embarrassment. "I'm sorry. I didn't mean to snap at you."

"Do you understand how isolated you are out here?" Alex asked.

"Cassie explained that to me."

"Did she also tell you this property sits at an intersection of major highways between Globe and Phoenix which smugglers use on their way to Tucson, and then to the border?"

Brenna shrugged. "What do you mean smugglers? You mean like drug smugglers?"

"Drugs, guns, people. This property is off the beaten path but close enough to the highway that it makes a perfect stopping-off point for people on the run, moving from one location to the next. There're been rumors in my community, people I know, some of my father's friends in the sheriff's department. And when I was out in the trees today, I saw evidence of campfires and trash. People have been camping out in those trees. Some of it may be from teenagers, but I'm sure some comes from people who are trafficking. And trust me, some of those people are dangerous."

Brenna looked out the broken window, to the dark grove, which had turned ash gray in the afternoon sun. She thought about Cassie's comment about teenagers, that even she'd come out to the grove to party when she was young. She remembered the coffee can by the front door with cigarette butts and other trash. She saw Alex watching her, Johnny waiting in the doorway. No doubt they thought she was helpless, unable to take care of herself. No doubt they felt inclined to protect her as people always had. She puffed her chest and crossed her arms. "As I said, I'm capable of taking care of myself. Thank you for your concern."

"If that's what you want," Alex said, "then I'll make sure we finish the road in the next few days."

"Thank you."

"So let's take a drive then." Alex tossed the photographs back on the desk and smiled.

For Brenna, that smile helped brush off the uncomfortable exchange.

The three left the room, and Brenna thanked Johnny once again for his help before she climbed into Alex's truck, waiting while the two talked. They conversed in Spanish but seemed to be whispering nevertheless. Brenna felt a tug of aggravation, thinking they were discussing their suspicion that she couldn't take care of herself alone on the isolated property. As she waited, she cast a glance up to the second story. That was strange, she thought. She was sure after Johnny'd plugged in the new lamp and tried it, he'd turned it off. But right then she could see a distinctive yellow glow emanating from the room containing the boxes and the old desk.

"All right, just to warn you, the access road is in terrible condition." Alex climbed into her seat. She looked through her windshield, following Brenna's gaze. "What is it?"

"I think I left the light on," Brenna said. When she looked again, she no longer saw the glow of light. "Guess it must be the way the sun was hitting the broken windowpanes."

But her memory of seeing a woman in the window a few days ago made her uneasy. She shivered, but tried to shake it off, thinking she was just being silly and illogical. She wasn't afraid to stay there by herself, and she wasn't afraid of smugglers either. Her greatest fear had already been realized, she knew. She'd lost her one and only child. Nothing could ever be more terrifying.

"I know a company that manufactures and installs new windows when you're ready for them," Alex said. "You'll want to get that done soon before we have any winter rain."

"Another cousin?"

Alex chuckled. "No, these are friends I met through Cassie. I'll get you their card later this week." She turned her truck toward the access road. "This grove is overgrown with weeds and grass, and the trees are massive, extremely dry, too. We need to get them down before someone's campfire starts the whole property on fire." She maneuvered around a bend in the road and began to pass the pump house.

Brenna saw the door was chained with a padlock. "I wonder why it's locked."

"Those wells under the irrigation mechanism can run deep. Keeps out animals."

"This land is on well water?"

"No, the wells connect to underground passages that connect to the canal system. Your water in the house comes from the city." Alex stopped her truck. "You want to get out and look? You'll be amazed how dark and thick it is."

Brenna agreed, exited the truck, and picked her way over the rough ground while following Alex into the trees. Once they'd gone a dozen yards, Alex stopped and turned around.

"See what I mean? It'll be slow going through this mass of trees." Her voice was muted by the dense canopy.

"I do see." Brenna looked around.

The trees hadn't been tended to in some time, hadn't been pruned or shaped. Most of them were dead even though brown leaves still clung to most of the branches, which reached many feet above and blocked any sunlight that might've tried to peek in. She peered through them, trying to see the house from where she stood, but the limbs and dead branches were too thick. Shrunken and hardened knobs of old citrus littered the ground; only a few dead or rotten pieces continued to hang from the branches. The air was still, no insects buzzed, no breeze blew. It was quiet but for the distant hum and rumble of the trucks still at work on the entry road.

"It's peaceful," Brenna said. "So quiet." The silence was indeed comforting for her. There were no sirens, no shattering glass, no splintering wood, no screaming wind. She felt the back of her neck. Her scar was cool to the touch.

"Yes, quiet," Alex said. "And when my crew knocks off and you're out here by yourself at night, that quiet will grow loud."

"You may not think that sounds pleasant, but believe me, I've needed silence for a long time."

Alex furrowed her brow. "I'd think the isolation wouldn't bring you much comfort. I guess I thought you'd want to be with people after your loss."

Brenna stepped around fallen branches. "I haven't been alone much since the accident. My sister and brother-in-law or ladies from our church are always with me. I know they mean well, but I can never relax, just be. It's hard because sometimes all I want to do is cry, sometimes scream."

She tugged at a beer bottle, half-concealed by dirt and debris. She turned it in her hand, tossed it back to the ground, and glanced at Alex who watched her, listened to her. She had no idea why she felt compelled to share something so personal with this woman, a stranger.

Alex cleared her throat. "Can I ask you something?"

Brenna nodded.

"How old was your son?"

"Six. He'd just turned six in February."

"I'm sorry, Brenna. That's a terrible tragedy, to lose a young child."

Brenna felt her jaw go rigid and her lips tighten into a thin line. "Have you ever lost a child?" She was aware of the bitterness in her voice.

"No, but I—"

"The worst thing in my life. It's something no mother should ever have to live through."

Alex buried her hands in her pockets. "No, no mother should have to."

Brenna turned away, feeling ashamed at her second outburst directed toward Alex. Clearly the woman was only being kind and didn't deserve to be attacked. She closed her eyes. The road equipment continued to rumble in the distance, and she stood still, soaking in the insulated sense of peace. The closeness of the trees calmed her and pulled the tension from her body. But the serene moment was broken when she heard a man's voice.

"Whore."

She opened her eyes, searched the trees, and caught a glimpse of muddy boots hurrying away from her. "Hey!" she shouted.

Alex hurried next to her. "What is it?"

"Are some of your men out here?" she asked, disturbed that one of Alex's men, the men Alex said wouldn't catcall her, had just insulted her.

"No, they're all on the entry road. Why?"

"You didn't hear that?" Brenna pointed in the direction where she'd seen the boots disappear. "Didn't you see someone just then?"

Alex frowned. "No, Brenna, I didn't."

Brenna squinted and dropped down to look between tree trunks. "There was someone there. A man. I heard his voice."

"I didn't hear it. Maybe it was an echo from the road."

Brenna shivered, certain one of the crew had followed them and had intentionally insulted her. She clenched her jaw more tightly and coughed with a closed mouth. Her throat felt thick, as if something was stuck in her windpipe. "I need to do some cleaning, if you don't mind." She walked back to Alex's truck while she touched the back of her neck and felt her scar, hot and throbbing.

❖

They didn't speak during the drive back, but once Alex had parked her truck in front of the house, she said, "I'm sorry about the way I reacted to you staying out here. I'm only concerned for you, nothing else. Sometimes I'm a little bossy and poke my nose in other people's business."

"It's nice of you to be concerned." Brenna tried to make her voice sound tender. She felt bad about having been bitchy earlier.

"You okay, Brenna?"

"I'm fine. Just tired." She looked into Alex's eyes. They were beautiful eyes, the same color as her thick, dark hair, which had a natural wave to it. Brenna wondered how soft Alex's hair would feel to touch.

They continued to watch each other, and Brenna was surprised she was able to hold Alex's gaze without blushing and tugging her own hair. She wanted to ask her about Cassie, to know if the two of them meant something to each other, but she figured it was none of her business. So she opened the truck door and slid out. "Thank you. I should get to my cleaning. See if I can get the floors swept."

"I'll see you Wednesday, but if you need something before then, give me a call." Alex leaned from her truck window. "And if Johnny can help with anything, feel free to ask. He's a good guy. You can trust him."

"Sure. Thanks." Brenna wondered if Johnny had been the one out in the trees, the one to insult her. She thought again about his tattoos and his devilish goatee.

Once inside with the door shut, she listened as Alex's truck headed away from the house. When she was sure she'd gone, Brenna sighed, slid down the wall, and plopped on her butt. She stared at the pile of supplies on the floor in front of her, wondering if she'd made a mistake. She felt sick to her stomach for some reason and tried to remember what she'd had to eat that morning. It was more than simple jitteriness around Alex, she was sure. It was this house, the grove, that man's voice. He'd called her a whore.

A whore.

She twirled her wedding band. She'd wanted to remove it months ago, but hadn't found the courage to do so yet. The guilt kept her bound to it. But she was going to change her name back, she thought. The ring should come off as well. After sliding it from her finger, she held it in her hand and looked at it. She thought of Debra then and their affair. Brenna knew she'd hurt her, had complicated her life, had almost cost Debra her marriage. She'd destroyed her own marriage in the process, hurting Edward. But he'd been so understanding, she remembered. Understanding but hurt all the same. He wouldn't punish her and take

Michael from her, he'd told her. But she'd lost her son nevertheless. A greater punishment in the end. She swallowed a number of times as the blockage in her throat threatened to send her into a coughing fit. Then she shoved her wedding ring into her pocket and began digging through her cleaning supplies and other purchases. There was plenty here to keep her distracted, she figured, and she began setting the other lamps throughout the house, putting in fresh lightbulbs in the kitchen and bathroom fixtures, and disinfecting the toilet plus the kitchen and bathroom sinks.

When she was done with all that, she went upstairs and examined the awful wallpaper in the second bedroom. She peeled a few strips to determine the work required to remove it. The paper had been applied over Sheetrock, and the adhesive had turned brown underneath. As she pulled away a strip from the corner by the window, she noticed in some places there were black splatters. She worried it could be evidence of mold from moisture getting in through the broken panes and leaky roof. The thought of battling mold spores disheartened her, and she felt too tired to continue with her cleaning.

So instead of carrying on with her plan to sweep and mop the floors, she started picking through some of the old documents and flipping through photos. She began gathering all the photographs into one pile and moving loose papers into another. Soon the sun shifted into late afternoon, making the room grow dim. She switched on her new floor lamp, then remembered she'd bought fuel for the oil lamp. She fetched the new wick and bottle of oil as well as a cloth. After disassembling and wiping down the antique, she inserted the wick and filled the basin with fresh oil. But she didn't have a lighter or matches with her. Temporarily stymied, she returned the lamp to the desk and switched on her new electric light instead, and resumed her inspection of the room's contents. After a while, she sat on the floor opposite the window while she dug through one of the file boxes. She found sales receipts for fertilizer, irrigation bills, and payments for freight. She also found another old photograph, stuffed between folders. She pulled it out and studied it. Like the others, this photo was a grainy black and white. It showed a gruff-looking man standing with a fair-haired, sickly woman. A younger man stood to one side of the couple, and a young towheaded boy on the other. He also looked sickly and resembled the woman a great deal. She flipped the photograph over. Someone had written on the back: *Poulsen Family 1924.* This was a priceless piece of history, she realized. It would be a perfect addition to the other photos, enlarged and framed, centered on the living room wall.

"The notorious Hadley Poulsen." She thought about Cassie's silly story.

Then as she studied the face of Hadley's wife and wondered what her name had been, wondered about the names of the assumed sons, the gruesomeness of the story rushed back to her, and she felt queasy again, thinking there might be a bit of truth to it. She stood and set the photograph with the others. By now it was dusk and the lamp's light reflected off the few remaining whole windowpanes. She went to the window to see if she could view the road crew from that vantage point and caught a reflection of long dark hair in the glass. Alex had come back. She turned around, happy she'd get to interact with her again.

But Alex wasn't standing in the doorway.

Brenna felt the scar on the back of her neck pulse while at the same time her hands went cold and she shivered. The small, cluttered room seemed to close around her, and she thought she caught the whiff of mold and mildew from the unsightly wallpaper. Perhaps that was what had her stomach sick. She coughed and switched off the lamp and hugged herself as she headed downstairs. She'd done enough for one day, she reasoned. She could come back tomorrow to continue her cleaning. She gathered her purse and jacket and headed for the front door, but stopped when she heard something. She paused and lifted her eyes. Something grated across the floor upstairs. It was faint, but the sound had come, she was sure, from the room with the desk. She turned away from the front door, looked toward the darkened stairway. Something was moving at the top of the stairs, something in the shadows. And this time, unmistakably, she heard footsteps, soft padded footsteps, landing on the steps, coming down the stairway. She grabbed her throat. She was certain Hadley Poulsen's wife was in the house and coming right for her. As her fear threatened to cut off her scream, there was a knock at the door.

"Brenna?"

She jumped and opened the door while holding her heart. Alex stood on the porch, her truck idling in the driveway.

"Hi." Brenna gulped breaths in short bursts. "You startled me. I didn't hear you drive up."

"Sorry about that," Alex said. "I just got back from checking on another job and noticed your van still out there. You need a ride back to it?"

"That would be great, thanks."

Brenna climbed into the truck, and as Alex pulled away, she looked at the second-story windows. They had turned dark now, the sun having set behind the trees.

"We have pizza and beer a few times a week when we finish for the day. You want to come along?" Alex asked.

Brenna looked over her shoulder, out the truck's back window, and watched the house. Her heart still raced and her mouth was parched as she swallowed nonexistent saliva. She must've heard Alex's truck pull up, she told herself, trying to dismiss the sound she thought she'd heard. Cassie's silly story and Alex's talk of smugglers had her tense. That was all. She covered her mouth and coughed.

"Are you feeling okay?" Alex asked.

"I'm good. I think."

"So, do you want to have pizza and beer with me and my crew?"

"I don't know, Alex. I'm not familiar with this area. I wouldn't know the way to get there or back to my hotel afterward."

"It's not far off the main freeway. Where you staying? I can give you directions as a backup to your GPS."

"Scottsdale, the Hilton." It was just now occurring to Brenna that Alex was asking her to socialize.

"Nice. Listen, I'll have one of my guys drive my truck and I'll go with you in your van to show you the way. Then I'll draw you a map back to your hotel. Come on, you haven't had dinner, have you?"

"No, I haven't." In truth, Brenna didn't feel like eating as her stomach was still upset. Still, Alex was asking her to do something, to spend time with her.

"It's not the fancy places Cassie may take you, but I know the family who owns the place. It's not a chain, and their pizza is from scratch. The beer's ice cold, too." Alex pulled alongside Brenna's van. "Will you come? We're a bunch of idiots, but we're all friendly. I'd like you to come."

That was all the encouragement Brenna needed. "Okay. I haven't had pizza in a while."

That seemed to please Alex, and after she'd told one of her guys to take her truck and meet them at the restaurant, she climbed into Brenna's van and grinned. "Great, I'm glad you're going," she said, and began to give her directions.

They drove off as the sun set on the grove. The trees stood silent, watching the house as a dim light flickered and grew, seeping from the upstairs window and onto the gravel drive below. The oil lamp was burning, the new wick sputtering, having soaked up the fresh fuel. And at the window, a figure stood. Her dark hair hung around her shoulders and her black eyes searched the trees as she looked in vain for that which she'd lost so many years ago.

CHAPTER FIVE

As Brenna drove, Alex talked about her work. Brenna was impressed to learn Alex was overseeing three other jobs around the Valley. Alex also mentioned she had prospects popping up in Peoria and one south of the Valley in Casa Grande.

"Sounds like you work all the time," Brenna said.

"Sometimes I do, even weekends. But for my crews who have families, I try to give them at least Sundays off."

"And how about your family?" She peeked at Alex's hands. "You married?" She'd guessed what Alex might answer, but hoped for some disclosure about Cassie and their relationship.

"Just me, my dad, and my grandfather at home."

When Brenna dared another glance, she noticed Alex smiling at her. "I'm sorry. I didn't mean to pry."

"That's okay. I know I don't live up to all the stereotypes."

"Stereotypes?"

"Most Latinas my age have a few kids by now, and the ones who don't are usually thinking about taking vows, being nuns." Alex chuckled. "Maybe not so much these days."

"You wanted to be a nun?"

That made Alex laugh outright. "No, Brenna, no nunnery for me. I'm not sure they'd take me at this point."

"But you're Catholic?"

"That stereotype I do live up to. And how about you? I heard you say something this afternoon about the ladies at your church."

Brenna clenched her jaw. "I was brought up Methodist, was married in the Methodist church, and baptized my son there. My husband was a deacon, so we attended a lot of church functions."

"I see."

"But I'm not religious. I don't believe in God. In anything. Not anymore." She was aware of how harsh she sounded, and like earlier that day, she regretted taking that tone with Alex, who she saw frown and look away. After a moment, she cleared her throat, swallowed the thickness that gathered there, and worked to sound more pleasant. "I've never known a woman in construction before, let alone one that owns her own business." She kept her eyes on the road. But she was aware Alex watched her, studied her.

"I've got a few gals working for me. Robin's a woman. She's a foreman, too."

"Interesting."

"And what did you do back home in Iowa?"

"Just a mother and wife," Brenna said, feeling self-conscious about her less-than-colorful life.

"Just a mother and wife?" Alex repeated. "I don't know about you, but I've seen my aunts and cousins raising children and running a household. There's no *just* about it. That's hard work. A ton harder than the hours I spend working roads and surveying land."

"I don't know about that."

Alex touched her shoulder. "Give yourself some credit, Brenna. Being a mother and wife is a big commitment."

Brenna clenched her jaw even tighter. "Yes, well I'm neither of those anymore. I guess I need to find a new career."

They rode in uneasy silence the rest of the way to the restaurant.

Inside the pizza joint, the crew from Brenna's job and the others from the job in Queen Creek were already there. They waved and motioned Alex and Brenna over when they saw them enter. Alex introduced her to each person, asked if she wanted beer, and then disappeared into the restroom to clean up. Even though she still felt apprehensive around Johnny and wondered if he'd been the one to insult her out in the trees,

Brenna sat next to him at the large round table. The other crewmembers studied her until finally one of the women addressed her.

"Johnny tells us you bought the old Poulsen place." She was the one Alex had introduced as Robin, the other foreman.

"My husband bought the land," Brenna said. "I'm getting it ready to sell to developers, maybe restore the home as a landmark."

"You know the story about that place?" Robin asked.

"A number of people have told me the story." Brenna produced her insincere smile and fought not to spit the words. She was tired of hearing the story of Hadley's headless wife.

The men and women at the table continued to gawk at her.

Then another man, Hector, said, "No worries, girl, every old place got a ghost story. Even the Delgados' restaurant got some old woman who haunts it."

"Which restaurant is that?" Brenna asked.

"Las Cinco Hermanas. It's the boss's family's restaurant. Her aunts and mother were the ones to start it, but her tía Marta runs it now," Johnny said.

"Best chimis in the state," Hector interjected.

"Tamales, too, and ah, the green chili," another woman remarked, and then she asked Brenna, "You like Mexican food?"

"Sure, I guess," Brenna said.

"Have Alex take you to Las Cinco Hermanas. It gets voted one of the top Mexican food restaurants in the Valley every year," the same woman said.

"And maybe you can see the old woman who haunts it," Hector added. "I've heard she appears to customers sometimes."

"She's an old vaquera, raised cattle back in the day," Johnny said. "Restaurant's built right on the site of her ranch home near the base of South Mountain. Had corral all around it. They say she waits until the cleanup crew sweeps and puts the chairs away before she starts practicing her lassoing right there in the main dining room."

Brenna refrained from rolling her eyes. What was it with Arizonans and their ghost stories? "Seems like your state has many ghost stories to go around," she said. "I was reading a magazine in my hotel room about the Lost Dutchman who supposedly haunts the Superstition Mountains. But like Hector says, every old place has a story, I guess."

"Hotel room? You're not from here?" Robin asked.

"No, Iowa. I'm only here to oversee the preparation of this property." Brenna hoped Robin wouldn't press for more.

"You and your husband those people who buy properties and flip 'em?" Robin leaned forward on her elbows.

Brenna bit her lip. "No, my husband, he—"

"Robin, that's the client's business, not yours." Alex stood behind Brenna, after coming to the table and catching the last bit of conversation.

"Sure, Boss." Robin went back to her beer.

Brenna looked at her. She felt at ease now she was there, but also nervous as Alex watched her before grinning and holding out a bottle of beer.

"You look like a girl who likes 'em light. Am I right?" Alex said.

"Light?"

"Your beer." Alex set the bottle in Brenna's hand and went around and sat across from her.

Johnny leaned in. "Boss likes hers dark. But I'm with you." He smiled, showing his two dimples. Then he hoisted his own bottle. "Salud!"

The group began talking about projects they were working on as well as family gossip and local sports rivalries. The pizzas came, and they dug in, continuing to talk with full mouths. While Brenna listened to the conversation and ate, she watched Alex who seemed to always be smiling and laughing. Alex glanced at her often, nodding on occasion, but she never held her gaze longer than a second. After the pizza was gone, the talk and laughter continued, along with some off-color jokes and remarks. But for the most part, everyone was pleasant and polite to Brenna, including her in the conversation, particularly Johnny, who patted her shoulder on more than one occasion. She noticed he kept looking at her, and when she turned to look at him any time he was speaking, he always held her gaze. She was certain now he couldn't have been the one out in the grove earlier that day. He was entirely too sweet, she thought. And she was beginning to understand something else about him as well. It had taken her a while because she was unaccustomed to a man's attention. Edward had begun dating her while she was still a senior in high school, and before that, she'd had no experience with boys. But now she could see it. Johnny liked her. At one point, he scribbled his phone number on a paper napkin and handed it to her.

"In case you need something," he said.

Alex shot Johnny a look that made Brenna realize Alex had seen Johnny's solicitous behavior, too.

When the group ordered another round of beer, Brenna excused herself to use the restroom. Still in her stall, she heard the bathroom door open and two women enter, talking.

"…and she's with your mom tonight?" It was Alex's voice.

"She's gonna take her to school the rest of the week and keep her overnight until I can get him out of the apartment." It was Robin, and it sounded as if she was crying.

"He needs a good treatment program, Robin. We need to get him into someplace, otherwise he'll just end up back on the streets using and selling," Alex said.

"I know that, but no place will take him because of his record. Shit, Alex, I can't let him be around her. She's too young to be exposed to this." Robin cried harder.

Alex's voice, softer, almost comforting, said, "Listen, I'll talk to my father. He'll know someone. We'll get him into treatment. Just keep Kylie with your mom until we can get him help."

Brenna heard Robin's muffled voice, assumed she must be hugging Alex as she spoke. "Thank you, I wouldn't be able to do this without you. And thank Rubén for me, too."

"Go see about the check. I need to pee and get to the smoke shop for Juan Carlos. I come home without his tobacco, he'll be heartbroken."

The stall door next to Brenna opened and closed. She didn't want Alex to know she'd overheard the conversation with her employee, so she flushed, then tried to wash her hands and leave. But the paper towel dispenser jammed, and just as she was about to wipe her wet hands on her jeans and escape, Alex came out of her stall. Brenna stared into the bathroom mirror at Alex's reflection.

"Sorry, I didn't mean to eavesdrop." She headed toward the door.

"Wait, Brenna. It's okay. Hang on a minute."

Brenna turned.

"We didn't get a chance to talk much." Alex washed her hands. "Johnny seems to be keeping you to himself." She smacked the paper-towel dispenser and pulled towels out. "Forgive him, he's harmless. But I think he's developed a little crush on you." She tossed her wet towels in the trash and leaned against the counter.

Brenna didn't know what to say. Her suspicions about Johnny were apparently correct. Alex, and probably the others at the table, had picked up on his flirtations. It made her feel good in a way. But she was developing an infatuation of her own, and it wasn't for Johnny.

"He's a sweet man, and so cute with those dimples and his devil's goatee."

"Ah, yes, his goatee." Alex chuckled. "He's been nursing it for months now. I think his mother would be happy to see it shaved off."

"I hope he won't be hurt if I don't—"

But Alex held up a hand. "No, Brenna, don't feel bad. He'll be fine. I had a talk with him, and I've told him, given that you're a recent widow, you're certainly not ready to be courted. Especially not by the likes of him." With those last words, she laughed.

"Right." Brenna noticed the bathroom lights glinted off Alex's face and eyes, lighting up the small room.

"I imagine it'll be sometime before you'd even consider dating again." Alex had grown serious.

Brenna began to stutter out an answer. "Well, I—"

But Alex added, "I mean, you're a young woman, and I'm sure you're still hurting, still missing your husband."

"And my son." Brenna shifted on her feet. People always assumed she was missing Edward. She anticipated the familiar wave of guilt that accompanied her silent awareness that she didn't miss her husband.

"Of course, and your son."

"Yes, well…" Brenna couldn't stop herself from tugging her hair. She tried to think of something to say, something to ask, and finally blurted out, "Your crew loves you. You're all like a big family. That's nice."

"Yes, we are. They're good people."

"I'm pleased Cassie recommended your company, and I'm glad I've gotten to know you." She flinched, sure she sounded like an idiot because she'd met Alex only three days ago. "It was nice of you to ask me to come along tonight, too. Thank you." She stuck out her hand, not knowing a way to end the conversation.

"I'm glad you did." Alex took her hand. "I'll lead you back to your hotel if you'd like. You can follow me in my truck."

"That's sweet, but some directions will do." Brenna noticed Alex kept her eyes fixed on her, squeezed her hand tighter.

Alex released her grip and pulled a paper towel from the dispenser and a pen from her pocket. "Right. Here, this should do." She drew a crude map as she explained how to get back on the freeway and toward the hotel in Scottsdale.

"I think between this and my GPS, I can find my way," Brenna said.

"Call me if you get lost. I'll be happy to come find you."

"I don't want to be any trouble."

"You're no trouble, Brenna. No trouble at all," Alex said.

Brenna lowered her eyes. She wanted to say more, but instead she could only stare at Alex's belt buckle.

Finally, Alex patted her shoulder. "I'll see you Wednesday at the Poulsen place."

❖

On Tuesday morning, Brenna drove off the lot of San Tan Jeep and Chrysler in a brand new cherry-red Jeep Wrangler, and it was loaded with every available option. Alex's cousin Victor could've sold the vehicle to her for the dealer's asking price and made a huge commission off the costly model, since she knew nothing about the process and game of buying a car. But since she'd asked for him by name and told him his cousin Alex had recommended him, he'd offered her the employee discount. Victor had laughed and told Brenna he knew the terror his cousin could be if she was crossed.

However, it'd been more difficult than Brenna had imagined handing over the keys to her minivan for the trade-in. She wasn't particularly attached to the vehicle, but it'd been the last ride she'd taken with her husband and son that fateful morning of the accident. It was gone now, behind her, as she drove toward the highway turnoff to her property. She'd purchased the soft-top convertible and Victor had shown her the way to roll the cover into the boot behind the backseat and along the safety bar. Now, speeding up the freeway with the sun bathing her skin and the autumn wind blowing in her hair, she was still in shock that the timid side of her nature had been pushed aside and this new bold woman had emerged. A cherry-red Jeep and a convertible? The soccer mom had shed her skin.

Before the turnoff to the highway, she made two more stops—one at a sporting goods store for a sleeping bag and air mattress and another at a hardware store. She purchased duct tape and a roll of thick plastic sheeting to use in sealing off the broken windowpanes until she could have them replaced. She also bought some lawn chairs, a small table for the front porch, primer, and paint along with rollers and brushes. Her goal for the day was to finish removing the boards from the windows, to seal off the broken panes with the plastic and duct tape, and to sweep and mop the hardwood floors as well as clean the debris from inside and around the house. She'd also take measurements for a refrigerator, and a bed for the downstairs bedroom, something she hadn't done the day before. If Alex's crew completed the entry road this coming week, she'd go ahead and purchase furniture to be delivered at the end of the week. Meanwhile, she'd prime and paint the downstairs bedroom. She was determined to work all day at the house, and if she felt comfortable, she'd spend the night. Alex would be back on the property tomorrow, and she wanted to be there as well, looking forward to another interaction with her.

After turning off the freeway onto the highway, she remembered the only food she had at the house was bottled water and a box of granola bars she'd left there the previous day. Her stomach had recovered, and she knew if she planned on working most of the day, she'd get hungry. So before she continued down the highway, she stopped at the gas station she'd noticed on her first trip out there to get snacks and ice for her cooler. As she parked her new Jeep, she saw a middle-aged man working on a tractor in the garage. He glimpsed at her, seemed to admire her new wheels, and went back to work. Inside, she was pleased to find a full convenience store with a dining area and deli counter off to one side. A few locals sat at one of the tables watching the news on a TV propped in the corner. She grabbed some chips and a six-pack of soda along with a couple cans of prepared pasta. The stovetop had gas—she'd checked the day before—and she could heat the pasta in the can if she was careful. It'd have to do until she bought some pots and pans. That reminded her, she hadn't purchased a can opener at the hardware store, and she wanted to get a lighter as well.

"Can I help you, miss?" a woman's voice asked behind her.

Brenna turned to face a large light-haired woman with calloused hands and broad shoulders.

"Do you have a can opener I could buy?" Brenna asked.

The woman motioned. "Over here with the auto supplies." She escorted her to the area. "That gonna do it for you?"

Brenna glanced at the deli. "Is the deli open?"

"I'll make you something." The woman stepped behind the counter. "What can I get you?"

Brenna read the handwritten menu, ordered, and waited as the woman built her sandwich. She glanced at the other customers watching TV and turned her attention to the news report:

Critics say the new bill is just the latest wave of racially biased legislation to come out of the Arizona House of Representatives. But supporters of the bill argue that demands on state resources are already stressed and claim denying undocumented immigrants access to health insurance and funding for education is one way to deal with the budget's shortfalls and further discourage illegals from crossing our borders for what one representative terms a free lunch.

"Just more of the same, am I right?" The woman slid the wrapped sandwich toward her.

"Excuse me?" Brenna had been paying attention to the broadcast.

The woman nodded her head toward the television. "These politicians and their crusades. You can always tell when it's election year. They gotta stir the pot." She headed toward the cash register while Brenna followed.

"I guess. I just moved here. I'm not familiar with local politics."

"Whereabouts you from?"

"Iowa." Brenna removed her debit card from her wallet and swiped the machine.

"Got some family from that part of the country." The woman started ringing up the food. "SpaghettiOs, cola, and barbecue potato chips. Sounds like someone's got the munchies."

"Could I get a large bag of ice as well?" Brenna asked.

Just then the mechanic came in through the propped-open door and began filling his cup with soda from the machine.

"Fernie, get this young lady a bag of ice," the woman said to him.

Fernie went out and grabbed the ice from the outside cooler and put it in the backseat of Brenna's Jeep. He came inside again and leaned against the counter while he flipped through a magazine.

"Having a picnic then?" the woman asked as she rang up the last of the items.

"No, just going down the road to work on a house I've inherited. Thought I'd need something to keep me going later in the day." Brenna punched in her PIN.

"Which house is that?" the woman asked.

Fernie put down his magazine, and he and the clerk exchanged glances.

"The one at the citrus grove, the old Poulsen place." Brenna reached for her bag. But the woman grabbed her hand as she reached.

"Honey, did you say the Poulsen place?" Her voice dropped, and Brenna noticed her peculiar expression.

"That's right. I'm renovating the house." She felt uneasy with the way the woman continued to hold her hand.

"You'd be better off having it all bulldozed," the woman said. "Place is nothing but an ugly reminder."

"No digas nada, mi amor," Fernie said.

Brenna didn't understand what he'd said, but it sounded like a warning. And then she realized it was probably Cassie's stupid ghost story again. She clicked her tongue. This ridiculous tale certainly had a long shelf life. "Are you referring to Hadley Poulsen's wife and her headless ghost?"

"Nelda Poulsen?" The woman looked baffled by Brenna's question. "No, honey, that old gal is buried in Mesa Cemetery. Her and her five babies. Poor thing. Now that's a heartbreaking story, but no, I meant that old fellow Owen, the caretaker that—" The woman stopped and stared at Fernie who was waving and gesturing at her. "Fernie, you know Brimhall wants his tractor ready by this afternoon. Quit your snooping and get back to work."

"I'm done, corazón. You don't need to be so bossy all the time. It's bad for your blood pressure," he answered. "Besides, this young woman doesn't want to hear your gossip and nonsense." He smiled toward Brenna and went back out.

The woman shook her head. "That man drives me to distraction." Then she leaned across the counter while she stole a glance at the two men engrossed in the television. "Listen, honey, don't believe none of that nonsense about Nelda's ghost. They been telling that yarn for longer than I've been around. It's nonsense, I tell you."

"I suspected as much."

"But Owen, poor old fellow," the woman continued, "he was the lackey of the chief deputy sheriff and his brother the state representative. They say he found out the truth about the family. You know, the excommunication, those suicides, all that."

At the word *suicide* Brenna yanked her bag from the woman's hand and backed away, shaking her head. "I don't know what you mean about suicide or excommunication. I don't even know this Owen. I just arrived in Arizona a few weeks ago, and I'm not familiar with any of—"

"You a churchgoing gal?" The woman eyed her.

The question felt like a slap in the face. The last time Brenna had stepped inside a church was at her husband's and son's memorial service and she doubted she'd ever go again. "I don't think that's any of your—"

"Well, listen," the woman interrupted again. "That land is cursed. You understand? The family had the money and power to cover it up at one time, and now those two grandsons, Julian Wilcox and his brother, Marcus, they gonna fight to keep those family secrets hidden. They have too much to lose."

Brenna stumbled backward toward the door. "I guess, but—"

"And poor Owen, I bet you a nickel he found out something. But you wait and see. The family doesn't have the power it used to. It'll all come out eventually."

Brenna walked through the open door. "What are you saying? I don't…" She shook her head, giving up on any attempt to learn more. She hurried to her Jeep, climbed in, and started it before even strapping herself in, but then yelped in surprise when Fernie, the mechanic, appeared at her passenger window. He watched her a moment before coming to her side of the Jeep.

"My wife likes to gossip. She means no harm," he said.

Brenna saw the name painted above the garage: *Fernando Flores, Owner*. "This is your place?"

He held out a greasy hand. "Sí, I am Fernando. But you can call me Fernie."

"It's nice to meet you, Fernie. I'm Brenna." She took his hand.

"It is a good piece of land you have," he said. "But perhaps a better idea if it is paved over."

She thought that was a strange thing to say, and although she knew she probably shouldn't ask, she needed to know. "Fernie, can you tell me what your wife meant about the caretaker, Owen? What happened to him?"

Fernie seemed to debate with himself before answering. "He was laying a concrete slab in the garage. Let me think…it has been about five years now. That is when it happened."

"When what happened?"

"We are not too sure, but the chief deputy sheriff said the old man had a stroke and lay helpless in the wet concrete for a day or two. A sad thing. Died a few days afterward in the hospital." Fernie shook his head. "Qué pena. A pity, it was."

"Is that why the doors are nailed shut?"

Fernie held up his hands. "This I do not know." He headed back to the garage, but stopped and turned around again, looking at her with a stern face. "My wife is right, señorita. That land is cursed. My people suffered greatly under the family, a lot of sorrow and misery that many of us wish to forget." He turned once more and disappeared inside the garage.

CHAPTER SIX

While she drove the highway toward the grove, Brenna thought about what the mechanic and his wife had told her. She also thought about what she'd imagined she'd seen in the upstairs window, the noises she'd thought she'd heard on the stairway. But she convinced herself she was letting Cassie's story and the remoteness of the property get the best of her. Hadley's wife was buried, presumably with her head, in the city cemetery. There was no merit to the local legend. And after all, she was a big girl and a pragmatic one as well, she told herself. She wasn't going to let her imagination run wild. But more important, she had to prove to everyone who continued to warn her and make a fuss, she was capable of taking care of herself and wouldn't be frightened off. Still the story about the caretaker had left her on edge.

As she approached the property, she saw Hector directing a large piece of machinery. She pulled over. When he saw her, he grinned and held off the man driving the equipment.

"Hey, Mrs. Taylor, the boss and Johnny are out in the grove. You want me to call them?" He fingered the radio on his belt.

"You can call me Brenna," she said. Then she asked, unable to hide her surprise, "Alex is here? She said she wouldn't be out until tomorrow."

"They're looking over some maps and grids. I'll tell them you're here." He used his radio and said something in Spanish.

She heard a woman's voice answer him in the same.

"They'll meet you by the house." Hector nodded his approval. "Nice Jeep. You get that from Victor?"

"I did."

"Sweet. Let me signal Kevin to pull the front loader over to give you room."

Brenna thanked him and drove around the large equipment and waved at the other crewmembers that waved back. She rounded the bend and the house came into view. Before she got out, she looked at the two second-story windows, where sun glinted off the broken panes. Next she considered the garage. She forced herself out the Jeep and walked over to it. She tugged on the doors, but they remained nailed shut. She thought about the poor man who'd died inside. It'd been nothing, she was sure, but an unfortunate event. The man was old, had stroked, and died at the hospital. There had to be a good reason why someone had nailed the doors shut. Maybe later in the week, Alex would get them open, as she'd promised, and Brenna would see there was nothing significant inside. She glanced over as two trucks rumbled over.

"Nice wheels." Johnny began checking out her new Jeep once he'd gotten out of his truck.

By now Alex had joined them. "Hi, Brenna."

"Hi." Brenna couldn't stop herself from taking all of Alex in, running her eyes from the top of Alex's head to her work boots.

Alex continued to watch her, smiling.

Johnny was over at her new Jeep. "Alex said you were thinking of going to see Victor. He give you a good deal?"

"I guess. I've never bought a car before," Brenna said, still looking at Alex. "My husband always took care of buying our cars. But Victor said he gave me the employee discount."

Alex nodded. "He did. I've already talked to him this morning."

"Thank you. Your cousin was very helpful."

"I'm glad he could help out." Alex began admiring the interior of the vehicle as well. "Lots of good stuff, I see. Whoa, satellite radio. Are those heated leather seats?"

"I went a little crazy. I probably didn't need the top of the line. But I've never bought a car before. It felt good to walk in and point to what I wanted and not worry about the price."

"I wouldn't know much about that sort of thing." Alex peeked into the backseat. "You want help getting these things inside? Johnny, start hauling these things in."

"That's not necessary," Brenna said.

"Nonsense. Let us help while we're here."

In moments, the Jeep had been unpacked, and Brenna offered cans of soda to thank them. Johnny declined and said he needed to get back to the road, but Alex took a can and sat on the porch steps. Brenna joined her.

"Beautiful sunny day," Alex said. "Strange weather for November. It's usually lots cooler."

Brenna gazed out at the wall of dead trees. "I thought you wouldn't be by until tomorrow."

Alex glanced at her and smiled before she spoke. "After Victor called to tell me about selling you that Jeep, I decided to swing by here. I hoped I'd run into you."

"Really? Why?"

"I wanted to see how you were doing. To say I enjoyed you being with me and the crew last night. To tell you you're welcome to join us anytime."

"I had fun, thank you." Brenna smiled, but it wasn't her fake smile this time.

"You looked like you were having fun. I think you even laughed a few times."

At this Brenna giggled. "I guess I did. It seems like forever since I've laughed."

Alex handed her the empty can, stood, and fished out her truck keys. "I bet it has been." Her voice sounded tender. "So listen." Her tone changed back to all business. "I see you bought a sleeping bag. Are you staying out here tonight?"

"Probably."

"I won't bother you again about staying in town, but keep your door locked. And call me if you need anything." Alex walked toward her truck.

"Alex?" Brenna stood as well. "Do you know much about this land? I mean, other than that silly ghost story. Do you know much about why the family stopped growing citrus?"

"Not much. Some rumors about low yield, not being able to harvest what they did grow, couldn't keep workers on the job. That sort of thing."

"Why's that? Why couldn't they keep workers?"

"From the stories I've heard people tell, the man who ran it the last years it was in operation was a bit loco. Didn't always pay the workers. But that's only what I've heard. Place shut down when I was a little girl."

"Have you heard anything about the caretaker who had a stroke?"

"No, when was that?"

"The man and his wife who own the gas station where you turn off the freeway told me he'd been laying a concrete slab in the garage and had a stroke, later died."

Alex glanced at the garage. "So I guess that was about five years ago. Cassie said the place had been boarded up that long. No, I don't know anything about that." She looked at the second story and out at the grove and back to the garage. Then she looked at Brenna, held her gaze before saying, "I'm going to worry about you out here alone, Brenna."

"I'm not afraid."

"I know." Alex began to say something more, but instead gave a little wave and smiled. "I need to get back to work. I'll see you tomorrow."

Brenna thanked her and watched her drive away. She felt flattered Alex had come by to see her, and she sat in her new lawn chair on the porch and thought about what it might mean. But she was sure she was making too big a deal out of the gesture. Besides she'd yet to establish the nature of Alex and Cassie's relationship and wasn't even sure her intuition wasn't misleading her. She pushed the quiet hope from her mind as well as the troublesome knowledge of the caretaker's death and got to work inside the house.

She spent the first hour downstairs, hesitant to go upstairs again after what she thought she'd heard the day before. But after glancing at the stairs a few times, she admonished herself for being uneasy and went up to the room with the desk and boxes. Again, she noticed the room seemed colder than the rest of the house. She decided she needed to seal the broken panes with plastic sheeting right away. But first, she found her lighter and rolled the new wick on the antique oil lamp, ready to light it for the first time. She froze, her thumb poised on the lighter. The tip of the wick was blackened as if it'd been lit before. She ran her finger over the charred cotton and rubbed it against her thumb while observing the soot. This made no sense, she knew. She'd only cleaned the lamp yesterday, not lit it. As she thought about this, she felt a whisper, a sigh against her ear. She swung around. But there was nothing, no one. She let out a breath and it created a misty smoke from the icy chill in the room. Her scar began to throb, her heart began to race, and she forgot about the lamp and hurried back downstairs and out to the porch and then to the gravel drive. She bent over holding her knees as she coughed and wheezed, chastising herself for getting spooked. That's when she realized the hum and noise of the road equipment in the distance scarcely pierced through the silence that surrounded her. Alex was right. It was a loud silence. It hadn't bothered her yesterday, but today she wished she'd purchased a radio in town as the silence made her uncomfortable. Instead, she found her MP3 player, plugged in the earbuds, and worked away for the rest of the day downstairs while listening to her favorite playlist of music. The upstairs could wait, she reasoned, and she needed to get the downstairs ready for a bed anyway. She kept her mind occupied on the music and forced herself to ignore the obvious incongruity of the lamp's charred wick.

❖

It was dusk when Brenna decided to clean herself up and have something to eat. By now her earlier nerves had calmed, and she felt the house was quite safe. She saw no reason not to spend the night. After heating a can of pasta on the stove, she went out to the porch to eat, watching the grove turn black under the deep purple desert sky. The air was unmoving with no breeze or noise from Alex's crew since they'd knocked off an hour before. She closed her eyes and let the stillness relax her. For some odd reason, the evening silence was less oppressive than the silence earlier that day. She spent the next hour on the porch contemplating, thinking about the house and about Alex, steering her mind away from her son and husband and Debra. When she began to yawn, she headed back inside to get ready for bed. She thought about showering first, but was too tired from mopping and cleaning. At least she'd removed the wooden planks from all the windows and patched them with plastic, except for the two upstairs. She'd have to do that in the morning.

After changing into sweatpants and plugging in her MP3 player to charge, she climbed inside her sleeping bag. Next to her on the floor, she'd set Michael's music box and the framed photograph of him and

Edward, along with her flashlight. For a brief second, she thought about going upstairs to fetch the antique oil lamp, to light it, and to watch the small flame as she fell asleep. But she decided against it; she feared she could knock it over in her sleep. She considered again how strange it was the lamp had appeared to have been lit at one time. She had an uncomfortable thought that perhaps someone had gotten into the house the night before after she'd left it. And now she wondered if she'd locked the front door last evening when she'd been frightened and startled by Alex's knock. She struggled with keeping that thought from her mind as she tossed and turned in her sleeping bag. She had yet to turn off the floor lamp by her place on the floor, wary about submerging herself into total darkness. From her position she could see the bottom step of the stairs leading to the second floor. She kept looking at that step and at the darkness beyond.

"This is ridiculous," she muttered.

She gathered her wits and switched off the lamp. It took a few moments for her eyes to adjust to the absolute blackness. Although the bedroom window wasn't covered, except for the few broken panes she'd patched with plastic sheeting, no light entered the room. No moon. No streetlights. Only blackness. She closed her eyes. Her sleep aid would kick in any moment, she was sure. But try as she might, she couldn't get comfortable on the air mattress as she wrestled with her exhaustion, struggling to fall asleep. She felt for her phone and pressed a button to see the time. It was after eleven thirty. Why couldn't she sleep? Ah, no wine, she told herself. She closed her eyes again and realized that perhaps the absolute stillness was too much. She switched on the lamp again and went to check her MP3 player. It had at least half a charge, enough to get her to sleep. She plugged in the earbuds, chose a playlist of classical music, hit random-repeat, and settled on her air mattress after turning off the light once more. Again the oppressive blackness swallowed her, but the music made it better. Now if she could only find the right spot, she'd fall asleep. But as she listened to the soothing music, focusing on relaxing her body, her mind began to pore over those details she most wanted to avoid. She didn't want to think about her son and husband tonight. She didn't want to think about that April morning in church when she'd first heard the tornado sirens in the distance. She didn't want to recall the sound of the wind, like a freight train bearing down on her.

She refused to think of those things, and she squeezed her eyes shut, trying to focus again on the events of the last few days, on her new acquaintances, but particularly on Alex Santana. She began to recreate the encounters she'd had with Alex, playing them over in her mind. She admired Alex's beauty, thought her voice and laugh were soothing. She remembered the way Alex had held her arm when she'd reassured her about the snakes and spiders, the way Alex had taken her hand in a firm grip, the way Alex had listened to her out in the grove as she rambled on about needing solitude. She imagined Alex's beautiful dark hair, her brown eyes, and her long fingers. Even as she lay alone in the darkness, Brenna felt her face warm at the thoughts she was having. But what was the harm in allowing herself to acknowledge her silly crush? Once the property was prepared, she would likely never see Alex again. Besides, thinking of her was a pleasant distraction from her grief.

With that thought, she began to consider other memories, some from childhood. She recalled the way she'd felt around her older sister's friends. She remembered wanting to be part of her sister's sleepovers so she could listen to the girls talk and admire their beautiful skin and hair. She'd carried those thoughts and feelings with her through high school and into her marriage. But she'd never discussed her feelings with anyone—not her sister, not her husband, no one. She'd always assumed everyone had these feelings at one time or another. Not to mention, her attraction had always been directed toward girls and women whom she admired more than anything. They'd always been confident people, smart and strong-willed. Qualities she lacked and wished she possessed. It was nothing more than hero-worship, she used to tell herself. Still, she'd always known the truth. But when Debra happened, she'd finally come face-to-face with the reality of who she was.

Brenna couldn't stop herself then as she began to obsess over that relationship, to replay the entire sad event from first kiss to the last screaming moment of their breakup. The affair had been born from the innocence of friendship. Debra and Allen Patterson were missionaries who'd been sponsored by her congregation. They were close to hers and Edward's ages, and since Edward was a deacon at the church, when the couple had returned Stateside, he'd invited them over a few times for dinner. Brenna had always found Debra attractive and envied the woman's intelligence and worldly experiences as well as her dominant personality, one that seemed to keep even her husband subservient to her wishes. After a few months of a growing friendship, of intimate talks and afternoon lunches alone while their husbands were off at work and other business, Brenna had found herself hopelessly infatuated. Then came Debra's surprising declaration of love, and for the first time in her life, Brenna found herself flying high on passion and romance, completely enraptured and ensnared. But as the affair reached its climax, Debra'd wanted more than Brenna could give. Would she leave her husband, Debra'd asked. Would she agree to move across the country with her? To leave Michael with Edward? To start a new life? Divorce Edward, yes. But leave Michael? She'd sooner die, Brenna had told her. Had this been just a game? Was she not worth the sacrifice, Debra'd demanded to know. Then she'd wept as she'd accused Brenna of destroying her life, her marriage, and her chance of spiritual redemption. Debra'd turned on her and had labeled Brenna a manipulative seductress, a jezebel, the Whore of Babylon.

Brenna shifted on her air mattress and wiped her eyes. *Whore*, she thought, *I'm nothing but a fucking whore.* She rolled over and cried herself to sleep.

Sirens screamed in the distance. She held her son to her chest and wove between pews. The door to the church basement was only a few feet from her, a few more steps.

"Where's Daddy?"

"Helping others."

"But I want Daddy."

The wind, the sirens, the wood beginning to splinter.

"Is he all right, Mommy?"

"Daddy will come."

An old woman fell to her knees.

"Hold Mommy's skirt. Let me help Mrs. Chambers."

Glass shattered, debris flew in daggers. She turned. He was gone. Ripped away, torn from her, body and soul.

"Michael!" Brenna shot straight up.

In the blackness she was disoriented, and her ears were dull. She pulled the earbuds loose and held her head. She was drenched in cold sweat and panting while her throat constricted, causing her to gag. Shaking, she ran her hand along the scar at the back of her head and neck. It was pulsing, hot to the touch, and the memory of the concussion made her woozy. And then, in that still darkness, she heard it. The click. The soft tinkling. The familiar tune. She gasped and reached for the lamp only to knock it over. She rolled from the air mattress and grabbed the flashlight, switching it on and beaming it at the music box. Her heart skipped beats and she cried out when she saw the music box gaping open and playing its sorrowful tune. She watched as the little mechanism twirled, and as she did, she had the feeling of someone standing in the darkness watching her. Did she hear someone breathing, crying? She waved her flashlight around the room. She was certain she'd find before her the ghoulish specter of Hadley's wife, headless and threatening. But there was nothing, only her boxes and suitcase.

She exhaled and shut the lid to her son's music box. She reasoned she'd bumped it in her sleep, thrashing about in her nightmare. But she wondered, when was the last time she'd even wound the thing? Still shaking, she stood and righted the lamp, turning it on. The room filled with light, and she stood a moment calming herself. She coughed a few more times and noticed her throat burned from screaming out in her nightmare. She went to the kitchen and pulled a bottle of water from the cooler she'd left on the counter. She continued to tremble, but her heart was slowly returning to normal. When she returned to the bedroom, she checked the time on her cell phone. It was three fifteen in the morning. Right then another sound reached her—scratching, sniffing, breathing. Her legs went numb and she held her breath and listened. There it was again.

"Crap."

She moved toward the bedroom door, where she listened again. The sound was more distinct now, and along with the scratching, sniffing, and breathing...no, it was panting...she heard a whimper. Coyotes. Alex had mentioned coyotes. With that thought, she wondered if it would be rude to call Alex this early in the morning. She'd already programmed her number into her phone. Hadn't Alex told her to call if she needed her? Or maybe she should call Johnny instead. The napkin he'd written his number on was somewhere, maybe in her jeans pocket. But she dismissed both ideas and admonished herself for being such a coward. She tiptoed to the kitchen and stood still in the dark,

holding her breath again, listening as her heart pounded. Scratch...
sniff...pant...The sound was right outside the front door. She hunched
commando-style and crawled to the picture window. She'd covered it
with plastic sheeting, but one corner was loose enough for her to peek
out and see the porch. However, it was still dark. Dawn was a good
four hours away. She pressed her ear to the corner of the window and
listened. It had to be a coyote or a wolf. Were there wolves in Arizona?
Had Alex mentioned wolves? Just then a mournful whimper, almost
a howl, came from the other side of the door, and she flipped on the
porch light and fell back to her knees to peer out again. She could see
fur—yellow, dirty and muddy—then a tail, a nose, a dog. She gripped
her heart and let out a sigh tinged with a giggle. She cracked open
the door to find a huge yellow mutt sitting on his haunches, panting
and looking at her. She watched him while he watched her back. She
opened the door a bit more. She saw he was caked in mud and had a
collar around his neck.

"Good boy, good boy," she cooed and opened the door wider.
"Where'd you come from?" She held out her hand.

The dog lowered his nose, sniffed her, and licked her hand.

"There now, good boy. You come from that cotton farm across the
highway?" She sat on one of the lawn chairs. "Come here, big guy. Let
me check your collar. You got a name or number?"

She reached around the dog's thick neck, feeling for a clasp on the
collar, but there was none. Instead she found a thick piece of canvas
looping, hooked together with two leather thongs. She bent to see if she
could untie it. When she did, she caught a whiff of his stench.

"Phew, you smell awful! What've you been into?" She giggled,
and the dog licked her hand again.

She couldn't remove the makeshift collar, but she did manage to
turn it and move the dog so the porch light fell on it. Stitched in the
canvas was a name, but it was muddy.

"Hold still, fella, let me see. Maybe it's your master's name." She
narrowed her eyes and rubbed her thumb over the stitching, scraping
off mud and debris. "Looks like, *M...I...G*...oh, it's Miguel."

The dog barked, narrowing his eyes and curling his mouth into a
goofy smile.

"Miguel. Is that your master's name or yours?" She patted his
head and smiled. But the smile dropped from her face. She recognized

the name Miguel. It was a Spanish name. In English it translated to Michael.

"Sometimes the universe is cruel," she said, and her tears dropped onto the dog's head, dampening his fur.

At this, the beast, as though he understood, whined and laid his muddy head in her lap and watched her with unusual golden eyes. She patted him and sniffed.

"You're a sweet boy. I bet you're hungry. Let me get you something."

Once inside, she rinsed one of the small buckets she'd used for cleaning earlier that day and filled it with water. She also cut a square of plastic sheeting and grabbed a half-eaten can of pasta from the cooler. When she returned to the porch, she saw the dog sitting at attention, looking into the pitch blackness of the grove.

"Here. I don't know if you'll eat this, but it's all I have." She spooned some cold pasta onto the plastic, stood, and watched to see if he'd take the food.

The dog sniffed the pasta, looked at her, and turned his head again to the grove. She followed his gaze, but she could see nothing past the dim glow cast from the porch light.

"What is it?"

She stared into the wall of darkness and shivered. When she looked again, the dog was eating. When he'd finished and had some water, he sat again on his haunches and turned his attention once more to the trees. She petted him and wondered what she should do with him, but decided she couldn't make him spend the rest of the night on the porch.

"I'm not letting your muddy self into my clean house."

As she observed the clumps of mud on his fur, he stood and began to wag his tail as if someone was approaching. She shot her attention to where he looked, and the hair on the top of her arms stiffened.

"Is there someone out there?"

No one answered. She shook herself, her nerves on edge from her nightmare.

"Okay, the only way I'm letting you sleep in the house is if you take a bath. Let me get some buckets of water and soap."

She turned to go back inside to gather the things she'd need, but the dog yipped and took a step off the porch. Her eyes registered the sight before her brain could comprehend. There in the circle of light cast from the porch lamp, she saw two bare and muddy feet. But before she could scream one sound, she watched the feet retreat and the dog follow after. She stumbled back in the house and slammed the door, banging the lock in place, and dropping to her knees to peer once more out the corner of the window.

"Shit, shit, shit."

She bit down on her knuckles and thought about crawling back to the bedroom and retrieving her phone to call Alex. But the dog returned to the porch. He came right over to the window, to the corner where she watched, and sat with his mouth in a goofy doggy grin, one that curled his lips and slit his eyes. She wondered if he was rabid or simply some manifestation of a demon come to taunt her.

CHAPTER SEVEN

Brenna had debated over an hour what she should do about the intruder on her property as well as the dog who continued to sit like a sentinel on the porch. Certainly, she thought, he had to belong to whoever had approached the house. Why hadn't the person said something? And why had he been covered in mud like the dog? She hadn't noticed any mud on the property the day Alex had driven her out to the grove, and neither had it rained since she'd been there. But once she was convinced the dog wasn't leaving and the person who'd approached the house wasn't returning, she got up the nerve to open the door again and step out onto the porch.

The dog wagged his tail and lowered his head as she came out.

"Is this your dog?" she called out to the darkness.

She waited for an answer, for the muddy feet to return, but again there was nothing.

"This is my property. You shouldn't be here."

Still nothing.

She considered the dog. He certainly looked harmless. She reached a hand and petted him, feeling him nuzzle against her. Perhaps the person had abandoned him on purpose, but she couldn't imagine why anyone would do so. And as she scrutinized him more, she could see just how filthy he was.

"All right, let me get you cleaned. We'll go hunting for your owner in the morning."

For the next hour, she worked her shampoo into his thick coat with buckets of warm water drawn from the kitchen sink. But all the water run through the old plumbing had loosened a coupling which linked the faucet pipes to the main water line. At five forty-five in the morning, she found herself on her back with her head and shoulders under the kitchen sink as she tried to fix the damage. Miguel, the dog, lay on his bath towels in the kitchen and watched her.

She cursed and crawled out from under the sink to switch out buckets. Water continued to trickle in a steady stream from the pipes. This constant flow required her to change out buckets every so often and pour the excess water outside. As she dumped the water in the gravel off the porch, she noticed the sky had turned a whitish blue. The sun would rise soon, and the construction crew would arrive as well. She wanted to be cleaned up before Alex showed later in the afternoon, but she didn't dare try to shower until she had the pipes under control. She had no idea what might happen with the change in water pressure when she ran the faucet in the bathtub.

"Come on, boy, let's see if I can fix it this time," she said to Miguel.

He followed her inside, had followed her each time she'd gone out and back, had followed her everywhere, even to the bathroom where she'd chided him to give her privacy.

When she saw the replacement bucket half-full, she groaned. "And I haven't even had a cup of coffee."

Miguel narrowed his eyes and curled his mouth into a smile, making her snicker. In the morning light, he looked less fiendish than he had in the wee hours of the morning.

"You're a funny dog. You're smiling, aren't you, silly boy." She petted his silky head.

Without the dirt, mud, and burrs, his hair felt like velvet, and it was the deepest yellow-gold she'd ever seen on a dog. He almost sparkled. She concluded by his color and shape that he must be a golden retriever and yellow Lab mix. But he was huge. His paws were as wide as her hands. She figured he had to have another breed mixed in to be so incredibly large.

She checked the time on her phone. She was sure Alex had said she wouldn't be coming by the property until afternoon. She had to stop the leak and get a shower before that, she knew. So back under the sink she went, and Miguel spread on his bath towels again and put his head on his massive paws to watch.

She tried once more with the pliers she'd purchased at the hardware store. She thought they probably weren't the right kind for plumbing work, but it was all she had.

"Okay, come on. Lefty, loosely and righty, tighty...tighty...tight." She strained against the handle of the pliers, grunted, and tried again. But the coupling wouldn't tighten, and water continued to trickle into the bucket. She smacked the pipe with the pliers. "Shoot, you dad gum piece of crap."

"Pipes respond better to actual curse words," a voice observed. "*Shoot* and *dad gum* don't usually get them to cooperate."

"What?" Brenna jumped and bumped her head when she heard the voice. She slid from under the sink to find Alex standing over her. "Alex, what are you doing here? I thought you wouldn't show until later." She got to her feet and tucked loose hair behind her ears. She was mortified to have Alex see her looking messy and unkempt.

Alex held two paper cups and flashed a huge grin. "No, I have some work I need to get to later today, so I decided to make this my first stop." She held out one of the cups. "I wasn't sure if you drank coffee or not, but I thought you might want something warm and comforting after your first night of sleeping in your haunted house."

"Something warm and comforting?" Brenna was confused, rattled. She'd wanted to be showered, her hair fixed, makeup on, and when she noticed her dirty hands, she stifled a groan. This was not the way she wanted their next encounter to play out.

"The coffee. I brought you coffee."

Brenna twirled a stray bit of hair. "Thank you, you didn't need to do that." She took the cup and added, "And the house isn't haunted. You, Cassie, and the others are just putting me on to see how long I'll last."

"No, Brenna, we wouldn't do that. I only meant it playfully."

Brenna didn't have a response to Alex's sudden sincerity. Instead, she glanced at Alex's work boots, and against her own will, her eyes climbed up Alex's legs, to her shapely hips, the wide belt, the open and unzipped jacket. She trailed her gaze to Alex's slender neck and paused on her full lips before looking into her eyes. She met her eyes, sucked in her breath, and looked away.

"Thank you again for the coffee," she managed to respond.

"You're welcome. And who's this handsome boy?" Alex petted Miguel who'd nuzzled his nose under her hand.

"He showed up last night, scratching at the door, and poor thing, he was covered in mud."

"Hmm, is that right? He sure is beautiful. What great eyes." Alex knelt and ruffled Miguel's ears.

"It was the strangest thing. Someone was out there last night. I think he's his dog."

Alex became still. "What do you mean? Who was out where?"

"I saw someone last night out front. But when I asked if Miguel was his dog, he didn't respond, never came back."

"Miguel?"

"Yes. See his collar? Looks handmade." Brenna tugged on the canvas collar for Alex to see. "All I can read on it is Miguel. I don't know if that's his name or his owner's."

Alex stood and smiled at the beast. "San Miguel Arcángel, defiéndenos en la batalla."

Miguel formed his goofy grin and let out a bark.

"I see," Alex said. "Our friend here understands Spanish."

"What did you say to him?"

"Part of a prayer I learned as a little girl. Translates something like, Saint Michael the Archangel, defend us in battle. Let's see, and the rest goes, *sé nuestro amparo contra la perversidad y asechanzas del demonio,* which means something like, be our protection and keep us out of the traps of the devil."

"That's pretty. I mean, the Spanish." Brenna thought the words were beautiful, and coming from Alex's mouth made them even more so.

"Ah, well, my first language." Alex petted Miguel a moment longer, seeming to deliberate on something. Finally, she looked up. "Brenna, the idea someone is out there in the grove watching your house makes me uncomfortable."

"Me, too."

"I'll have some of my guys drive out there later and see if they spot anyone, see if the dog is theirs, tell them to get off your property."

"Thank you."

"Sure." Alex pulled a handful of sugar packets and creamers from her jacket pocket and tossed them on the counter. "I brought these. I wasn't sure if you liked your coffee black or not. I guessed you'd like it sweet."

"I do like it sweet." Brenna giggled. "But two or three would've done it." She continued to giggle while she dosed her coffee.

Alex leaned close. "I guess I overdid it with the sugars. You do seem sweet enough already."

Brenna felt her face grow warm, and she tugged at a strand of her hair while she stared at the countertop. She wasn't sure, but that had sounded like flirtation.

"What's going on with your sink?" Alex asked.

"I don't know. I can't get the pipe thingy to tighten. I ran so many buckets of warm water last night trying to get him clean"—she pointed to Miguel—"and I think something has worked loose."

"You want me to take a look at it?" Alex started to remove her jacket.

"No." Brenna held up her hands. "Thank you, but I want to fix it myself. I need to be able to do things on my own."

"Okay, but"—Alex pointed to the pliers she'd dropped on the floor—"those aren't water-pump pliers. You're going to strip your coupling. And it may be tight enough. You may only need a new washer."

Brenna picked up her pliers. "I don't understand."

"Listen, I have a toolbox in the truck. I've got the right tools. Why don't I let you borrow them?"

"That's nice of you, but I know you're busy and all."

"Brenna, you won't get anywhere with this." Alex touched the pliers in her hand. "Let me get my toolbox. I'll be right back."

When Alex left the kitchen, Brenna groaned out loud, embarrassed because she knew she smelled after having worked all day yesterday, bathing the dog that morning, then working on the sink.

"Here we go." Alex returned and set a toolbox on the counter. She opened and unfolded it to four levels. It was packed with a wide variety of tools, making Brenna feel humbled by her few measly wrenches, screwdrivers, and hammer.

"Try this one." Alex held out red-handled pliers. "If it's a washer, you can tighten it all you want and it still won't seal the leak."

Brenna took the tool and climbed under the sink. But she was so flustered and distracted by Alex's presence that with one left turn, a force of water sprayed in a torrent down her face and soaked her head and upper body. She screeched when the water hit her. At the same time, Miguel stood and barked.

"Oh, damn!" Alex stifled a laugh while she ran out to the side of the house to the main water valve. "Did you drown yourself?" she asked as she came back in.

"Almost." Brenna giggled and shook her arms away from her body. Her T-shirt was soaked.

Although Alex had been laughing at Brenna's surprise shower, she stopped midchuckle and rested her eyes on Brenna's chest. And while her skin was a deep tan, her cheeks flashed red and she looked up to gaze into Brenna's eyes.

As soon as Brenna realized Alex's eyes were on her, she folded her arms across her chest. She hadn't bothered to put on a bra yet that morning and the wet T-shirt clung to her full breasts. "I should go change."

Alex swallowed. "Yes. You should."

In the bedroom, Brenna shut the door and searched in her suitcase for dry clothes all the while thinking about the way Alex had just looked at her. She'd seen that look before in Edward's eyes when they'd first been married, in Debra's eyes each time they'd been intimate. And now Alex. She couldn't help but smile, thinking as unkempt and pale as she was from her months of mourning, she might've caught Alex's attention after all.

After she'd changed clothes, combed her hair, and made herself more presentable, she returned to the kitchen only to find Alex had removed her jacket and folded Miguel's bath towels, and was now lying on her back inspecting the sink.

"You don't need to do that, Alex."

"Just looking for you. I think it is stripped." Alex turned the pliers, and when she did her core tightened.

Brenna stared at the place where Alex's T-shirt had come loose from her jeans, where the waistband of boyshorts hugged her middle. She felt her face burning again, and she had to hold the countertop for support.

Alex slipped out from under the sink. "Looks like you did strip the coupling, but the washer is rotten, too. Both will need to be replaced." She held out the damaged pieces. "I can have Johnny run to the hardware store and pick these up this afternoon if you'd like."

"I can go. Really." Brenna tried not to stare at the obvious definition in Alex's arms, especially her forearms.

"You won't be able to get down the road until later. We have the trailer with a backhoe parked on it right now and two track loaders are off in the ditch. I'll give these to Johnny and have him pick them up at lunch." Alex put the pieces in her jeans pocket. "Besides even though you have a fancy four-wheel drive out there, I wouldn't want you trying to barrel through the desert just yet and ruin that sweet red paint job."

"It is a bright red, isn't it?" Brenna giggled. "My husband always insisted on white or silver cars. Something about speed traps."

Alex nodded. "Your husband? I see. He probably fixed the leaky pipes, too."

"No, he'd just hire a plumber. Anytime I tried to fix something at home, he'd get frustrated and say it cost more to fix what I messed up."

Alex nodded again. "Well, I have to say, I respect you for wanting to be self-sufficient, Brenna. Many women, and a lot of men, too, would rather let other people do it for them, rather than doing it themselves. It's admirable you're trying to make your own way."

With that compliment, Brenna managed to make eye contact again. "Thank you."

"You're welcome."

Brenna shrugged. "All right, if you wouldn't mind having Johnny get the parts, I'll install them. I can't have the water off all day. I'm going to need a shower eventually."

"I'll have him go at lunchtime. Speaking of lunch, do you like onions and jalapeños on your chili cheese dog?"

"What chili cheese dog?"

"The one I'm buying you from Della's lunch truck. Della has the best chili cheese dogs. Makes her own chili from scratch. I take mine with onions and jalapeños. It's great going in, but not so much on the way out. Still, it's worth the price." Alex patted her stomach and laughed.

"Alex, I don't expect you to buy me lunch."

"But Della's famous around town. You *have* to try one of her chili cheese dogs."

"Okay, but no jalapeños, just onions."

"Right. And just a dog and bun for you, mister." Alex patted Miguel's head. "Don't want the lady here to suffer through your stinky farts."

"Do you think whoever left him here last night is still out there?"

"I don't know, but I'll have some of my guys check it out, like I said. If we don't find anyone, he's yours to keep."

Brenna petted his head. "I have to admit, I wouldn't mind keeping him. He's been great company."

"He certainly is a beautiful dog." Alex glanced out the kitchen window and grabbed her coffee cup. "Let's go catch the sunrise. It should be hitting Red Mountain about now. Come on, you won't believe how magical it is."

Alex pulled her by the arm, and Brenna allowed herself to be led, taking her coffee with her and following Alex to the front porch with Miguel right behind her.

As the three watched, the sun crested the top of the house, bathed the dead trees in bright light, and crawled across the shadowy land to begin its illumination of the mountain Brenna had observed her first time at the property. In silence, they sipped their coffee and watched the event. The mountain first turned from a dull gray to a light pink and finally a deep crimson as the sun eventually embraced it fully.

"Wow," Brenna said.

Alex was right. The sunrise on Red Mountain was magical, and the moment felt magical, too. She could smell the fresh desert air, feel the warmth of the morning sun as well as the sensation of Alex's forearm as it grazed against her own. She found the courage to turn and look at her, only to find Alex watching her in return. She held her gaze, determined she wouldn't look away.

"Beautiful," Alex said.

"Yes," Brenna said. Then, although she'd changed into dry clothes, she shivered.

"Wait here." In an instant, Alex had returned with her jacket and wrapped it around her shoulders.

The gesture was so innocent, polite, and full of tenderness, Brenna nearly burst out crying, but she forced herself to sip her coffee and turned her attention to the mountain once again.

After they'd stood silently for a while, Alex said, "I always thought it looked like a breast with a hardened nipple."

Brenna shot her a glance and giggled.

Alex blushed again as she'd done in the kitchen. "In high school, we used to come out here a lot. We called it Titty Mountain because everyone thought that, not just me."

"I see it. I thought the same thing when I drove out on Friday."

"In high school, Cassie and I hung out with this girl, Nicole, and was she something. Poor girl was so conservative and proper. She couldn't say the word *breast*. When they served chicken breasts for lunch in the cafeteria, she couldn't ask the lunch lady. Instead, she'd say, *Could I have the chicken front?*" Alex laughed and her smile filled her face.

She continued with her story while Brenna gazed at her, adoring the way the morning sun now bathed her long dark hair and sparkled in her eyes.

"What a hoot she was. We'd tease her about climbing Titty Mountain and doing a dance on the nipple. And she'd get mad at us for making her blush. It was fun to tease her." Alex cocked her head and smiled. "You remind me a little of Nicole."

"How so?"

"I don't know. She was quiet, shy. A little too clean-cut for our generation. Innocent, I guess."

Brenna dropped her eyes. "I'm far from innocent." She hung her head and realized just how true it was.

"Hmm," was all Alex replied.

They stood awhile longer, the two women and the golden dog, and then Alex checked the time on her phone.

"I need to get out there and make a few stops. I'll send Johnny to get your parts and Hector and a few others to search the trees for your intruder. Then I'll see you around one for lunch." She turned to walk to her truck.

"Wait, your jacket." She removed it and offered it back. "Thank you." She was reluctant to part with it; the jacket had a scent, like freshly washed linens, sun dried on a clothesline.

"Anytime."

"And thanks for the coffee and for saving me from drowning."

"You are more than welcome, Brenna." Alex climbed into her truck. She started the engine and rolled down the window to lean out.

Brenna noticed Alex hadn't put back on her jacket, and her bare arm with her brown skin soaked up the rays of the sun. "How will I be able to thank you for everything you've done for me?"

Alex pointed to the red Jeep, which gleamed brightly in the morning sunlight. "How about when we finish this road, some Saturday afternoon you and me go for a spin in your new ride, four-wheeling in a dry river bottom?"

Brenna had never been four-wheeling, but with Alex she wanted to try. "Sure, I'd love to take you for a spin."

Alex barked out a laugh and raised her eyebrows. "Is that right? Okay, I'll see you at lunch." She backed out, waved, and headed down the gravel road.

"What is wrong with me?" Brenna moaned, realizing the way her comment must've come across, and she watched until the truck disappeared around the bend. "Come on, Miguel, let's clean what we can." She motioned for the dog to follow, and as she walked back toward the house, she was lost in thoughts about Alex. "Jeez—*I'd love to take you for a spin*—what an idiot I am." She turned when she reached the door. "Come on, boy." She saw Miguel sitting in the gravel driveway, his head raised, looking at the second story. "Miguel?"

The dog looked at her.

"What is it?" She stepped off the porch and lifted her eyes to the spot where he'd been looking. She saw nothing but the dirty, broken panes of glass. "There's nothing. Now come on. You're giving me the heebie-jeebies."

Miguel followed her inside and sat at the base of the stairs while she began to clean the mess in the kitchen. Absorbed in her thoughts of Alex and in her worry over some person out in the trees, she didn't notice Miguel stand and wag his tale as he looked at the top of the landing. And neither did she notice the dark-haired woman who descended and stood petting the dog while she watched Brenna with black eyes.

CHAPTER EIGHT

Brenna had been preparing the downstairs bedroom walls for primer when she heard tires roll up the gravel driveway. She checked herself in a compact mirror—she'd dug around in her suitcase earlier and found her makeup bag. Satisfied she looked as good as she could, she went to the front porch to greet Alex, who carried a tray of food with drinks as well as a paper bag under her arm.

Miguel ran out to meet her, lifted his snout, and sniffed.

"Hang on, boy. Let's get the sink fixed first," Alex said to him. She stepped onto the porch and held the tray of food out to Brenna. "I hope orange soda is okay. It's my favorite."

"Orange is fine." Brenna took the tray.

Alex held the door and brandished the paper bag. "And here are your parts. You want to put these on first and make sure we can get the water running before we eat?"

Brenna agreed that would be a good idea.

In the kitchen, Alex demonstrated how the pieces fit together and handed them to her along with the water-pump pliers. "After you get them hand-tightened, use the pliers just enough to make a snug fit. Don't overtighten."

Brenna took the items, crawled back under the sink, and began to install them.

Alex got on one knee and peeked under the sink. "Let me get the flashlight out of my truck."

"There's one in the bedroom." Brenna lifted her head to watch as Alex went to fetch it. She seemed to be gone longer than it should've taken, so she called out, "Did you find it?"

"Got it right here." Alex returned, knelt again, and directed the light onto the pipes.

As she worked, Brenna felt Alex lean in and place her hand on the floor between her legs.

"The picture by your sleeping bag," Alex said after a bit.

Brenna stopped fiddling with the pipe and peeked at her.

"Your son and husband?" Alex asked.

"Yes."

"He was handsome, your husband."

"He was." Brenna went back to tightening the coupling.

"Your son," Alex continued, "he looked a lot like him, but your son was colored like you, blond, green eyes. He was a beautiful child."

Brenna dropped her hands. "Yes, I know." She stared at the pipe above her. The titillation of what she thought had been Alex's earlier flirtation vanished as the weight of her loss pressed down on her. Then she felt Alex's hand touch her thigh. She raised her head.

"I'm sorry, Brenna. I noticed the picture when I went in the bedroom. I shouldn't have been nosy."

Brenna forced her insincere smile and with some hesitation reached out and patted Alex's hand. "No problem. I'm okay." She let her hand rest there until she felt Alex squeeze and release her.

"You almost done?" Alex asked.

"Hang on." Brenna went back to tightening while she wondered about the affectionate gesture.

In a few moments the pipe was reassembled, and Alex leaned forward. "Is it tight?"

"Maybe."

"Let me see. Let me test it."

"With your fingers?" Brenna asked, and she saw a smile begin to form on Alex's face. She stuttered. "Or...I mean...this? The pliers?" She held up the tool.

"Fingers." Alex reached under the sink, over Brenna's head, and tested the coupling. "It feels tight enough." She pulled her hand back out. "Now give it one turn with the pliers."

Brenna tried to hold the pliers, but her hands shook, and the pliers slipped from her grip.

"Here, open them wide, all the way." Alex took the tool from her hand and held her by the wrist.

Brenna did as Alex instructed and within seconds the repair was complete. Alex stood while Brenna scooted out from under the sink. As she began to hoist herself to a standing position, she felt Alex take both her hands and lift her. She'd been taken off guard by the quick movement, and now she stood chin to chin with her.

"I think you did it," Alex said.

"What?"

"I think you've fixed the sink. Let me go turn it on." Alex still held her hands.

"Turn what on?" Brenna stared at Alex's lips.

"The water." Alex leaned forward, and when she spoke, her breath blew across the skin of Brenna's cheek.

Miguel barked.

Brenna giggled and stepped away, tugging on a strand of hair and feeling the heat in her face. "I guess he wants his hot dog."

"I guess he does. Okay, you watch it, and I'll turn it on." Alex disappeared out the door and to the side of the house. In a moment, she called out, "How does it look?"

Brenna examined the pipes, tried the faucet. "I think it's good."

"And we have water," Alex said as she came back inside and checked under the sink and tried the faucet as well. "Okay, let's eat." As she washed her hands, she asked, "Do you want it inside or outside?"

"Do I want what inside or outside?" Brenna felt her cheeks flush once more.

"Your chili cheese dog."

"Outside. It's such a pretty day." She blinked and tried to clear her head.

They took their meal to the lawn chairs on the porch and watched as Miguel sat at their feet and devoured his plain hot dog in minutes.

"Have your guys checked the trees yet for his owner?" Brenna asked.

"Yes, before I sent them to lunch, I had Hector and two others walk back by the area where I'd seen signs of a campfire."

"And no one?"

"Nope, not a soul."

"So whoever it was just abandoned him here?" Miguel was such a well-behaved dog. It seemed strange for someone to give him up.

"Sometimes people can't care for a dog, don't have the means. If it was a group moving through, maybe they figured he'd be better off with you."

"Then I guess I need to get him some dog food later." Brenna petted him. It would be nice to have him around, she realized, to have the company and companionship.

"You can drive the road later this afternoon. We'll knock off about three."

"So the road's done?"

"Nah, we'll need another day, but we'll move the track loaders off to the side so you can have access. I want to finish and start surveying by the end of the week. Next week's a short one, so we'll be a little behind schedule."

"Short? Why's that?"

"Thanksgiving, I give my crews Thursday and Friday off." Alex took a bite of hot dog and chewed while watching her. Then she asked, "Are you flying back home for the holidays?"

Brenna didn't answer at first. She'd promised her sister she would, but she'd never had any intention of doing so.

"I don't think I want to," she said finally.

Alex chewed another mouthful. After she swallowed, she said, "You can't spend Thanksgiving out here by yourself. I won't allow it."

"Alex, it's okay. The day doesn't mean anything to me." But she was lying. This would be her first family holiday without her son.

"You shouldn't be alone, not on a holiday."

"But I am alone." She remembered saying those exact words to her sister weeks ago.

They ate in silence, and thankfully, Brenna still had enough of her hot dog left she could chew and swallow, disguising the fact she was swallowing the rush of tears pushing against her throat.

Miguel laid his head at her feet and whimpered.

They ate without talking a bit longer, and Brenna assumed the matter was dropped. But Alex surprised her. She reached out, took her shoulder, and turned to level a steady gaze at her while she spoke.

"That's not true. You're not alone, Brenna. No one's truly alone."

Brenna was unable to look at her. Instead, she watched Miguel, swallowed the last bit of food, and cleared her throat, which felt thick again, blocked somehow.

"This will be the first Thanksgiving without my son." Her voice shook. "I'd rather spend it by myself. Thank you."

"I can see how difficult this will be for you, every holiday, his birthday. Yes, I understand."

Brenna hung her head.

"Still, I want you to come to my family's Thanksgiving. I won't let you stay out here by yourself."

Brenna clenched her teeth, coughed into a closed mouth.

"Listen." Alex let go of her shoulder, stood, and talked with her hands as if she wanted to emphasize her point. "We close my family's restaurant to the public, and everyone—my aunts and uncles, cousins, second cousins—shows up. And my aunts start making tamales three days before, and we roast a whole pig, and some of my cousins have a band, and my cousin Raymond is a DJ, and we clear the main room for a dance floor. The kids have a piñata, and we drink tequila shots, well the adults, not the kids, and it goes until like two in the morning. And don't worry, we have turkey and dressing, too, but the desserts, you won't believe the spread. We have pie and cake and empanadas and flan and…" Alex stopped and sat again. "Brenna, I'm sorry. Don't cry. Please, I didn't mean to upset you."

Brenna leaned into her hands and sobbed. "What do I have to be thankful for? What?"

Miguel pushed his massive head between her bent arms and nudged his nose against her face. That made her giggle, and she hugged the dog and continued to weep while Alex waited. Finally, when she'd managed to get some control, she looked at Alex and saw her eyes were full of concern.

"You're sweet to ask me, but I can't go. Please understand."

"All right," Alex said. "Then I'm coming out here to spend the day with you, and I'll box us up a whole feast to bring with me. I'm not going to let you be alone on Thanksgiving. It's not right."

Brenna was taken back by this, and she studied Alex's face, noting how serious she looked with her lips drawn and one eyebrow raised.

"You can't miss your family's Thanksgiving. That's ridiculous."

Alex's eyebrow arched higher. "You leave me no choice. I have a mission to make sure my clients are well taken care of."

Brenna felt the heat creep into her face again. Why was it she couldn't help blushing around this woman, she wondered. "Are you telling me you'd do this for any of your clients?"

"Maybe." Alex grinned now, relaxing the stern look on her face.

"You would not." Brenna playfully slapped her leg.

"Okay, maybe just for the pretty ones."

Brenna gulped her orange soda and squirmed in her chair. This confirmed it, she was certain. The flirtation wasn't only in her mind. But Cassie? What was their relationship?

"Will Cassie be there? At your Thanksgiving party?"

"Sure, she and Kelly both. They always come."

"Her business partner?"

Alex frowned before breaking into a smile. "I think you know better than that, Brenna. Kelly's her wife. Her domestic partner."

"Of course." Brenna looked away and took her time sucking down the remainder of her orange soda, draining it. She removed the lid from the cup, scooped some ice into her mouth, and began to chew while she thought about this and wondered what Alex had meant. *I think you know better.* She spit the ice back into her cup and said, "The day I first met you, I thought you and Cassie were together. There seems to be this connection between you, and when she and I were at lunch the other day, she talked about you the whole time. I figured the two of you were a couple."

"We were, a long time ago when we were teenagers. She was my first. I was hers."

"High school sweethearts?" Brenna smiled at the thought, thinking it seemed innocent and romantic.

"Something like that."

"And now?"

"Best friends. She's been my rock. In high school, she'd defend me when other kids called me names, made fun of me for being Mexican, for coming from a family of migrant workers. She was there for me when my mother died, got me through it. She's the best friend anyone could ever hope for. I love her, can't imagine my life without her."

"Yes, she said something at lunch the other day about your mom. How old were you when she died?"

"Seventeen, a junior in high school." Alex twirled her cup, rattling the ice, while she crossed one leg over the other and bounced a foot.

Brenna realized she'd touched on something still painful. She was about to disclose her own loss, the unexpected and tragic deaths of her own mother and father when she was twelve, to commiserate with

Alex, to let her know she understood how hard it was to lose a parent. But she remembered after Edward's and Michaels' deaths, how women from her church, other parents from Michael's school, would try to share some personal loss with her as if they could identify with her pain. She'd resented those attempts at sympathy. Mostly because she felt she didn't deserve the tenderness and understanding.

So instead, she replied, "I'm sorry to hear that, Alex. You were young. It isn't fair."

"Little in life is," Alex said and checked the time on her phone. She began cleaning up. "I need to run again if I'm going to make it to the other side of the Valley by four. I'll see you tomorrow, but it'll be afternoon." She gathered the trash and stood while searching her pockets for her keys. "Think about my invitation, Brenna. I'd like you to come, for you to be my guest."

This comment made Brenna wonder. If Cassie wasn't with Alex, then who? There had to be someone special in Alex's life. She was too beautiful, too charming to be single.

"I'm embarrassed to ask this," Brenna said, following Alex to her truck.

"Ask what?"

Brenna began to twirl a strand of hair again, but stopped as soon as she realized Alex had picked up on her nervous habit. It occurred to her she must've been giving herself away the whole time.

"What did you want to ask me, Brenna?"

"You're a nice person."

"Thanks."

"I'm guessing you're probably dating someone right now. I don't want to cause any problems for you." She wanted to hide right then. Could she have been less smooth, or more presumptuous?

Alex chuckled and made a contorted face, a silly face, and whistled air through her teeth. "I'm not seeing anyone at the moment. It's been a few years. Got a little burned last time out." She laughed and ran her hand down the back of her ponytail.

Brenna inwardly cheered, but outwardly she shrugged. "I see. Okay, well then, I'd love to be your guest for Thanksgiving. You're right. I probably shouldn't spend the whole day alone."

Alex patted her arm. "Thank you. I'll be honored to have you as my guest."

"No, thank you for asking. I hardly know you and in the last few days you've gone out of your way to be friendly and make me feel welcome."

Alex patted her arm once more. "You're easy to be friendly to, Brenna." She looked past her to the house, turned and looked out at the grove. "Listen, keep your door locked, and call me if any more unexpected visitors show up."

"No worries. I have a watchdog now." She petted Miguel, and he nuzzled against her leg.

"Yes, you do." Alex pointed to the dog. "Protégela. Mantenla a salvo."

Miguel wagged his tail and pawed her jeans.

"What did you say to him?" Brenna asked.

"I told him to watch after you and keep you out of trouble." Alex held out her hand. "You have my number. I'm serious, call if you need me for any reason."

"I will." She regarded Alex's hand and thought it was such a formal way to say good-bye after what they'd shared that morning and afternoon, but she took her hand, nevertheless, and felt Alex's long fingers grip her and pull her in a little.

"Good then." Alex released her and walked backward to her truck. "I'll let my tía Marta know I've invited a guest for Thanksgiving, and I'll see you tomorrow afternoon."

Brenna watched her once again climb into her truck, wave, and drive down the road. She gazed after the plume of dust kicked up by the truck's tires and wished Alex hadn't gone, wished she could've stayed there the rest of the afternoon and into the evening. She wanted Alex to talk to her, speak Spanish to her, look at her the way she had in the kitchen.

She looked at Miguel. "What does she mean about keeping me out of trouble? I'm not the one who rolled in mud last night."

Miguel wagged his tail.

"You know what? I'm going to take a picture and send it to Jess. Show her I can't possibly come home for Thanksgiving now that I have a dog to care for."

She retrieved her phone from inside, returned, and focused on the dog. She took the picture and pulled the phone away to look.

"You must've moved. Hold still, Miguel."

She raised the phone again, making sure he was in the frame, and pressed the button. But when she looked at the second take, all she'd gotten was a sharp reflection from the sun. She played with the phone's camera settings, and this time, she moved to shadow the dog with her body, lined up the frame, and snapped the picture. But all she could see in the photo was her own shadow cast against the gravel driveway. Miguel *must've* moved, but when she looked, he was sitting in the same spot. When she looked at the last picture again, she saw a soft yellow glow to one side of her shadow, almost like an aura.

"What's going on?"

But she was neither ready nor able to allow her mind to reach the obvious explanation. Instead, she went back inside the house to continue priming the bedroom walls and preparing them for paint.

CHAPTER NINE

By the time Brenna had finished in the bedroom, it was past dinnertime. She knew she needed to run over to Fernie's store and get some dog food, but instead she was enjoying watching the sun set behind the grove and Red Mountain. Miguel lay at her feet, and she stroked his back while she lounged in a chair and yawned. It was one of the more peaceful moments she'd experienced in a long time. But the longer she sat there, she noticed her head began to ache, and she thought perhaps she hadn't allowed for enough ventilation while she'd worked. And now she wondered at her rush to seal the windows with the heavy plastic. Before beginning to apply the topcoat of paint, she knew she needed to peel some of the plastic back and allow for airflow.

She rubbed her temples, her shoulders and felt the tight muscles. A sudden sense of exhaustion flooded her right then. She hadn't slept well the night before thanks to her squeaky air mattress and Miguel scratching at the door. And all the excitement earlier that day with Alex's two visits and apparent flirtations had left her spent, limp almost. But Miguel needed food and she could use something for her headache as well. Still, she was unmotivated to move, and although her head continued to ache, she was enjoying her time watching the way the changing light altered the landscape around her while she fantasized and daydreamed about Alex.

She caught herself smiling, and while she wondered how she could possibly be feeling the feelings she was, how she could be feeling alive again, she also struggled with guilt. Did she even have the right to feel this way? After all, in the last months, she'd resigned herself to never being happy again, believing she no longer deserved it. She'd cheated on Edward, she'd broken Debra's heart, and she'd lost her son because she'd failed to protect him. It was simply selfishness, she thought, allowing herself to be intrigued by Alex.

Right then she caught a glimpse of movement out in the grove. She stood and took a step off the porch and stared, trying to discern what she'd seen. City lights still glowed on the western horizon, but the trees were covered in a dense darkness by now. She started walking toward the tree line. It could be Miguel's owner coming back to retrieve him, having changed his mind after all. She grunted with disappointment; she'd grown fond of the dog in just the short time he'd been with her, and she dreaded the thought of giving him up.

But another thought occurred to her. What if it wasn't the dog's owner? What if it were one of those smugglers Alex had warned her about? Someone, one of Alex's crew, she was sure, had cursed her that day she was out in the trees with Alex. She looked over at the road. The equipment was silent. The crew had gone home hours ago.

She paused but kept her eyes on the area she'd thought she'd seen movement. Perhaps it'd only been shadows or a flock of birds moving to nest and sleep. She continued then, Miguel by her side. But as she grew closer to the edge of the grove, he began to herd her, cutting in front of her, causing her to stop and walk around him. He did it a few more times, and she giggled.

"For goodness sakes, Miguel. What are you doing?"

When they reached the edge of the grove, he positioned himself between her and the trees. She petted his head and listened while she squatted and looked through the narrow rows of trunks. But it was too dark for her to see anything.

"What do you think, boy? You see someone?"

She stood and tapped a shriveled knot of what had once been a grapefruit hanging on a low branch. When she did, it snapped from its dead stem and dropped with a thump to the dirt below. She gave it a little kick with her shoe.

"Come on, I need a shower and to get to Fernie's for your food."

She shivered as she walked back toward the house, but she came to a dead stop when she heard a rustling sound, then a tap-tap-tap. At her feet, the shriveled grapefruit, the one she'd only seconds before snapped from its branch, rolled to a stop. She turned around, and

Miguel circled in front of her, guarding her. His hair stood on end and a deep growl came from his throat. She gripped his canvas collar and realized Miguel wouldn't be reacting as he was to his owner, returning to retrieve him. It had to be an intruder, a smuggler, the man who'd cursed her and called her a whore.

"This is private property. You're on private property. Leave before I call the police." She tried to shout it as confidently as she could, but her voice shook and came out shrill.

She listened for tramping feet, as the trespasser ran off, but only silence came from the trees. Miguel growled again and tugged at her hold.

Then she heard what she thought was a contemptuous laugh, so soft and muted she wasn't sure she'd heard anything. Miguel broke free and tore into the trees. He barked, not as if he was alarmed, but rather as if he were attacking.

"Miguel!" She started to rush after him, but feared who or what she might encounter.

Right then the sky turned darker as a colony of bats sprung up from the trees and swarmed. She screeched, sank to her knees, and covered her head. But within seconds the colony had moved on and Miguel was back, licking her arms and face.

"Well, shit." She hugged the dog's neck. "Stupid bats."

Miguel nuzzled her and smiled his goofy grin.

"Thank you, brave boy. I'm glad you're with me."

She stood and kicked the dried grapefruit back toward the line of trees and then returned to the house. Inside, she locked the door and peeked out the window covered with plastic before resigning herself to the fact she was nothing but a baby being so frightened and startled by bats. She called him to follow and went to shower. While stripping off her dirty clothes, she decided that in addition to dog food and aspirin, she'd pick up a six-pack of beer, perhaps a bottle of cheap wine. Anything to steady her nerves and help her sleep through the night.

❖

She opened the passenger door of her Jeep and motioned. "Let's get you some food and me some beer."

But Miguel continued to sit on the porch.

"Come on, silly, let's go for a ride. I'll buy you a special treat."
She pulled his collar, but he wouldn't budge. "You stubborn mutt. Fine.
I'll go without you, but stay right there and wait for me."

She turned her Jeep around and began down the road. Alex's
crew had finished more than three-quarters of it. At this rate, they'd be
finished by the end of tomorrow, and she'd be able to shop for some
furniture and a decent bed to be delivered. She'd be happy for that, a
decent bed.

At the gas station, both Fernie and his wife, whose name Brenna
learned was Patricia, greeted her and asked how renovations were
going on the house. She made polite chitchat and told them about
Miguel. While Patricia made her a sandwich in the deli, she talked
about her marriage to Fernie, their children and grandchildren. But
when she asked Brenna about her life, Brenna froze. After a moment's
awkwardness, she revealed she was a widow and had lost her only child.
Patricia shook her head and made small expressions of sympathy. She
reassured Brenna that she, Fernie, and their oldest son, Luis, the night
manager of the store, would be happy to help her out with anything she
might need. Before Brenna could get out the door, Patricia had given
her a container from the deli to be used as a dog dish and a larger cooler
to store more food until she had a new refrigerator delivered. But the
most useful item Patricia insisted she take was an old radio Fernie had
used in the garage but no longer needed.

The drive back toward the citrus grove was as beautiful as the
sunset had been. The desert sky, a purple black with only a sliver of a
moon, wrapped around her like a cloak of stars, and she could see the
shadow of Red Mountain on the horizon and thought about how that
morning, she and Alex had stood on the porch and watched the sun light
the unusually shaped peak. For the rest of the twenty-plus mile drive,
she allowed herself to daydream about Alex once again.

When she pulled in front of the house, she realized she'd forgotten
to leave any lights burning, but she could see Miguel waiting under
the awning. Now out of the Jeep and on the porch, she strained to find
the keyhole in the door handle. When she opened the door, the house
was pitch-black. Her heart raced as she knew she'd have to enter the
blackness and search for a light. Once again she was thankful to have
Miguel by her side as she stumbled toward the kitchen and found the
switch. She let out a sigh once the light came on, but knew she was

being silly. There was nothing to be afraid of, nothing but a colony of bats and maybe a few snakes and spiders as Alex had teased when they'd first met. Still, the house was quiet. Too quiet. All she could hear was her own breathing and the swish of Miguel's tail on the hardwood floor. She plugged in the radio, and after settling on a station, she fixed the dog some dinner and stood in the kitchen eating her sandwich while watching him wolf his food.

After cleaning up and changing for bed, she called to check in with her sister and tell her she wouldn't be coming back to Iowa for Thanksgiving. She knew this was going to be a difficult conversation.

"Thanksgiving should be spent with family," Jessica said.

Brenna could hear the hurt in her sister's voice, but she managed to control herself, not snapping back that her family was dead. Instead she offered to fly Jessica out at Christmas when the boys had time off from school.

"We could drive up and see the Grand Canyon," Brenna said. "Mason asked me about it before I left. It would be fun." She tried her best to sound upbeat and positive.

"And what do you even know about these people you've just met?"

"I told you, Jess, she's a friend of the Realtor Edward was working with, and she owns the company that's preparing the property. She's nice and said it wouldn't be any trouble to have me over. And besides, like I said, I have this dog now. I can't ask someone to take care of him while I'm away."

Jessica agreed finally although she still sounded hurt.

They talked another hour, but mostly Jessica chattered about all the people she and Brenna knew in common and the things Tanner and Mason were doing in school. Brenna felt bad for not being more interested. She'd only been away from Davenport for five weeks, but she felt as if it'd been years since she'd lived there.

After she got off the phone, she stretched and rubbed her shoulders. She'd tensed while talking with Jessica. It wasn't a new feeling either. When the affair with Debra had been at its most intense, she'd thought Jessica might've suspected something. Jessica would corner her and ask probing questions, suggestive and even accusatory questions. The interrogations would leave Brenna tense and edgy. But she'd always managed to maneuver around those questions. She wondered just how much Jessica knew. But that mattered little now, she thought. Debra was gone, back to her husband and their mission in East Africa, and Edward and Michael were dead. She slumped against the wall as the old suspicion, that taunting whisper, accused her once again. If she hadn't cheated on Edward, if she'd stayed a faithful wife, if she'd not tried to...

Miguel pressed his head against her leg and pawed her arm.

She wiped tears and held her head, which had started to pound again despite the aspirin she'd taken with her first bottle of beer. She needed to sleep, she knew, so she took another dose with a sip of her third beer before sending Miguel out to do his business. After locking up, she brought him back into the bedroom where she took her sleep aid, swallowing it with one more swig of beer. She settled inside the sleeping bag and patted the ground next to her.

"Come lie with me, boy."

Miguel, who'd been sitting in the doorway watching her, came close and lay down.

She switched off the lamp, wrapped an arm around his neck, and nestled her face against his shoulder.

"This is nice. I've missed having someone to hold." She felt herself beginning to drift.

It was comforting to have him there with his rhythmic breathing and warmth. And the sleep aid, mixed with the alcohol, eased the jitteriness she'd felt the night before, had felt just that evening. Within minutes, she was asleep. But her last thoughts were not with Alex and her growing infatuation. Instead, they lingered on the mistakes she'd made, on her errors of judgment, which she believed had cost her son his life. She had made so many mistakes, and she continued to pay for them still.

Chapter Ten

The floor broke apart beneath her.
"Hold my dress," she shouted over the roar.
"I want Daddy."

She yanked his hand and forced him to take the edge of her dress. "Goddamn it, Michael, I said hold my dress!"

Splinters hurled at their faces, and she flung her skirt, which had transformed into a giant flowing curtain, over her son's body. He'd be safe there while she helped the old woman.

But it wasn't Maribel Chambers at her feet. Instead it was Debra, her face contorted. "Who will you save?"

Brenna clutched her flowing skirt. There were so many folds, so much material. She was frantic as she unfolded the garment only to find Michael gone.

Wood cracked, glass shattered, and the scream of the tornado siren merged into her own.

She bolted up yelling his name as she'd done every night since she'd lost him. She was drenched in sweat and sobbing. She fell back on her pillow and pulled her hair while she continued to cry and cough, choking on her tears. What she would give to be spared this nightmare for only one night, just one night. She reached for Miguel, but couldn't feel him. Then she heard his feet on the hardwood floor, his familiar panting and swishing tail. She hoisted herself to her knees and switched on the floor lamp to see him standing in the bedroom doorway looking, not at her, but at something next to her.

"Do you need to go out?" She coughed and wiped her eyes.

But he only continued to sit, watching.

The radio had gone to static. Perhaps the noise was hurting his ears. She switched it off.

"Miguel?"

The dog followed something with his eyes.

"What are you looking at? Don't do that, it gives me the creeps." She strained to see what she hoped would be a moth or fly.

There was nothing.

She looked back at him. "What is it?"

Then, the click.

She dropped her mouth open as her eyes went to her son's music box. The lid lifted. The small mechanism rotated. The little teeth plucked out the tune. As the melody swirled around her, she felt someone watching. But she couldn't move. Fear paralyzed her. The box had opened on its own, an action she knew was impossible. As the music box made a second rotation, she turned her head to see Miguel smiling at someone and wagging his tail.

"Who...what are you looking at, you damn dog." Her tears came from panic now, not sorrow.

She pulled her legs to her chest and cowered. But she couldn't stand to hear that tune play through again. She slammed the box shut, staring at it, praying it wouldn't open again. Then she watched as Miguel seemed to follow someone out into the living room. The lamp from the bedroom shone into the area outside the door, and she could see he'd paused at the foot of the stairs, turning and watching her while his golden eyes glowed in the reflection of the bedroom light.

She gaped at him, at the music box, and back to him. He'd been on the floor next to her when she'd fallen asleep. He must've bumped it. It must have a sprung latch. That was the only possible explanation.

Miguel whined.

"Do you need to go out? Is that it?"

She rubbed her arms around herself. She would accept the explanation of a sprung latch because anything else was too ridiculous. She pull herself up on wilting legs and went to the kitchen where she turned on the light, then the light in the living room, and finally the porch light. She opened the door and held the rickety screen.

"Hurry up. I want to go back to sleep." She wondered what time it was.

Miguel turned and stared up the dark staircase.

"Miguel, damn it, come on, hurry." She was harsh now, impatient, her nerves on edge.

Then she heard something else, something that knocked the air right out of her—a loud thud just above her head. Her legs went to mush while a whimper escaped her throat. She stared at the dark steps. Another noise, less intense, but a definite sound of movement, scraped across the floor above. She grabbed her throat. Her heart was climbing out her mouth and she couldn't breathe. Then she spied her keys on the kitchen counter. She had to grab those keys and the dog, and get the hell out of there. Someone had broken into the house while she was sleeping and was in one of the upstairs rooms. Maybe there'd been someone out in the trees earlier, not just the bats. Maybe it was a smuggler as Alex had warned.

"Miguel." She motioned for him.

But he wagged his tail and climbed the stairs.

"No, no, no. Damn it, Miguel."

He stopped at the top of the landing and turned, his eyes beckoning her to follow.

She didn't know what to do. She didn't want to abandon him, afraid the intruder would harm him. She snatched her keys and the hammer she'd left on the counter with the rest of her tools. It was against her better judgment to climb those dark stairs, but she wanted to protect her dog.

"Is there someone there?" she asked as she approached him.

She paused after each step to listen for more noises. There were none. Finally, she reached the top of the landing. She gripped the hammer, blinked, and waited for her eyes to adjust while she stood as still as her frantic breathing allowed. Now she wished she'd brought the flashlight with her. The one room, the empty one, was dark. Anyone could be hiding in the shadows, and the lamp was clear across the room. The room with the desk and boxes was also dark and—

Why was the door shut? She hadn't shut it when she'd been in there the day before.

She debated if she should go back downstairs for the flashlight or simply risk dashing in and switching on the light. Or maybe she should just pick up the dog, if she could, and run for it. But another sound assaulted her. It came from behind the closed door, the room with the desk.

"Shit!"

She grabbed Miguel's collar, pulling him back toward the stairs. But Miguel was not cooperating. And even more interesting, he wasn't growling nor was his hair on end.

"Miguel, please."

Abruptly, a thin slice of sickly yellow light cut through the gloom of the hallway and beamed under the closed door. Someone had turned on the light inside the room.

She wanted nothing more than to run as fast as she could from the house right then, but the rush of fear and terror kept her from finding her feet. She fell backward onto her butt and crab-crawled away from the door while she bit her lip to keep from screaming. She knew the intruder would be coming through that door any moment, and all she had to protect herself with was a hammer. She felt her stomach turn and convulse as fright gripped her. She juddered and shook, watching the light under the door, waiting to see a shadow pass through it. But there was nothing.

"Miguel?"

He went to the door, nudged it.

By now her heart raced so brutally, she was sure she'd faint. But as the door opened, she saw no one stood inside. She jerked up on trembling knees and entered the room. As soon as she did, she gasped and held her chest. Her heart thudded to a stop and began again. There on the desk the antique oil lamp glowed with a flame burning at its wick, the little flare flickering in the room. As she stared at the flame, her rational mind told her an oil lamp couldn't spontaneously catch fire. Someone had to have lit it.

"This is crazy."

She moved to switch on the floor lamp in the corner, but she couldn't take her eyes off the small spark bobbing and hissing on the cotton wick. She flinched as she reached out and turned the little knob on the lamp to snuff out the flame. When she did, an ethereal wisp of smoke twisted up through the top of the glass chimney and dissipated. She heard Miguel behind her and saw him watching with intense eyes. Then something occurred to her. Perhaps the intruder had slipped out the window and fallen to the gravel drive below. But the lever which opened the window was in its locked position. She wiped sweat and tears from her eyes and stared out into the darkness. All over her body, she felt little hairs stiffen and her skin turn clammy while the scar on the back of her head and neck pulsed.

"We need to go back into town. I'll find a hotel that takes pets, and we'll go back into town. I was foolish to think I could stay out here by myself."

She started to leave the room, but her eyes fell to the desk. The day Cassie and she had first explored the house, she'd opened the drawers to the desk, all but the largest drawer, which wouldn't open. But now, the drawer was open an inch. She leaned on tiptoe and peered inside. She could see something shiny. She pulled on the handle and the drawer opened all the way, revealing two silver necklaces.

"What's this?" She pulled out a silver rosary and a small silver medal, both untarnished.

She brought the pieces over to the floor lamp to have a better look. The rosary was an elegant piece in a primitive way. The silver looked hand-forged and shaped, the beads worn in places from repetitive finger strokes. At one end, the crucifix. At the other, a medallion with a representation of the Virgin. She was familiar with most religious iconography, but this image was different. She examined the small medal next. It was a silver oval, strung on a silver chain with a broken clasp. On one side was a man, no, an angel. She wasn't sure. It looked as if he was holding something in his hand. Across the top were words, worn, but readable.

She leaned closer to the lamp and read, "San Miguel." She looked at the dog. "You've got to be joking."

She checked the drawer once more, but it was empty. She thought that for such a big drawer on the outside, it certainly was shallow on the inside. She shut it and looked around the room. There was no simple explanation for all of this, she knew. The thumping and shuffling, the oil lamp burning, the drawer opened. And now these two silver pieces shining as if they'd just been polished—she knew silver oxidized if not tended to. If these pieces were pure silver, which she suspected they were, they should be black with tarnish, but instead they glinted. Whatever the explanation, she didn't want to spend another moment in the house. She patted Miguel's head.

"Let's go."

But as she began to leave the room, he yipped, causing her to turn.

He stood on his hind legs and perched against the window. She looked past him, out to the blackened grove; she'd yet to put the heavy plastic on these broken panes. She came close and saw a pinpoint of orange light in the distance, a campfire on the back acreage. It could be smugglers, she thought. Maybe one of them had gotten into the house after all. How he'd gotten out made no sense. Or maybe it was teenagers, just as Cassie had mentioned. Then she remembered what Alex had said about the trees being so dry they could easily go up in flames. The fear of an uncontrolled fire that could sweep the entire property was enough to sideline her anxiety about smugglers and the mystery of the oil lamp. In fact, she'd released so many endorphins during her moment of fright she felt almost energized. She switched off the lamp, went downstairs, and pulled on shoes and a jacket. She placed the two silver necklaces on the kitchen counter and headed out the door while motioning for the dog to follow.

"Are you coming with me this time?"

Miguel seemed eager to follow and leapt into the front seat of the Jeep without her opening the door.

"Good boy."

She turned on the bright lights and turned toward the back access road. As she drove, she realized this road was in worse condition than the main road in. Although her Jeep had plenty of clearance, she took her time, slowing for the deep potholes while keeping her eyes on the campfire in the distance. The farther she ventured, the air grew colder and the darkness thickened. She drove around the bend, passed by the pump house, went a bit farther until she was a dozen yards from the campfire. She put her Jeep in park and listened. She could see people, but she couldn't hear any laughter or loud talking typical of drunken teenagers. The thought crossed her mind it might be drug smugglers, and perhaps they were watching her approach, ready to accost her. But whoever they were, she had to get them to douse their fire. She shifted into drive and approached. As she advanced and her headlights illuminated the group, she noticed these people weren't teenagers and didn't look like the type to be trafficking in drugs. They were adult men, sitting on stools, overturned tubs, and stumps of trees. They didn't even look toward her as she approached. She put her Jeep in park and stood on her seat.

"Hello?"

Miguel jumped out and went toward the group. He wagged his tail as one of the men began to pet him.

"Is this your dog? Does Miguel belong to you?" She saw he was going from person to person. "Excuse me, but if he's your dog, that's fine. I know one of you left him last night."

Nothing.

She groaned, got out of her Jeep, and went over to them, hoping to get one of them to speak to her.

"Listen, this is private property. I don't care about you being out here, but the fire has me worried. The trees are dead. It would only take a spark."

Miguel sat with the silent men and waited.

She sighed in frustration and searched the faces she could see in the firelight. None made eye contact with her. That's when she noticed how tired these men looked, how worn-out they appeared. They were dressed in work clothes, wore boots covered in dried mud and dirty caps or cowboy hats on their heads. Then, in the firelight, deeper in the shadows, she caught glimpses of bare legs and feet. As her eyes adjusted she realized they were women and children. Some of the women hugged infants while others held belongings, rolled-up blankets, sacks, and canteens. From what she could see, at least a dozen people crowded around the fire. She was sure it was a family of migrant farm workers, perhaps more than one.

"Do you need help?" Brenna asked.

One of the men took off his sweat-stained hat. "Sí, usted nos puede ayudar."

"I'm sorry, I don't speak Spanish."

"He says you can help us." It was a woman's voice, accented and ancient.

Brenna peered toward the fire. She was uncertain who'd spoken. "How? Tell me what you need."

The men stood and parted while an old woman dressed in a faded red skirt and a black shawl pulled around her head, stepped into the light. Her face was hidden in the hollow of her mantle and she held a large, ripe grapefruit in her hand. Brenna wondered where'd she'd found it, for all the trees were dead. There was no live fruit.

"You will help us?" the woman asked.

Brenna cringed without meaning to. The woman's voice sounded menacing. "Of course. What can I do?"

"He has not returned. You must find him."

"Who hasn't returned from where?"

"Pedro, my grandson."

Brenna examined the crowd. She could see small children, their faces dirty and noses running. Her heart sank as she imagined a little boy, separated from his mother's protective arms, gone astray somewhere in the dark. She coughed as something tickled her throat.

"Your grandson? Is he lost?"

"He went to the house to free his mother, my daughter. But he has yet to return. You must help." The woman fingered the grapefruit in her hand.

"Of course I'll help you. How long has he..." Brenna stopped. "Wait a minute." She pointed in the direction of the house. "You don't mean that house?"

"Sí."

"I'm afraid you've made a mistake. There's no one in that house but me and this dog." Brenna pointed to Miguel.

"Dog?" The woman turned her hidden face toward Miguel. "No, señorita, he is not a dog."

Brenna frowned. Clearly something was being lost in translation. "I need to call someone who can help you. We're not communicating. I've got my..." She reached inside her pocket for her phone and realized she hadn't brought it. "Damn, my phone. Let me go back to the house and get it."

The old woman took a step forward. She held the grapefruit between her hands as if to split it open. "You will help us." It was a statement, not a question.

"Yes, of course. I said I would," Brenna said. "I don't want your grandson out there in the dark afraid."

The fire surged as if someone had sprayed it with fuel. The old woman dropped the grapefruit and drew back her shawl. Brenna stared into black eyes, mesmeric eyes, among the folds of the woman's wrinkled face. Something about those eyes, that face, made her draw in a quick breath. When she did, she choked and coughed while covering her mouth. The rest of the family, all standing now, stepped closer. They formed a semicircle around her and watched her with solemn and sad faces. Their worried expressions moved her, for she knew what it was like to be concerned for a child.

"Don't worry. I'll find him," Brenna said. "But let me call a friend who can help us. In fact, why don't you"—she reached her hand to the old woman—"come with me and you can talk to my friend. She speaks Spanish."

"We have no permission to the house. Only Anabel, my daughter, is permitted."

"It's okay. You can come to the house. It's my house." Brenna continued to hold her hand out.

But the grandmother ignored it. Instead she stepped closer and looked to either side of Brenna. She began to shake her head as her black eyes widened and filled with tears. "Ave María Purísima!" she exclaimed and covered her mouth.

"What is it?" Brenna asked, confused, a little afraid.

The grandmother reached out and placed her hand on Brenna's cheek. "Such sorrow."

"What?" Brenna pulled away.

But the grandmother stepped closer. "Ay, mija, how you suffer. It clings to you." She put her hand to Brenna's chest.

Brenna would've pulled away again if her feet hadn't been rooted to the ground. She felt heat rush from the woman's hand. Her chest began to burn, her throat to blister. Something clawed inside her, like tiny talons slashing at her windpipe.

"What...what are you doing?" She grabbed her own throat and wheezed.

"Sí, such sorrow, but anger and bitterness also." The grandmother wept. "It clings to you, swallows you."

A muffled echo of something off in the distance, the sound of men shouting and horses whinnying, reverberated against the dense trees. Abruptly the people began talking, their voices panicked. Women hugged infants and toddlers to their chests, children shrieked and held each other, men picked up shovels and long sticks, and Miguel went on guard as his hackles rose.

"What's happening?" Brenna asked.

The grandmother stared at her with wide eyes. "You have called him back. Your shame has drawn him." One of the men took the old woman's arm and began to lead her off, but she turned back to Brenna. "We will not leave without Pedro and Anabel. You must find him, find Pedro. He went to the house to free his mother. She is in the house. She is in the house." She turned with the others and vanishing into the trees.

"Wait. Please, I don't understand," Brenna shouted after them. Within seconds the grove was empty of people and silence pressed around her while the firelight cast shadows against the wall of dead trees. "Hello?" She noticed Miguel watching. "Were those your people?"

He leapt back into the Jeep and waited for her as she kicked dirt onto the flames and doused the campfire as best she could. Shaken, she joined him, turned her vehicle around, and started back on the road to the house with one hand on the steering wheel and the other resting on his back. He had to be their dog, she was certain. It had to have been one of the men or perhaps one of young children who'd dropped him off on her porch last night. The best she could figure, they were migrant farm workers, working the farms and groves in the area. Or perhaps they were simply passing through to another farm or grove. No matter, at least they weren't smugglers, she thought. She cursed as she passed the pump house. She felt frightened, but didn't understand the source of her fear. She was confused as well. None of what happened made any logical sense to her. And the old woman, what had she meant about her shame drawing him back? She swallowed and coughed, her throat tingling. By the time she'd pulled in front of the house, her fright and confusion had given way to frustration. She needed to call Alex, to have her come out in the morning and talk with these people. And that would mean she'd likely be giving up Miguel.

"You need to be with your people, Miguel."

She turned off her Jeep and thought about the boy, Pedro, and wondered where he could be. She could certainly sympathize with the grandmother and the others. Here they were sleeping outdoors with children and babies, out in the elements and worried for the boy and his mother to return. But they had to be mistaken, she thought. The mother, Anabel, must be over at the house on the cotton farm.

"Don't worry. Alex will help us figure this all out. The boy and his mother can't be far." She frowned. "Miguel?"

He sat in the front seat of the Jeep, but his head and shoulders were on point, his eyes directed toward the second story of the house. Brenna raised her eyes. In the room with the desk and the ugly wallpaper, a light came on. Her throat seized shut, and she sputtered a hushed cry as she saw the face of a woman appear in the window. The woman's raven hair fell around her shoulders and her dark eyes watched Brenna. They were beautiful eyes, black as onyx, like the grandmother's, and nearly as hypnotic. Brenna gripped her keys in one hand and the handle of the Jeep door in the other. She couldn't take her eyes from the woman who stood in the window gazing at her.

"Anabel?" And then she had a thought. "Nelda?" But the woman was dark, not fair like the woman in the old family photograph.

The figure pressed her hand against a full pane of glass and continued to watch Brenna, her expression seeming to plead for help.

"Miguel," Brenna said without looking at the dog, "is that Anabel?"

He whimpered.

"I need my phone." She started walking toward the house, all the while watching the woman, who in turn, watched her.

But the house had been transformed. She went up onto the porch, and as she reached for the screen, her hand met the handle of the door instead. She searched the outline of the door. The screen was missing. Then she saw the door was polished oak, not weather-beaten and faded. She turned the knob. It was locked.

"What the…"

She walked backward off the porch. To her disbelief she was standing in front of a house she didn't recognize, a house painted in bright blue with white trim.

"I'm dreaming…sleepwalking…this is crazy." She began to hyperventilate. Her stomach knotted, and she felt as if she'd throw up. "Miguel?" She called his name, hoping desperately he'd start licking her to wake her. She had to be dreaming in her sleeping bag. It had to be a nightmare. "Miguel!"

She backed away from the house and looked at the window again. But the woman was gone. Brenna searched for Miguel, but he was gone, too. Had he run off? But when, where? She gaped at the window, saw shadows swerving in the light. A man's voice, deep and threatening, snarled from within the room. A woman's, pleading and begging, countered his. Then Anabel fell against the window and scratched at the glass. Her panicked eyes looked at Brenna as someone yanked her by the hair and pulled her away from the window. Anabel shrieked out incomprehensible things, cries of desperation, which pierced Brenna's head, driving into her gut.

"Oh God, oh God, oh God!" She sobbed as she cupped her ears.

She clambered into her Jeep and fumbled with her keys. But just as she was about to turn the engine over, the screaming stopped. Then she heard stomping, as if someone bolting down the stairs inside the house. She watched the front door swing open before she scrambled to the passenger side, slipped out, and ducked to hide from whoever, *what*ever was coming out that door. She fell prone onto the gravel driveway, closed her eyes, bit down on her knuckles, and held her breath. The scar on the back of her neck and head pulsed with each heartbeat. She could hear the crunching sounds of someone, large and heavy, walking across the gravel away from the house. She heard a grunt and a creaking sound as if a door was being opened. Then silence. She peeked under the Jeep. But there was no one she could see. She got to her feet and climbed back into her Jeep and started it, checking the time on the dash display. But the incandescent glow of the clock only revealed blinking numbers: 3:15. She tapped the display, punched the little buttons. The clock wasn't working, and she wished she knew the time. She looked around one more time, back to the window, which, as she saw now, was perfect with all the panes whole and unbroken. But to her horror, she also saw what looked like handprints, bloody handprints smeared in streaks down the glass. She couldn't determine any longer if she was dreaming. Right now her terror was real. And where was Miguel? Why had he run off when she'd needed him? She threw the Jeep in gear and turned it toward the road, but she slammed on her brakes before she'd gone more than a few yards. It was the garage. The doors, the ones that had been nailed shut, stood wide open. A light from a kerosene lamp filled the space, and although she was certain she'd seen a bloody hand and a foot lying on the dirt floor of the garage, she wasn't about to investigate. She stepped on the gas and flew across the ungraded portion of the road, onto the portion Alex's crew had finished, onto the highway, and straight to Fernie's store.

Chapter Eleven

Brenna pulled to a screeching halt in the store's parking lot. Inside, she found a man leaning against the counter. He looked like a younger version of Fernie, but she had no time for introductions.

"Call the police," she shouted. "A woman's being beaten to death."

He stared at her.

"Did you hear me? Call 9-1-1!"

"Okay, lady, calm down. Here, here's the phone." He pulled a landline phone from under the counter and set it in front of her.

She dialed, waited for the pickup while tapping her foot.

"9-1-1, what's your emergency?" A woman's voice spoke on the other end.

"My name is Brenna Wilson, I mean Brenna Taylor. I live at the Poulsen grove off McKellips Road, east of the freeway, I think." She felt sweat drip down the side of her face, and she panted while she spoke, trying to control her voice and breathing.

"You're Brenna?" the young man asked, but she shushed him.

"What's your street address, ma'am?" the operator asked.

"What's my street address? I have no idea. There isn't one. I don't know." She looked at Luis. "What's the street address of the Poulsen property?"

"I don't know. We just know it as the Poulsen grove."

"I don't have an address," Brenna said into the phone.

"Ma'am, the computer indicates you're calling from eighty-nine hundred East McKellips Road, is that correct?"

"What's the address here? This store?" she asked Luis.

He ran off the address, and she confirmed it to the operator.

"And this is your residence?" the operator asked.

"No, I'm at a gas station. Listen, a woman is being hurt on my property. I heard her screaming in my house, and I think her family is out in the grove, and they're missing a boy. Please, you have to send the police." She began crying into the receiver.

"Ma'am, I need you to remain calm. Who's the woman? And where's the boy?"

"I don't know!" She pounded the counter.

A pause registered on the other end of the line, and the operator said, "Ma'am, the location where this incident happened is not the same as from where you're calling. Is this correct?"

"For God's sakes, yes." She held her head

"You say this incident happened on the Poulsen property twenty-three miles east of your current location?"

"Yes, the citrus grove, hurry."

"I'm connecting you with the Maricopa County sheriff's office," the operator said. "That location is not within the jurisdiction of Mesa police. Please hold."

Brenna heard elevator music. "What? No!"

But within seconds another voice answered. "Maricopa County sheriff's office, how can I direct your call?" a man's voice asked.

"Listen to me, there's a woman being harmed. She may be dead by now, on my property, at the Poulsen Citrus Grove. I need help." She gritted her teeth.

"What is your name, ma'am?"

"Brenna Taylor, for the second time, and no, I'm not calling from the house. I was locked out. I'm calling from Fernie's Garage. Will you please send help?"

The operator confirmed the address and said, "I'll dispatch a deputy immediately. Remain at your present location until he arrives."

She slammed the receiver down and held her face as she tried to get a grip on her emotions. She raised her head to see the young man staring at her.

"You're Luis?"

"Yeah, and you're Brenna. My mom and dad told me about you."

"I'm sorry for being crazy, but it's been a bizarre night." She tried to smile, but she was still shaking and couldn't muster more than a weak grin.

"I can see that. I was just getting ready to make the first round of coffee. You can have yesterday's pastries, too, if you like. The bakery truck won't be here for another hour." He picked up a carafe and headed to the area behind the deli.

"Thank you, Luis, just coffee for now. My stomach's tied in knots." She sat at one of the tables in the deli area and focused on breathing. Her heart still hammered against her ribs, and her hands and knees throbbed from falling prone when she'd hid behind her Jeep.

Luis returned and began preparing the coffee. "So tell me what happened. Do you know the woman? Who was harming her?"

"I'm not sure. I think her name is Anabel. Does that sound familiar to you?"

"No, I don't know any Anabel."

"Her family was camping in the grove, waiting for her and her son. The boy had run off or something." Brenna tried to piece together in her mind what might be going on. "The grandmother said Anabel was in the house. That didn't make sense to me. But when I came back, she was there, and the house…It just doesn't make any sense. The door, the windows, the paint." She rubbed her scar at the back of her head. "And then I heard a man yelling and her screaming. God, she was screaming as if she was being murdered. And she was in my house, but it wasn't my house."

Luis sat while the coffee brewed. "I don't understand what you mean it wasn't your house."

"I don't know. It was as if I were hallucinating or something. Maybe the primer fumes or…" Brenna began thinking out loud. "The oil lamp was burning. It doesn't make sense. And the night before last, I woke up and my son's music box…" She concentrated on the tile floor while she spoke. "And then again tonight it was playing. It spooked me. My son. His song."

"My mom told me about your son and husband. I'm sorry to hear about that."

"Thank you."

"Did you say primer fumes? You know, when you paint you need lots of ventilation."

"I'm aware of that."

"And that property is probably gas."

"It is."

"You should call the gas company. If you have a slow leak, you wouldn't even smell it. But it could still be poisoning you, but real slowly, so you'd have weird sensations and stuff."

"You have a point." She hadn't smelled any gas. She'd been able to use the gas stove to heat the canned pasta, and she'd had hot water from the gas water heater when she'd showered. But something had to explain the bizarre happenings. Primer fumes mixed with gas fumes was a logical explanation.

Luis poured the coffee and brought it over along with dispensers of sugar and cream. "Just something to think about."

Brenna prepared her coffee and wondered if these last two nights she'd been sleeping in noxious fumes. What if everything she'd experienced was nothing more than a delusion brought on by poisonous air?

"Thank you, Luis. I'll call the gas company and have that checked." She sipped her coffee and wished she'd brought her phone with her. She so needed to call Alex, but she didn't know her number by heart. "Do you have a phone book?" she asked. "I was going to look up a friend's number along with the gas company."

"Sure." Luis went behind the counter and dug around. When he stood, he glanced out the front windows of the store and made a face.

"What is it?"

"I can't believe they sent him."

"Sent who?" Brenna joined him at the counter.

A sheriff's cruiser pulled next to her Jeep, and a large, mustached man with a prominent belly and beefy arms hoisted himself from the seat of his car. He held a clipboard and admired her Jeep.

"The deputy?" she asked, not liking the look of the man. "What's wrong, Luis?"

"That's not just a deputy. That's Marcus Wilcox. He's second in command, the chief deputy sheriff of Maricopa County."

"I didn't expect them to send someone so high ranking." She watched the large man circle her Jeep and jot down what she assumed was her temporary license plate number. She noticed he had small, mean eyes and a cruel mouth partially hidden by his mustache.

"It makes sense. That was his family's property," Luis said.

She did a double take from Luis to the officer. "That's a Poulsen?"

"Yep, Hadley Poulsen was his great-grandfather." Luis shook his head and added, "The man and his brother, the state representative, are bullies." He turned to her. "Be careful, Brenna. Some people, my dad's relatives particularly, they say he's el diablo...the devil."

Marcus Wilcox entered the store. "Someone here call in an emergency?" He looked Brenna up and down, smiling a sick smile, and glanced at the younger Flores. "Luis, you pranking me, boy?"

Brenna could tell he'd bristled with being called boy.

"No, Chief Deputy. This woman called, not me," Luis said.

Wilcox turned to her, again ogling, making her skin crawl. He tipped his head toward her even though he wasn't wearing his white doeskin cowboy hat. "Ma'am, how can I help you?"

Brenna glanced at Luis, who she thought had shaken his head in a silent warning. "Well officer, I—"

"It's Chief Deputy Sheriff Wilcox, ma'am. Chief Deputy will do," he interrupted, preening with the use of his title.

She rolled her eyes and began again. "Yes, Chief Deputy, I was out at the Poulsen property, and I saw a campfire in the distance, and—"

"I thought my granddaddy sold that property to a fellow from back East?" Wilcox interrupted again while he poured himself a cup of coffee.

"He did. That was my husband."

He turned and studied her again, paying particular attention to her hips. "Is that right? And where's your husband now?"

"He's dead. He died in an accident seven months ago." She placed her arms across her chest to block his lecherous stare.

The deputy apparently hadn't anticipated her answer and stopped midway from taking a sip of coffee. "I see, so you're the fellow's widow. Hmm." He narrowed his beady eyes. "You ain't living out there in that house are you, ma'am?"

"I am. I'm fixing it up, renovating, and restoring it."

"What the hell for?"

Brenna returned to the table where she'd left her coffee and sat. "I'm not sure."

Wilcox watched her, looked over at Luis again, and examined his clipboard. "Dispatch says you think a woman was being harmed out there. Tell me about that."

Now Brenna wished she hadn't called for law enforcement. "Some people were camping in the grove, and I went out to talk to them. They were worried about one of their boys and his mother. Then something frightened them and they ran off. When I got back to the house, I heard a woman screaming and I drove here."

Wilcox checked the prepackaged doughnuts. "Hmm, yep, sounds like illegals. They probably got spooked by their coyotes coming to look for 'em. Sometimes they don't pay up and manage to get away. Woman was probably getting a beat down. Some of them coyotes pimp out the women, the children, too, if they can." He settled on a package of doughnuts, opened them, glanced over at Luis, smiled, and shoved a bite in his mouth.

Brenna watched with disgust. "I don't know what you mean about coyotes. You don't mean the animal, I take it."

Wilcox smacked his lips. "You ain't heard of coyotes? They traffic in drugs and a whole host of other things, people, too. Take a down payment, usually all the money a person has, and arrange to sneak 'em across the border, holding 'em at gunpoint in a drop house and demanding more money. But sometimes they keep 'em out in a field or in the desert."

"Coyotes smuggle people across the border?"

"Smuggling's not the word, more like trafficking. Lot of the time they keep part of the family in one location, pimping out the young children and women, while making the men work. It's a dirty business." He took another bite of doughnut.

Brenna grimaced. "I don't think these people were being trafficked, or whatever. I think they were migrant farm workers, maybe from the farm across the highway from me."

"Not likely. Cotton's not high for another month."

"Whoever they are, they need help. Someone was hurting that woman."

"You see the woman?"

"I saw her briefly in the upstairs window."

"Upstairs window?" Wilcox narrowed his eyes. "She was in the house?"

Brenna nodded.

"Why was she in the house? Did you let her in?"

"I don't know how she got in the house unless she came through the grove looking for her son and found my door open while I was out talking with the rest of her family."

Wilcox tapped his clipboard on his thigh. "Seems reasonable." He finished off another doughnut and gulped his coffee then wiped his hand across his moustache. After examining his notes, he walked to the soda cooler and took out a bottle of cola, opened it, and sucked down half before belching and patting his large stomach.

Brenna saw Luis grit his teeth. She realized he wasn't able to do a thing about the deputy's thievery.

"You don't know these people out in the grove?" Wilcox asked. "Never seen the woman before? Maybe offered them work or a handout recently?"

"No and no. I don't know who they are and I've never seen or talked to them before."

"So tell me, ma'am." Wilcox wiped the back of his hand across his mustache again. "Are you staying out there all alone?" He gave her a greasy smile.

She knew what he meant. She understood his implication, and it made her sick. "No, I'm not. Not after this morning. I'm picking up my sister and her husband and my nephews at the airport this afternoon. They'll be staying with me through the holidays."

"Huh, all right then, let's go check it out." He turned to Luis. "Tell your folks I stopped by and thank them for the coffee." He held the door. "After you, ma'am. I take it that's your fancy Jeep? I'll follow in my cruiser. Be right behind you." He smiled while he ogled her once more.

Brenna didn't want to be alone with this man. Her intuition was screaming a warning inside her head and stomach. She glanced at the digital clock on the shelf by the cigarette display. It was four forty-five in the morning. Alex's crew had gotten to her place around five or five thirty yesterday morning.

"Thank you, Chief Deputy. I'll be right out. I need to get some toiletries."

He grunted and went to his car.

"Luis." She turned to him as soon as the deputy was outside. "Please help me. Find the number for Santana and Sons Survey and Grading. They should be in the phone book. If not, call information.

Get ahold of the owner, Alex Santana. Tell her what's happened and ask her to send someone from her crew to my property as soon as she can."

"I'm on it. I saw one of their trucks yesterday morning when they stopped in for coffee. I know what company you mean."

"Thank you." She grabbed a box of tampons, which she didn't need. "Listen, I don't have my wallet, but—"

"Don't worry about it. You want me to call my dad to meet you out there? You shouldn't be alone with that bastard. He's got a bad reputation with women."

"No, call Alex Santana. I'll drive slowly and give her time."

Brenna exited the store and saw the deputy watching her. She climbed into her Jeep, took her time cinching her seat belt and backing out onto the highway. She hoped to see the sun peeking over the horizon, but the sky was still a pale blue white just before sunrise. Time seemed off somehow, she thought. Everything seemed turned on end. She glanced in her review mirror and saw the deputy's car following right behind her.

"Please, Alex, please hurry," she said as she drove slowly toward the grove. She hoped Alex would get her message in time.

CHAPTER TWELVE

A pproaching the turnoff for the property, Brenna saw two trucks parked along the highway and two men leaning against their open tailgates sipping from thermoses. It was Johnny and Hector. She pulled up, and Johnny came running.

"Brenna, Alex called and told me to meet you here. She's worried about—" He stopped when he saw the sheriff's car pull close. "Alex told me to stay with you while he's here. Let me get in with you." He went to the other side of her Jeep to climb in, but stopped again when he saw the deputy roll down his window.

"What you boys doing out here? Harassing this young woman?" Wilcox sneered.

"No sir, Chief Deputy. We're part of the crew working on the road. We're with Santana and Sons." Johnny pointed to the sign on the side of his truck.

The deputy made a face. "Ah, right, Santana and Sons. Yes, I know all about your boss and her father. Well get on with it. I'd like to get home for breakfast."

Johnny jumped into the Jeep. "Alex told me you have to call her. She's worried sick and said she'll be here as fast as she can."

"Thank you, Johnny. That man is such a creep," Brenna said.

"You got that right." His phone buzzed. "It's Alex." He answered, speaking Spanish then English. "Here, she wants to talk to you."

Brenna took the phone and steered with one hand. "Alex?" She was trying not to burst into tears.

"God, Brenna, what's going on? Are you okay? My office said you'd called for the sheriff because some woman was being hurt out there."

Brenna could hear the panic in Alex's voice.

"It's complicated. I don't know what's happening." She pulled in front of the house. Johnny climbed out, came around and stood by her side of the vehicle, and watched while the deputy was still back on the ungraded portion of the road.

"Johnny's there with you," Alex said. "He's going to stay at your side until I get there. I'm about fifteen minutes away. You stay close to him. Don't let Wilcox get you alone, do you hear me?"

"Okay, I won't. I'm sorry. I don't mean to be such a pain." Brenna wiped her nose on her jacket.

"Stop. You're not a pain. Now hang on. I'll be right there. Give the phone back to Johnny."

Brenna handed Johnny the phone, and he began conversing in Spanish again. She figured he was reassuring Alex he'd watch over her. While they talked, she climbed out of her Jeep and looked at the upstairs window. No one was there. She scanned the house. It was as she knew it—dirty, faded and peeling blue paint, with broken windows and a weathered door covered with a rickety screen. She glanced at the garage. The doors were shut. She walked over and tugged on them, but the doors didn't budge. Just then she heard a familiar bark, and she turned around to see Miguel running toward her with his tongue hanging from his mouth.

"Miguel!" She met him halfway, falling on her knees and hugging the large beast. "You dumb dog, I was worried about you. Where did… oh my goodness, you stink."

He was covered and caked in mud, just as he'd been the night before.

"Ugh, look at me." She stood and examined the smear of mud down her front. "Damn it, these were my last clean clothes."

But before she could scold him any more, her sweet loving companion transformed into a snarling vicious brute, curling back his lips and exposing his canine teeth, growling and barking.

"What is it?" She took a step back, frightened by his sudden change. Then she turned and saw the deputy had just pulled up in his car. "Miguel, stop." She tugged on his canvas collar, but the dog was focused on lunging at the deputy's car.

"You call your goddamn dog off right now or I'll put a bullet in his head," Wilcox yelled through his cracked window.

"For heaven's sake, he's just protecting me," Brenna yelled back, and she motioned Johnny over. "Help me get him in the house." The two of them managed to pull Miguel onto the porch and push him inside.

Johnny shut the door. "That's a good dog."

Wilcox came onto the porch. His eyes shifted back and forth. "Place looks pitiful. Take my advice, ma'am, and bulldoze these buildings along with the trees."

"I'd think you'd be sentimental about your family's estate," Brenna said.

Wilcox glared at her. "Estate?" He took a breath as if trying to calm his temper. "I watched my mother and father slave over this grove, losing money year after year. Fruit went foul, trees stopped producing. Cost my father his health and my mother her sanity." He shook his head and scowled. "I'm glad Granddad sold it off. He should've done it long ago."

"Except for the area under the tennis court and the house, until my husband and his broker managed to convince your lawyer." She was interested why Wilcox seemed so bitter.

"He's got his reasons. Some family business is private." He wiped his mouth and straightened his shoulders. "Besides you got the house now. Thought we'd hold on to it. But my brother Julian's making a run for governor next term. Granddad figured he'd need the funds." He studied his clipboard. "This woman you saw in the house, the one being attacked, she still in there? That dog's inside, so I'll let you two check it out."

Brenna said to Johnny, "Come with me?"

Johnny nodded and the two went inside.

"Some great police work, lazy bastard," Johnny said as they entered the house.

Brenna sighed, pleased to be away from the deputy's gaze. She noticed all the downstairs lights she'd turned on hours before still glowed, and Miguel sat waiting in the living room with clumps of mud smeared about the once-clean hardwood floors.

"Great, now you've brought your muddy mess inside." She bent and hugged him. "But you're a good boy protecting me like that."

He grinned and licked her face.

"Where'd you find these?" Johnny lifted the two silver necklaces from the kitchen counter where she'd set them.

"Upstairs in a desk. That one's a rosary, isn't it?"

"Yes, with a Nuestra Señora de Guadalupe. Our Lady of Guadalupe."

"What's the other?"

Johnny turned the medal over and back. "A San Miguel. These look old."

"That's what I thought."

Wilcox yelled from outside, "Hurry it up in there."

Johnny returned the two silver pieces to the kitchen counter. "Let's look around and get rid of him."

Brenna checked the bedroom and bathroom, then met Johnny at the stairs. "Hey, do you smell gas?" she asked.

Johnny sniffed the air and went to the kitchen, bent over and smelled along the stove. "Nah, I only smell wet dog. Why? Have you been smelling gas?"

"I don't think so, but what happened seems so bizarre, and I was thinking, given the house is old, maybe there's a gas leak somewhere."

"You want, I'll call the gas company." Johnny pulled his phone out. "You shouldn't mess with stuff like that."

"Don't you need to wait until they open?"

"They got a twenty-four-hour emergency number. I got it programmed because sometimes we come across gas lines when we're working. Here let me call real quick." He hit a few buttons and began speaking to someone on the other end, giving them the location and Brenna's name.

Upstairs, they first checked the empty room, then the other where she saw neither the electric lamp, nor the oil lamp burning. There were no signs of a struggle either, and at the window, no smears of blood on the fragments of glass.

"I heard her screaming," Brenna said. "I saw her at the window. I'm sure of it."

Johnny stroked his goatee. "I believe you, Brenna. But she's gone now. Maybe she got away." He wrapped his arms around himself and chattered his teeth.

She shivered, too. The room was colder than it'd been a few days ago. Abruptly, the sound of screeching tires and a roaring engine reached them. Both she and Johnny looked out the window. Alex had just arrived. Brenna watched as Alex emerged from the truck. Her hair was down, not pulled back in its ponytail. Instead it was wavy and wild. And she didn't look like the same woman Brenna had seen just days ago for the first time. It wasn't the sweet joyful Alex with the warm brown eyes and generous smile. This was an angry Alex, a protective one. It reminded Brenna of the old cliché of the mama grizzly protecting her cubs.

"Shit, she's pissed," Johnny said.

Brenna could tell he no doubt had experience with this Alex and was afraid of her.

"See the way she's standing? And I know that look. Damn," he added.

She watched Alex stride toward Wilcox, who leaned on his open car door talking on the radio. When he saw her, he came to attention as if he was being approached by a drill sergeant.

"Let's get out there," Johnny said.

Brenna followed, anxious to see Alex and to be reassured everything would be okay.

When she got downstairs, she asked Johnny to wait a moment. "Let me hold my attack dog while you open the door."

"I wouldn't mess with him." Johnny patted Miguel's head.

She held Miguel tightly by his collar, but the dog pulled, eager to go outside. "No, you stay, Miguel. Good boy for protecting me, but you stay. Alex is here now. It's okay."

Miguel seemed to understand because he ceased pulling and sat at attention although he continued voicing a muted growl.

When Brenna walked onto the porch, her gaze went to Alex, whose eyes dissolved into large pools of worry and concern. Brenna smiled and waved, and Alex nodded her head toward her before turning back into angry Alex and facing off with the deputy once again.

"As I told you, this hasn't got a thing to do with your crew, Ms. Santana," Wilcox said. "I was called out on a legitimate case. And no, there isn't a conflict of interest here."

"You'll find any goddamn reason to harass them and me, Marcus, and you know it." Alex stood inches from him, dominating his space. "And you want me to believe the chief deputy sheriff of Maricopa County, second in command, is out driving a beat at four o'clock in the morning?"

Wilcox folded his beefy arms across his large stomach. "Your kind is always suspicious of men in uniform, aren't they, Ms. Santana."

"What kind is that, Marcus? The spic, the wetback, or the dyke? That's what you want to say, isn't it? That's what you mean." Alex spat the vulgar words at him.

He glared at her and fingered his clipboard. Finally, he looked away as if he couldn't tolerate her forceful stare. "You done the name-calling, not me." He smirked as he turned his attention to Brenna. "Well, ma'am, let me suggest you do a better job of vetting your hired help from now on. This company has numerous violations of the Legal Arizona Workers Act, and—"

"That's a lie and you know it," Alex said.

Wilcox ignored her. "And the owner here has been cited a number of times for civil disobedience and disturbing the peace."

Brenna puffed her chest and took a step next to Alex. "This company came highly recommended to me, Chief Deputy, and I'll thank you to focus your attention on the whole reason I called for law enforcement."

"Your dollar, lady," Wilcox said. "So, tell me, did you find the woman in your house? Any sign of a struggle or violence?"

"What woman in your house?" Alex asked. "Brenna, what happened?"

Brenna turned to her. "Last night I went out to the grove because I saw a campfire. When I got out there, some people where camping and—"

"You went out there by yourself in the middle of the night? Shit, Brenna, do you have any idea the kind of people that...ay Dios!" Alex pressed the bridge of her nose.

"Alex, wait. Let me finish." Brenna hadn't expected her to react this way and could see she was on the verge of tears as well. "I had Miguel with me. I was fine. Anyway, I found these people out there. It looked as though they were camping and they told me one of their boys had gone missing and his mother was in the house. So I told them—"

"Why would his mother be in your house?" Alex interrupted again.

"I don't know. I was wondering the same thing."

Wilcox looked from one woman to the next. "Probably running from someone, found your door open, and went inside to hide."

"Maybe," Brenna conceded. "Anyway, when I returned to the house, I tried to get back inside to call you, to see if you could translate, I was having a hard time understanding them."

"So now you offer translation services to your clients, Santana?" Wilcox asked.

Alex paid him no attention and asked Brenna, "And why didn't you call me?"

"I locked myself out. I didn't have my phone. Then I heard the woman screaming. I freaked out and..." Overcome with the emotional intensity of the scenario she'd experienced, Brenna covered her mouth and fought for control.

Alex waited for her and seemed to soften her stance and voice. "It's okay. You can tell me later. I get it. You went and called 9-1-1. I'd have done the same thing." She turned to Wilcox. "So now what? Are you driving out to the grove to see if you can find them, talk with them?"

Wilcox looked out across the dead trees. "How far out did you see them?"

"Past the pump house right to the fence by the tennis court," she said, and she thought of those awful little white houses she'd observed in the photograph upstairs, the ones Johnny had shown her a few days ago.

Wilcox went stiff. He stroked his mustache, and Brenna could see his mean, little eyes narrow.

"Well, I need to see if any of them are still camped out." He eyed his sheriff's cruiser. "How bad is the road?"

"I hit a few deep ones in my Jeep. It's pretty broken up," Brenna said.

Alex looked upward and rolled her eyes. "Get in my truck, Marcus. I'll drive you out there."

Wilcox scowled. "Guess it's better than tearing out my transmission." He climbed into the passenger side of Alex's truck and waited.

Alex turned to Johnny and Brenna. "You two stay here. I'll be right back." She looked at Brenna, opened her mouth as if to say something more, but shut it again, climbed into her truck, and drove off.

"Is she mad at me?" Brenna asked Johnny, once they'd gone.

"Nah, don't worry, she gets like this when she's pissed. She and Wilcox got a history."

"A history, what do you mean?" She'd been wondering why the two seemed hostile to each other.

"He likes to harass us. Demanding to see our visas and green cards even though most of us are citizens, born right here in Arizona. He tries to cite her for not filing the electronic verifications even though she does. Makes her resend them, stuff like that. Anything to hassle her."

"Why pick on Alex?"

"Cause she's the shit, man." Johnny chuckled.

"I don't understand."

"It's like this, for years her and her father's been protesting the stupid bills Wilcox's older brother is always trying to push through the state legislature. First it was that damn proof-of-citizenship bill. Lately, it's been this new thing about keeping immigrants from getting health insurance or money to go to school. It's always something, and Alex and Rubén, they fight back every time. The bastard's just getting back at her. That's all."

"He acted afraid of her." Brenna thought about the way Wilcox had come to attention when Alex had approached him.

"She's got a reputation. People don't mess with her."

"Has she really been convicted of civil disobedience and disturbing the peace?" This side of Alex was not something Cassie had divulged.

Johnny chuckled again. "It's not as bad as Wilcox makes it sound. She got the charges reduced."

"What happened?"

Johnny motioned her over to the porch and began to explain. "A while back, we were at the capitol protesting the bill that forces people like me to prove we're citizens anytime we're pulled over. Anyway, these skinheads were marching on the other side of the street. You know, like a counterprotest supporting it. Everything was okay at first, but then one of those jackasses decides he's gonna come across the street. He starts yelling all sorts of crap at us and spits on this little girl. Then bam!" Johnny clapped his hands together. "Here comes the boss and she bears down on this skinhead and starts beating the shit out of him. Took three guys to pull her off."

Brenna's mouth dropped open. "She attacked a skinhead?"

"Yep, broke the bastard's jaw, too. Lucky for us, though, the Phoenix police were right there and kept it from being a full-on drag-out fight. They took her in, but the judge reduced her charges because she was defending the little girl." Johnny shook his head. "You ever gotta go into a dark alley, take the boss with you. She gets pissed, she goes loca."

"I'll remember that," Brenna said, gaining new respect for Alex. Then she wondered about something Johnny had said. "This latest bill you referred to, I heard something on television about it."

"Yeah, just some bullshit, more of the same. Economy takes a dive, all of sudden it's brown people's fault there's not enough money for schools and no one can afford to see a doctor."

She'd never bothered with politics much, but recognizing Alex's interest and involvement, she listened attentively as Johnny continued.

"Look, people forget most of us here didn't cross the border. Our families go back generations. And they also forget most of those who come over the border just want to work and make a better life for their families. It isn't like they want something for nothing. They work hard, and they just want to keep their kids healthy, get them a decent education. This shit Wilcox and his brother keep pushing is nothing but racism."

"Sounds like it."

"Don't get me wrong, there's bad people who come across the border all the time. But there's bad people everywhere, and not all of 'em are brown."

He continued voicing his opinion about the controversial legislation and recounting a few other episodes of Alex's political protests and arrests. Brenna learned Alex, along with her father, had become a thorn in the side of the two Wilcox brothers. Rubén Santana, who'd worked alongside César Chávez to bring justice to farm workers in the seventies, was a leading figure in the local Mexican American community. His influence reached deep, drawing the ire of business leaders and politicians who'd aligned themselves with corporate and conservative interests.

As they continued to talk, a gas truck pulled up and a service man climbed out. "Are you Brenna?"

"Yes, thanks for coming so quickly," she greeted him

"Can't take a chance with gas. So you think you have a leak?"

She explained how she'd had some unusual sensations and knew the house was old. The serviceman didn't seem to think her concern was unwarranted and asked her and Johnny to stay outside while he checked the line and the gas appliances.

"I should restrain my dog. Give me a second," she said.

Inside, she searched for something to keep Miguel under control. She found a belt she'd packed away in her suitcase and made a makeshift leash, then led him to the porch.

While the man got to work, Johnny patted Miguel on the head, turning his collar to examine it. "So you think he belongs to those people you saw out in the trees?"

"That's my guess."

"He's a strange-looking dog."

Brenna cupped her hand under Miguel's chin and turned his face to her. She looked into his beautiful golden eyes while he smiled at her. "You're such a goofball." She giggled. "And a good boy, too. I don't like that mean old deputy either."

"Dogs know," Johnny agreed.

Another ten minutes went by before Alex's truck came around the bend in the road. She pulled close to the house, and Wilcox got out and went to his car while she came onto the porch.

"Why is a gas truck here?" she asked. "And why is the dog covered in mud?"

Miguel tugged at his makeshift leash and growled as soon as he saw Wilcox, still busy back at his car.

"And why are *you* covered in mud?" she asked Brenna.

"I called the gas company, Boss," Johnny said. "Brenna thought there could be a leak."

"Well shit, Brenna, what's going on and why's he growling?" Alex pointed to Miguel.

"He doesn't like the deputy." Brenna tugged Miguel back to a sitting position. "Stop it now, Miguel. Alex is here. No one's going to hurt me."

"That's right, Brenna. No one's going to hurt you. I'll see to that," Alex said as though it were an oath. "But explain to me why you two are covered in mud."

"I was happy to see him, so I hugged him. But I don't have any idea why he's caked in mud. Ask him. You said he understands Spanish." She wanted to force Alex to smile. She needed to see that reassuring smile and know Alex wasn't angry with her.

Johnny turned his head away and covered a snicker while Alex stood back and put her hands on her hips. It looked to Brenna as if she was about to reproach her for her smart-alecky reply.

Right then, the deputy started toward them. "Okay, I got all I need." He took a step onto the porch.

Miguel lurched and snarled, while he jumped back, not having seen the dog as Alex was blocking his view.

"Goddamn it, I told you to get that dog under control," Wilcox snapped.

Brenna struggled to keep Miguel at bay.

Alex intervened. "Siéntate! Cállate! Déjalo!" She pointed, and he fell silent and sat at attention.

Brenna handed Johnny the makeshift leash and went to the deputy. "Did you find anyone?"

"Nope, didn't think I would either. My guess is whoever they were, they're long gone. I'll file this report. Here's the reference number." He handed her a slip of paper. "I'll check back in a few days."

"She's fine, Marcus," Alex said. "I'll have a man on site twenty-four hours from now on."

"Well, it's an MCSO case now, Ms. Santana. Regulations require we check back." He addressed Brenna. "You said your sister and family would be here this afternoon?"

"Yes, I pick them up later today," she said, and she saw Alex frown.

"All right then, keep your eyes open for anyone who shouldn't be on the property. And call it in if you do spot anyone." Wilcox smirked at Alex, before turning to his car.

"Thank you, Chief Deputy," Brenna said.

He waved a hand at her but didn't look back. The three watched as he squeezed himself into his cruiser and left the property.

Brenna let out a breath of relief and waited for Alex to look at her. When she did, Alex's face had changed, looking tired and concerned.

"Brenna, I was worried sick," Alex said. "You don't know what I was thinking and—"

"Brenna?" It was the gas man.

"You found something?" Brenna asked.

"I did. Main line is good, but your furnace needs to be replaced, the water heater, too. Both have slow leaks. And I'd guess your stove is on its way out as well. I've turned off the gas at the main valve. I suggest you open the house to get some airflow and see about replacing those appliances ASAP."

Alex cursed under her breath.

"Was it enough of a leak to cause hallucinations?" Brenna asked him.

"Hallucinations? Did you have any?"

Alex's mouth fell open.

"I don't know, but there were a few things." Brenna was embarrassed to reveal the bizarre events and visions she'd had.

"Mostly you should have a headache and be sick to your stomach, but maybe hallucinations," he said. "If you have someplace to stay tonight, I'd do that and wait until you get those new appliances hooked up. You'll need to schedule a service call to have us come out and turn the gas back on once everything's in place."

Brenna asked a few more questions about the appliances, signed a form, and said good-bye to the serviceman. All the while Alex sat on the lawn chair listening, and Johnny petted Miguel.

When the man left, Alex got up and walked toward her, taking her by the arm. "I want to talk to you." She looked over at Johnny. "Johnny, go back to the office and get the RV. Call your mom and tell her you'll be onsite for the next two weeks. Hang on, and I'll give you a ride back to the highway."

"Yes, Boss. I'll see you later, Brenna." He brought Miguel over, handing her the leash. "He's a great dog. I hope you get to keep him."

"He is a great dog, and thanks for your help and for staying with me," Brenna said.

"De nada. Not a problem." He smiled and climbed into Alex's truck.

"And you," Alex said to her. "You get yourself in the house, pack what you need, and wait for me on the porch." She turned toward her truck.

"You're not *my* boss, thank you," Brenna said.

Alex pivoted around. "What did you say?"

Brenna crossed her arms and met Alex's intense gaze. "I said you're not my boss, Alex."

The two stood in a stare down until finally Alex smiled. Her first smile since she'd arrived that morning.

"No, I'm not your boss," Alex said.

Seeing Alex's smile made Brenna smile. "So don't boss me, okay?" She twirled a strand of her disheveled hair.

"Yes, ma'am. So can I suggest you wait on the porch with your dog until I return?"

"I'll think about it."

Brenna turned toward the door and glanced back to see Alex climbing into her truck and talking with Johnny. She wondered what they were saying, why they were smiling and watching her as they backed out and drove off. She also wondered what the little power struggle had meant, but decided it must be a good thing because when she'd turned and saw the way Alex was watching her through the truck's windshield, she could've sworn Alex had that look again, the one she'd given her in the kitchen the morning before. Brenna hoped it wasn't a gas-induced hallucination.

As soon as they were out of sight, she dashed into the house, brushed her hair and teeth, washed her face, and changed into another dirty shirt, but minus the mud. She gathered the things she'd need to give Miguel another bath and returned to the porch.

"Where'd you find all that mud, bad boy? It hasn't rained, and I didn't see any mud last night."

While she went back inside to fill the bucket with water from the sink, she thought more about the interaction she'd just had with Alex. Watching her with Johnny and the deputy, Brenna had realized Alex was used to giving orders and being in charge. For most of her life, she'd acquiesced to the stronger personality. She'd done so with Edward, she'd done so with Debra, but this morning, she'd stood up for herself and had met Alex's challenge. She enjoyed Alex's take-charge attitude and was tempted to fade into that docile person she'd always been, but she was determined she wouldn't let even this beautiful and charismatic woman dominate her. She vowed right then, no matter what transpired between them, she wouldn't allow Alex to boss her around. Back on the porch, however, she began to doubt herself as soon as she saw Alex pull up, park, and get out of her truck. Alex walked toward her with her eyes fixed and her face void of its usual joyful glow. Brenna stood and waited for her to speak, thinking the whole time Alex seemed different somehow. And for a moment, Alex's loose dark hair caused her to flash on the image of Anabel she'd seen only hours before.

Chapter Thirteen

"Are you okay?" Alex asked.

"I'm better now."

"Your sister and her family are flying in today?"

"No, that was a lie. I didn't want Wilcox to think I was alone."

There was a pause before Alex responded. "Smart woman, quick thinking." She walked toward Brenna while keeping eye contact.

Brenna stood unmoving. She couldn't read Alex's face and was worried she'd launch into a lecture about going into the grove at night alone and involving Marcus Wilcox. But none of that happened. Instead, Alex walked the few steps onto the porch and came close, so close the tails of Alex's untucked shirt brushed against her.

Brenna held her gaze. "Are you mad at me?"

Alex shook her head.

"I'm sorry, I didn't know about you and Wilcox. I didn't mean to—"

"Stop." Alex touched Brenna's face, pulled her close, and wrapped her arms around her shoulders.

Brenna was surprised at the display of affection, but she didn't resist. She wrapped her arms around Alex's waist and held her in turn, enjoying the scent of her shirt and hair. It was the same cleanly washed and sundried linen scent she'd smelled on the jacket the morning before. Then as they stood on the porch in that tender embrace, she felt Alex trembling, heard her sniffling.

"Alex, are you crying?"

Alex pulled away, walked off the porch, and turned her back while she covered her face. "Give me minute."

Brenna didn't know what to do, didn't understand why the strongest woman she knew had broken down in tears. And this, the same woman Johnny had said had broken a skinhead's jaw.

Alex turned back around, wiping her eyes. "I get emotional when everything quiets down. I'm great in an emergency, on top of everything, but as soon as the situation calms down, I fall apart."

"Okay."

"Would you mind making some coffee? I saw yesterday you had a coffeepot."

"Sure, come in while I put it on." Brenna went inside, followed by Alex and muddy Miguel. She brewed the coffee while Alex stood in the kitchen and watched her.

"I should've checked your gas appliances. I could kick myself for overlooking that," Alex said.

"You couldn't have known. Cassie sent an inspector after all. And you heard the gas guy, they're tiny leaks. You might not have found them."

"I was in the shower when my phone rang." Alex rubbed her forehead. "I got out and saw I had a message. It was Susan from the office. Her message didn't make sense, something about a guy from a convenience store calling about you. That you were in trouble and some woman had been hurt and Wilcox was with you and..." She wiped her hand across her eyes. "Shit, I had no idea what that meant. I called her back and she said she didn't know either, so I called Johnny and Hector and told them to get out here. Johnny called back as I was tearing down the freeway, telling me you weren't at home, and"—she hung her head and squeezed her eyes—"I was scared and I couldn't drive fast enough." She turned her face away again.

Brenna touched Alex's shoulder. "I know you don't want me to say I'm sorry. But I want you to know, I had no idea Wilcox would show up, and I had no idea you two had such an antagonistic relationship."

"I know you didn't mean for any of this to happen." Alex looked around the room, visibly collecting herself. She pointed to something on the counter. "Where'd these come from?" She picked up the rosary and other necklace.

"I found them in the middle of the night."

"Found them? Where?"

Brenna began to tell Alex everything from the moment she'd been startled awake, to thinking there was an intruder, to finding the two silver necklaces, to seeing the campfire, and so on until she'd brought her up to date. But she left out certain details—the oil lamp burning, the way the house had been transformed, the open garage. She feared Alex would think she was delusional. While she related the tale, she fixed two cups of coffee, and as she finished her story, she and Alex sat together on the porch sipping their beverages. During her whole retelling, Alex had watched her while nodding her head and listening.

"And so Johnny and I checked out the house and found no sign of her or a struggle. Then you drove up," Brenna concluded.

Alex studied the rosary and the San Miguel medal she'd been holding as Brenna had told her story. "My mother's rosary is similar." She rubbed her thumb over the image of the Virgin and added, "This rosary is valuable, the San Miguel, too, but the rosary was precious to someone." She looked at Brenna. "Let me take a look at that desk."

Brenna led her to the upstairs room, where Alex examined the desk and the large drawer. Then she picked up the stack of old photographs and shuffled through them.

"That's the Poulsen family." Brenna pointed to the picture she'd found. She flipped it over to show Alex the writing.

Alex nodded and continued looking through the old pictures. None of the rest had images of people, only landscape and buildings.

"Do you think the rosary and medal belonged to one of them?" Brenna asked when Alex had returned to the photo of the family.

"No, these are Catholic symbols. The Poulsens were Mormon, at least until the brothers were excommunicated."

"Yes, Patricia at the gas station, Fernie's wife, mentioned something about that. Do you know why they were excommunicated?"

Alex examined the photo of the small white houses and kept looking out the window in the direction where they'd stood a long time ago. "No idea. It was before I was born. But it must've been bad."

Brenna stepped closer. "You keep studying that photo with the houses. What do you see?"

"I don't know. That tennis court seems peculiar." Alex put the photos down and inspected the silver once again. "The strange part is you found these in this desk, which had been locked in this house for at least five years. But who'd have locked them away and why?"

"Maybe they belonged to the caretaker."

"Maybe, but I'm guessing not. The Nuestra Señora de Guadalupe, although not exclusively for women, is something a woman would most likely have, and this San Miguel is smaller than most. Many young boys receive this medal for their confirmation."

"They look old to me."

"Yes, but freshly polished. Silver tarnishes easily."

"I thought the same thing. I'm sure they're precious to someone, as you said."

"Very precious to someone, I'm sure."

Brenna shivered as a stream of cold air wrapped around her. She leaned toward the window, felt the warmer air seeping in from the broken panes. She had no explanation for her next thought, felt as if an outside influence shoved it into her mind.

"I'd like to find who they belong to and return them."

"How are you going to do that?" Alex asked.

"I don't know. Could they've belonged to some of the migrant farm workers, maybe from back when the grove was still running, producing fruit?"

"I guess they could've."

Brenna sifted through the loose papers on the desk, opened boxes, and thumbed through files. "Do you think there's a record of the families who worked here?"

"Unlikely. But the nearest church may have a record. Many of the migrant farm workers were from Mexico, and most were Catholic. They'd have sought out the local priest, the closest parish for confession, communion, that sort of thing."

"So it's possible we could find someone to give them to? Maybe a relative of the original owners?"

Alex chuckled. "We?"

"You're going to help me, aren't you?" Brenna came back over to the window where Alex stood. "You did say anything I needed."

"I did say that."

"So how should we start? Maybe you can ask around to see if anyone remembers someone who'd been employed by the family. I'll ask Fernie at the gas station. He said something about his people suffering here."

"Suffering?"

"Yes, I don't know what he meant."

Alex frowned and turned the rosary over in her hand. "My parents were farm workers when they were young. My aunts and my grandfather, too. It was hard work, I know, from the stories they tell me. Harder still, I think, for those who worked before the reforms. Records weren't always well kept. I'm not sure we can dig far enough back to find an heir to these pieces, Brenna."

"Maybe not, but I want to try." When she voiced her determination, Brenna felt the cold air around her abate, and she was filled with warmth almost as if someone was holding her in a blanket.

"Okay." Alex pulled Brenna's hands toward her and placed both necklaces in her upturned palms. "I'll help however I can." Then she pointed toward the grove. "But right now, we need to find that family, track down where they headed. From what you describe, I'm afraid it sounds as if they're being held by coyotes."

"Is what Wilcox said true? Do they sometimes force the women and children into prostitution?"

"I'm afraid so."

"God, Alex, we have to help her." The memory of Anabel's sad eyes haunted Brenna, nearly as much as the sound of her screams, and the idea she might be suffering a more terrible fate weighed on her.

"We'll help them, Brenna, I promise. But for now"—she put her hands on her hips and cocked her head—"this is a suggestion, not a direct command. Johnny'll be staying on-site in the company RV. He'll be here and can look after Miguel. You saw the way they got along. He'll feed him and keep him out of trouble."

"You want me to go back into town."

"You can come back during the day and supervise the installation of your new appliances, continue painting, whatever. But until the house is safe, until we know what's going on with that family, please, Brenna. I'd sleep much better at night knowing you were safe in a hotel room."

"You're right. I need to wash clothes anyway and I need a good night's rest."

"Thank you. I thought I'd have to get all bossy on you again." Alex laughed and Brenna joined her.

"I sort of liked it. Funny thing is, the old me would've allowed you to boss me around all you liked. But now, it's important for me to do things on my own as much as I can, to make my own decisions. Do you understand?"

"I do."

Brenna smiled and looked Alex in the eyes. She felt they'd grown closer over the last two days, particularly after the trauma of the morning.

"Alex, what you did, you coming out here to rescue me…" She shook her head. "I'm sorry. When it all happened, when I saw Wilcox, I was scared, and the only person I could think to call was you. And here you are."

"Yes, here I am."

"We only met last Friday, and yet you've asked me to Thanksgiving, helped me with my sink, come and rescued me this morning."

"I've told you, my father taught me to care for my clients' needs as best I can."

"I see. I'm just another job to you."

"I think you know better than that." Alex took her hand. She appeared to be weighing her words before she spoke. "Brenna, I know things have been difficult for you, your life turned upside down. I have a lot of sympathy for you."

"I don't want your sympathy." She tried to pull her hand away, but Alex held her.

"And I was going to say, I also have a lot admiration."

"Admiration? Why would you admire me?" This shocked her. No one had ever admired her before.

"Because you haven't given up on life." Alex squeezed her hand. "Have you?"

Brenna cringed inside thinking about the many times she'd wished she were dead. It wasn't only since Edward's and Michael's deaths. There were times before, times as far back as her childhood. She forced her insincere smile; she was feeling like an imposter. Alex's admiration was misplaced.

"No, Alex, I haven't given up."

"Good." Alex released her hand. "Now let's go figure out the kind of appliances you need to order. I'll give you the names of a few wholesale warehouses where you can get a good deal."

"More cousins?"

"Of course. Don't you know some stereotypes exist because they're true?" Alex laughed.

After examining the furnace, water heater, and stove as well as writing down some specifications for Brenna to take with her when she ordered new models, Alex checked the time and headed for the front door.

"I need to get across the Valley, and the morning traffic is growing thicker the longer I wait."

Brenna followed her to the truck and waited while Alex unzipped her jeans and tucked in her shirt.

"I don't know what happened here last night, Brenna. But I'll get some of my guys on it. See if we can't find out what happened to Anabel, see if we can find Pedro." She finished clasping her belt.

"Thank you. I can't stand to think of that woman being beaten. Her screams were...it was terrible."

Alex pulled her hair back into a ponytail and secured it with a tie. When she'd finished, she stepped closer. "We'll get to the bottom of this, I promise you. We'll find those folks and make sure whoever was hurting Anabel is punished. And we'll find Pedro and reunite him with his mother, too." She reached out and touched Brenna's cheek. "I always keep my promises. You should know that."

"I have no doubt."

Alex opened her truck door.

But Brenna reached out and took her arm. "I want to ask you something."

"Yes?"

"I know I'll be having dinner with you next Thursday, with your family and all. But I was hoping you'd agree to let me take you to dinner tonight. I want to thank you for all you've done for me."

"I can't."

"Of course." Brenna backed away, feeling foolish for even asking.

"No, I mean I can't tonight. Friday night is better, but I get to pick the spot. I know Cassie's been taking you to all those fancy places in Scottsdale, and I don't want you spending that kind of money on me."

"Money isn't an issue," Brenna said, feeling relieved Alex hadn't turned her down. "But I'll let you pick. I don't know much around here."

"Great."

"Yes, great." She spontaneously hugged her. When she stepped away again, she noticed Alex's eyes were wide and she had a silly grin on her face.

"I'll call you later." Alex climbed into her truck, waved, and pulled away.

Brenna turned to find Miguel standing at the edge of the grove. She joined him and gazed into the trees. Even with the full rays of the morning sun, the interior of the grove remained dark and dense. She wondered if the family was still out there, still hidden. Perhaps they were watching her right then. But when Miguel began to growl softly, her instincts told her to get away from the trees. She tugged him by the collar.

"Come on, you're getting a bath."

Back on the porch, she bathed him as she'd done before. But all the while, he continued to watch the grove, growling every now and again, causing her to look and stare. But there was nothing, nothing at all she could see. Yet her scar began to pulse, and it was warm to the touch.

Chapter Fourteen

B renna sank to her neck in the bubble bath. Her body ached from sleeping on the air mattress for the last two nights, and before she'd left the property that afternoon, she'd washed the dog and somehow managed to paint the entire downstairs bedroom. She'd said good-bye to Miguel once Johnny had shown up with the RV, then headed back to the same five-star hotel in north Scottsdale. She'd been embarrassed when she'd checked in because she was dirty, with paint on her hands and in her hair, but the desk clerk had remembered her. He'd told her a single room wasn't available, but Ms. Leighton had called earlier and made arrangements for her to be put in a suite. She wondered how Cassie knew about her change in plans. Clearly, she and Alex had already talked.

After soaking and relaxing in the tub, she ordered dinner along with a bottle of wine. While she waited for her meal, her phone rang. It was Cassie.

"I wasn't going say I told you so," Cassie said, "but Brenna, for goodness sake, I told you so. I wish you'd listen to me and not tried to stay out there."

"I know."

"And I'm sorry about the gas. My guy checked it, but he didn't have the instruments to detect tiny leaks."

"No, Cassie, it's okay. As I told Alex, there was no way of knowing, and besides, I'm fine now."

"Yes, but what if they hadn't been small leaks? Do you know how responsible I would've felt if you'd fallen asleep and never woken up again?"

Brenna didn't respond. She'd hoped for that very thing many times.

"I'm glad Alex was there, especially with that creep Wilcox," Cassie added.

"Me, too."

"And that poor family. Alex told me about them," Cassie said. "But don't worry, she's the most dependable person I've ever known. She'll find them and help them. I know she will."

"I know she will, too. She's a wonderful person."

Cassie went silent, and Brenna wondered how much she and Alex had been discussing her.

Finally Cassie said, "She told me you'll be with us at Thanksgiving."

"I will."

Another long pause and then, "She likes you, Brenna. You do know that, don't you?"

"And I like her." Brenna swirled the wine in her glass. Her limbs tingled. Having Cassie confirm Alex's interest in her was thrilling. "Did she tell you I asked her to dinner?"

"She told me."

"We're going out Friday night."

"Sounds good." Another long silence, then Cassie asked, "Brenna, have you been involved with a woman before?"

Brenna gulped her wine. "Sort of."

"I had a hunch."

Brenna began to protest, but realized she'd had the same hunch about Cassie the morning they'd met in her office. "I'm that obvious?"

"Let's just say sometimes I have a sense about people."

Brenna giggled, her head beginning to float from the wine and her excitement over Alex. "And why do I feel as though you've been playing Cupid this whole time?"

Cassie giggled as well. "Something tells me my influence was minimal in this exchange." She added, "Listen, since you two are going out Friday night, why don't you and I have lunch and go shopping Friday afternoon. Maybe you'd like to get a few new outfits? Maybe a few pairs of tight-fitting jeans, some boots or heels, a couple of silk shirts? What do you think?"

"I guess." Brenna thought about the contents in her suitcase. She'd brought nothing with her other than T-shirts, sweats, and ratty old mom jeans. "Yes, I probably need something nicer for Thursday, too."

"You don't need to get too dressed up. Nearly everyone wears jeans, everyone but Alex. She goes all out in a dress and heels. She's absolutely stunning."

"Alex puts on a dress and heels?" The picture of Alex in something other than jeans and work boots intrigued her.

"She does. She says it's her night to shine because family get-togethers are the only opportunity she has to dress up. And she dances. Everything—salsa, rumba, mambo, you name it, she can do it. I can't wait for you to see her. She's so funny when she does the Macarena. Be ready to laugh until you wet your pants. And she pulls all of us out onto the dance floor, too. It's so much fun."

"I don't dance," Brenna said, feeling at once excited and petrified. She'd never liked dances, had avoided them in high school. For her wedding, she'd tried to learn because Edward had insisted they look natural when they danced for the first time as bride and groom. Those sorts of appearances had been important to him. "Seriously, I don't dance."

Cassie laughed. "You will. Trust me. Alex is a good and patient teacher. If she can get Kelly to follow her in a salsa, then she'll get you out there."

The two talked longer about the property. Cassie indicated she'd lined up a number of new housing investors interested in turning the grove into single-acre mini-mansion lots. She also suggested Brenna have the Mesa Historical Society come to the house to collect the boxes in the upstairs room. There could be something of value in them among all the documents and photos. Brenna agreed that might be a good idea.

After getting off the phone, she Googled the historical society, and while surfing their website, she discovered the organization had an extensive archival library of original legal documents, civil contracts, personal journals, and newspapers. The archives were open to the public for research by appointment. This gave her an idea about finding an heir to the two silver pieces. Maybe she needed to start from the present and work backward in time, seeing if she could piece together the history of the Poulsen grove from its inception. Maybe she'd be able to discover the family to whom the silver belonged.

After another glass of wine, her fourth, she prepared for bed. She felt dizzy from the amount she'd consumed and wondered if she should forgo her sleep aid. Dying in her sleep didn't feel quite as appealing as it had, not since she'd met Alex. But she feared the nightmare, the replay of that Sunday morning in April. For the last two nights, the dream had forced her awake, and she dreaded facing it again tonight.

While sitting on the bed, she wondered when she'd be able to sleep through the night without the dream haunting her. She picked up Michael's music box, which she'd brought from the house. She'd taped it shut with some painter's tape, and as she held it in her hands thinking of her son, she also began thinking about Anabel and her family looking for the boy, Pedro. Perhaps Anabel had taken it on herself to go looking for him. She must've been worried for her son out in the darkened grove at night. Perhaps she'd been trying to protect him from the coyotes and traffickers. Brenna rubbed her thumb over the tape, which held the box shut. She'd tried to protect her son as well, but she'd failed.

By now the wine and the excitement of the last night's events caught up with her. She lay back and watched the pattern of television light on the ceiling while replaying her strange encounter with the migrant family. And then something occurred to her, something about the grandmother's words. *He went to the house to free his mother,* the old woman had said. *She's in the house.* It was Pedro who'd gone looking for his mother, not the other way around.

"Why were you in the house in the first place, Anabel? Why did he need to free you?"

The wine and her exhaustion hit, and she fell into a deep sleep.

For the first time since Edward's and Michael's deaths, Brenna woke without the weight of dread and despair. She lay in bed and allowed the sensation to wash over her. Her doctor had said the first months of grief were the worst, but she'd find ways to cope, and each day would be better than the previous one. But he'd warned her, too, that she'd always have those days when she'd fall into depression. This morning wasn't one of them, however. She had things to do, and knowing she might see Alex later in the day excited her. She cleaned up and headed out to find the warehouses Alex had told her to visit for her new appliances.

It was a warm November day, and she'd yet to put the top up on her Jeep since she'd purchased it. Enjoying the sunshine, she cruised through an industrial district of south Phoenix with the wind in her hair. She found the places easily, and the men were helpful. After she told them she was a friend of Alex Santana, they guaranteed the appliances would be delivered and installed by the next Tuesday morning. After accomplishing that task, she retrieved the address for the Mesa Historical Society she'd programmed into her GPS. The place was on the other side of town, but it was a beautiful day, so she didn't mind the drive.

Forty-five minutes later, she pulled up to the old adobe building in downtown Mesa. Inside, she spoke to a receptionist about her find at the Poulsen property, then had a brief discussion with the society's director. He was interested in the documents and photos and told her he'd send one of the volunteers to the house after the Thanksgiving holiday to take a look. She asked about using the archives to do some research, and he was happy to give her access, particularly after she offered a large donation to the historical society's general fund. At the back of the building where the archives and stacks were located, she looked around, unsure where to begin. She decided to ask for help from the library's research desk.

"Excuse me, miss?" Brenna said. "I'm trying to find something, anything, on the Poulsen Citrus Grove."

The young woman typed a few things on her computer, studied the screen. "I think there may be some legal documents, a few newspaper articles. I could pull them for you if you'd like."

Brenna read her name tag. "Thank you, Sadie. Have you volunteered here long?"

"A few semesters. I'm a history major at ASU. This work counts toward my practicum."

"Listen, Sadie, I'm sure you have tasks you need to accomplish as part of your work here, but if you could put in extra time and find information on the property, on the family, on anyone who worked for them, I'd be willing to pay you in cash."

Brenna exchanged phone numbers with her, thanked her again, and slid her some large bills as a down payment. Back in her Jeep, she prepared to drive to the property. It was coming up on noon, and she couldn't wait to see her dog. And she hoped Alex was on-site as well.

❖

When she pulled onto the property, she was pleased to see the entry road completed and noticed a new colony of heavy equipment—a huge excavator, two small bulldozers, and a backhoe had been delivered. She looked around for Miguel, called for him, but was disappointed when he didn't come running. She peered into the thick trees and saw the glint of sunshine flash off a windshield. Alex's crew was out there. She drove toward the back acreage where the crew was working and found their trucks parked alongside the pump house. After parking her Jeep, she inched her way toward the interior, trying not to trip in the tall weeds and the gnarled roots. She was approximately at the same spot where she'd seen the family camping the night before. But at her feet, she couldn't discern any evidence of their campfire or where she'd kicked dirt onto the flames. Ahead she saw the tennis court and the chain-link fence, which cut across the property marking off the portion of land that hadn't been included in Edward's original purchase. Yards in front of her, she spotted Alex talking with some of her men. As she stepped forward, she snapped a stick underfoot, causing Miguel, who'd been resting at Alex's feet, to let out a happy bark and come running in her direction. He reached her within a few bounds, and she dropped to her knees to hug him.

"Now that's a welcome everyone deserves." Alex picked her way over.

"I know. That's one of the best things about dogs," Brenna said. "They're always happy to see you and greet you as if it's been years."

"I meant the way you greeted the dog. I wondered if I was going to get that kind of warm hello."

Brenna stood and tugged her hair. Alex's smile was already undoing her. "Well of course." She hugged her.

"So what's up?" Alex asked.

"Well, I've ordered the appliances and paid for them. They'll be delivered and installed on Tuesday. If I have the gas turned back on Wednesday morning, I can move back in Wednesday night and maybe get the rest of the downstairs painted so I can order some furniture."

Brenna told Alex about her plans to have new windows installed and an alarm system put in as well. She wanted to finish the upstairs, too, she explained, but knew removing the unsightly wallpaper in the one room would be a two- or three-day job.

"How long are you planning on living in the house after you've restored it?" Alex asked.

"I don't know. I guess I need to look into what steps to take to list it as a historical home, to get it registered, that sort of thing."

"And then you'll go back to Iowa?"

"I haven't thought that far ahead, to tell you the truth." When Brenna answered, she noticed Alex smile.

They watched each other, neither speaking. Alex's men leaned against trees, and one of them said something in Spanish and chuckled. Alex scowled and spoke something back to them, causing all four of them to jump like scared rabbits.

"I need to get back to this. If we can map this sector, we can start leveling the trees and hauling them off within the next few days."

"Sounds great. But I wanted to check with you. Anything about Anabel or Pedro?"

Alex shook her head. "I sent Johnny and Hector out to the surrounding farms in the area after lunch to ask about them, but they haven't returned yet."

"I hope we find a clue soon." Brenna looked around the dense groves. "What if we don't? What if the boy or his mother—"

"We'll turn something up," Alex interrupted. "I'm sure of it."

"I'll let you get back to work then."

"Okay, and listen, I'm going to be crushed these next few days, so if I don't see you around, I'll see you Friday night."

"Looking forward to it." Brenna let her gaze linger on Alex before motioning for Miguel. "Come on, Miguel, come help me measure for a bed."

The beast rose to his feet, trotted over to her vehicle, and jumped into the open Jeep window without effort.

"How old do you think he is?" Brenna asked. She'd noticed his agility the night before as well and was amazed at his nimbleness, especially for his size.

"Haven't a clue," Alex said. "He's a strange one though. For most of the night, Johnny said he slept against the garage doors. And since we've been out here, he's whimpered nearly the whole morning by the pump house. I finally had to scold him and invite him to stay with me."

"He's missing his people. I want to find them and help them, but I don't want to let him go. I guess I'm being selfish, aren't I?"

"I can't imagine you ever being selfish. Not one bit."

Brenna looked away. "You'd be surprised." Then she took her leave and drove back to the house.

In the downstairs bedroom, she jotted down measurements for a bed. She realized she'd only be able to fit, at most, a full-sized bed, not a queen as she'd hoped. But she figured that would do. As she'd told Alex, she didn't have any idea how long she planned on living in the house once it was restored. With that thought, she speculated on just how long she planned on staying in Arizona, and wondered, if things with Alex developed as she hoped they would, if she might stay longer than she'd planned.

Afterward, she spent some time on the porch with Miguel, petting and talking with him. He was a good companion, and once again she felt a tinge of sorrow thinking about having to return him to his people. Nevertheless, she wanted to find them and help them. She continued to delay on the porch, all the while hoping Johnny and Hector would be coming back soon, and she'd have some word on the missing boy and his mother. But after an hour, she decided she needed to head back to her hotel and see about getting her clothes washed and perhaps see what she could piece together about the Poulsen family once she'd heard from Sadie, the volunteer at the historical society.

Back inside, she snagged the rosary and medal she'd left in a kitchen drawer the day before and went back upstairs to get the Poulsen family portrait, still stacked with the other photographs on the desk. While in the room, she considered the nasty wallpaper once again. She wasn't looking forward to stripping it, worried she'd find the presence of mold, which would require her to treat the sheetrock before she could prime and paint. At the corner by the window, she peeled away a bit more paper from the place she'd inspected days ago. She managed to work a large strip of it free and was intrigued to find the dark stains behind it had a peculiar pattern. She examined them more closely, tearing more paper away. A familiar shape began to form. It was…it couldn't be. She tugged, tore, and shredded before stepping back and holding her hand to her mouth. She blinked, trying to comprehend what she saw, then stepped closer and placed her hand over the image of another—a dark, splattered outline of a human hand, a small hand like her own. In fact, it was the exact size as hers. Was it paint, she wondered. Perhaps whoever had papered the wall had left the print. The oil from the person's skin might have caused rust or discolored the adhesive, or was it…

Her phone buzzed in her pocket, and she answered it.

"Hey, Brenna, this is Sadie. I looked up some stuff, just a little. But I've already found some interesting newspaper articles, some old ones in the archive."

"Okay." Brenna wondered why her stomach felt sick again, why her head was pounding. She was sure the fumes had dissipated by now.

"Yeah, well some of this stuff is disturbing," Sadie said.

"Disturbing? How do you mean?" Now Brenna could feel her scar prickling.

"Apparently one of Hadley Poulsen's sons shot himself there in the grove."

Brenna picked up the family portrait from the desk. There was the gruff man, the sickly woman, and, on one side of them, the slight young boy. But there was the other man as well. She studied his face. Was this the son, she wondered. She brought the picture closer and narrowed her eyes. She hadn't noticed before, but he had a visible sneer on his face.

Chapter Fifteen

Brenna found Alex's home in a working-class neighborhood in south Chandler. As she drove the street and inspected the house numbers, she noticed people sitting on their front porches. Many of the neighbors smiled and waved at her. Once she found the right house, she parked her Jeep across from the ranch-style home built of red brick with huge mesquite and Palo Verde trees in the front yard. She checked her hair and makeup in her visor mirror. Where had this woman been for so long, she wondered. She couldn't remember the last time she'd made herself up so well.

As she walked the path of stepping stones set in the desert landscaping, she adjusted her tight-fitting jeans and smoothed her green top she'd purchased that morning while shopping with Cassie, who'd told her green went well with her eyes and hair. In addition to the new jeans and top, she also had on new ankle-cut boots. She liked the way she could sway her hips in them, and also liked the extra two inches they gave her. At the front door she took one more breath to calm her nerves, rang the bell, and waited. The door opened, and she heard a man's voice through the screen, which blocked her view of the interior.

"You must be Brenna, Alejandra's friend. How glad I am to meet you," the voice said.

It was such a deep and resonant voice, full of kindness, and when the screen opened, she looked into familiar brown eyes. The man, in his late sixties, was handsome with wavy black hair, gray at the temples.

"I'm Rubén, her father." He held out his hand.

"Mr. Santana, it's a pleasure to meet you."

"Please, you're my daughter's friend. You'll call me Rubén." He put an arm around her shoulders, leading her into the entryway. "Alejandra is still dressing. She arrived home late from a job in Peoria. It's nearly halfway to Los Angeles." He laughed. "Please come inside and meet my father-in-law, her grandfather, Juan Carlos."

As they passed through the living room, she noticed a shrine in the corner. The lit candles adorning the shrine cast an amber glow over a statue of the Virgin Mary and a framed photograph of a beautiful Latina who looked a great deal like Alex. A silver rosary hung draped across the photo's frame.

In a room off the main hallway, sitting on a recliner, was an ancient man, small, frail, and leprechaun-like. His hair was white, cut short, and he had a clean-shaven face with large brown eyes. He rested forward on a cane watching the door as she and Rubén entered.

"Bienvenida, mija." He laughed and held his hand out.

Rubén guided her hand into the old man's, for as she now realized, Alex's grandfather was nearly blind.

"Padre, esta es la amiga de Alejandra, Brenna," Rubén said. "Brenna, this is Alejandra's grandfather, Juan Carlos Delgado."

"It's nice to meet you, sir." She caught the scent of pipe tobacco hovering in the air around him.

"Sí, sí, tú eres bendecida en mi casa." Juan Carlos patted her hand.

"He gives you his blessing," Rubén translated.

And then Juan Carlos began speaking so fast and with so much joy Brenna wondered what all the fuss was about. He laughed, smiled, and patted her hand. Rubén interjected Spanish and laughed as well, nodding his head. She smiled, not knowing what they were saying, but she hoped it was good.

Rubén touched her shoulder. "Juan Carlos says you're the most beautiful young woman our Alejandra has brought home. He says he now understands why she's been singing so loudly in the shower these past few mornings. You must have brought her much joy."

Alex appeared in the doorway. "Hey, Brenna."

Brenna turned to see nothing less than perfection. Alex wore a pair of khaki pants that fit her every curve, and a black knit top, low cut and buttoned in the front. She wore black leather boots with a heel, and she'd styled her hair into soft curls, which hung around her shoulders.

She also wore a silver necklace with matching bracelet that set off the sparkle of the silver-hooped earrings dangling from her ears.

"Alex, you're beautiful." Brenna felt her cheeks warm with the declaration.

"Thank you." Alex grinned and her eyes traveled the length of Brenna's form before she said, "And you look fantastic."

Brenna glanced at Rubén and Juan Carlos to see if they were uncomfortable, but neither man looked bothered. Apparently the greeting between Alex and her was normal and commonplace. She envied Alex right then for being her own self and still accepted by her family.

Alex hugged and kissed her grandfather, said something to him in Spanish. When Juan Carlos responded, Alex took Brenna's hand and brought it back to him once more. Then Juan Carlos became solemn, saying something long and measured. When he'd finished, Rubén and Alex both said, "Sí, sí."

"We're going now, Papá," Alex said. "Remember, Tía Marta put your dinner in the bottom shelf of the fridge. Three fifty for only thirty minutes or the tortillas will harden."

"I can handle dinner tonight, mija." He hugged her and walked them to the door, where he took Brenna's hand once again. "You're always welcome in this house, Brenna." And then he turned to Alex. "Remember, Alejandra, you have to be in Casa Grande tomorrow by seven in the morning. Don't drink too much and be home in bed by midnight."

"Papá, I'm thirty-two years old. You can't set my curfew anymore."

Rubén smiled at Brenna. "Ah, she's my baby, Brenna. But a father never stops fathering even when his baby is a grown woman."

As they walked to the Jeep, Alex chuckled. "It's embarrassing. He still treats me as though I'm his little girl. I guess it doesn't help I sleep in the same room I grew up in."

"The same room? That's amazing. Is it the same bed, too?"

"Yes, but I ditched the Spider-Man sheets when I graduated high school."

Brenna giggled and reached for the passenger-side door, opening it for the woman with whom she was becoming more captivated.

"Thank you, that's sweet," Alex said, climbing into the Jeep.

"So tell me what your grandfather said at the end. He sounded serious." Brenna buckled in.

"He was reminding us we have invited you into our home, and you are now like a daughter to my father, a granddaughter to him, and a sister to me. We must always remember our vows to our family and care for those who need our help just as the Blessed Mother cares for us in our need."

"My goodness, Alex, that's beautiful." Brenna was taken aback. It seemed so formal, so special, so unusual.

"Well, he's old and half blind, but he's still head of our family. It's tradition to extend the bond of family to those we invite into our home. He blessed you when he met you, didn't he?"

"Yes, your father said that."

Alex touched her shoulder. "Whether you like it or not, you're under the protection of my family now. We'll be here for you whenever you're in need."

"That's the kindest thing anyone has ever said to me." Brenna's heart felt warm. In all her life she'd never heard of such a thing, had never felt so honored. She glanced at Alex again, noting how stunning she was with her hair curled and eyeliner accentuating her eyes. "Okay, where'd you pick for dinner?"

"A little pub by the city center you passed on the way to my house."

Brenna put her Jeep in drive and followed directions while Alex pointed out various landmarks—the community center where her father and grandfather still played dominos, the local Catholic church where they attended Mass, her elementary school, the burger shack where she'd had her first paying job. Brenna loved listening to her talk. Alex's memories all seemed genuine and happy. There was nothing bitter about her childhood that she could see. At the restaurant, they settled in one of the booths, and Alex greeted most of the servers and the bartender—everyone there seemed to know her. They ordered a round of beer and fell silent. Brenna ran a finger across a divot in the table as she sipped her beer. There was so much she wanted to know, so many things she wanted to ask. And on top of that, she had some interesting, yet disturbing, information she'd obtained about the Poulsen family from Sadie. She was anxious to share those findings with Alex. She took a long draw off her beer while she watched Alex watch her with her steady eyes. It made her heart race and she giggled.

"I had so many things I wanted to say, to ask you, and now I don't know where to begin," Brenna said.

"Okay, then I'll start. Tell me what you were like when you were a little girl."

"I don't know, Alex. I don't want to talk about me anyway. I want to talk about you."

"That's not fair. Cassie's filled you in on plenty of tales about me and my exploits."

"She and Johnny both. You were quite the rabble-rouser, weren't you?" Brenna smiled as she sipped her beer. "So tell me about Alejandra—I had no idea that was your name."

"Yes, Alejandra Clarita María Santana-Delgado." Alex emphasized each name.

"How did they fit all that on a birth certificate?" Brenna giggled again. "I'm plain Brenna Ann Taylor."

"Wilson?"

"Right, Wilson." She fell silent and extended the fingers on her left hand. It'd been a week since she'd removed her wedding ring. "I'm changing my name back, I told you. Back to Taylor." She thought she saw Alex's eyes sparkle. "Anyway, I'm confused. Which is your last name? Santana or Delgado?"

"Both. Delgado is my mother's maiden name. Santana-Delgado is my legal surname, but lots of people don't understand how we take our father's and mother's names. So for business, I drop my mother's name."

"And your first name?" Brenna could see Alex was somewhat self-conscious about it.

"It's the Spanish version of Alexandra. My father picked it. I think he'd hoped I'd be a boy." Alex chuckled. "My mother said it meant the defender of man, and she knew that was what I was born to do." She stared past Brenna as if lost in a moment of thought, then shrugged. "Most of my friends and the younger family members call me Alex, but to the older generation, I'm still Alejandra."

Again they fell silent. And then Brenna thought about the shrine and the candles she'd seen in the corner of the living room. "Was the shrine for your mom?"

Alex explained in most Catholic homes, particularly among the Mexican American community, there were small shrines in their houses where they'd pray and light candles in remembrance of someone or for someone in need. She told Brenna how her mother, Clarita, had grown up with four sisters, one of whom was her twin, and how the family had lived in El Sahuaro, Mexico, and traveled across the desert a number of times a year to work on farms and in groves in the United States. One harvest season in the late 1970s, Alex's mother along with her sisters and their father, Juan Carlos, traveled to a small farming community outside San Diego where they'd attended a UFW rally led by César Chávez, and she met Rubén Santana at that rally.

"My father was born in a city along the border in Sonora, Mexico, and had seen some of the worst treatment of workers before Chávez and the reforms," Alex said. "He managed to get himself and my mother's family citizenship, and you know, their story is the real American dream. My mother and aunts cleaned houses and scraped together enough money to open the restaurant, Las Cinco Hermanas, in Phoenix. My father built his business. And all of us first-generation kids have gone to work in family businesses, opened our own, found good-paying jobs, even attended college. I have cousins who are nurses, teachers, policemen, fireman, and even two lawyers."

"Is that the restaurant where your family's Thanksgiving is held?"

"Yes, mostly my tía Marta runs it now, but my other aunts still cook there on occasion."

"She's your mom's twin, you said."

"Yes." Alex peeled the label on her beer bottle. "I can't wait for you to meet her, Brenna. She's special to me."

"I bet she is." Brenna sensed the wash of sadness that'd come over Alex, and she realized, as she'd suspected earlier in the week, Alex still mourned her mother's death after all these years.

Alex continued to peel the label on her bottle. When she spoke, her usually confident and playful voice had softened. "My grandparents, they were migrant workers and, you know, poor. There wasn't much in the way of medical care, certainly no prenatal care. My grandmother, mi abuela, died a few days after giving birth to Marta and my mamá. And Marta, well, she was born first. Mamá, she was never as strong. It wasn't until she was a teenager they discovered she had a heart defect."

"It sounds as if she managed to live with it for most of her life."

By now Alex's eyes were damp. "She did. But after having me, the doctors told her she shouldn't have any more kids. Having me stressed her heart."

Brenna reached across and took one of Alex's hands.

"It was hard on her, though," Alex continued. "She and my father always wanted to have a big family. I wouldn't have minded a brother or sister either, but, you know, I have many cousins instead. Marta's kids, Angel and Marissa, we're close in age, so they're like my brother and sister, and they were like a son and daughter to Mamá as well."

"I'll get to meet them on Thursday?"

"Yes, and everyone's excited to meet you, too." Alex wiped her eyes and smiled, seeming to shake off her melancholy. "Marissa and Angel in particular. I've told them all about you."

Brenna choked on a sip of beer. "No pressure there."

They laughed as the server set their food in front of them, and soon they'd settled into eating while the conversation turned to lighter topics as Alex shared more about her close-knit family as well as some of hers and Cassie's exploits as teenagers. Brenna laughed often at the things Alex told her. Cassie'd been right—Alex was a big goofball with an outrageous sense of humor. When their plates were cleared away and the server went to fetch dessert and coffee, Alex said it was Brenna's turn to share. But Brenna had nothing she could think of worth sharing.

"Tell me about your parents," Alex said.

Brenna felt the levity of the last hour dissipate. "I wanted to tell you earlier."

"Tell me what earlier?"

"That I lost both my parents when I was twelve."

With this statement, Alex sputtered and covered her mouth. "Ay, Dios! What happened?"

"Car accident. They'd just dropped me off at church camp outside Cedar Falls. On their way home they were in a multicar pileup. They died at the scene." Brenna dug at the divot on the table with her fingernail.

Alex shook her head. When she spoke, her voice faltered. "You've lost so much, Brenna, more than one person ever should."

"We both have."

"And where did you go live after?"

"With my sister, Jessica. She's eight years older, and she'd been married for a few months, so I went to live with her and her new husband, Bill. When I was nineteen, I married Edward. And after that—"

"You lost him, too," Alex finished her thought.

"Yes, and Michael."

Alex leaned in. "Can you tell me about your husband and son? Or is it still too raw?"

"I can, I think."

And she began to tell Alex of the way she'd met Edward when her brother-in-law had brought him home from the office for dinner. How Edward had decided they'd be married, how her sister and brother-in-law thought it was a good idea. She told Alex about their attempts to conceive children, her miscarriage. She talked about giving birth to Michael, how for the first time she felt unconditional love for another person, how being a mother gave her the deepest joy she'd ever experienced.

"And the day they died, can you tell me about that?" Alex asked.

Brenna looked off into space and began to relate the sad event, her voice flat and monotone as if she were reading off a grocery list.

"It was a Sunday, the first week of April. Tornados had been spotted the day before and we were on watch. We were in church when the sirens blared. I heard them in the distance. No one panicked. If you live in Iowa, any of those states, you get used to the drill. The minister directed the elders and deacons to proceed with the emergency plan. Edward was a deacon, so he gave Michael a hug and told him to go with me. He told me he'd join us in moment. Then I carried Michael toward the basement."

She stopped, stared at the wall. She pictured the doorway that led to the basement, the elderly woman who'd tripped and fallen, the sirens, the freight-train wind bearing down, the shattering glass, the splintering wood, her son wanting his father. He was afraid, and she'd set him down to help the old woman. He was supposed to hold her skirt. Why had he let go? Why had he run back to Edward? And then the twister hit the church full force. A heavy wooden pew whipped up and crashed down on human flesh—on Edward's flesh. He'd thrown his body over his son's, but it hadn't been enough.

"Brenna?" Alex shook one of her hands.

Brenna blinked and refocused her eyes on Alex's face.

"The last thing you said was you headed to the basement."

"The basement…" Brenna rubbed her temples. "I don't know but somehow Michael got away from me and ran back to Edward. They were crushed in the debris."

Alex visibly shuddered. "I'm sorry. I didn't mean to make you relive it. I only wanted to understand."

Brenna sipped her beer and refocused on the divot in the table.

"I want you to know," Alex continued, "I understand you must struggle every day. And I'm here for you when you need someone to talk to, someone to cry with. No matter what, you can depend on me to be here for you. Just as my grandfather had me vow earlier this evening, you're now part of my family, and I'll be here for you when you're in need."

Brenna took another swig of beer and dropped her head. This wasn't the date she'd imagined. And Alex's pity was not the emotion she'd hoped to arouse in her that night.

They took their coffee and dessert surrounded by a somber mood and spoke about the progress on the property. But Brenna was in no mood to report the peculiar and uncomfortable facts Sadie had dug up. Instead they discussed the prospects of having the property prepared for lots and the possibility for economic development in the area. Alex told her she stood to make nearly triple the amount Edward had invested if things played out right. But Brenna felt ambiguous about making money from the land. The house and the silver she'd found were more pressing for her.

When the meal was over, Alex suggested they walk to the city center where every Friday and Saturday night during the fall and winter months, local residents held a farmers' market with fresh fruit and vegetables, arts and crafts, and entertainment. The trellises and the ramadas in the city center had been strung with lights, some of them Christmas bulbs. The two strolled along the booths and checked out the vendors' wares. Brenna began to feel her spirits lifting, especially after the few times Alex brushed her hand or leaned close while they walked. As the night passed, Alex's mood seemed to lift as well. She told Brenna more stories of her youth, more funny tales, and Brenna loved hearing all of them. Before long, both were smiling and laughing again, enjoying each other's company, the earlier conversation fading away.

"And tell me again how it's possible you're still single with you being so charming?" Brenna asked. They sat on a bench listening to a young man play his guitar.

"You think I'm charming, huh?"

"You know I do. Don't play coy. I'm apparently an open book since both you and Cassie were able to figure me out."

"I haven't got you all figured out." Alex brushed her fingers against her leg.

"I'm not so complicated," Brenna flirted back, taking Alex's hand.

"Somehow I suspect that's not true."

"But it is. I'm just a simple gal from Iowa."

Alex scrunched her brows together, apparently perplexed. Brenna waited, wondered what she was thinking.

When the guitar solo ended, Alex turned to her. "When did you know about yourself? Was it before you married your husband or after?"

"I probably always knew. But I finally admitted it to myself a year ago."

"What happened a year ago?"

Brenna pulled her hand away.

"Did you meet someone?" Alex asked.

"Sort of."

"Who was she?"

"A woman at our church, a missionary."

"And?" Alex turned to face her directly.

Brenna folded her arms across her chest. "And we became close and I liked her. I'd never felt that way about Edward. I realized then what was missing in my marriage, why I wasn't altogether happy in it. That's when I finally admitted it to myself."

"Were you in love with her?"

Brenna bit her lip. "At the time, I thought so." She felt Alex watching her, knew she was waiting for more. She covered her mouth and coughed. She felt her shame climbing up her throat, tasted the guilt in her mouth. Other than Edward and Debra, no one knew of her betrayal. She'd never told Jessica, never had a friend to confide in, and now the pressure of her transgression threatened to choke her. She swallowed the thickness in her throat. "I'm not proud of what I did." She grunted once the words left her lips.

Alex didn't respond right away, but finally said, "I'm the last person in the world who'd judge you for anything you've done, Brenna. I haven't always made the best choices in relationships either and I've regretted quite a few."

"Like the last one?" She was curious why it had resulted in Alex not dating for the last number of years.

"Yes, the last one. I think I rushed in. I should've been more cautious, taken things slower."

"I suppose you'll want to take things slow with me." It made sense, Brenna knew. After all they hadn't known each other long.

Alex took her hand and brought her up. "You've been through a lot, lost a lot." She started leading her toward the Jeep. "I want to give you time and space to grieve your husband and son. And as I told you the night we went for pizza, I figured it would be sometime before you were ready to date again."

They reached the Jeep and Brenna held the door for her. "I didn't know I was ready until I met you."

Alex shook her head. "But I don't want to be your distraction. I want your feelings for me to come from a genuine place."

Brenna waited to respond until she'd gotten in and buckled her seat belt. Before she started her vehicle, she turned to Alex and searched her eyes. She could see her point, understood her hesitation. "I don't think of you as a distraction."

"No?"

"There's something about you, about your smile, your face. That first day we met, it was as if a beam of sunlight was coming right out of you. That sounds silly, I know, but I felt something cut through the darkness in my head that day, as though something woke me up."

"I remember how sad you looked that day."

"I *was* sad. I have been for months. I've been dead inside, walking around completely numb. And when I haven't been numb…" Brenna rubbed her eyes, lowered her voice to a mere whisper. "Do you know, for the first month all I did was scream. And if I wasn't screaming, I was crying or cursing."

Alex touched her cheek. "Lo sé, lo sé, bella. I know."

"I never thought I'd feel this way again, the way I do now," Brenna continued. "Never thought I'd be able to laugh and look forward to the next day. But part of me feels…" She looked away. She didn't want to cry, not now when everything seemed to be going the way she'd hoped it would.

"Go on."

"Part of me feels as if I don't deserve to feel alive again. Maybe I deserve to be miserable for the rest of my life." Brenna felt Alex cup her chin and lift her gaze.

"You don't deserve any such thing, Brenna."

"Maybe."

Brenna squeezed her eyes shut to ward off the tears before putting her Jeep in gear and driving back to Alex's house. Once she'd parked under the street lamp, she turned off her engine and waited to see what Alex would do. Would there be a good night kiss? Or was Alex determined to take things slowly as she'd said earlier? But instead of saying good night and getting out, Alex continued to watch her, not opening the Jeep door, only removing her seat belt.

"You should know my feelings for you are genuine, Alex. Genuine and real. And I don't care if it's only been a short time. My feelings are no less valid." Was this what Alex needed to hear?

"But you don't even know if you'll remain in Arizona after you're done with that house."

"And you don't know I won't."

In the open Jeep, they gazed at each other. A dog barked in the distance, insects hovered around the streetlight above, and the temperate November air caressed their exposed skin, the touch barely noticeable. Brenna risked moving one of Alex's dark curls off her shoulder.

"I don't mind taking things slowly. Getting to know each other is part of the fun. But I want you to understand, I don't think of you as a distraction. I've grieved for Edward and Michael every day since I've lost them, and I suspect, like you feel about your mother, I'll grieve for them every day of my life."

"That's fair." Alex moved her hand to Brenna's thigh. "Yes, I'd like to get to know you better. There're lots of things I'd like to know about you."

"Like what?"

Alex smiled, lightening the mood. "Your favorite color, what you wanted to be when you grew up, if you had any pets when you were a child. That sort of thing."

Brenna stared at Alex's lips as she answered. "Aqua blue. We always had cats, no dogs, and I think at one point I wanted to be a gypsy and travel with a circus, but I settled on being a farmer and to raise hogs and chickens on my grandparents' farm."

"Ah, I see. A sweet little farm girl from the Midwest." Alex chuckled and stroked her thigh.

"Yes, I fit the stereotype as well." She giggled. "And what about you? Do I get to know your favorite color, what you wanted to be, how many dogs and cats you had?"

"Yellow, followed by orange. And let's see, I think I wanted to be a safari guide when I was little, but there's no jungle here in the desert. And no cats that I recall, but we've had two Rottweilers, four mutts, and three Chihuahuas."

"That's a lot of dogs."

"Most were strays. Mamá was always taking in strays. She'd take them in, get them healthy, and find them good homes. But she did let me keep Taco, one of the Chihuahuas. I had him until I was twenty-five. Still miss the little booger."

"You named your dog Taco?"

Alex grinned. "Nah, his name was Chico, but I called him that when I took him for a walk. It always made the neighbors laugh."

"You certainly make me laugh."

"See, I am a distraction after all."

"A gorgeous one." In the dim light, Brenna was sure she detected a blush on Alex's cheeks.

"Thank you. I think you're beautiful, too," Alex said.

They fell silent again, looking at each other, and looking away quickly. Brenna played with the seam of her own jeans with one hand, while her other hand now rested on Alex's as she continued to hold her thigh.

"I should go." Alex opened her door. "I have an early morning and a long weekend."

"When will I see you again?"

"I'll be down south for the weekend, may not be back in the Valley until late Monday, and then I'll need to be on-site Tuesday and Wednesday at the Peoria job."

"Then when?"

"Thursday for Thanksgiving."

"I'll miss you." Brenna felt vulnerable to admit it, but it was true.

"I'll miss you, too, but we'll talk on the phone." Alex moved to leave the Jeep.

But Brenna reached and held her by her arm. "Okay, but…"

Alex waited.

"I should walk you to your door."

"No, I'm fine. It's late." Alex leaned forward and placed a kiss on her cheek. She lingered close and said, "Buenas noches, mi hermosa, mi bella." Then she stepped out of the Jeep and onto the porch. She delayed there with the front door open, until finally she waved and went inside.

Brenna touched her cheek and stared at the closed door. It wasn't the kiss she'd hoped for, but they were taking it slow after all. She drove back to the hotel replaying the entire night in her head, even the difficult parts, and giggled again at some of the things Alex had told her while remembering how her face beamed anytime she smiled.

CHAPTER SIXTEEN

Longtime Mesa resident Owen Charles Brock died of natural causes in a Mesa hospital. He was ninety-eight years old. Brock moved to Arizona in 1922 where he worked in the Old Dominion Copper Mine in Globe before becoming employed by the Poulsen family citrus grove.

Brenna read a photocopy of an obituary as she sat in the living area of her hotel suite with her laptop, a selection of documents, the silver rosary, and the San Miguel medal spread out before her on the coffee table. She'd ordered breakfast and a pot of coffee and had the television playing in the background for company. She'd been awake since early that morning even though she'd gotten back to her room past midnight. She'd tried to sleep, but had lain awake, thinking about dinner, still feeling Alex's soft kiss on her cheek. Since she couldn't sleep and couldn't stop fantasizing about her, she'd decided to get up and go over the material Sadie'd found—newspaper articles, court documents, bills of sale, financial records, and property deeds. She was looking for something, anything that might lead to the owner of the silver necklaces. She reread the caretaker's obituary and did the math in her head. He would've been about fifteen when he'd moved to Arizona, and as a young man, would've worked for the Poulsen family. He'd have known Hadley and Nelda, known something about the families working the grove, perhaps the ones to whom the rosary and San Miguel belonged. The obituary, however, didn't mention anything about surviving family members. There was no one with whom she could follow up. Then she wondered when Nelda had died and skimmed the newspaper article about their son's death.

> *Dallin Poulsen, eldest son of Hadley and Nelda Poulsen, veteran of the Great War, wounded at the Battle of the Argonne Forest, recipient of the Badge of Military Merit, shot himself...He succumbed to his wounds. He is survived by his younger brother, Lanny.*

The article was dated 1928. If Lanny was Dallin's only surviving relative, that meant both Hadley and Nelda had to have been dead by 1928. On a piece of scratch paper, Brenna made a crude timeline indicating Brock's death along with the others, stretching the decades back to the early 1900s. Cassie had told her Hadley had homesteaded the property before Arizona had become a state, which a quick Internet search told her meant he had to have settled on it before 1912. She considered her timeline as she stroked the beads on the rosary. She realized she was looking at a hundred years' span of time. The heirs to the silver might not even live in Arizona any longer. Perhaps it was futile to keep looking for a clue. She had, after all, the house to focus on. The house and Alex.

She glanced up at the television as a familiar name caught her attention:

State Representative Julian Wilcox continues to draw criticism from his fellow lawmakers, including those of his own party, with his crusade to pass what he calls his No-Free-Lunch legislation, Arizona House Bill 1180.

She sat forward on the sofa. Julian Wilcox was that creepy chief deputy's brother.

The news report continued: *Wilcox, who announced his gubernatorial run earlier this year, argues his bill will address much of the state's budget shortfall by denying children of illegal immigrants state aid for education, including in-state tuition, and by limiting their health-care coverage to federally funded emergency Medicare. However, recent investigative reports have uncovered that one of Wilcox's privately owned businesses, Southwest Fabrics and Textiles, has been fined twice in the last five years for employing workers with undocumented status. The business is a subsidiary of Poulsen*

Enterprises, which was founded by real estate mogul Lanny Poulsen, Representative Wilcox's grandfather.

Brenna pulled up Cassie's number on her phone and placed the call. "Cassie, can you arrange for me to speak to Lanny Poulsen?"

Cassie sputtered on the other end of the line. "Brenna, it's six thirty in the morning!"

"Oops. Sorry. I didn't mean to wake you."

"And why would you want to meet with that old geezer?" Cassie asked.

"I need to talk to him. You met him, didn't you, when you and Edward purchased the property?"

"No, I only met with the lawyer. I never spoke to Poulsen."

"But just now, on the news, there was a story about a fabric company, part of Poulsen Enterprises. He's still alive, still around."

"Certainly not for long. The man's in his nineties, if he's not a hundred yet."

"Do you think he has all his faculties? I mean, he's not in a nursing home, is he?"

"I don't know. I don't think so. But why in the world would you want to speak with him? If you want the rest of that land, Brenna, we'll have to talk to the lawyer again. And at this point, I think we need to concentrate on getting what you have ready to sell—forget the back acreage."

"No, this has nothing to do with the land. I need to know the names of the migrant families who worked the grove when it was still in operation." She heard Cassie groan.

"Right. The rosary and that other piece. Alex told me." Cassie was quiet before adding, "It seems like a long shot, I'll tell you that. I'm not even sure what pretext I can give to get you in to see him, but I'll see what I can do."

"Thanks, Cassie, this means a lot to me. I can't explain it, but I feel strongly about finding someone to return these necklaces to."

"They're an interesting find, that's for sure," Cassie said. Then she lowered her voice. "So spill it, Brenna, tell me about dinner with Alex last night."

Brenna giggled. "As if you haven't already gotten her version."

"Of course I have, but now I want yours. What can I say, I'm a voyeur at heart, and I'm dying to know how it went from your point of view."

Glad to have someone to share her excitement about Alex with, Brenna told Cassie the highlights. But when she'd disconnected from the phone call, she continued to sit on the sofa while she wondered once more whether she even deserved this feeling, whether she deserved Alex. The rosary was still in her hand, and she stroked the beads while she considered her worthiness. Alex was a good person, kind and honest, but she was…She shook her head as she thought about the things she'd done, her past, the way she'd talked to her parents, treated Jessica, cheated on Edward, and the promises she'd made to Debra, only to break them. She'd been selfish. Nothing but selfish. She stood and tossed the rosary onto the coffee table and forced the shame from her mind. She'd been feeling too good in the last few days, and she didn't want to sink back into depression and self-condemnation. But when she stood, the Poulsen family photo slid from the table. She picked it up and studied each of their faces. She hadn't noticed before, but the young boy, whom she now knew must be Lanny, not only looked sick, but also scared. And inspecting the face of the older brother, Dallin, she saw his image looked different than it had yesterday afternoon. He was sneering, that was the same, but now he was also smiling with that sneer. A smile that made her scar tingle and burn.

She wasn't sure what made her decide, but later that afternoon she found herself driving to Mesa Cemetery. At first the idea had been repellent to her, having last been to a cemetery in Davenport to watch her husband and son interred. But something other than her scar itched. It was a thought, an intuition she couldn't shake.

At the cemetery, she found no mausoleum stood for the Poulsen family. There weren't huge headstones either. In fact, the burial plots were quite plain. At one end was Hadley Poulsen, born 1881, died 1926, and Nelda next to him, born 1883, died 1925. Five smaller headstones trailed after the parents. Brenna stared at those headstones, read each child's name. The birth and death dates were in close succession, the earliest 1899–1904 to the oldest 1912–1915. Fernie's wife, Patricia, was right. Nelda Poulsen had lost her children one right after the other—one of them only months old, the oldest three. Brenna couldn't help but hurt for her; she understood the pain a mother's heart experienced in losing a child, and this poor woman had lost five. Finally, she came to the eldest son's grave, which lay after all the smaller ones. Dallin Poulsen had been born in 1898, died 1928. She remembered something she'd read in the article about his death. He'd fought in a battle…what was it? But she couldn't recall and decided to take some pictures of the headstones with her phone before returning to her property and checking on Miguel.

Thirty minutes later, she found him sulking by the garage. When he saw her pull in, though, he was up and at her side, wagging his tail and smiling. Johnny and some of the crew were taking a break, and she spent some time talking with them, asking if any more clues to Anabel's and Pedro's whereabouts had surfaced. But no clue had been uncovered. The family had vanished, it seemed, into thin air. When the crew went back to work, she got busy and prepared the living room area for primer, while Miguel lay at the foot of the stairs and watched. By late afternoon, the workers had called it quits and were departing the property, and she figured she needed to head back to her hotel as well. But she went upstairs first to see if she could view what they'd done so far that day.

From the window of the wallpapered room, she could see an area where trees had been taken down. It wouldn't be long before the entire landscape was bare. While there, she straightened some of the loose papers and stacked boxes as she knew a volunteer from the historical society would be out next week to take a look at the items. But she didn't inspect the wallpaper any further. Something about those black stains the other day had unnerved her. Still, she went to the window once more before she left and placed her hands on the few whole panes that remained. She gazed out at the grove, growing darker as the sun faded, and thought about Anabel standing in that exact spot while her black eyes pleaded for help. Brenna remembered her screams, too. They'd pierced the early morning air, had driven right into her head and gut. As she replayed the horrible night in her mind, she slid her hand down the window, paying no attention to the jagged edges of broken glass. She flinched when she felt the cut and brought her finger to her mouth. The injury oozed blood. Just as she'd been prompted to visit the cemetery earlier that day, she felt another curious urging and wiped her bloody finger against the glass, then stood back to inspect it. There'd been bloody streaks down the window. Anabel had clawed at the glass. Brenna knew she and Johnny should've found that evidence at least. She fought with herself then. She didn't want to look, but the impulse was too strong. She turned to the wall in the corner where she'd stripped the wallpaper and placed her hand with the bleeding finger over the black splatter. She knew now the stain was blood.

She looked at Miguel, now standing in the doorway where he'd been lying watching her. He was staring at her as he'd done the night she'd discovered the silver. She closed her eyes and shook her head. She knew what she was thinking was absurd.

"Come on, Miguel. I need to head back to town."

But as she turned to leave, she glanced at the oil lamp sitting on the desk. What she saw made her stomach knot. Nearly half the fuel she'd put in it days ago had been consumed, and the wick had been rolled and blackened even more.

❖

She knelt in the gravel and talked to Miguel, telling him to be good and she'd see him tomorrow. She was trembling inside, having the uneasy feeling return to her stomach and head.

"Thanks again for watching him," she said to Johnny.

"Not a problem. Like I said, he's a good dog. Since we can't find the family, I guess he's yours."

"The family," she mused and glanced at the window. "Johnny, do you think that family is here illegally as Wilcox said? Do you think they're on the run?"

"I wouldn't doubt it. It happens a lot."

Brenna waved to him and Miguel as she turned her Jeep toward the road. From the entry road, she pulled onto the highway and looked once more at the grove. From the fence line, she could see the area the crew had cleared that day. But she did a double take. One of the crew was still out there, watching as she drove past. She slowed. What was wrong with his face? And as she watched, he turned and disappeared into the trees.

❖

On the drive back toward her hotel, she continued to fight her nausea and headache. What had started out as a fairly pleasant day had turned worrisome. It wasn't her usual depression about Edward and Michael or even her self-torture and blame over Debra. No, this was something else. It was the property, the sad story of Nelda Poulsen and her many lost children, the suicide of Dallin Poulsen, the strange appearance of the family, and their even stranger disappearance. But most disturbing was the assault on Anabel, which Brenna knew she'd witnessed, but now doubted. And those damn black smears, those handprints of blood. Whose blood?

A tremendous jagged web of horizontal lightning burst across the desert sky, followed by a shaking boom. Brenna jumped and swerved in her Jeep. Rain clouds gathered all around the panoramic stretch of the mountainous horizon, and by the time she pulled into the hotel's parking lot, a steady cold rain hammered the pavement, and the warm temperatures plummeted. After getting some help from one of the staff to secure her Jeep's top, she returned to her room, taking shelter from the unusual storm. She cuddled in a blanket, as the temperature in her hotel room had dropped as well, despite her calls to the front desk and her fiddling with the thermostat. She ordered room service, avoiding the wine this time, tried to eat to calm her stomach, but gave up after a few bites. She took something for her headache and rolled up again in a blanket on the sofa. The rain outside her hotel window came down in a steady hiss and her room grew colder. Exhausted from her late night with Alex, she stretched out and dozed off watching television. As she fell asleep, the image in her mind of the Poulsen house blended and merged into the interior of a church.

The sanctuary was empty and dark, and she walked the center aisle to the front and gazed at the altar.

"Where are you, Mommy?"

She turned to see him wandering through the nave, moving between pews. She reached him and held him to her, weeping with joy at the familiar feel of his little body, the smell of his hair. Then glass shattered, fragments shot like bullets across the open room. He cried for his father, but she reassured him and struggled against the powerful wind to make it to the basement door. But the door was nailed shut, and she tugged and screamed in frustration, her son clinging to her.

"My son, my son, I have to save my son!"

An old woman crouched at her feet.

"Hold Mommy's skirt. Don't let go." She lifted the woman's shoulders, and dark eyes bore into her as black hair cascaded around her.

"My son, find my son. You have promised," the woman growled. She began to smile and laugh while her face transformed into a disfigured one with the bottom half of her chin missing. It was no longer a woman, but a monster, and it lunged.

"Whore," the monster sneered as it choked her. "You fucking, dirty whore."

Brenna shot up gasping for air and holding her throat. She wheezed and struggled to breathe while her limbs tingled. Outside the rain still poured and inside the room felt even colder than before. She checked the thermostat and made hot tea in the room's microwave oven. Sitting back on the sofa, she hugged the blanket and cursed her nightmare. She regretted not ordering wine after all. On the coffee table, the rosary lay with the other documents and photograph. She picked it up, curious to find the usually cool metal felt warm, almost hot to the touch. When her phone rang, she jumped.

"Hey." She smiled into the phone, relieved to see Alex's name appear on the screen.

"I was afraid you'd be asleep," Alex said.

"No, I was waiting for your call."

"You okay? You sound out of breath."

"It's nothing. I just woke up from a bad dream, that's all." Brenna wiped sweat from her face, but she shivered all the same.

"So you were asleep. I'm sorry."

"It's okay. I'd fallen asleep on the sofa. This kind of weather always makes me sleepy."

"What do you mean this kind of weather?"

"The rain. Aren't you getting soaked? A storm rolled in around sundown and hasn't let up."

"No, it's perfectly clear here. Hmm, that's strange. Oh well, so tell me about your bad dream."

"It was nothing, just the same thing. The church, the tornado." Brenna winced at the taunting image of the dark woman transformed into a monster.

"I'm sorry, Brenna. Do you have the dream often?"

"Almost every night."

Alex sighed into the phone. "I guess that's to be expected."

"I don't want to talk about my nightmares. Tell me about your day. Tell me everything, where you went, what kind of job you're working on, what you had for lunch, for dinner."

For the next hour they talked—mostly Alex talked and Brenna listened. The details were inconsequential, but Alex's voice and her laugh were enough to draw off the tension in Brenna's shoulders and ease her headache and stomach. Before long she was giggling at Alex's stories as well as yawning.

"I'll let you get to bed. You sound tired," Alex said. "And maybe since you've had a bad one already, you'll dream only sweet dreams for the rest of the night."

"Talking to you has been a big help. Thank you."

"Like I said at dinner last night, I'm here when you need someone to talk to, someone to cry with."

"You're not only a gorgeous woman on the outside, Alex Santana, but on the inside, too. I've never known someone as kind as you."

"Thank you, Brenna. That's sweet. And I want you to know… actually I hope you aren't offended, but last night after you left, I lit a candle for you, said a prayer to Our Mother, and asked her blessing to help you heal and gain some peace."

"You prayed for me?"

"I did."

Brenna tried not to let her voice sound bitter, but it did. "Thank you, Alex, but you shouldn't have bothered."

After getting off the phone, she sat a long time on the sofa while she ruminated and stewed with the old anger. And all the while, the silver rosary grew hot in her hand.

CHAPTER SEVENTEEN

Sunday was rainy, cold, and bleak, and Brenna sank into depression once again. The twist in her nightmare, missing Alex, and the circumstances and events surrounding the property—all of these worked on her, and she found herself reading and rereading the material Sadie'd photocopied for her as well as viewing the pictures of the gravestones she'd taken the day before. She was aggravated, on edge, and short tempered. She barked at the woman who'd brought back her clothes from the laundry, complained about something insignificant to the staff that brought her dinner. She was in a dark mood, a black mood, an angry mood. In the evening, she took a hot shower, trying to draw off the chill she still felt from the storm. She couldn't understand why she was so cold, cold right to her bones. She'd lived her whole life in the Midwest, suffered through countless snowstorms, but had never felt the sort of penetrating cold she experienced now. After her shower, she bundled in a robe and decided to call for room service to see about getting a bottle of wine, something that would help her fall into a deep sleep. She wasn't about to have a replay of this newest version of her nightmare. But before she could call for room service, her cell phone buzzed. She answered, seeing it was Alex.

"I was wondering if your room service was there yet," Alex said.

"My room service?" Brenna asked. "I was about to call for a bottle of...hey, how did—" And then she heard a knock. "Hang on." She tightened her robe, opened the door, and found Alex, dripping rainwater from her hair and clothes. In her hands, she held a small pot of miniature sunflowers with a tiny scarecrow adornment. Brenna fell against the door with surprise. "I can't believe you're here. I thought I wouldn't see you until Thursday. You weren't even due back until tomorrow."

Alex laughed. "Do I get to come in or not?"

"Yes, of course." Brenna pulled her in and hugged her. "Alex, you're soaking wet. Why'd you drive back in this storm?"

"It was completely clear until I hit Highway 10, but when I came up on the city, I was in the middle of it suddenly." She held the small pot of flowers, which also dripped rainwater. "Here you go. I saw these at a stand just before the freeway outside Eloy, and I couldn't resist. I decided to bring you a bit of sunshine with a little scarecrow to chase away your bad dreams." She flicked the tiny straw figure and chuckled.

"Sunshine? You brought me sunshine?" Brenna knew Alex could have no idea of the word's significance.

"I hope those are happy tears."

Brenna took the flowers. "You can't begin to imagine." She looked at them and back at Alex, whose smile was as radiant as the sun. "Thank you, Alex, thank you for these."

"You're welcome."

Brenna tugged her robe. "Let me go change." In the bedroom, she called to Alex from behind the closed door. "Pick out what you want from the menu by the phone. I was getting ready to order some wine, maybe some dinner." She came out dressed in sweats and carrying a towel.

Alex flipped through the booklet. "Brenna, I can't let you buy me dinner again, and besides there're no prices listed."

"I know, just pick what you want." She handed Alex the towel. "Here, see if you can dry yourself off a bit. I don't want you catching cold."

Alex rubbed the towel on the outside of her wet clothes. "You should turn up the heat in your room."

"I have. The thermostat's broken, I think. It reads seventy-two, and I've called a dozen times downstairs for them to do something about it."

"Well, it's colder inside this room than out in the hallway." Alex handed her the damp towel. "You okay? You seem out of sorts."

"Just one of those days, I guess. Go on and pick something to eat. I'll call it in and have some extra blankets sent up, too."

"Like I said, you don't need to buy me—"

But Brenna put her finger to Alex's lips, shushing her. "I won't take no for an answer."

After some coaxing, Alex agreed to stay and allowed Brenna to order dinner. They sat on the sofa, snuggled together with a blanket across their laps and one around their shoulders and ate while Brenna showed Alex everything she'd uncovered in the last few days with Sadie's help.

"Owen Brock was the last person who'd have known any of the families working for the Poulsens, at least that's what I thought," Brenna said. "And then I heard something on television about Lanny Poulsen's corporation and realized the man's still alive. I don't know why that never occurred to me to begin with. He has to remember some of the families who worked the grove. Cassie's going to get me an appointment to talk to him."

"I don't know, Brenna. Even if he agrees to see you, I mean, he's a really old man. My grandfather's eighty-nine and forgetting things, you know, a little dementia setting in."

"Based on my calculations"—Brenna held the family portrait—"I'd say he's in his midnineties. If he's still involved with his corporation, he might still have most of his faculties." She tossed the photograph aside and picked up the rosary. She fingered the beads and wondered who'd once held the piece and what her prayers had been.

"It's important for you to find someone to give this to, isn't it?" Alex took the necklace from Brenna's hand.

"Yes. But I don't know why. It just is."

Alex ran her fingers across the beads. "My mother's rosary is similar, like I told you, but it isn't all silver. It has the Nuestra Señora de Guadalupe on it as well. She had it in her hands when she died, although for the last few days of her life she never regained consciousness." Alex rubbed her forehead and lowered her voice. "But I made sure she held it in her hands. I thought about burying it with her, but my grandfather told me I needed to keep it, to pray with it, and remember her."

"Do you pray often?" Brenna could sense Alex's growing sadness.

"I pray, but I haven't been to confession or communion in years. The official church doesn't have a place for people like me. But I'm respectful of it. The beliefs are important to my father and grandfather as well as my aunts and cousins, and Our Lady of Guadalupe was special to my mother. She's special to me, too."

"Tell me about her."

Alex continued to stroke the beads as she spoke. "The story goes, she appeared to Juan Diego, a peasant in Mexico. She asked him to have a church built in her honor. There's more about the miracle of the flowers, the roses he found growing out of season and gathered in his cloak, and how she embedded her image within it. Anyway, for many Catholic Latinos, she's our patroness, our miracle. There're tons of festivals and shrines in her honor. Even for the most agnostic among us, she's special. My cousin Eddie, he became a Wiccan, but even he still prays to her."

Brenna considered this information and her ignorance when it came to beliefs outside her own. She pointed to the medallion. "I don't think I've seen a version of Mary like this before. What's she standing on?"

"That's the moon. See, and there's a little angel holding it up." Alex rubbed along the bottom. "Something people don't realize is she's unique to the cultures of South America. For the native people of Mesoamerica, the moon was the god of darkness. By standing on him, Our Lady shows she has defeated him, overcome him."

"Hmm, interesting." Brenna took the medallion from Alex and scrutinized it. "And her robe, what's on it?"

"Stars. In the original image on Juan Diego's cloak, her mantle is blue and turquoise, the sign of royalty. The stars set within the mantle show she's the queen of heaven."

"That's unusual. Being brought up Methodist, there was never mention of anyone other than the angry and vengeful male God."

"I'll tell you a secret," Alex said.

Brenna giggled at Alex's sly smile. Alex was trying to remain upbeat even though her eyes indicated otherwise. "Okay, let's hear it."

Alex glanced around the room as if she were a spy, looking for enemy surveillance. She raised her eyebrows in a silly way and Brenna giggled once more. Then she leaned forward to whisper. "Most of us pray to her almost exclusively. My aunts, particularly my tía Marta, believe she is the Supreme Being, the first cause."

Brenna leaned back. "Really?"

Alex nodded. "But it's heretical, so we don't advertise it, if you know what I mean."

"Huh." Brenna cocked her head, examined the piece once more. "And these lines, what do they represent?"

"Ah, the sun's rays," Alex said.

"The sun?"

"Yes, you see for the native people, the sun was their most powerful god. But Our Lady stands before the sun, in front of it, dominating it. And it looks as if the rays shine from behind her, but in fact, they shine from within her. She's the sun, our mother, the bearer of all life and love."

Brenna blinked. "The sun. I see."

"My tía Marta says every woman carries a ray of her light within them, a spark of her flame. Each of us has a piece of her within us. We are all mothers, so to speak."

Brenna lowered her eyes. "Some of us better than others."

"Why do you say that?" Alex took her hand. "I bet you were a terrific mother."

Brenna pulled her hand away and leaned forward on her knees while she held her head. Determined not to cry, she gritted her teeth and squeezed her eyes shut.

"His death was an accident, Brenna, a terrible thing. You did all you could. You told me you tried to get him to the basement." Alex caressed the small of her back and waited.

But Brenna didn't move, didn't respond. What would Alex think of her if she knew the truth?

"You know"—Alex cleared her throat—"Mamá used to tell me nothing was stronger than the bond between mother and child. No power can equal it. And when she knew she was close to dying, she reminded me daily, *No voy a dejarte nunca, Alejandra. Nunca.* I will never leave you, Alejandra, never."

Brenna looked up when she heard Alex's voice break.

"And you know," Alex continued, "it's true. I feel her with me often." She wiped her eyes.

Brenna nodded, but looked away. She'd never had that sort of bond with her own mother.

After an uncomfortable silence, Alex said, "Talk to me, Brenna. Don't shut down." She rubbed Brenna's shoulder.

But Brenna pulled away from Alex's touch, reached for the television remote, and turned the unit on. "You want to watch a movie?" She flipped through channels and settled on something before tossing the remote on the table. She leaned back, but crossed her arms across her chest. Still, it didn't prevent Alex from scooting closer and putting an arm around her. At a commercial, she said, "Do you know how insurance classifies a tornado?"

Alex shook her head.

"As an act of God." Brenna turned her attention back to the television and fell silent.

Alex stayed only a bit longer. She told Brenna she was tired from her work over the weekend as well as the drive and needed to get to bed. At the door, they hugged, and Alex kissed her on the cheek.

"I'm worried about you," Alex said.

"I'm fine." She wasn't.

Once Alex was gone, Brenna took the pot of sunflowers into the bedroom and placed it next to her son's music box. She touched the decoupage image of the sun on the box and caressed the petals of the little sunflowers in the pot. She thought about Alex and her mother, about what Clarita had told her—a mother's love for her child was a powerful force. But her own love for Michael hadn't been enough to save him. As a mother, she'd failed him when he'd needed her the most. She retrieved what was left from the bottle of wine at dinner. Not bothering to pour it into a glass, she guzzled what remained and swallowed not one, but two sleep aids. She would, at least, sleep through the night, numb from her pain, numb everywhere except for the thickness that gathered in her throat.

Brenna didn't see Alex over the next few days, but was able to talk with her often on the phone. Meanwhile, she kept herself busy, painting the living room and kitchen of the Poulsen house. Each afternoon she'd go out there, visit with Miguel, check in with Johnny, and then get to work. She avoided the upstairs rooms, however, except for having Johnny help her place heavy plastic over the two windows. It was still raining, still icy cold, and she figured once the new furnace was installed, she'd want the house to warm up without losing any of its heat. With Johnny's further help, she sealed off the downstairs windows with plastic sheeting as well.

On Wednesday morning, the furniture-delivery followed by the appliance-delivery men showed up and installed her new purchases. By afternoon, a serviceman from the gas company arrived and turned on her gas. He checked all the new appliances and gave her the okay. And now with the house warming up, her new sofa and television along with the new bed, nightstand, and dresser, the house seemed almost cozy and livable.

Later that evening, she checked out of her hotel suite and brought back her suitcase of clean clothes along with all the documents she'd collected from Sadie. She unpacked her clothes and set the music box along with her little pot of sunflowers on the nightstand next to her bed. She debated whether she should put the photo of Edward and Michael there as well, but it was the only picture of her son she'd brought with her. She placed it with the other items and went to make Miguel some dinner. On her way back to the property earlier that evening, she'd stopped off at Fernie and Patricia's store, and Patricia had made her another sandwich. It wasn't the high-class cuisine of the Scottsdale Hilton, but she enjoyed it as she sat on her new sofa with Miguel there for company in front of her new big-screen television. She felt more upbeat than she had for days. It helped as well tomorrow was Thanksgiving and she'd get to spend it with Alex. Not seeing her since Sunday evening had been difficult even with the phone calls each night.

By the time Alex finally called that night for her regular check in, it was past bedtime. "Sorry, bella. I know it's late, but I needed to get some paperwork done."

Brenna smiled into the phone. Alex had taken up calling her *bella*, and she liked it, knew it meant beautiful, and felt it was Alex's careful way of being romantic without rushing things. "It's okay," she said. "I figured you were slammed with work."

"These short workweeks are murder." Alex groaned. "I need to get to bed and get some sleep since I'll be up at dawn and down at the restaurant to start the pit for the pig. My cousin Marco always goes short with the mesquite. Need to make sure he gets it right, you know."

"Do you boss around your cousins, too?"

Alex chuckled. "I boss everyone."

Their conversation continued for another hour. At one point, Brenna asked Alex about her living arrangements and wondered if she ever wanted to live on her own. Alex explained living with her father and grandfather was a benefit to them all, and she enjoyed the close relationship with them.

"But do you think you'll always live with them?" Brenna asked.

"No, someday I'll find my own place." Alex paused on the phone as she yawned, then said, "I always thought I'd like to have some horse property by Red Mountain. You know, girls and horses. I've always wanted a horse. But it's more than that. I love the desert, and if I could wake up every morning, walk out on my porch, and see the sun hit that mountain, well, I'd believe I was living in paradise."

They said good night, and Brenna went outside to see if she could spot Red Mountain in the dark. Its familiar outline was visible since the rain had let up a bit and a breeze had dissipated some of the clouds. She gazed at the mountain and remembered the morning, not long ago, when Alex had first shown her the sunrise. And she realized she'd love to see the sunrise every morning on Red Mountain with Alex by her side.

The light in Johnny's RV came on and he stepped out, waved, and called out good night. She waved back, happy he was there. With him and Miguel, the isolation didn't seem quite as profound. She waited while Miguel stepped off the porch into the darkness to do his business, then she led him back inside and climbed into her new bed. She patted her blankets and called for him. He jumped up and curled next to her.

"Let's give this another try. I haven't slept one night through in this house." She kissed his nose, flipped off the light, and rolled over, pulling the blankets around her.

It was as black as ever in the room, but the heat from the furnace, along with Miguel's rhythmic breathing, soothed her. She was tired from her physical labor of painting over the last few days. Getting to sleep, she hoped, wouldn't be a problem even without her sleep aid or wine, which she craved, nevertheless. But the dream woke her.

"Mommy?"

"I'm here, Michael."

"I'm scared. I want Daddy. Where's Daddy?"

"He'll come. Now hold my skirt."

She set him down, and he was gone. She screamed and tore at her hair. She could feel the sharp pain of something slamming into the back of her head, splitting her skull.

"Mommy? Where are you, Mommy?"

She could hear him, but she couldn't reach him. He was lost, and she couldn't raise her head to see.

She sat up in bed when Miguel licked her face. She pushed him away as she wept into her hands before wiping her eyes and nose. Miguel jumped off the bed.

"You need to go out?"

She switched on the lamp and sat a second to focus on the present, to push the nightmare from her mind. Then she started to swing her legs out of bed, but she went stiff instead. She'd heard something. She watched the music box. It didn't open. She heard the noise again, but this time it wasn't inside the house. It was outside her bedroom window.

"Mamá? Dónde estás, Mamá?" a child's voice called.

"Oh, hell," she said. It was Pedro, she was sure, still looking for his mother. She followed Miguel to the front door and listened again. He clawed at her leg. "Okay, okay. You need to learn to hold it, for heaven's sake."

She turned on the porch light and opened the door, but jumped and fell back shrieking as Johnny beamed his flashlight in her face.

"Sorry, I thought I heard you call me," he said.

Brenna held her heart. "No, wasn't me. I think it's the boy, Pedro."

"He can't still be out there."

Brenna grabbed his flashlight, pushed past him, and began waving the light around. "Pedro? Where are you? Please come here, honey. We want to help you."

Silence.

"You think it's that kid?" Johnny asked.

Brenna narrowed her eyes as she peered into the darkness. Even with the waxing gibbous moon, she couldn't see past the porch light, and the beam of the flashlight did little to illuminate the darkness. "Would they have left their boy behind?"

"No, Brenna, we don't leave our kids. Unless…"

"Unless what?"

"Unless they couldn't get to him. Maybe they got moved before they could find him."

Her teeth chattered and she hugged herself. She was reluctant to go back inside and leave Pedro out there especially in this cold weather. But she doubted she and Johnny could find him even with a third of her property stripped of trees.

"Leave your light on, Johnny. I'll leave my porch light on. Maybe that'll draw him to us. I don't know what else to do but hope he'll come to the door and ask for help."

She called Miguel along, headed back into the house, and got her phone from her nightstand. Maybe she needed to call Alex and let her know. But when she saw the time on her new alarm clock, three fifteen in the morning, she decided she'd wait and call after breakfast. So to pass the time, she grabbed an extra blanket and plopped in front of the television. As she surfed the channels for something to watch, thankful she'd had a satellite dish installed, she thought of poor Pedro out there, of Anabel somewhere being held by coyotes, of the old woman and her worry for her daughter and grandson. And her scar pulsed to the point of making her dizzy.

CHAPTER EIGHTEEN

It was four o'clock in the afternoon when Brenna arrived at the south Phoenix restaurant, Las Cinco Hermanas. The adobe building was framed in timber beams, painted turquoise, and strung with Christmas bulbs, and a banner hung across the eaves: *The Delgado Family Thanksgiving, Private Party*. She parked her Jeep at the far end of the full parking lot and walked toward the building while she noticed some teenagers hanging out at their cars smoking, talking, and listening to music. They watched her as she walked by. Nearly everyone smiled and a few waved.

One teenage girl jogged over. "Are you Brenna? My cousin said you'd be coming. Go inside, we're gonna eat soon."

Brenna thanked her and weaved her way between cars to the front. She passed an ornate fountain and a koi pond that looped in and under the entry bridge leading to the main doors. The front patio was lined with Saltillo tile, which wrapped around large cottonwood trees, providing an intertwined canopy of branches and leaves. Music, laughter, and conversation seeped from the open front doors, and she could smell a wonderful aroma, almost like barbecue but not quite. When she entered the foyer, the lights were dimmer than the late-afternoon sunlight, and it took her eyes a moment to adjust while she looked around for a familiar face. The restaurant was crowded with children and old people, adults and young teens. Rubén and Juan Carlos sat to one side at a table on a raised platform. A stream of people were walking up and shaking the two men's hands. Then Brenna spotted an attractive young woman who made eye contact with her, smiled, and headed her way. As she approached, Brenna thought she looked familiar—she had long dark hair, dark eyes, and a radiant smile. It could've been Alex's younger sister if she'd had one.

"Brenna? Hi, I'm Marissa, one of Alex's cousins. Welcome to the Delgado family Thanksgiving." She pulled Brenna into a hug.

"Hi, Marissa, thank you," Brenna said. "I didn't realize there'd be so many people."

"We have a large family, but if you count all the extended family and the multiple generations, we could easily populate our own small country." Marissa laughed and led her by the hand to the raised platform. "Alex is on the back patio with some of the guys. She likes to supervise the pig roast. I'll take you out there, but first you need to greet our abuelito."

Rubén reached out and embraced her when he saw her. "Brenna, my dear child, welcome."

Juan Carlos pulled himself up with his cane. He grinned and reached for Brenna's hand, which she extended to him. He said something to her, and Marissa translated. "Grandfather says again he blesses you and welcomes you to his family. He hopes you will search your heart and find much to be thankful for this Thanksgiving day."

Brenna smiled, but she had to force it a bit. It was the first Thanksgiving without Michael, and as she'd told Alex once before, she didn't feel she had much to be thankful for.

"Thank you, Abuelito," she said, using the term of affection Alex had told her meant grandpa. "I am happy and honored to be here with you and your family."

Juan Carlos nodded his head and said something more to Marissa who replied in Spanish before excusing herself and Brenna.

Back at the bar, Marissa patted a man on the shoulder. "Hey, babe, this is Brenna. You know, Alex's Brenna."

He extended his hand. "Hi, I'm Justin. We've been waiting for you. Glad you could join us. And don't worry, this is only my third Delgado Thanksgiving, and I'm still getting used to it."

Brenna thanked him, noticing Justin's T-shirt printed with the words *Phoenix Fire Department* and the logo of a phoenix bird. As she scanned the other people at the bar, she noticed one of the two men Justin had been talking to also wore a similar shirt.

"Are you a fireman?" she asked.

He pointed to the other man. "Yep, me and Angel. We serve at the same station. I'm a paramedic and Angel's our captain."

Angel came right over and embraced her. "Alex was right. You are beautiful. But my cousin has always had good taste in women."

She could see such a striking resemblance among Marissa, Angel, and Alex. In fact, Angel could've passed as Alex's twin brother.

The other man sitting with them elbowed Angel's ribs. "And you have good taste in men. There must be a family connection."

Angel introduced the man as his partner, Philip.

Brenna stood with her new acquaintances and exchanged small talk. While they conversed, she noticed a huge framed black-and-white photograph hanging as the centerpiece on the bar's wall. It showed five beautiful Latinas standing in long white dresses with their black hair pulled up in buns. Sitting on a stool in front of the women was a handsome middle-aged man. Brenna recognized him. It was Juan Carlos, and the women behind him, his five daughters. The middle two daughters resembled each other, and she noted one of the twins was definitely Alex's mother; she looked nearly the same as the photograph of her by the family shrine. The group continued chatting, until finally Marissa took her by the arm again and began leading her down a back hall.

"You can put your purse and jacket in the office and we'll go out on the back patio and see if Alex is done supervising the pig," Marissa said.

When Marissa opened the door to the patio, the smell of roasted meat washed over Brenna. It was delicious, different from anything she'd ever smelled. But more delicious than the scent of succulent roasted pork was the sight of Alex standing by the fire pit giving directions and supervising the operation. She wore a two-piece dress, the skirt layered and flared at the bottom, almost like a peasant skirt, but of a shinier aqua-blue material. The top was made of the same material and was held up by one strap over her left shoulder, the other shoulder exposed and bare. The low cut of the top was lined with embroidered flowers. The skirt was short, just above her knees, and she wore black heels and sheer black hose as well. Alex had accessorized the dress with a large onyx-beaded necklace and dangling onyx earrings. Her dark hair was curled, and she'd put on extra makeup, her eye shadow highlighting the aqua in her dress.

Alex glanced up, saw them, and walked over. "Brenna, I wondered where you were." She gave her a quick hug and added, "And you've met Marissa."

"I had my eye out for her," Marissa said. "Saw her walk in with that stunned look and knew it had to be her."

"I wasn't expecting so many people," Brenna said.

Marissa patted her arm. "Don't worry, you're not required to learn everyone's name. I have second and third cousins whose names I still can't remember." She pointed to the door. "Alex, I'm heading back in to see if Mamá needs some help."

After Marissa went inside, Alex said, "Welcome to my family's Thanksgiving." She held Brenna at arm's length. "And you look wonderful."

"And you look...wow." Brenna couldn't find the words. This was such a different look from the Alex she was used to seeing.

"I don't look slutty, do I?" Alex twirled her skirt.

"For heaven's sake, no. You're gorgeous. I can't think of the right words. Striking, appetizing, delicious even."

"Delicious? Hmm." Alex brushed a lock of hair from Brenna's eyes. "I want to introduce you to my aunts. And Marissa's right. Don't worry about everyone's name. Just have fun."

The two proceeded to the kitchen, but every few feet someone stopped Alex to hug her and be introduced to Brenna. They'd invariably hug Brenna as well. Finally, Alex swung open the kitchen doors and brought her into an area full of women chatting, cooking, and preparing food. It was a picture of organized chaos.

First, Alex introduced Brenna to her mother's oldest sister, Sofia, a pretty woman who, Alex explained, spoke little English, like her grandfather. Alex translated her welcome: "We are happy to have you in the family." From there, Brenna met two of Alex's other aunts, Imelda and Lucia. The family resemblance to Sofia and to Alex was striking. Each hugged her in succession and welcomed her in turn. Finally, Alex pulled her over to a woman stirring a large pot of gravy. She looked so much like the photograph of Clarita, Brenna already knew who she was.

"And this is my sweet tía Marta, my mom's twin," Alex said.

The woman looked right into Brenna's eyes. A delayed response, almost awkward, caused Brenna to cringe. Marta stopped stirring, wiped her hands, and came close.

"Brenna Taylor." She introduced herself and held out her hand. Something seemed different about this aunt. Marta took her hand, but palm up, and studied it before closing her own hand over it.

"Lo veo. Lo veo," Marta said, shaking her head. She continued to hold Brenna's hand and stepped back to take her all in before pulling her into a hug. When she ended the embrace, she touched Brenna's cheek, held her hand there, and searched her eyes. "Alejandra, you did not tell me she was this pretty," she said. She had the same mild accent as the other aunts, only her voice was deeper, more authoritative.

"Thank you, Marta, you're very kind," Brenna said. She felt apprehensive.

"Hmm." Marta patted her cheek and moved both hands to Brenna's shoulders and patted them as well as she shook her head and muttered something in Spanish.

"You look so much like the picture I saw of Clarita, your sister," Brenna said.

"Yes." Marta continued to hold her by the shoulders.

From her side vision, Brenna saw Alex was frowning.

"Your son and daughter look so much like Alex as well." Brenna smiled, but her lips quivered with nerves.

"I have been blessed with two beautiful and generous children and doubly blessed because each of them has found a companion who adores them," Marta said.

"Qué pasa, Tía?" Alex asked.

But Marta waved Alex off. "A mother always wishes the best for her children," she said. "And now I see my dear niece, a daughter to me as well, has found someone special. We are happy to welcome you into our family, Brenna." She returned to supervising the gravy.

"Thank you," Brenna said.

Alex gripped her hand to lead her away when Marta spoke once more.

"I hope you will allow your heart to heal, mija. The burden you carry is too great even for one as strong as you."

Brenna saw Alex's face redden and her lips draw tight. She pulled her from the kitchen into the main dining hall.

"Did I say something wrong?" Brenna asked.

"You're fine. Come. I want you to sit over here." Alex brought her to a table and pulled out a chair. "I'll get us something from the bar." She placed a kiss on the crown of Brenna's head and left.

Brenna watched her go, but Alex didn't go to the bar. Instead, she headed back toward the kitchen. She worried she'd done something to insult Marta and wondered if it'd been such a good idea to accept Alex's invitation after all.

"Brenna?" Cassie's voice cut through the clamor.

Brenna jumped up and embraced her. "Finally, someone I know."

"I'm glad you're here, you're in for a treat." Cassie turned to the woman by her side. "Brenna, this is my partner, Kelly."

Kelly held out her arms. "Hugs. I hear you've been adopted into this family like Cassie and me, so we gotta hug."

Brenna accepted the hug. "I've heard a lot about you. I'm glad we're finally meeting."

"You're all I've heard about for weeks," Kelly replied. "And this one"—she pointed to Cassie—"and Santana are on the phone every other hour talking about you. I bet your ears have been burning something fierce."

Brenna looked sideways at Cassie. "Is that right. Every other hour?"

"I confess." Cassie held up her hands. "But I told you, I knew the second you walked into my office."

"She plays Cupid for all our single friends, Brenna. She can't help herself," Kelly said.

Cassie looked around. "Where's Alex?"

"She went to the kitchen," Brenna said.

"You meet all her aunts? Marta?" Cassie asked.

"I did."

"I bet they were all happy to meet you."

"I guess so." She looked past Cassie and wished Alex would hurry back.

Cassie and Kelly excused themselves to grab drinks at the bar, and Brenna sat again and watched in the direction of the kitchen. Soon she saw Alex heading her way, carrying two bottles of soda. Apparently she'd stopped by the bar.

"I wasn't sure, but I thought you'd want to start with a soda first. We usually do beer and tequila after we eat," Alex said.

"That's fine." Brenna took the bottle and noticed Alex studying her. She appeared tense around the shoulders, her mouth pursed. "Did I say something wrong to Marta?"

"Of course not," Alex said. "She thinks you're beautiful."

"Then what?"

But before she could press for more, Cassie and Kelly joined them, and Alex's whole demeanor changed.

"Oigan, chicas," Alex said and hugged each woman.

"Damn, girl, way to outdress everyone," Kelly said.

"You look hot, woman," Cassie interjected. "You're gonna burn up that dance floor like you always do, I can tell."

Alex put her arm around Brenna. "We both are."

Brenna's stomach clenched with apprehension. "Alex, I can't dance. I told you."

"Don't worry," Alex said. "I'm a good teacher."

Another half hour passed with people arriving and greeting each other. Brenna saw everyone went to pay respects to Juan Carlos and Rubén before beginning to mingle. Eventually, Marissa and Justin joined them at the table along with Angel and Philip.

"When's the chow?" Kelly asked.

"Another few minutes," Alex said. "They're moving a microphone over to Juan Carlos's table right now."

In moments, everyone was seated, and Brenna watched as two men moved a microphone close to Juan Carlos. Without any command, the restaurant fell silent as mothers hushed their children, fathers tapped their teenagers' shoulders, and old people turned in their chairs.

"Familia, bienvenidos," Juan Carlos said into the microphone. "Que Dios los bendiga."

"Welcome my family," Rubén interpreted. "God's blessing on all of you."

And then Juan Carlos continued while Rubén translated every few lines. The benediction went on for twenty minutes before the little man brought it to an end.

Rubén translated: "And let us not forget those who have left us to be cradled in the arms of Our Blessed Mother, held in the hollow of her mantle, in the crossing of her arms. They wait for us, and there will be a great celebration when we are reunited with those we love once again."

Brenna stifled a sigh. That earned her a troubled look from Alex, who covered with a smile and a pat on her leg.

Then Juan Carlos raised one hand while Rubén steadied him. "Los bendigo, mis hijos. Vayan con Dios."

The entire restaurant exploded with applause as if the old man had just given a Carnegie Hall performance. Rubén bowed to him, helped him take his seat, and then spoke into the microphone. "Let's eat."

A slow progression, each table in turn, went to the kitchen, and every person was served buffet-style as each walked along the counters. The feast consisted of not only the traditional Thanksgiving spread of turkey, stuffing, potatoes, and gravy, but also a large tray of shredded pork, which had just been removed from the whole pig. A good dozen cold and hot salads, half a dozen different breads and muffins, along with flour and corn tortillas graced the counter. As Brenna tried to decide what to take, she realized there was no way she'd be able to sample it all.

"Have some tamales." Alex put one on Brenna's already full plate. "My aunts work on these for days. And have some beans and rice, too," she said, spooning on the food.

"Alex, I can't eat that much." Brenna giggled.

"This is just the main meal. Wait until dessert comes out."

"I'll burst." She giggled again as Alex continued to pile her plate.

"Don't worry. I'll have you burning it off dancing." Alex winked, and they continued down the line.

With food dripping from their plates, Brenna, along with Alex and her friends, returned to their table. Raymond, the DJ, played norteña music in the background, and everyone began talking and eating. During the dinner conversation, Brenna learned a great deal about Alex's cousins, how Justin had met Marissa through Angel's unit, how Philip flew for an air-rescue and emergency-transport company, and how he and Angel had been together for six years. She was also impressed to learn that Angel had the distinction of being the first openly gay Latino in Arizona to serve as captain of a fire station. However, for all of the conversation and history they shared with her, no one asked about her family or background. She decided either Cassie or Alex had told them, and they were being respectful of her privacy.

As the meal came to an end, Brenna saw young children head to the front door. "What's going on?" she asked Alex.

"The kids hit a piñata after dinner while my aunts clean up and prepare the dessert table. You want to go out on the patio and watch?"

"I'm sorry, but no. I don't think I can." Brenna could see children, some Michael's age, in the stampede toward the door.

"I get it. You don't have to explain."

Then, as the children and their parents made their way out the door, one little girl broke away from the group and skipped over.

"Prima, you come, too?" she asked Alex.

"You go on, mija. But be careful not to hit your brother with the stick this time." Alex hugged the little girl and turned her toward Brenna. "Jacquelyn, meet my friend. This is Brenna. Can you say hello?"

"Hi." The girl smiled.

"Hi, Jacquelyn. I'm pleased to meet you."

"You're pretty," Jacquelyn said. "I like your gold hair."

"Thank you, and I think you have beautiful eyes," Brenna replied.

Alex gave the girl a playful swat on the bottom. "Go see if you can hit that piñata before your cousins destroy it."

"Te quiero, Prima," the child said and skipped away.

"You're good with kids," Brenna said, leaning close while she rested her chin on her hands. "It's cute. I guess they don't mind your bossiness, do they?" She laughed at the perturbed expression on Alex's face.

"Well, I've babysat most of the little ones here, and even some of the older ones, too."

"Do you think you'll ever have a child of your own?"

Alex raised her eyebrows. "I don't know. I never thought much about it."

"You're still a young woman."

"I am."

"So what did she say to you when she left?"

"Jacky? She said, I love you, cousin."

"I love you?"

"Yes, *te quiero* is I love you," Alex said. "Well, not the intimate form, but what you would say to a friend or a family member."

"And how do you say it the other way? The intimate form?" Brenna leaned closer.

"It's…it's *te amo*." Alex diverted her eyes.

"*Te* what?"

"Te amo," Alex repeated. She fidgeted with her soda bottle until she excused herself to the restroom, where she seemed to be long delayed. As Alex returned and headed toward the table, a blast of music erupted from the band, which had set up in the corner of the main hall.

"They've started playing music for dancing. You ready?" Alex asked.

"Alex, seriously, even if I could dance, I'm too full. You go on and dance. I'll watch."

Alex grinned. Whatever awkwardness there'd been between them when she'd explained the expression *I love you* was now gone. Brenna pushed away from the table.

"Wipe that grin off your face, Alex. I told you I won't dance. I need to use the restroom anyway."

Brenna laughed to herself as she wove in and out of people toward the restroom. Something told her Alex would convince her otherwise about dancing. But at this point, she figured she didn't mind. At least the earlier tension between them had dissipated, and Alex was back to her silly self. When she returned to the table, Angel was delivering a tray of tequila shots along with a bowl of lime wedges.

He passed a shot to each of them. "Salud!" He grinned, swallowed the shot, and bit into a slice of lime.

She'd never done tequila shots before, and after watching the rest, she decided to try it. But even though Angel had snagged the more expensive Patrón, she grimaced and shook her head as the liquid burned its way down her throat. The others laughed when they saw her face.

"Wow, look at you shooting tequila like a pro." Alex chuckled as she gave Brenna's shoulder a squeeze.

Brenna coughed and pounded her chest. "Right. Like a pro."

The others laughed some more.

The band began to play a fast salsa, and Alex told her to have a seat and watch while she and Angel took the dance floor along with Marissa and Philip and two dozen other couples. Brenna sat back and watched as the shot of tequila began warming her limbs and her brain began to shiver. She watched Alex dance, her leg muscles flexing through the sheer black hose, her skirt swirling around her. Brenna blinked, trying to comprehend how Alex and Angel managed to move their feet so quickly, to gyrate their hips, legs, and shoulders so smoothly. She hadn't seen many Latin dances before, and to see these two together, both such attractive people, astonished her. She watched spellbound while Alex's hair flew around her as Angel dipped her and twirled her away. Then she heard a piercing trill escape Alex's lips. Others on the dance floor cheered the two cousins and answered Alex's trill with their own.

"She's warming up for you, Brenna." Cassie patted her on the arm. "Didn't I tell you she was something?"

Brenna couldn't believe how smoothly Alex danced, how seductively. And as the tequila coursed deeper into her system, she felt the urge and throbbing in her own body, teased out by the spectacle of Alex dancing. The song came to an end and the band went right into another number. Marissa motioned for Justin to join her, and he plodded out to the floor while Angel and Philip took a seat and chugged their beer.

Alex turned to her and held up her hand. "Let me help them. I'll be right over to get you."

As the music began, Marissa took the follow position while Justin took the lead. But Alex came behind Justin, lined his arms up to Marissa's, and pressed into his backside to direct his movements. Justin looked mortified, Brenna thought, being sandwiched between the two. But he allowed Alex to move him, and in no time, the two were doing a modified rumba. Alex broke off from the couple and came back to the table. Brenna could feel the heat steaming from her body.

"See what I mean? Justin is up and moving. I'll get you out there, too," Alex said.

"No, no way. I can't dance like that." Brenna shook her head, but she giggled all the same. The tequila was not only making her feel relaxed, but also silly.

"Don't worry, bella. We'll start off with a bolero. It's a slower dance, almost like a waltz."

Alex went over to the band, gained the attention of a guitar player, and whispered something in his ear. He nodded and passed on Alex's message. The current song ended, and Raymond spoke into the microphone, announcing a song, while more couples crowded onto the dance floor. Alex returned and held out her hand.

"Señorita, favor de bailar conmigo."

Brenna took her hand, felt her stomach tighten with anxiety, and followed Alex to the dance floor. Alex positioned her and looked into her eyes.

"Don't look at your feet. Watch my eyes, feel my hands. You can tell which foot to step with by the pressure of my hands"—Alex demonstrated—"and by my hips and thighs. Just imagine our bodies are connected at the hips and shoulders. Relax and let me move you."

Slowly, timidly, Brenna began to move, feeling Alex's body moving her. But she was nervous, thinking too much, not allowing the natural rhythm of the dance and Alex's movements to reach her.

"I'm sorry," she said, after stepping on Alex's feet for the third time.

"You're doing fine. Try not to anticipate, just accept my touch." Alex tightened her grip on Brenna's hip.

"Let me help you, girl." Marissa came behind her.

Brenna felt Marissa's hands on her hips, her breasts against her back, and her legs moving against her own. Her eyes went wide and her face burned as she swallowed a few times. The sensation of being pressed between Marissa and Alex while their bodies moved against her, guided her, and stroked her was unbelievable.

"It's okay, she'll help you." Alex stifled a laugh. "Just let us move you. Relax."

Brenna surrendered and allowed them to move her body to the slow rhythm of the music. While the song progressed, she looked into Alex's eyes and saw she was pleased. That silent approval gave Brenna the burst of self-assurance she needed, and before she knew it, Marissa had backed away, and she was dancing with Alex unassisted. Once the song ended, Alex brought her to a standstill.

"You did it, Brenna. You danced."

"I did, didn't I?" She hugged Alex around the neck.

Within seconds the band resumed playing, and the crowd let out a whoop as dozens more people piled onto the dance floor and lined up.

"You'll love this," Alex said. "It's the Macarena. It's like line dancing." She pulled Brenna to the center of the dance floor. "Just watch me and the others and you'll pick it up in no time."

Cassie and Kelly joined Brenna on one side and Marissa and Justin on the other as the music picked up. She laughed as she watched Alex doing the goofy moves, exaggerating her arm and hip movements, and singing along. Then Alex turned and did her moves facing her and the others. She made faces and added her own distinctive moves, causing everyone to laugh. Brenna became so tickled, she could hardly follow the group, and by the time the crazy song ended, she was panting and sweating with exertion as well as laughter. Alex took her hand, leading her back to the table, and after Brenna sat, Alex plopped herself on her lap and wrapped an arm around her neck.

"You got it, bella. See, I told you it'd be fun."

Angel appeared with another tray of shots and passed them around. The second shot went down a little more smoothly than the first for Brenna, but still she made a face.

"I think you're growing to like this stuff," Angel said.

Alex held her hand up. "Slow 'em down, hermano. She's gotta drive home later."

Right then someone came over and told the table the desserts were ready, and some of the group headed for the display.

"I don't think I can eat any more," Brenna said.

"Just a little flan." Alex pulled her along. "We'll come back and dance some more, and I promise you'll burn it off in no time."

Brenna went willingly and allowed Alex to pile another plate full with desserts. Back at the table, the group talked and snacked while the music continued to play. But soon the dancing resumed, and Cassie and Kelly went out to dance, as did Marissa and Justin. Philip also danced with Alex, and Brenna watched as the two did a masterful bachata. She couldn't help but envy Philip when Alex balanced her leg against his hip while he held her at the thigh and twirled her away from him.

"I don't understand something," Brenna said to Cassie once she and Kelly had returned to the table. "Two women can dance, but not two men?"

"It's not uncommon in their culture for women to dance together. At most events, they outnumber the men," Cassie said.

Brenna glanced around at the faces of the large extended clan. She was curious as to how both Alex and Angel were able to be openly gay in such a traditional family. "The family accepts them?"

Cassie wagged her head from shoulder to shoulder. "Well, to a point. I'm sure some of the family disapproves, and certainly their church is not going to approve. But her grandfather has accepted them and the few others who have come out, so no one's going to do or say anything to contradict him."

"Interesting." Brenna looked over at Juan Carlos.

"Yes, well, family is important to them. As Alex says, as her grandfather says, family comes first. Those bonds are more important to them than anything."

"Family," Brenna echoed.

The music was loud, and the tequila had both alleviated much of her hesitation about dancing and being social and lifted her spirits. But thinking about what Cassie had said brought her down when she thought about Edward and Michael, about the seemingly picture-perfect image of a wholesome, happy family they'd presented to the outside world. She thought about her sister, too, about her parents, and how her sense of family had been shattered when she'd been so young. And she thought about the migrant family, possibly on the run, whom she'd met over a week ago in the grove. They could've moved on, but they were not about to leave behind the boy, Pedro, and his mother, Anabel. She realized then she was envious of them, of Alex, and of Cassie and Kelly who'd been adopted into the Delgado tribe. She wondered if she could believe what everyone had said to her that afternoon. Was she a part of this family, accepted into the fold? When the song ended, she watched Alex coming toward her, and questioned once again if she deserve her, was worthy of her.

"You good?" Alex plopped again in her lap.

"Watching you dance is amazing."

"Well I have more lessons for you," Alex said with her lips pressed to Brenna's ear.

Brenna felt her face burning and wondered if it was the tequila or Alex's subtle flirtation.

Angel came over with another tray of shots and held it out to her. "One more, no? We still have plenty of time to get you sober for your drive home."

Alex took two shots from the tray. "This is it for her," she said to him. Then she handed Brenna a glass and said, "Right? I get the sense you're a lightweight with this stuff."

"Sort of, I guess. I'm not much of a drinker." But Brenna knew the statement was false.

"Ah, well." Alex raised her glass. "Salud!"

Brenna downed her third shot and bit the lime Angel held out to her. When she opened her eyes, she noticed Alex looking at her with a smile on her face. With the liberating effect of the alcohol, she almost allowed herself to lean forward for a kiss. But the band picked up again, and Alex held out her hand.

"You ready for another dance?"

Brenna ran her hand over her eyes. The dark thoughts she'd experienced moments ago had vanished, and she took Alex's hand and followed her to the dance floor once again. But this time Alex switched their positions.

"I'll let you lead now," Alex said, and the band must have seen her cue because they offered another slow-paced tune.

"I don't think I can do the opposite." Brenna felt her body stiffen.

"Yes, you can. Just think about what I did to you, and you do that to me," Alex instructed. "Here, I'll help you, but look at my face, not my feet."

"Alex, I can't." Brenna struggled with frustration as she tried to move the mirror opposite of what she'd done before. "I'm better at receiving than giving." She smiled at the double meaning of her words.

Alex put her mouth to Brenna's ear. "Trust me, I think you'll be good at giving if you just relax and do what comes naturally."

"Is that right?" Brenna felt tipsy from her third shot of tequila.

Thankfully, though, Angel came behind her before she trampled on Alex's feet any further. "Here, Brenna, let me give you some help. This one's too hot to handle your first time in the lead."

And he, like Marissa before him, leaned in to her. Just as before, she relaxed and soon found the look of approval in Alex's eyes enough to give her the boost of confidence she needed to grasp the movements. Angel pulled away, and she began to lead Alex on the dance floor.

"I knew you had the right touch," Alex said.

Brenna stumbled momentarily. "Well, not quite." She giggled.

"Are you having fun?"

"Yes."

"Do you have any idea how beautiful you are when you smile? I mean, really smile, not the fake smile you showed me that day in the trees."

Brenna felt her body go liquid, and she wondered if she was dancing as well as she imagined. "Mmm, yes, my fake smile. Well, no fake smiles around you," she said, slurring her words.

Alex chuckled. "Okay, you're cut off from the tequila for the rest of the night."

"But it gives me courage to dance with you."

"I see."

"And to kiss you good night." Brenna thought she'd said those words in her head, but the look on Alex's face told her they'd come from her own lips.

The song ended, but instead of leading her off the dance floor, Alex held her in place and asked, "Do you need courage for that?"

Brenna teetered, giggled once more. "Maybe. I guess we'll see."

CHAPTER NINETEEN

For the rest of the evening, Brenna couldn't take her eyes off Alex, couldn't keep from touching her hand, shoulder, or hip. Brenna danced with her again and again, becoming better at both the lead and the follow positions. Alex taught her new moves, different styles and always complimented her on her ability to pick up the steps so quickly. With her new burst of self-confidence, she also danced with Cassie and Kelly. Angel, then Philip, took her out on the dance floor as well. And although she felt shy about the way Marissa had helped her learn to move, she danced with her, too. Even Justin got in on the action, and the two of them managed to pull off a decent dance although they were both novices. As the evening became nighttime, people began to leave. By ten o'clock most of the little children and their parents had gone home, and so had Rubén and Juan Carlos. Before the two patriarchs left, however, Brenna thanked them again for welcoming her into the family. And it was a heartfelt thanks, she knew, for she was allowing herself permission, just a little bit of self-forgiveness, and was willing to think she did belong with this family, with Alex. By one o'clock in the morning, the band had packed away its instruments, and Raymond had put on a CD mix of music for the rest of the night. The tables stood mostly cleared and wiped down, but the fire pit still smoldered on the back patio, and beer bottles and paper products littered the floor. By then Alex's aunts had finished cleaning the kitchen and prepared to go home. The women made their rounds to their children and grandchildren and hugged them all good-bye. When they came to Alex's table, the aunts hugged Brenna along with the others. But Marta was the last to take her leave and waited to tell her good night until everyone else had started toward the door.

"I will pray for you, mija. I will light a candle and pray." Marta kissed Brenna's cheek.

"Thank you, that's nice of you." Brenna felt her tongue go heavy, and she cringed inside thinking she must sound like an idiot.

Thankfully, Alex pulled her aunt into an embrace, and Brenna observed the two of them whispering. But to her dismay, she saw Alex's face draw tight again as she kept glancing over at her. Once Marta had left, Alex seemed to shake off the tension, and she pulled Brenna on her lap and hugged her.

"Marta thinks you're sweet." Alex kissed her shoulder.

But Brenna felt there was something Alex was withholding, and when she saw Alex exchange a glance with Marissa and Angel, she was certain something was wrong.

Another hour later, Angel and Philip excused themselves. Angel kissed her cheek and held her at arm's length. "I'm glad to know you, Brenna. I know things have been hard for you. Alex told me. But seeing you here tonight, dancing and having fun, I see you're starting to embrace life again."

She stood speechless in his grip and gazed into his eyes, Alex's eyes.

He kissed her cheek once more. "Give yourself time, girl. We're all here for you. Remember that."

She watched him and Philip leave and wondered about what he'd said. And when she looked over at Alex, she saw her watching her with an expression that was hard to read. She couldn't tell if Alex was angry, sad, or scared.

The rest of them talked for another hour. Brenna told them about Anabel and Pedro as well as the mystery of the rosary and the San Miguel medal. Soon Justin began yawning and said he needed to rest and sober up for his shift. They all headed toward the office for their jackets and purses, and she said good-bye to her new friends, hugging each one, giving an extra special hug to Cassie.

Outside, Alex accompanied her to her Jeep and held her hand as they walked to the far end of the parking lot.

"Thank you for coming," Alex said.

"Thank you for asking."

"This was the best Thanksgiving ever."

"It was wonderful."

When they were a few feet from the Jeep, Alex turned to her. "I liked dancing with you, Brenna."

Brenna squeezed her hand. "Cassie was right, you're a good teacher."

Alex shrugged. "It helps to have a willing student." She looked pensive again and gazed up at the night sky. It was heavy with clouds, but the rain had held off for most of the day.

"What is it, Alex? You seem uptight tonight. Are you sure I haven't done something?"

Alex continued to gaze upward. "No, you're fine. It's just that..." She chuckled and shook her head.

"Just what?"

"If someone had asked me a few weeks ago if I believed two people in less than two weeks from such different worlds could..." She shook her head again. "This breaks all my rules, all my promises to myself not to rush in." She looked at Brenna. "I don't want to make promises I can't keep. I don't want to set you up, set me up for heartbreak. But more important, I don't want to get in the way of your healing."

"I am healing, Alex. Every day I'm getting stronger."

"I hope so."

Brenna saw the trepidation in Alex's eyes. "You're scared, aren't you?"

"Scared shitless," Alex said.

"Me, too." She traced her finger along the hem of Alex's single-strapped blouse, along the top of her shoulder. She had no idea where her confidence to do so came from. "You're beautiful when you dance." She watched the vein in Alex's throat pulse, the hollow of her neck quiver. "Absolutely beautiful."

"Brenna, I'm not sure we—"

But before Alex could finish, Brenna wrapped her arms around her neck and pulled her into a hard, closed-mouth kiss. But she lost dominance of the kiss when Alex pushed her against the Jeep, pulled her wrists to her sides, and pinned her in place. Alex controlled the kiss now, and Brenna had no choice but to surrender while her body flooded with lust. When the kiss ended and they continued to stand close, noses touching and their breathing ragged, Brenna was the first to speak.

"First a plumbing lesson, dance lessons, and now a kissing lesson. What will you teach me next?" She spoke as seductively as she knew how.

Alex kept her face close, searching her eyes. "Don't you know you've taught me something as well?"

"What could I have possibly taught you?"

"Courage, mi hermosa. Courage and strength."

As Brenna drove back to the property, she played her radio and sang along. She'd done more than survive her first Thanksgiving without Michael even though she'd missed him and felt the sting of his loss. She'd laughed and taken risks, overcome her shyness about dancing, asserted her desire to be with Alex, and had kissed her, not once, but many times. They'd stood against the Jeep for a long while kissing and whispering, and before she'd left, she'd asked Alex to come back to the house with her. But Alex had explained she was responsible for disassembling the fire pit and helping get the restaurant ready for the next day, Black Friday, when shoppers would be out in masses and stopping in for lunch. But Alex had suggested something which eased her disappointment.

"How about I come over tomorrow, early afternoon? I'll bring a box of leftovers and we can watch a game, maybe a few movies. And I'll bring my overnight bag if it's okay with you."

Brenna had felt her pulse quicken. "I'd love that."

"Then it's a plan. Now you drive home safely. It's been a few hours since you had a drink. You should be fine." Then she'd added, "And you know Johnny's in Glendale with his mom for the holiday, so you're going home to an empty house."

"I'm okay. Miguel's waiting for me. Besides, it's after two thirty in the morning. I doubt I'll hit any traffic, and it isn't raining at the moment." She'd given Alex another deep kiss before leaving.

Now, as she made the turn off the freeway onto the highway toward her property, she noticed Fernie's place was dark. She wondered about this—Patricia had told her the store was open twenty-four hours, even holidays. When she was minutes from the entry road, she reached inside her purse for her phone. She thought she'd give Alex a call and let her know she was home. That's when she noticed she had four missed calls and two voice mails. She slowed to retrieve them. The first message was from Jessica, wishing her happy Thanksgiving. Brenna chided herself. She'd been so excited all day about going to Alex's, she'd forgotten to call her sister. Then the next message came through from Sadie.

"Hi, Brenna, this is Sadie. I meant to call you last night, but I was up all evening making pies with my mom. Anyway, I happened to be over at the county archives in Phoenix and found this interesting document about Hadley Poulsen."

Brenna pressed the phone to her ear.

"Yeah, so anyway, you know I couldn't find his and Nelda's marriage license. I know you'd asked me to see if I could locate a copy, but they'd have been married out of state most likely. I don't know. Anyway, he applied for another marriage license about eight months after she died in nineteen twenty-five."

Brenna turned onto her access road and drove toward the house. She could see the glow of the porch light and was anxious to see Miguel.

"The application lists a nonresident, a woman named Anabel Gonzales."

Brenna's stomach lurched.

"And he'd also filed to adopt her child, too. It looks like…um, a ten-year-old boy, also a nonresident, named Pedro Gonzales."

Brenna stopped the Jeep in front of the house, turned off the engine and lights. But she remained in her seat.

"Anyway," Sadie's message continued, "looks as if the application for the marriage and adoption were both declined. I don't know why. I thought it was interesting because you'd told me about those people you were trying to help. And I thought you'd said their names were Anabel and Pedro. Kind of a weird coincidence, don't you think?"

Weird wasn't close to describing it.

"I know you're probably with family or friends for the day, but give me a call Friday and I can scan and email these things to you. Talk to you later." Sadie finished her message with a cheery voice.

But Brenna didn't feel cheery, not one bit. She pulled the phone away from her ear and stared at the screen while trying to wrap her mind around Sadie's words. The time on the phone read three fifteen. She climbed out of her Jeep and looked to find Miguel. He sat in the beam of the porch light with his golden eyes watching her. Then, as her eyes adjusted, she caught a glimpse of two bare feet, dirty and muddy. The dog was sitting while someone petted him.

"Miguel?" Brenna could barely speak his name; her throat seized and her tongue grew heavy.

When Miguel stood, she could see the person, a young boy, about ten years old. He watched her, and she saw he'd been crying. Right then, terror and fear snatched away her strength, and her legs threatened to buckle beneath her. Although it made no sense, she knew who the boy was.

"Pe-Pedro?" She sputtered his name.

The boy walked toward her. Without meaning to, she took a step away from him.

"Please," he said in an accented voice.

"What do you want?" She wept, her confusion intense.

"Help, please. I come to free my mother."

"Anabel?"

Pedro stepped off the porch and pointed upward. "She is in the house."

She looked, following his finger, and watched as a light came on in the upstairs room. Now she understood. She'd never been alone in the house. Anabel had been with her the entire time.

They were green eyes, not brown, which looked at her with such sadness her rational mind shouted he was a real flesh-and-blood boy, not a ghost or apparition from 1925. She began shivering. The air was not only colder, but also changed. An electric pulse charged around her, and an echo, an impression, a memory began to form. The light was on upstairs. It must be Anabel, but she wasn't at the window as she'd been the time before. Brenna looked again at the young boy with green eyes and dark hair. He was covered in mud, and stank.

"Pedro," she said as calmly as she could manage, "I'm going to call a friend of mine. She'll help you and your mother, okay?"

She brought her phone up and noticed the screen was black. She turned it on, then off, and the incandescent glow sparked and the screen reappeared. She speed-dialed Alex's number and brought the phone to her ear. Silence. She looked at the screen and saw no bars, no signal. She moved backward and to the side, holding her phone in the air, trying to get a signal, but none was to be found. The boy watched her, waiting. Then Miguel turned and focused his attention on the front door. The hackles on his back stood from his neck to his tail, and a deep guttural growl issued from his throat. Pedro stared at the window, and that's when Brenna heard the voices—a man's voice, a woman's voice. He was yelling, cursing. She was sobbing, begging.

Pedro began crying and turned to Brenna. "Again, it comes again. Please, help."

She glanced from him to the window where she thought she saw shadows, movement. When she looked again at Pedro, he'd changed. Where was the mud? He'd just been covered in mud. She'd seen it, smelled it. But he was not all that had changed. She took another step away from the house and saw, as before, it had been transformed. The windows were unbroken, no plastic sheeting. The frame was painted, the wood unweathered, and the screen door missing.

"What's going on?" She held her hand to her heart and swallowed the sick feeling in her stomach.

"It comes again." Pedro grabbed something around his neck and began to mutter prayers.

"What comes again? Pedro, you were just covered in mud and now you..." The boy fingered a small silver medal around his neck. "The medal. It's yours." The implication of what she saw knocked the air from her lungs, and she struggled for a breath.

He looked up from his prayers just as a piercing scream issued from the house, and Brenna saw Anabel appear in the window. She clawed at the window and cried out. Someone was attacking her from behind, yanking her by her hair.

"Mamá!" Pedro screamed, and his green eyes widened. "I get my uncles. Please stop him!" He ran toward the grove with Miguel following.

"Stop. Wait. Pedro, Miguel!"

Brenna ran after them, and as she did, she saw the glow of a campfire spark in the distance. The family had returned. She knew she needed to reach them, enlist their help to storm the house and free Anabel. But Anabel shrieked again. She stopped running and looked back. She could see shadowed movements in the window and hear the crashing, cursing, and begging. She glanced at her Jeep and back to the house. Someone was killing Anabel, and she realized she had no time to get help. She had to decide. Although Alex thought she was courageous, Brenna had never thought of herself as brave or heroic. She'd only once tempted death on that April morning when she'd run against the torrent of wind and flying glass and wood to reach her son who lay dying under the weight of his father's body and a heavy wooden pew. She'd leapt with all her strength, falling inches short of grabbing his little hand, which lay twisted away from his body. She'd crawled while the glass and splinters cut into her knees and hands until finally she'd clutched the little fingers, only to feel them go limp. Now, as she stared at the lighted window, she recognized whatever was in the house hurting Anabel could never be as terrifying as the experience she'd lived through months ago.

She saw for the first time the garage doors stood open and ran to the building. A lit kerosene lamp hung from a beam inside the door, and along the walls were garden tools, gas cans, and old tires.

She grabbed a shovel and ran back to the house. First she tried the front door, but it was locked. Anabel continued to shriek and plead. Brenna knew she was running out of time, so she faced the picture window and heaved the shovel over her shoulder and swung it through the glass, which shattered in one large sheet and fell in brittle shards to the porch and inside the house. She wasn't thinking of her own safety nor was she trying to make sense of the fact her furniture was missing. Instead, the interior of her house was decorated with an area rug and furniture that was not her own. No, those thoughts were of no use to her. She thought only of barging into that room and stopping whoever was attacking Anabel.

She ran, gripping the shovel, and bolted up the stairs two steps at a time. Halfway, she heard stomping and labored breathing. Although she couldn't see anyone, she felt a force and heard a man's grunting. She tried to push forward, but was shoved backward and tumbled down the steps. Her head slammed on the wooden floor, and she winced with pain and dizziness. But she wasn't going down without a fight. She swung her shovel wildly and blindly, determined to strike whatever had pushed her. But her shovel only whistled through the air, not landing a blow. She rolled to her side and tried to get to her feet, but her fall down the steps had shaken her and her legs gave way. She forced herself to her knees, using the shovel to steady herself, and saw the front door stood open. As she crawled toward the open door, she heard the muffled sound of grunts and curses. A man's voice. But when she peeked outside, she could see nothing but the eerie glow of the kerosene lamp hanging in the open garage.

She pulled herself to her feet, walked onto the porch, and listened. She could still see the campfire in the distance and wondered why Pedro hadn't returned with his uncles. Then the garage doors swung shut, and she heard the sound of heavy footsteps on gravel. Invisible footsteps from an invisible devil came her way. She scrambled off the porch and ran to the side of the house to hide and catch a glimpse of the unseen force. But she could see nothing. Finally, the footsteps tracked away from the house, and she sat panting and sweating with her back against the wall. Her head throbbed from her fall, and her scar burned. But the adrenaline rush dulled the pain just enough to give her the will to continue.

Then in the distance, she heard hoofbeats, the whinnying of horses, and men shouting. Someone was coming. She crept toward the garage, peeked inside, and in the flickering light, saw Anabel lying motionless. Brenna looked again at her Jeep. She could leave, find an open store, and call Alex. But soft moans, a gentle cry made her look again to see Anabel moving. Brenna slipped through the doors and approached her. She smelled the kerosene now as well as the sweat and blood that seeped from the injured body before her. She knelt and bit back her fear as she touched the pulse along Anabel's neck. And as Brenna reached, Anabel grabbed her hand.

"Mi hijo, mi hijo," she whimpered, trying to rise from the ground.

"Anabel? Who did this to you?" Brenna lifted her head. Anabel's eyes were swollen nearly shut, but still, Brenna caught a glimpse of their blackness.

Anabel focused on Brenna's face and tried to speak, but she managed only a grunt. She gripped her hand tighter, her own hands bleeding and oozing. Brenna gazed at her and tried not to shrink away from the bloody disfigurement of what she remembered had been a beautiful woman. Not only were Anabel's eyes swollen, but also her bottom and top lips were split open, the top one clear to the base of her broken nose. Her teeth were stained red with blood, and Brenna could see she struggled to breathe as blood pooled in her mouth. Along her hairline, a gash, clear to the bone, clotted with blood as fluid seeped from her splayed ears. Brenna shook as she wiped blood from Anabel's mouth. She knew she needed to get her into the Jeep and to a hospital.

But as she tried to lift her, she felt Anabel pull away and take both her hands.

"Please, my friend," Anabel said in a heavily accented voice. "My son, he will kill my son."

"Who? Tell me who did this." Brenna wept as she held the dying woman's hands. She could see how hard Anabel fought to hang on. She was a mother, like herself, a mother wanting desperately to protect her child. Then the sound of the massacre reached them. In the distance women and children screamed, men yelled, and the sound of gunfire and horses whinnying penetrated the walls of the garage.

Anabel opened her mouth and wailed, broken-hearted and beaten. "No! No! No! Que Dios nos ayude!"

"What is it? Tell me what's happening. Tell me what to do."

Anabel turned her head and managed to pry open an eye and focus on Brenna one last time. She attempted to smile through broken teeth, the deep gashes of her lips gaping wider.

"Please," she said as the last of her life drained from her. "We are as sisters now, you and I. Find my son...avenge our deaths... promise"—she choked on blood—"your promise...mi hermana...tu promesa."

Brenna closed her eyes and sobbed. "I promise." She realized Anabel held something, and when she pulled her hand away and opened her palm, she found a solid silver rosary resting there. "How?"

But Anabel didn't answer. Instead, she opened her mouth in a silent scream, looking past Brenna's shoulder.

"What is it?" Brenna asked, frightened.

"I thought I killed you, you filthy whore," a man snarled.

Brenna turned and caught a glimpse of a belt buckle and something black and threatening. It was a pistol, and it pointed right in her face. She felt the blast, the shockwave echoing and bouncing off her. She fell as a searing pain tore at the back of her head, and the sound of a freight train wind-tunneled through the church, shattering glass and splintering wood. She screamed for her son, screamed so loudly her throat burned. She reached him, and as she gripped his hand and met his eyes, he seemed to recognize her. He blinked, but when he opened them again, his eyes stared back at her, empty. She would've continued screaming but for the pain at the base of her skull driving her into blackness, tumbling her into oblivion.

❖

The first sensation she recognized was the gravel beneath her cheek. Then she heard the familiar whimper and felt a wet tongue across her face. There was that smell again—the reek of foul mud and rancid water. She opened her eyes to find a black nose poking her.

"Miguel?" She could barely speak. The pain radiated from her temple through her head and down her shoulder.

The dog clawed at her, swiping his massive and muddy paw across her.

"Ouch. Okay, okay." She rolled onto her back. That made the pain in her head worse. She blinked as the icy wind blew across her face. She covered her eyes with her hands and tried to remember what'd happened.

She'd been driving home from Thanksgiving. Alex had kissed her, and then Sadie's message…Brenna sat up. Had she run off the road while trying to fiddle with her phone? Had she crashed? But when she looked around, she saw she lay on the gravel by the garage. All around her were yellow shards of glass. The few remaining panes of glass, which had filled the small windows above the garage door, lay shattered around her. She looked at Miguel, who seemed to be watching her with concern, and noticed he was covered in mud. Her memory came rushing back right then—the muddy boy, his mother, the medal, the rosary. Anabel was dead. She'd held her hands as she lay dying. Then she remembered the shadow of the pistol pointed at her head. She raised her hand to her forehead. Her fingers went right to the wound, which ran along her temple and behind her ear. The injury felt moist and painful to touch, and when she looked at her hand again, she saw blood. A wave of nausea hit her, and she lurched, spitting and coughing. She'd been shot in the head, but how badly she couldn't tell.

She pulled herself to her knees, wobbled, and looked toward the house. It was as she knew it, old and peeling paint, with taped-up windows. She crawled to her cell phone on the ground a few feet from her. It had the full strength of bars and a signal, she noticed, but the time read seven thirty-eight in the morning. She'd lost four hours. She rose to a standing position, swooned, and caught herself against the garage. She leaned against it and forced herself to stay conscious. As she did so, she examined the doors and saw they were nailed shut. She touched her wound again. None of this made sense, she knew. The garage had been open, Anabel had been dying, she'd made her a promise. She began to untangle the events as a fine mist of rain began to fall. She looked at her dog...the mud...his face...those eyes.

"You know, don't you?"

He whimpered and nuzzled her hand.

"You're his dog. You know what happened to those people, to Pedro. You know who killed Anabel."

She laughed. It hurt because it rattled her head, but she had to laugh, remembering the night he'd shown up at her door and she'd fed him the only food she'd had on hand. What sort of ghost eats SpaghettiOs? When she tried to move away from the garage, toward her Jeep, she swooned and caught herself again. She realized she was hurt much worse than she'd first thought, and she knew she needed to get help, to get Alex. She steadied herself as she raised her phone and punched the speed dial. The phone rang so many times, she was sure it would go to voice mail. Alex was probably still asleep.

The call connected.

"You're up early." Alex's sleepy voice came through. "You wake up with a hangover or something?"

"Alex...my head...I'm bleeding."

"Brenna?"

"Anabel, Pedro...dead. Alex, please..." Her head swam, her stomach flipped and turned, making her feel weaker and more disoriented. Her knees gave out, and she collapsed.

"Brenna? Brenna?" Alex's voice shrieked through the phone as it lay feet away from Brenna's reach.

But she couldn't answer or call out, for she was fading, dying, she was sure. Finally dying, finally through suffering the loss of her little boy. As she slipped into unconsciousness, grateful to be done at last, she felt Miguel lay on top of her. The last thing she heard before she went under was a howl, a long resonant howl as if some great horn were sounding off in the distance.

"I love you, Mommy."

"I love you, too, baby." She kissed the top of his head and wept.

"Don't be scared. Daddy's with me." He began to pull away as he pointed down a sunlit road which wound through the grapefruit trees.

"Michael, stay with Mommy. Please, baby, don't leave me." She held him tighter, but he glided out of her arms like a strand of mercury, bright and liquid.

"It's okay, Mommy. I'm not afraid. You don't be afraid either."

"Michael, please." She sobbed and shivered in the cold wind.

She opened her eyes and turned her head, meeting the most beautiful golden eyes. Miguel licked her face. "Eww, you stink."

She pushed away, sat up, and grabbed her phone. It was after eight thirty in the morning. She'd been unconscious for only forty minutes. She touched her wound, but it was no longer bleeding. In fact, she felt no pain at all. Instead she felt revived, rested, and hungry. Right then, she heard the roar of an engine and tires screeching down her entry road. Alex's truck and another swung into her driveway, and Alex jumped from her vehicle and raced to her.

"Brenna!"

She'd been crying, Brenna could see.

"Keep her seated," Angel said as he ran to them. He was joined by Justin running over with his kit.

"What happened?" Alex cradled her.

"How did you know to come?" Brenna asked.

Alex leaned her against her shoulder while Justin shined a light in her eyes. "Don't you remember calling me? You were mumbling and then I heard you fall, and then there was this earth-shattering wail, a howl, or something," Alex said.

"Brenna, follow my finger. Can you track my finger?" Justin said.

She did as he asked, but she was confused.

"Did you hit your head, Brenna?" Justin cupped her head and palpating her skull.

"Here." She pointed to her temple. "But it doesn't hurt anymore."

Angel helped Justin pull her hair away, and they examined the area where she'd pointed. Then they leaned her forward, and Alex lifted her hair from her neck.

"There's no mark there," Angel said. "Are you sure you—"

"Brenna, where'd you get this scar?" Alex asked.

"I was hit by debris in the tornado. Took over thirty stitches to close it up."

"Let's get you inside." Angel and Justin hoisted her to her feet. "Check you out a bit more."

As they stepped through the front door, Brenna looked at Miguel. "You're a muddy mess. You stay here on the porch until I clean you up."

He tried to follow them inside, but Alex shooed him out, leaving the screen door open so he could sit and watch.

The men put her on the sofa, and Justin continued to check her vitals. But Angel motioned Alex out on the porch again and the two stood close together, whispering. After a few moments, they came back inside, and Angel sat next to her, taking her hand and smiling.

"Can you tell me about last night?" he asked. "Do you remember being at the restaurant?"

After she recounted the prior evening's events, Angel asked her the current year, the current president, the year she was born, and a few other factual questions. She answered them all correctly.

"Then I guess you'll live." He laughed, and for a moment, Brenna saw his face light up like Alex's.

"Good to know." She saw Alex watching her.

"Well you don't have a concussion," Justin said, packing his kit. "Blood pressure's fine, oxygen level's fine. But you need to see a doctor on Monday, get checked out. Will you do that?"

"Okay."

"Thanks, Justin." Alex hugged him. Then she hugged Angel. "Gracias, hermano. I owe you."

"Yes, thank you both," Brenna said. She felt embarrassed about all the fuss.

"No problem. I'm glad we were here to help." Angel smiled at her again, and then he turned to Alex and leaned in as he whispered something once more.

"Sí, lo haré," Alex answered him.

Brenna felt her face flush. She knew they were talking about her. Then Alex walked them to their truck, and the three stood in the soft rain and talked while she sat on the sofa and wondered what they were saying about her.

"I'm sorry," she said once Alex came back inside. "I didn't mean to get Justin and Angel involved. They're dressed for their shift. I didn't make them late, did I?"

Alex shook her head. Her hair hung loose, damp from the rain. She looked disheveled as if she'd just rolled out of bed. "They were heading in when I got your call. And no worries—they're happy to help. They're worried about you. So am I."

"Worried?" Brenna blew air from pursed lips. "Maybe you should be." She was beginning to doubt what she'd experienced. But it'd been too real to have been a tequila-induced hallucination, she was sure.

Alex sat, took her hands, and began to sob. "Brenna, I'm sorry I let you come home alone last night. I should've followed you."

"I'm fine, Alex, please don't cry." Brenna put her arms around her while she gained comfort from the clean sundried-linen fragrance clinging to Alex's hair and sweatshirt.

Alex continued to weep. "When you wouldn't answer…and that howl. I knew you were hurt and I almost called 9-1-1, but I was afraid Wilcox would hear the call over the radio and arrive before me. So I called Angel and he got Justin and raced over here to meet me and… I'm sorry. I shouldn't have let you come home alone. I don't know what I was thinking."

"It's okay, I'm fine. I can't explain it, but my head is fine."

Alex slipped to the floor and knelt while still holding Brenna's hands. "What happened? I don't understand what happened to you."

Brenna hesitated as the images of the tragedy flashed in one still-frame shot after the other in her mind. She could still smell Anabel's broken body, feel her bloody grip, hear her desperate plea.

"Does *pro-may-sah* mean promise?" Brenna asked, pronouncing the Spanish word as she remembered it from Anabel's lips.

"Yes." Alex frowned and wiped her nose. "Why do you ask?"

Brenna knew she had to tell Alex what happened, or what she thought had happened. But she suspected Alex wouldn't believe her and would chalk it up to the delusions of a grief-stricken mother who'd finally snapped. In fact, she was sure Alex and Angel had been discussing that very thought out on the porch while Justin had attended to her. Nevertheless, she had to try. She had to hope Alex would believe her because she'd promised Anabel, and she wasn't about to break that promise. And if Alex wouldn't believe her, how would she, on her own, be able to help Anabel and Pedro?

"Okay." She thought about how to begin and looked into Alex's brown eyes. "Okay," she repeated, "I need you to listen and try to understand. Please, I need you to keep an open mind."

"Go on, Brenna. I'm listening."

"Thank you. Let me tell you what I think happened."

Chapter Twenty

"...And I felt the gunshot, felt myself fall. But I don't remember after that," Brenna said. "When I opened my eyes Miguel was poking me, and I was certain I was bleeding. Then I passed out again, and well, now I'm fine."

She sat with Alex on the sofa. In the last twenty minutes as she'd recounted her story, Alex had barely blinked and neither had she nodded nor indicated one way or the other how she was receiving the tale. Miguel watched from the porch, and Brenna found it easier to look at him through the screen as she spoke rather than at Alex. She could see something in Alex's eyes, and it unnerved her.

"I'm not sure what happened after that," she continued. "I don't remember calling you, but I remember this strange sensation as I passed out again."

"What sensation?" Alex asked.

Brenna touched her temple where she was sure she'd been shot. "It was strange. I felt Miguel lie on top of me, and this is silly, but I think he howled. And then Michael was with me, and he was telling me not to be afraid. When I woke up, you and Angel and Justin were here."

The rain had started again with more force, and with the front door open, the sound of it hitting the gravel outside drowned out the silence that ensued. Alex held Brenna's hand and rubbed the bridge of her nose with the other while closing her eyes.

"You believe me, don't you?" Brenna asked.

"Yes, I believe you."

Brenna let the air out of her lungs and hugged her. "Thank you. I was worried you'd think I'd lost my mind."

"It's not your mind I'm worried about."

"I don't understand." Brenna could see Alex was now on the verge of crying again.

"I think you experienced those things just as you described them to me, right down to the last detail. I believe you experienced it all."

Brenna narrowed her eyes. "Then what's wrong?"

Alex shuddered, wiped her eyes. "Please understand, Brenna, I'm not discounting the details of your experience. It's only I doubt your interpretation."

"My interpretation? What does that mean? Those people were murdered on this property. Hadley Poulsen killed them all. Don't you see? Cassie's silly story, that stupid urban legend, had a nugget of truth in it after all. It wasn't Nelda he killed, but Anabel, her son, her entire family. They've been trapped on this property for all these years."

Alex stood and pulled Brenna up with her. "Go take a shower. Change out of your muddy clothes, and while you do, I'll give Miguel a bath. Then you can pack a bag and we'll go to my house. Miguel can come, too. He'll like my backyard. It's big."

"He won't leave this property, and I won't either, not until I've finished what she's asked of me." Brenna pulled away, realizing Alex intended to stop her from fulfilling her promise.

"Brenna, I need to get you away from this house, from this property. I need to get you someplace safe." Alex used her authoritative voice and held her by both wrists.

"You can't make me leave." Brenna tugged on Alex's grip. "I won't leave until I find Anabel and Pedro and the others. We have to find them, Alex."

"You need to get away from here!"

She now saw the true fear in Alex's eyes. Her hands trembled as she gripped her, and her lips quivered as she fought off tears. "There's something you're not telling me."

Alex shook her head and muttered in Spanish.

"Alex, tell me what the hell is wrong." She felt a new panic grip her, and she pulled her wrists free. "Tell me."

"My aunt, she saw it. Saw something clinging to you."

"What does that mean?"

"It means something is trying to destroy you, Brenna. Some evil has attached itself to you. You're cursed—el susto, the fright. Whatever it is, Marta saw it around you, hovering around you like some black cloak about to swallow you whole."

A cold stab pierced Brenna's chest and her throat tightened as she backed away. "What the hell are you talking about?"

Alex spoke through shallow gulps of breath as she wept. "You told me you saw your son and husband die. You saw them, Brenna. That sort of terror sticks to you, weakens you. And now you're vulnerable to anything that wants to attach itself to you. This Anabel, this woman you think you saw, you don't know really what you saw. It could be a demon, some evil spirit trying to draw you into its own hell."

"She is not a demon, she's a mother. A mother who has lost her son."

"That's what it wants you to believe. It knows you're missing your own son, and it's using it against you."

"Bullshit!" Brenna hurried to the bedroom where she retrieved the two silver pieces she'd put in her nightstand drawer the day before. She returned to the living room and shoved them in Alex's face. "These are religious symbols, Alex. Pedro prayed with his. Anabel held hers in her hands as he beat the life out of her. Why would demons do that?"

"The devil is a tricky fucker, Brenna."

"I don't believe in the devil. I don't believe in God either. But I know those people need my help."

"Madre de Dios!" Alex flung her arms and hands as she spoke. "You don't even know if it is those people. It could be deceiving you, using your own sympathy against you. Don't you see? You ran into that family a week ago and got frightened out of your wits. And since then you've been preoccupied with finding an heir to the silver and—"

"It's all here, Alex. All the clues," Brenna insisted. From the kitchen counter, she grabbed the stack of documents and photographs she'd been obsessing over the last few days. Like the silver, she brandished them in Alex's face. "I know what happened. Hadley killed them. I don't know why, but he did. Maybe Anabel refused to marry him after Nelda died. Maybe he flew into a rage because she loved someone else. Maybe he thought she was a whore!" She sucked in her breath, caught herself on the counter. A clearer vision of what had happened last night rushed back to her. "He called her...me...a whore. He called me a whore." Her head began to swim again, and she felt as if she might throw up.

Alex pulled the documents and photos from her and set them on the counter. "Brenna, look at me. Please look at me." She took her shoulders.

Brenna held her head and shivered as she recalled Hadley's cruel voice condemning Anabel, or was it her?

"I need you to listen to me." Alex shook her.

But Brenna continued to cover her eyes.

"I need to get you out of here. If I have to, I'll pick you up and drag you. But I'm not letting you stay a moment longer."

"Her blood is on the walls upstairs." Brenna fell against Alex's shoulder. "She's real, Alex. She's not a demon. She needs me and I won't abandon her. You have to help me because I can't do this by myself."

Alex stifled a sob. "There's no blood upstairs, Brenna. I've been in that room, remember? It's just another trick."

"Behind the wallpaper." She took Alex's hand and pulled her up the stairs. "I'll show you. You'll believe me. You've got to believe me."

Upstairs, she threw open the door and tugged Alex over to the corner by the window. Rain had come through the plastic sheeting, and the room smelled musty and acrid. She pointed to one of the dark spots.

"See? It's a hand. Her hand." Brenna placed her own over the splattered outline. "And look." She pulled away another strip of paper. When she did, she revealed another dark smear. "More of her blood." She turned to Alex. "He beat her in this room, Alex. Beat her so badly she was bleeding from her mouth and nose and ears. And her hands, her hands were bloody, and she was clawing at the wall, at the window for someone to see her, to help her."

Alex's mouth hung open, and her eyes gaped wide as she made the sign of the cross.

"I need you to help me, Alex. She's lost her boy. I know what she feels, I know how she hurts. And she called me her friend, her sister." Brenna touched Alex's arm. "She needs me as much as I need her. I need to help her and I can't do this without you."

"What do you want me to do?"

"Uncover her body. She's in the garage under the concrete slab."

"And if there is no body? Will you come back to town with me?"

Brenna was sure they'd find Anabel's remains. So to buy herself time, she said, "Yes, I'll go back with you."

Alex held her arms around herself and shivered. "Go take a shower then. I'm going to call Marissa and have her bring out my bag and some food. I'm going to call my aunt, too. She can help you, Brenna, if you'll let her."

"Help me how?"

"She has her ways. If you trust her, she can get you through this."

"And Anabel? Can she help her?"

Alex led her from the room and down the stairs. "Yes, bella, if Anabel is who you think she is, Marta will help as best she can. But right now, all I care about is keeping you safe."

❖

While Brenna showered, Alex washed Miguel. Afterward, they sat on the sofa together waiting for Marissa to show, sipping coffee and watching television, a football game, with the volume low.

"Did you tell Marissa what happened?" Brenna asked.

"No, I left it that you'd passed out and hit your head."

"It's just as well. Your whole family will think I've gone off the deep end."

"You haven't gone off the deep end, Brenna. And if you do, I'm diving in right after and saving you. I won't let you go under."

Miguel sat at Brenna's feet, and he lifted his head and laid it on her knee while he watched her with his bright eyes. She petted him, taking comfort in his calm gaze.

"He's been trying to show me this whole time. But what I don't understand is why the grandmother said he wasn't a dog."

Alex furrowed her brows. "The old woman with the family? Tell me again what she said to you the night you saw them."

"That Pedro had gone to the house to free his mother, that he hadn't returned," Brenna recalled. "She also said they couldn't leave without them. I understand now. It's strange but it's almost as if they're all caught in some sort of weird purgatory, as though the nightmare just keeps repeating and repeating"—she closed her eyes—"and repeating. I know that feeling. The nightmare just never stops."

Alex put her arm around her and kissed her hair. "I know."

Brenna looked upward. She knew Anabel was in that room even now, waiting and watching. "She's been trying to contact me from the first day. I saw her in the window the day Cassie and I first came out."

"Did the grandmother say anything else to you?"

"No, well...yes, she said something strange I didn't understand."

"In Spanish?"

"No, she touched my face and said she could see how sad I was as well as..." Brenna let her words trail as she thought about her encounter over a week ago. What was it the old woman had said? About her sorrow, her anger, calling him back? "Well, damn." She went to the kitchen counter and began flipping through the stack of papers and photos. She brought them over to the sofa and spread them on the coffee table. "Look. This is Hadley." She pointed to the Poulsen family photo. "She told me I'd called him back, my anger had called him back."

"The grandmother told you this?"

"Yes. He's in the grove, Alex. I've sensed him there and so has Miguel."

Alex rubbed her forehead. "Por Dios! Brenna, this is dangerous shit."

Brenna touched the place she'd been shot. "Yes, Alex, I know."

Marissa showed up two hours later, bringing with her Alex's overnight bag and a box of leftovers from the day before. She and Alex spoke on the porch while Brenna heated plates of food, and then Marissa said good-bye to head back to the restaurant to help with the crowds. But before she left, she hugged Brenna and told her to please trust her mother, Marta. Brenna understood Alex must've related the entire story to her.

"You said earlier Marta could see darkness around me," Brenna said after Marissa had gone. "Is she a psychic or something?"

They were eating their meal at the sofa while the television still murmured at a low volume with another football game airing.

"Not really a psychic, more of a healer," Alex said.

"I don't know if I believe in curses, but I guess I've felt as if my whole life has been one big plague. First my parents, then meeting Debra, then losing Michael."

"Debra?"

"The woman I told you about, the one from my church."

"Right." Alex wiped her mouth and set her plate away. "I'm not sure it's an actual curse like an hechizo. There are other maladies, afflictions we can bring on ourselves. Seeing something terrible or having intense anger can harm us as well."

"I guess I have both of those." Brenna lowered her head. It was true, she knew. She'd not only been dealing with her grief over Edward and Michael, but also a penetrating rage that sometimes boiled over. She was angry at many things—at her parents for dying, at her sister for sweeping her off to marry Edward, at Edward for his mild manner and lack of passion, at Debra for blaming her and demanding she leave Michael, at her church, her minister, the gaggle of gossiping church ladies, and at fate for taking her son. But most important, she was angry with herself, feeling responsible for Michael's death. She maneuvered into Alex's arms and rested her head on her shoulder. She stared at the television, but paid it no attention.

"Tell me about your aunt. How does she heal? How will she help me and Anabel?"

Alex began to explain how the magical and mystical were embedded in her Mexican culture, a mix of ancient and indigenous practices mingled together with Catholicism. The healers, many of them women, were those who understood the use of plants and herbs as ways to right the body, mind, and soul. They were revered and sought out for all manner of healing from digestive and menstrual disorders, to more serious maladies such as extreme fright or a curse like the evil eye.

"Marta is a yerbera and a curandera," Alex said. "She's well-regarded in our community and considered quite powerful." She lifted Brenna's face. "I suppose all this sounds fantastic to you, an outsider. But believe me, I've seen the results of her healing many times."

"And how did she acquire her powers?" Brenna had never been superstitious and certainly never cared for anything religious, but she believed Alex and trusted her.

"She is, as I told you, my mother's twin. She was born first and was always the stronger of the two. But I don't know why she is the way she is. Some say it's because she absorbed her mother's, my grandmother's, wisdom when she died. When she was still a young girl living in Mexico, a man, a curandero, approached her and told her he'd had a dream about her and he was required to teach her his ways before he died."

"So she's like a shaman."

"Yes, something like that."

"When you spoke with her on the phone, did she indicate how she would help?"

Alex held her tighter. "She will do all she can for those lost souls, but what I really care about is her helping you. I won't lose you to this darkness. I won't let you go."

The rain pattered on well into the afternoon. The two continued to sit on the sofa and talk, waiting for Marta to call back. When she did, she told Alex she wouldn't be able to make it out to the property until the next evening and suggested they come back to town. But Alex told her aunt that Brenna was determined to remain at the house. Against Marta's better judgment, and Alex's, too, Brenna had committed herself to stay and to see about uncovering Anabel's remains the next morning. And Alex would not leave her to face the task alone.

By late afternoon Brenna could hardly keep her eyes open. "I'm tired. I think I'll go take a nap if you don't mind."

"That's a good idea." Alex kissed her forehead.

"You want to join me?"

Alex chuckled. "I think one of us needs to stay on guard."

"She won't harm us, Alex. I'm sure of it."

"You may be sure, bella, but I'd rather keep my eyes open. Besides, I need to call Johnny and see about him meeting us tomorrow morning with a circular saw so we can cut away the garage doors."

"You're going to tell him?"

"Like I've told you before, he's a good guy. We can trust him."

Brenna went to her room with Miguel following. She could hear the new furnace blowing, fending off the cold and damp in the house, but still she buried herself under blankets and cuddled against Miguel. She wondered, as she drifted off to sleep, where Alex planned on sleeping that night. On the sofa? With her? And she was amazed at herself for even having those thoughts given what she'd lived through in the past twenty-four hours.

She opened her eyes to a dark room, but the flicker of the television screen filtered into the bedroom through the open door. Her nightstand clock beamed nine o'clock in the evening. She'd slept the entire day.

She rolled over and faced the wall and considered going back to sleep. But she felt Miguel wag his tail, thumping it on the bed. She turned over to see Alex sitting close. Her hair hung around her shoulders, and her face was hidden in the shadows with the television's glow backlighting her.

"You let me sleep the whole day," Brenna said.

Alex touched her face.

Brenna shivered. "I should turn up the heat. Your hand is freezing."

Alex stroked her cheek.

"Did you talk to Johnny? Tell him the whole story?"

Alex didn't respond. Instead she fiddled with something in her lap.

Brenna reached and felt her son's music box in Alex's other hand. "That's Michael's. He was my little sunshine. The light of my life."

She saw Alex bob her head as if she were acknowledging that thought. Then she felt Alex's hand move to pull back the painter's tape, which secured the sprung latch.

"Alex, please don't. I can't bear to hear that song."

But Alex ignored her and lifted the lid. The sorrowful tune began to play as she leaned forward, close to Brenna's face.

"Your promise. Do not fail me."

Brenna flailed in her bed as she clambered out of her blankets just as Alex appeared in the doorway and flipped on the lamp.

"Brenna, who are you talking—" Alex fell back against the door and crossed herself with shaking hands.

Anabel swirled away from the bed while Miguel hopped down and went to her side. She watched Brenna and Alex, turning her head from side to side.

Brenna held her chest, feeling her heart racing and her throat constricting. She stared at Anabel and blinked. She wasn't bloody and broken, but whole and dressed in a white linen gown with a sheer shawl drawn around her head and shoulders. When Michael's music box began another cycle of the melody, Brenna shut it and glanced at Alex who'd gone ashen in the face. She turned once more to Anabel and was snared by the power of her dark gaze. The woman was beautiful, hypnotically beautiful.

"It was you. You kept opening it," Brenna said.

Anabel nodded.

"You know it was my son's. You know I've lost him."

Again Anabel nodded.

"Brenna," Alex said as she held her position, as if transfixed by Anabel's specter.

"It's okay, Alex. She doesn't want to harm us. She only needs our help. Isn't that right? You need me to uncover your body and your family's. I know where you are. In the garage. And your family, they're under the tennis court where their houses once stood."

Anabel nodded once more.

"But your son, Pedro, I don't know where he is."

"Ayúdame, por favor. Tu promesa," Anabel said.

Brenna looked at Alex who translated. "She says please help her, your promise."

"I'll keep my promise, Anabel." Brenna got up from the bed and came close to her. "I'll find Pedro."

Anabel turned to Alex, seemed to consider her a long moment, then said, "Hermana, venganza. Ayúdame. Mi venganza."

"Shit," Alex sputtered and crossed herself once again.

Anabel looked at Brenna. "Venganza," she repeated and swirled and thinned, dissipating into nothingness.

For a beat, the two stared at where she'd been. Then Miguel came over to Brenna and leaned against her leg. She cocked her head and looked into his eyes. When she looked at Alex, she was gaping at Brenna and the dog.

"I told you she doesn't want to harm me," Brenna said. "You can see, can't you, how much she needs me?"

Alex heaved and pointed to where Anabel had stood.

Brenna went to her, taking her into her arms. As she held her, she felt Alex trembling. "What did she say to you there at the end?"

Alex tried to speak, shuddered once more before answering, "She said, *Sister, revenge. Help me. My revenge.*"

"Her revenge?" Brenna shook her head. "But he's dead. Hadley Poulsen is dead."

"I don't know, Brenna. I'm just telling you what she said. She wants revenge."

Brenna grew still and her eyes widened. "His son, the friends, Owen Brock. Oh my God, Alex." She pulled away and ran to the kitchen and returned with the stack of documents and papers, placing them on the floor, arranging and rearranging.

"What are you doing?" Alex asked.

Brenna stood and pointed to the array of papers. "She's asked others before me. Others who didn't do as she requested."

"I don't understand. What are you getting at?"

Brenna picked up the family photograph and considered the frail image of the young boy who grew up to be Lanny Poulsen. "This family and property have seen more tragedy than we've realized."

"What does that mean?"

"There've been others, I think. Others she's tried to convince to help her. But they didn't listen." Brenna leveled her gaze at Alex. "Even if I didn't care for her, I'd be compelled to help her. I have no choice now." She weighed her words, but decided to speak the obvious. "If I don't, I'll end up dead like the others."

Alex faltered on her feet and let out a muted cry.

CHAPTER TWENTY-ONE

It took some convincing on Brenna's part to make Alex calm down and see reason. She kept repeating Anabel would not harm them if they did as she requested, but Alex was frantic and kept demanding they leave right then, to leave the dog even if he refused to go with them.

"She called you sister, too, Alex. She begged you to help. We can't abandon her," Brenna said. "And even if we left the property, it won't matter. She has a farther reach than you'd expect."

"What are you talking about?"

"Let me show you."

Brenna pulled Alex to the bed and began to weave together a tragic tale, spun out of the fragments of events she'd pieced together from the material Sadie'd found. First she showed Alex the newspaper report on Dallin Poulsen's suicide. She followed with three news blurbs about Dallin's friends who'd returned from war with him, and who'd gone to work for the Poulsen family. Shortly after Dallin's death, each of them in turn had met with tragedy and untimely death from accidents, everything from being hit by a train, drowning in the Salt River, to falling from a ridge in the Superstition Mountains. Alex listened, squirming on the bed and glancing out the doorway toward the stairs. But as Brenna continued to talk, she started to settle down.

"What war? World War One?" Alex asked.

"That's right." Brenna retrieved her laptop from the living room and typed a few words. She studied something she found on the Internet and turned back to Alex. "The four of them fought in the Battle of

Argonne Forest. It says here it was one of the bloodiest battles our country has ever seen. Known for something called the Lost Battalion where over half the men were killed or went missing. Dallin and his three friends were some of the survivors. And when they returned to the States, they came home to work in his father's citrus grove."

"And you think he knew about the killings?"

"I do. And I think Anabel tried to get them to do something about it, to find Pedro, to reveal the crime. But they ignored her, so she killed them."

Alex gulped.

"And look here," Brenna said. She picked up another article off the floor. "The property was managed by Nelda's brother for a time before Lanny was old enough to take over. After growing up, he returned to the property, married, and tried to run the grove. But it failed constantly. Then his wife died giving birth to his second child, who died a few days after."

"Anabel did that?"

"I'm not sure. But it was tragic nevertheless. Lanny had to have known what his father did. Perhaps Anabel wanted him to come forward when he reached manhood, but he didn't. So I think she punished him."

Alex picked up the rough outline Brenna had made days ago. "But according to your timeline, he was only a boy at the time of the murders. Why would she punish him?"

"Like I said, she wants this crime uncovered and her boy found." Brenna handed Alex another document. "And look here. I think your creepy deputy sheriff and his equally unsavory brother know something."

Alex read the paper and sighed. "So Lanny Poulsen's only surviving child, a daughter, returns to the property years later with her husband, Evan Wilcox, to raise her two sons and restore the family business."

"Yes, but again, the trees underproduce, and they can't keep any workers. Migrant families come and in a short time leave, refusing to return. Fernie told me the other day the working conditions were terrible. He had aunts and uncles who slaved under Wilcox, apparently. Then for no obvious reason, Lanny's daughter has a breakdown and is put into a mental hospital in Phoenix where she later hangs herself. And her husband has a heart attack a month later out in the grove."

Alex circled the rest of the papers and photographs. She rubbed her neck as she bent and read something, then stood and circled some more. "You think Marcus and Julian know what their great-grandfather did?"

"I'm not sure."

"And this Owen Brock, the caretaker?" Alex pointing to the man's obituary.

"When Lanny took his two orphaned grandsons and moved to Scottsdale, Owen was put in charge of the place. He'd worked for the Poulsens since he was a teenager. He must've known about the murders."

Brenna contemplated the arrangement of clues before her, thinking she needed to see Lanny Poulsen even more urgently than before. He must know where Pedro was buried, and she wondered if Cassie had come up with a good scheme to get her an audience with him. But of course, now it wasn't to question him about the names of migrant farm workers who'd been employed by his father, but rather about a long-forgotten massacre which had wiped out an entire family. She looked upward, thinking once again about Anabel there in the room, about the bloodstains behind the atrocious wallpaper.

"I don't think Owen or Lanny was necessarily at fault for their deaths," she said. "They were too young, too innocent. But I think they knew, and I think she tried to convince them to help her as well, but they didn't. She grew impatient, and she punished them. Owen died in that garage while he covered her unmarked grave with concrete. He was covering her up, covering up everything, and she wasn't happy."

Alex lifted her by her shoulders and turned her so they were face to face. "How will we find her son?" Alex asked. "You told me he wasn't with the family, and she doesn't know either. Am I supposed to dig up the entire property?"

"I'll dig myself if I have to, anything to end her suffering."

Alex hugged her. "Damn if you aren't stubborn. Stubborn and brave."

Brenna laughed and stood back. "That's quite the compliment coming from the woman who broke a skinhead's jaw."

Alex shook her head. "I act rashly out of anger. But you, mi hermosa, drove across the country alone, went out to a dark grove by yourself to confront strangers, and swung shovels at evil spirits. Not to mention you shoot tequila as if it's lemonade."

Brenna laughed again.

"You have some big cojones, mujer," Alex said, holding Brenna's face. "Courage like I've never seen before."

She gazed into Alex's eyes. She saw the admiration there, and she hoped something else as well. "I haven't always been this way. That's a recent development." She remembered her old self, the quiet and docile girl who'd been easily led into a loveless marriage, the woman who'd allowed herself to be seduced into a forbidden affair.

"Well, I like this development." Alex stroked her hair.

"The old Brenna was a pushover."

"Is that right?"

"She let other people make decisions for her and never asked for what she wanted."

"I see. And does she know what she wants now?"

Brenna sucked in a breath. Alex was flirting outright. "I know exactly what I want." She pulled Alex into a kiss, forcing her tongue against hers, sucking on her lower lip, and biting it as she pulled away.

Alex's eyes went wide and her chest heaved.

"I want to please you, Alex. You'll show me how, won't you?"

Alex began to answer, stuttering out some incomprehensible sound.

"You'll teach me?" Brenna pulled Alex by the hand toward the bed. "Like dancing, you'll teach me how to move, how to please you?"

"Yes, but..."

"But what?"

Alex pointed upward. "Anabel. She's in the house and..." She pointed to Miguel who'd jumped up on the bed. "And that dog. I can't make love with you when that dog is watching. It's all kinds of wrong."

"That's not just a dog."

"That's what has me worried."

Brenna turned to him. "Miguel, give us privacy."

He jumped down, went to the living room, and curled at the base of the stairs.

"Okay?" She pulled on Alex's sweatshirt.

"Are you sure?"

"Very sure."

Brenna moaned as Alex wrapped her arms around her and began kissing her, tugging at her jeans as Brenna tugged at Alex's. They fell on the bed while they scooted all the way out of their clothes. At one point, she tried to reach and switch off the lamp, but Alex pulled her down.

"I want to see you, to watch you move," Alex said.

"But, Alex, I've had a child. My body is—"

"Stop." Alex held up her hand. "You're beautiful. I haven't stopped thinking about you since the moment I saw you. The way you blush, the way you tug your hair, your sad smile." She began weeping, and she wiped her eyes as she gazed at her. "You broke my heart the first time I saw you, Brenna. Your sorrow, your despair. I wanted nothing more in the world than to take your pain from you. And that day, when I drove you out into the trees for the first time, ay, bella, mi hermosa, you looked so small and broken standing in the shadows of those trees. And all I could think was I wanted to bring light back into your life, sunshine and joy once again. To see you smile with sincere joy. And I have thought of nothing else since."

"And you have brought sunshine back into my life." With that statement, Brenna gave herself over, letting Alex lead.

But unlike dancing, Brenna had had some experience with a woman, and lacked any hesitation. Still, she was surprised—although she wondered why she should be. Alex had after all much more experience than she did. She couldn't help but be amazed at the way Alex skillfully built her excitement as she whispered into her ear, sometimes in English, other times in Spanish. She could hear herself moaning at Alex's touch, as she stroked her sides and along the inside of her thighs. Alex teased her until she could've brought her legs together and squeezed, certain she'd climax from that movement alone. But there would be no rush. Alex would take her time and continue the slow tortuous buildup, working Brenna's anticipation higher. And as if Alex held marionette strings, Brenna began raising her hips in a steady rhythm, aching for Alex to touch her.

"Please," she said into the mane of dark hair covering her face. "I need you."

Alex must've thought she'd played long enough because she instantly went inside her, moving and pushing, pulling and gliding. Brenna cried out and met those fingers halfway, thrusting into them as they thrust back. And when Alex curled her fingers and crooked her elbow at just the right angle to allow a steady in-and-out motion,

Brenna convulsed, close to release. She panted with an open mouth and felt herself reaching the top more quickly than she'd expected, sensitive from the foreplay. This was nothing like the monotonous sex she'd had with her husband, nothing like the awkward and clumsy lovemaking with Debra. This seemed fluid, natural, and right.

"How are you doing that?" she asked, not understanding how Alex prolonged her building pleasure.

She saw Alex smile just before she bent her head and began teasing her nipples with her tongue while at the same time her thumb began to stroke her as her fingers moved in and out. That was all Brenna needed, and a blast of heat shot through Alex's fingers and tongue, sending her into a meltdown as the first wave of her climax overtook her followed by another, dragging out her repressed desire and need, milking every ounce of pleasure and sensation from her. She was screaming, she was sure. That had to be her voice, she knew. And she could hear Alex, too, moaning as she held her while her fingers kept moving until she'd convulsed so intensely she clamped down and managed to turn to her side, closing herself. She gripped Alex's forearm, felt the muscles and tendons tighten as her long fingers moved. She held her arm, slowing her, trying to pull back. Finally, Alex stopped her movements and simply lay rigid inside her, filling her and echoing back the pulsing of her inner walls. Brenna's breath came in ragged gulps and her head felt light and dizzy. Alex was still inside her, but she was cradling her now, kissing her cheeks, whispering something in Spanish.

She took a long breath. "Is it supposed to feel that way? That hard, for that long?"

"When you truly care about someone, that's how it feels." Alex pulled out and lay on top, kissing her. Then rising on her elbows, she showed a cocky smile. "Don't think I'm done with you. I've only gotten started." She kissed Brenna again and began kissing her neck, her shoulders, along the crook of her elbow, her breasts, and hips until she rested between her legs.

Brenna watched Alex's slow descent, knowing what was coming. "Alex, I'm not sure. I can usually have only one." She felt her cheeks flush for having admitted her limitation.

"Don't be so sure." Alex parted her. "Now lie back and let me have you." She held one of Brenna's breasts, her other hand entering her again.

Brenna moaned as Alex's strong tongue touched her and began to move over her. Any anxiety she might've had about her inability to climax a second time dissipated as she felt herself building to the top again. It was a slower buildup, but it was coming. Alex was doing this to her, and she couldn't stop it, didn't want to stop it, and Alex's tongue showed no sign of weakening or slowing. She let her body go and allowed Alex to drive her again into another powerful orgasm. She cried out a guttural, animallike cry as the pleasure, verging on the unbearable, rippled through her body. She held Alex's head, pulling her hair, and arched her back. Her body was no longer her own, she realized. She'd given over not only the physical properties, but also the secret parts that cried out to belong to another. No matter what, from that point on, she knew she belonged to Alex. Only Alex.

In the aftermath of the climax, Brenna curled into a fetal position as Alex held her in her arms and comforted her. They lay that way a long while, whispering and giggling, stroking and kissing, breathing in the comfort of each other's scent. Then, although she should've been tired from the experience Alex had put her through, Brenna felt a rush of energy and pulled herself on top.

"Brenna, it's okay. You don't have to," Alex said.

"Yes, I do. I want you." Brenna began to imitate Alex's moves.

Alex's breath hitched in her throat.

"Like this?" Brenna asked.

"Yes."

"And this?" She was heady with the sensation of being in control of Alex's body.

"Yes, yes, like that." Alex closed her eyes and lifted her hips to the rhythm of Brenna's touch.

But Brenna didn't need instruction. She knew what to do because she'd paid close attention to the way Alex had touched her. She felt elated and proud to be the one to give her this feeling, that Alex was accepting it and allowing her to lead. And it wasn't long before Alex cried out her name, arched and bucked. And as Alex had done to her, she didn't stop until Alex had grabbed her wrist and pulled her away. She felt Alex's walls pulsing around her fingers, and she watched and waited until Alex was able to focus once more.

"I don't think I expected this from you." Alex panted for a breath.

Brenna smiled and began sliding down her body.

Alex tried to wave her off. "You don't have to mimic me down to the last…" She groaned then whimpered as Brenna moved into her with her tongue.

The sound of Alex's vulnerability drove Brenna crazy with desire, and she concentrated with unusual intensity and vigor. It wasn't long before Alex cried out and bucked up from the bed once more. When she finally stopped and climbed Alex's body, she was lightheaded with the exhilaration.

"That's an incredible feeling, giving that to you." She kissed Alex along her neck.

"Yes it is…incredible…*you're* incredible." Alex gulped and swallowed.

Brenna propped on her elbow and smiled, watching Alex and adoring every movement, gesture, and sound.

Alex simmered down and gazed at her. "What?"

"I don't think I'm done," Brenna said with an apologetic smile. She craved the power of Alex's touch and had found the confidence to ask directly for what she wanted, no longer fearing her body would be unresponsive.

Alex wrinkled her brow. "Are you serious? You are! Por Dios, Brenna! You're gonna kill me." She laughed and rolled her over, positioning herself behind, pulling Brenna's bottom against her and cupping one of her breasts while sliding fingers up the inside of her thigh.

Brenna squealed when Alex moved her into position, and now she waited, turning her head and looking over her shoulder. She saw Alex lick her lips. "I'm not sure I know this move," she said and giggled.

"It's like dancing, bella. Relax and let me move you, and if you're a good girl, I'll let you lead next time."

Well into the night they continued, and their lovemaking was indeed like a dance, lilting and rhythmic as they easily transitioned from one position to another, from one leading while the other followed and back again. Finally, as the early hours of the morning approached, Brenna felt sleep tugging. The events of earlier, Anabel's unexpected visit, and now the intense lovemaking had left her consumed. Alex allowed her to switch off the lamp, pulled her head to her breast, and stroked her hair.

"Sleep now, mi amor, sleep. But no more nightmares for you, not while you're in my arms."

Brenna relaxed into Alex's embrace. She welcomed the sleep and the peace that came from knowing she was safe and cared for. It was everything she'd ever wanted, everything she'd ever dreamed. And those shadows which had hung about her began to break apart. Even the deep anger and guilt felt lighter as they diluted and thinned under the purity of Alex's love and light. But she stirred from her near sleep as she heard Miguel move out by the stairs. She sat up and looked at the clock. It was three fifteen in the morning. Just then she felt a stirring and peered into the darkness as a soft shimmer began to grow before her. Alex turned away and began snoring. Miguel hopped onto bed, his eyes glowing golden. And now Anabel stood beside the bed looking at her. Brenna held her gaze, mesmerized by the depths in the woman's eyes, the pure blackness and beauty. Anabel touched her cheek with a cool hand, moved her hand to Brenna's heart, and then to the music box on the nightstand. But she didn't open it this time. Instead she smiled, almost sadly it seemed, and scattered into a thousand sparks of light as if a dandelion had been caught in the wind.

Brenna wiped the sudden sweat from her brow. She stared into the dog's eyes and listened to Alex's soft snore. It was the time, she realized, the time it had come before. Yet the house was quiet. There were no signs, no echoes of the tragedy. And she wondered, the grandmother had said she'd called him back. Perhaps, she thought, he would not come while love filled her heart. She spooned Alex and nestled against her back. As she began to fade once more into sleep, she touched her cheek, then her heart while remembering the sensation of Anabel's cool hand. At that moment she understood she'd come to love not one, but two women in a matter of weeks.

Chapter Twenty-two

B renna stood away from the flying bits of wood as Alex and Johnny labored to cut out the doors on the garage. Miguel sat at her feet. It was early afternoon, and the rain had retreated, leaving plenty of sunlight to complete their mission. But she kept checking the time on her phone. It was taking longer for Alex and Johnny to get the doors down than she'd anticipated, and she wanted to get to Anabel, to show her she was serious about keeping her promise. At first she'd suggested they simply demolish the entire structure, but Alex had insisted they leave the garage intact if they could.

"If we do find her remains," Alex had said, "it would be a good idea to have them protected. The county medical examiner and her forensic team will need to do a thorough investigation, and we don't want her unmarked grave compromised by the weather or scavenging animals."

Brenna had agreed that made some sense, and now she waited and watched as the two worked to remove the doors. Twenty minutes later, Alex set the saw on the ground, wiped her face, and then together, she and Johnny brought the doors out and maneuvered them to the side of the building. Brenna stared into the dim space almost expecting to see Anabel standing there.

"You check for spiders," Alex said to Johnny.

"Sure, Boss."

Brenna came close to her while Johnny was inside shining a flashlight. She wiped sawdust from Alex's cheek, and noticed she looked apprehensive. "You okay?"

"I'm fine," Alex said. "Just don't care much for snakes and spiders, especially the spiders."

Brenna clicked her tongue.

"What?" Alex turned to her.

"And you were trying to be all tough about that very thing the first day I met you, telling me not to worry, that you'd take care of it."

"I said my guys would take care of it."

"You're really afraid of spiders?"

Alex averted her eyes. "It's the legs. Those creepy, disjointed legs."

"All clear." Johnny came out, pulling spiderweb from his hair.

"No spiders?" Alex asked.

"Smashed a few black widows, but most of the webs were abandoned," he said.

Brenna looked at her, saw it was a true phobia, and regretted teasing. "It's okay, Alex. I'll go check." She took the flashlight from Johnny, entering the garage before Alex could protest.

She threw light on the concrete floor. She could see a strange pattern in the swirls, and she got on her knees to run her hand across the dusty slab.

"What is it?" Alex asked, coming behind her.

"Look at this pattern."

Johnny had retrieved another flashlight from his truck and now held it high, illuminating the small area a little more. He yelped as soon as his light joined with Brenna's, and Alex crossed herself while Brenna stood and raised her flashlight higher. In the strokes Owen Brock had made as he'd laid the slab was the image of a body, twisted and anguished.

"Is it Owen or Anabel?" Brenna asked.

Alex shook her head. "Probably a little of both." She turned to Johnny. "Get the 27SR parked by the bend in the road next to the pump house. Its bucket is small enough to get inside here and we'll use its break force to smash the slab. It'll go a lot faster than jackhammers."

"You sure about this?" he asked. "Maybe we need to call someone."

Alex held his shoulder. "We don't know what we'll find. But we need to uncover all we can before we go to the authorities. If Wilcox gets wind of this before we're ready to expose what happened..." She shook her head.

"I get it, Boss. I know. He'll throw us in a cell pending investigation."

"Yes."

Johnny held his own religious medal he'd pulled out from under his collar. "Okay. Be right back."

Alex turned to Brenna. "I don't think you should be in here when we uncover her remains. Go back in the house and wait."

"No, I'm staying," Brenna said. "I held her hands when she died, and I want to see her when you uncover her. I want to return this." She pulled the rosary from her pocket.

"Brenna, it isn't—"

"Please, Alex, I'll wait on the porch, but don't try to protect me from seeing her."

It didn't take long to break away the concrete. It'd been a homemade job, not professionally done. The slab hadn't been poured deeply or evenly. What took the most time was the steady peeling away of each layer of dirt. Alex directed Johnny as he worked the backhoe, and every so often, she'd stop him, kneel to brush away dirt with her gloved hands, dig with a small shovel, and then redirect him to keep digging. Brenna watched from the porch with Miguel. The sun was sinking lower into the late afternoon, and she worried they might lose the light after all. Then she saw Alex stand and give Johnny the sign to kill the backhoe's engine. He jumped down and bent over the area with her. They were up to their waists in a narrow ditch, and Brenna went to them with Miguel at her heels.

"Alex?" She came closer.

Alex stood, her face drawn. "We've found her, Brenna."

Miguel pushed past them and jumped into the grave as Brenna came to its edge. They'd uncovered a hand and part of a shoulder poking from rotten material, the remains of her dress. Miguel sniffed and circled a few times before lying alongside the bones and putting his head against the partially mummified fingers.

"He's her dog?" Johnny asked.

"I'm not sure who he is." Brenna reached for Alex's hand and lowered herself down alongside Miguel. She knelt in the dirt and petted him. "Let me see her, big boy."

Miguel shifted to allow her closer. She looked at the mummified hand with the fingers upturned and remembered holding that hand. She looked at the shoulder bone and tattered remains of her dress. It was real now, she thought. There in front of her were the remains of Anabel, beautiful Anabel.

"I want to see her face."

Alex hesitated.

"Please, Alex. Let me see her."

Alex moved to the area where the remains of Anabel's head would most likely be and began to scoop dirt. The first thing becoming visible was the black hair. Both Johnny and Alex grunted, and Alex closed her eyes and made the sign of the cross once again before continuing. In moments, Anabel's skull, shrunken and decimated with her black hair still attached, became visible. Johnny clutched his medal and prayed. Alex hung her head. But Brenna gazed into the empty sockets and remembered those eyes, the pleading in them as Anabel lay dying. She reached and stroked the black hair.

"It's okay, my friend," she said. "We've found you, and I promise we'll find your son and the others. Now be at peace."

She wiped away tears and placed the rosary into the upturned fingers. When she did so, a gust of wind swirled inside the garage, and Anabel's skull shifted on its bony neck. The hollow eyes and open mouth turned toward Brenna. Alex jumped and Johnny squeaked. But Brenna didn't budge. She continued to gaze into those sockets, stroking the hair. Then with Alex's help and a hand from Johnny, she climbed out and called Miguel out, too.

"We should cover her. Give her some dignity."

She went to the house and returned with a blanket. Together they covered Anabel's remains, placing gravel at the corners to hold the blanket in place.

She petted Miguel's head. "Guard her. Keep her safe."

The dog took his position alongside the grave where he stayed as commanded.

Brenna paced back and forth in front of the garage. Every now and then, she'd stop and look at the upstairs window, back out at the grove, and then continue pacing. It was night and the only light, other than the moon, came from the porch. Alex sat there watching her while Miguel, still on post, followed her with his golden eyes. After a good hour of this, she finally gave up, petted Miguel, and came to sit with Alex.

"I keep replaying it," she said, "but I can't think of anything that might help us locate Pedro's body."

She pulled her lawn chair close and took Alex's hand while she watched the line of trees and replayed the horrible scene in her mind. Since that afternoon, since finding Anabel, she'd been gradually sinking into a bitter mood against her will—she wanted to hold on to the wonderful feeling of being with Alex. Yet she couldn't keep the sense of foreboding from pecking at her. It was as if Marta's description of darkness, like a thick cloak surrounding her, swallowing her, was becoming real.

"You okay?" Alex kissed the back of her hand.

"Just frustrated. I'm worried we won't find Pedro, and I promised her."

"We'll find him."

She squeezed Alex's hand. "Are you willing to help me dig up every inch of every acre until we do?"

"Every acre, every inch."

Brenna leaned over and kissed Alex's cheek. "I knew I could depend on you. And I was thinking, maybe we need to tackle the slab tomorrow. You've brought in all that heavy equipment. Do you think we could smash through the tennis court and start uncovering the others first thing in the morning?"

Alex shifted in her chair and rubbed her forehead. "That may not be the best idea, Brenna."

"Why?"

"Technically, you don't own that land. I'd be trespassing. And believe me, Marcus Wilcox will use anything he can to throw me into one of his holding cells."

"I'd bail you out. I have the funds."

"Not until I'd been in there overnight."

"Wouldn't that just add to your otherwise colorful police record?" Brenna winked.

Alex chuckled. "It would." Then her face and voice turned serious. "But I'm not willing to risk it. Wilcox has a bad reputation with female prisoners."

Brenna grimaced. "You're not telling me—"

"I am. But the old bastard never gets called on it. You know, powerful family, old money."

"That makes me sick." Brenna withdrew her hand and folded into herself. She'd felt the chief deputy sheriff's lecherous gaze on her, and knew as well Hadley Poulsen had probably done much worse to Anabel than beat her. She wondered if the sickness had been passed from great-grandfather to grandson. She pulled her phone from her pocket and brought up Cassie's number. "I want you to tell Cassie what happened. She'll believe you. I'm not sure she'll believe me." She handed Alex her phone.

"I wasn't planning on bringing her in on this."

"Just tell her, Alex. And when you're done, hand me the phone. I have an idea."

Brenna listened as Alex and Cassie talked. It was strange to hear the story told from someone who hadn't witnessed the events. She could tell from Alex's side, Cassie was hesitant to accept the bizarre tale, even thinking Alex was having her on. But finally, Cassie came to accept the story, as Johnny had earlier. And just as Brenna had asked, when Alex finished, she handed her the phone.

"I guess you can tell me you told me so," Brenna said.

"This is crazy," Cassie responded. "All these years, all those times I went out there as a kid."

"I know."

"So you need to uncover the others and find Pedro. How can I help?"

"I want you to contact Poulsen's lawyer, the one you and Edward worked with. Tell him I'm so pleased with this property that I'm interested in other investments, perhaps even seeing about making a large donation to his grandson's gubernatorial race. Tell him it's imperative I meet with Poulsen himself on Monday."

"Brenna, it's a holiday weekend."

"Email, call, text, whatever you need to do, Cassie. Make sure you let him know we're talking a large amount of money. I need to see that old man right away. He's got to know where Pedro is buried. I have to find him soon. I promised her."

Cassie agreed to do what she could, pledging to get Brenna in to see Lanny Poulsen first thing Monday morning. When Brenna got off the phone, Alex shook her head and smiled.

"What?" Brenna asked.

"You're not only beautiful and brave, but a schemer as well."

"We have to move fast on this, Alex. Don't ask me why I know this, but I do. We have to find Pedro and expose this as soon as we can."

"I know. Otherwise Anabel will come after us."

Brenna turned her attention to the dark mass of trees. "No, I'm not worried about Anabel any longer. I think she and I have this connection. I don't think she'll harm me after all."

She stood and walked to the end of the porch where she watched the trees in the moonlight. He was out there, she knew. He hadn't attacked last night. Would he try again tonight? Or the next? She couldn't bear the thought of Anabel and Pedro or the others reliving their nightmare again.

"He's waiting. Watching and waiting. He knows we've found her, and I think he'll try to stop me from finding Pedro."

Alex joined her on the step and stared off at the trees as well. "Brenna, my aunt sensed a darkness around you, as I said. She thought, like I did, it was the grief over your son. But now I'm worried it may be something more. Something more dangerous than despair."

"What? Hadley Poulsen?"

Alex brought her into a tight hug. "You said the grandmother told you that you'd brought him back."

"Yes, she said that."

"And what if he's determined to take you, too?"

"Take me where?" Brenna stood back and looked into Alex's troubled eyes.

"To hell."

"To hell?" Although she didn't intend to, Brenna smirked. "Don't worry, Alex. I've been to hell, and it doesn't scare me in the least."

Chapter Twenty-three

That night they made love once more. For Brenna it was an effective distraction from the growing unease she'd been feeling since uncovering Anabel's body. And as they'd done the night before, she and Alex continued making love well into the early hours of the morning until they fell exhausted into each other's arms. But unlike the night before, Anabel didn't make a bedside appearance. Nevertheless, Brenna startled awake at three fifteen and waited for her apparition to appear. After an hour of no sign, she went out on the porch and over to Miguel who kept his silent vigil over Anabel's bones.

"You're a good boy, Miguel. You'll keep her safe, just as you kept me safe."

She scanned the trees. There was no sign of the family's campfire, yet she couldn't shake the feeling he was out there watching her. She left Miguel to keep his guard and climbed back in bed alongside Alex. But she wouldn't sleep. Instead she continued to replay the night of the attack as she'd witnessed it, and wondered why Pedro had never made it to his uncles, and where he'd ended up. By morning, she was exhausted and sullen. She felt herself pulling away from Alex, and Alex kept asking if she was okay, suggesting once more Brenna go back into town while she and Johnny, and perhaps Hector, began to look for Pedro.

"No, Alex, she asked me. Me," Brenna said. "I'm the one that made the promise, not you." She heard the impatience in her voice and realized she'd barked out her words.

Alex pulled back. "I'm worried about you, bella. You seem to be unraveling."

"I won't go. You can't make me leave her." And Brenna shut herself in her room the rest of the morning and occupied herself with calling her sister and Sadie.

Later that day, she convinced Alex to head into town for more groceries, something Alex was wary to do.

"I don't feel right leaving you alone."

"It's the middle of the day. Nothing happens in the middle of the day."

"Promise me you'll stay in the house."

"I promise."

But now with Alex gone and Miguel on his watch, Brenna felt pulled toward the grove. She strolled along the tree line and glanced over her shoulder to see Miguel watching her.

"You stay with her, boy. I'm taking a walk."

But she hadn't gone more than a few yards when she noticed the dog with her. As he'd done once before, he began to herd her, stepping in front of her and forcing her to change directions. But she was undeterred, and in a matter of minutes she found herself in the midst of the trees with only fragments of sunlight piercing through the dense branches. Miguel panted and circled while he whined at her. But she ignored him and searched around, wondering where Pedro might've ended up. In one direction she could make out the clearing where Alex's crew had stripped some of the trees. Opposite that was the access road that led to the back acreage toward the pump house and to the fence line where the concrete slab lay. She headed in that direction and the sunlight grew dimmer the farther she ventured in.

"I'm okay, Miguel," she scolded him after he'd tried to herd her again. "It's broad daylight. Nothing can harm me."

All at once, she broke through a clearing where a few trees had been cut down long ago. She examined the stumps and the area around them, looking for signs of a possible grave. But there were none. She sat and felt herself gulping to breathe. Without the shade of the trees, the sun gleamed down on her, almost oppressively, and with the rainfall of the past few days, the humidity seemed to suck the oxygen out of the air. She wiped sweat from her eyes and peered through the thick branches around her. It occurred to her then she was turned around and was uncertain in which direction the house, access road, or pump house lay. She panicked, stood, and circled around as she debated which way to head. Suddenly Miguel went on point, his head hunkered low, and the fur on his back bristled. He began to growl, and she dropped down to look at what he'd discovered. Her eyes focused on something deep within the grove. Was it a fallen tree limb? She blinked. Had it moved? But there was no breeze, no wind. She strained her eyes more, then stifled a scream when she saw the leg and the jeans covered in mud, in blood, or both. She stood to run, and when she did, she saw a boot attached to the end of the leg. It had taken a step closer to her, and now she saw a hand reach forward.

"Miguel!"

Miguel erupted into a vicious bark and dove into the trees. She tripped over a stump, clawed her way up, and took off running. She kept tripping on limbs and roots, falling into branches. She could hear Miguel snarling and her own breath coming in big gulps. Then she heard his voice. He was not yelling words or screaming anything comprehensible. Instead, he howled like a lunatic ready to pounce, an inhuman shriek tinged with manic laughter. She sobbed as the monstrous voice closed in on her and screamed again when she fell, her ankle caught in a gnarled root. She was certain he'd caught her and gripped her in his hand, ready to drag her back into the trees. But she pulled herself free and continued to plunge through the grove as dead branches slashed her, cutting into her face. She flailed her arms and ran without any purpose other than to find a way out. She could hear Miguel barking and gnashing his teeth. And that ungodly howl would not stop; the malevolent laughter only grew louder. She reached out when she caught a glimpse of her Jeep's windshield. With one final burst of will she dove forward and landed, skidding across the gravel into the clearing. She cried out as she half crawled and half ran toward the house, then fell on the porch steps and labored to breathe, while calling Miguel.

"Miguel? Miguel? Oh God, Miguel!"

He emerged, limping, with burrs and mud clinging to him. He came to a stop in front of her and panted in great heaves, drool dripping from his open mouth.

"I'm sorry," she cried and gripped him around the neck.

When she looked past him, her frantic breathing came to an abrupt stop. At the edge of the trees he watched, smiling, but not smiling, his face misshapen, the lower jaw hanging disjointed and loose. Then he turned and faded back into the grove.

❖

Brenna held the washcloth to the deep slash on her left cheek. The others had been shallower, and Alex had managed to doctor them properly. But the one laceration still oozed. At the moment, she sat on the porch while Alex drank beer and muttered in Spanish. She would not look at her, and Brenna was sure the mutterings were curses. Alex had been angry when she'd returned from the store to find her weeping on the porch steps, her shirt torn, and her face and hands bloody. Alex had cared for her wounds and ordered her to sit on the porch and wait for Marta to show. They wouldn't have to wait long, because once Alex had called her aunt and divulged all that had happened, Marta had found someone to cover her shift at the restaurant and was presently on her way over.

Alex opened her second beer and pulled a long draw from it.

"Alex, I told you, I'm sorry," Brenna said. "I don't know what came over me. It was as if I was being pulled, beckoned almost into the trees." She drank a beer as well, but she had no appetite for it. It was only the coolness of it soothed her throat, raw from screaming.

"I knew I should have gotten you out of here."

"But Marta's on her way. You said she can help."

"I don't know if she can stop all this, Brenna." Alex finished off her beer in one long gulping motion and set the bottle aside. "This could be beyond even her."

Miguel had gone back to his post after Alex had returned. Brenna had checked him over and found he'd been cut and slashed about the head and one of his paws was torn as well. Alex had tended to him, too, but assured her his wounds were superficial. Now Brenna watched him watching her, thinking he too was disappointed in her for her foolishness.

When Marta's car came around the bend, Miguel followed it to the spot where it pulled to a stop. Marta got out and turned, not to Alex and Brenna, but to Miguel who approached head down and eyes up. At first Brenna feared he would launch into an attack. But he didn't. Instead he sat at Marta's feet, his head still lowered while she considered him. She managed to stoop, using her open car door for support, and cup his head and lift his face. She nodded, said something to him. He wagged his tail and returned to guard Anabel. By now Alex was off the porch and Brenna joined her.

Marta looked them up and down and rested her gaze on Brenna. "We have much to do."

Brenna pointed to Miguel. "The dog? Is he theirs? Does he belong to them?"

"He belongs to no one," Marta said. "He is simply a sentinel, a guardian. They called and he answered."

"I don't understand."

"Perhaps we are not meant to." Marta pointed to her backseat. "Alejandra, please, this box, bring it to her remains."

"Sí, Tía." Alex retrieved it.

Marta took Brenna's hand. "I want to see her. Show me."

Brenna led Marta to the garage and pulled back the blanket which covered Anabel's bones. Marta shook her head while she crossed herself. Then she and Alex began conversing in Spanish, and Brenna watched as they set a shrine on the surface of the garage floor. They placed a small statue of the Virgin, the same depiction as she'd observed on the rosary, they lit candles, and Marta placed a vase with fresh flowers among them. Then she and Alex knelt in the dirt, Alex helping her aunt, and prayed. Brenna watched the spectacle and felt like an outsider. When they finished, Alex helped her aunt to her feet, and again they conversed in Spanish, shutting Brenna out, or so she felt. Then Marta took her hand again.

"Show me the house. Show me where she appeared to you," Marta said.

Brenna led the way as Alex began to retrieve other items from Marta's car—a linen bag from the front seat, and from the trunk, a bundle of chopped wood and a small barbecue grill. In it, Alex began preparing a fire just off the front porch.

Inside the bedroom, Brenna recounted the first night when she'd awakened to the sound of her son's music box, the night she encountered Miguel. She also told Martha about the next night when she'd found the oil lamp burning, discovered the rosary and medal, and had spoken with the family out in the grove. Brenna knew Alex had already divulged to her the rest of the events.

Marta touched Michael's music box. "You have been blessed, mija. These lost souls have chosen you as their champion. And Anabel, she feels a bond with you, with your broken heart which aches for your own son."

"She said we were like sisters."

"Sí, sisters of sorts," Marta said. "Now, show me the desk, this oil lamp of which you speak, the bloodstains."

Brenna once again led the way, and Alex, who'd left the wood to burn down, joined them upstairs. At first Marta walked around the room without giving anything much attention. She stood a moment with her eyes closed, as if listening to something, then touched the desk and lamp, looked through the other pictures cluttering the desktop, and leafed through boxes before studying the bloodstains on the wall. Finally, she turned and faced Brenna.

"You said the young woman, Sadie, found a record of Hadley Poulsen applying for marriage and adoption licenses, but they were denied. Do you know why?"

Brenna shook her head.

"I sense something." Marta began to examine the desk again. She slid open the large empty drawer.

"What is it?" Brenna asked.

"I am unsure, but we are missing something." Marta put her hand inside the drawer and ran it along the edges.

"I was thinking it strange, too, he wanted to marry her, especially since his wife hadn't been dead long," Brenna said.

"Sí, strange." Marta took Brenna's hands in her own and turned them, running a thumb over the palms. Then she gazed again into her eyes before starting to smile. "Ay, ya veo. You are meant to find them."

"The family?"

"The pictures." Marta pulled Brenna over to the large drawer. "Draw it out. Turn it on end."

Brenna pulled the drawer all the way from the desk and flipped it, dropping out a piece of balsa wood which had been fitted as a false bottom, along with three old black-and-white photographs hidden beneath.

"What's this?" Alex asked.

She and Brenna went to their hands and knees, arranging the photos in a line. Marta brought reading glasses from her dress pocket and reached for the photographs, and the three huddled together to inspect them. The first was of Anabel and a young Pedro. The second was of Pedro, as Brenna knew him, standing arm in arm with a fair-haired boy around the same age.

"That's Lanny," she said. But the third photograph leapt out at her. "Oh. My. God." She covered her mouth.

It was a family portrait, not too dissimilar from the one of the Poulsen family. But in this photograph, Hadley stood with his arm around Anabel, and between them stood Pedro. Hadley held the young boy's shoulder. To one side of Anabel stood Lanny, and to the other side of Hadley, stood Dallin. Nelda was missing from the picture.

"He was going to marry her and adopt her son," Marta said. "Why kill her? Why beat her to death? Look at the smile on his face. He is not the killer."

Brenna studied the photo again. She noticed only three of them were smiling: Hadley, Anabel, and Pedro. The look on Lanny's face, as he stood off to one side, was sad. But nothing compared to the cruel expression on Dallin's face.

"This picture had to be taken not long before they died," Alex commented.

"I don't understand," Brenna said.

Marta flipped through all three photos again. She pointed to Hadley's face. "This man had every reason to love the woman and her son. Look at the boy's resemblance to him. And look at this one. Can you not see the resemblance between the two young boys?" She held up the photo of Pedro and Lanny.

"Brothers?" Alex asked.

"Half-brothers," Brenna said, visualizing the timeline of Pedro's birth. Nelda must've been alive when Anabel had become pregnant. "If Hadley didn't do it, then who?"

"Look again. Look closely, mija," Marta said. "Did not Cain kill his brother Abel, out of jealousy?"

"Lanny?" Brenna knew that was absurd—he'd have been too young. How could he have beaten a grown woman to death? Arrange for the death of her entire family?

"Look again." Marta pointed to Dallin's image. "Do you not see the eyes of el diablo, the devil, looking back at you?"

Brenna shivered. She'd seen that look before, those cruel, beady eyes. They were the same eyes on Dallin's great nephew, Marcus Wilcox, and the same on the monster that had hunted her in the grove.

❖

She sat on the sofa and held Alex's hand. The revelation of Pedro's parentage had upset her, but she didn't understand why. And apparently Alex was done being upset with her; she held her close and listened while Marta spoke.

"The full story is buried with the family," Marta said. "But we do not need to know the full story. As you and Alex have concluded, I am confident the others are under the concrete slab. We need only find Pedro."

"Can you communicate with him? With Pedro?" Brenna asked. She shivered again, though it wasn't particularly cold in the house.

"No. I am sorry. I sense Anabel, feel her watching us," Marta said. She turned to look at Miguel, who'd come onto the porch and was watching through the screen door. "As well as this old one." She pointed to Miguel. "And I have some sense of the family." She looked past the dog toward the trees.

Brenna studied Marta's face. "You sense something else, don't you?"

Marta nodded.

"Tell me."

Marta rubbed her forehead, much in the same manner Brenna had seen Alex do. "There is betrayal here. Betrayal and regret and guilt. So much guilt."

Brenna twisted in her seat.

Marta continued. "It is apparent to me the woman and man loved each other. I can see it in the photograph and I can feel it from her."

"He was married to Nelda," Alex interjected.

Marta looked at her niece then at Brenna. "We love who we love." She kept her eyes glued to Brenna, who twisted and squirmed again.

"The timeline." Alex got up and found it shuffled among the papers on the coffee table. "Look, Tía, Pedro would have been a few years older than Lanny based on this. And if that were the case, old Hadley was having an affair with Anabel for at least ten years."

"It would appear so." But Marta wasn't looking at the timeline, she was still watching Brenna.

Brenna couldn't hold her gaze and looked at her hands. They were cold and shaking.

"I wonder if Anabel was married as well," Alex said, engrossed in studying the timeline and the photographs. "Maybe to one of the other workers. Or if Hadley was the only one to be unfaithful."

Brenna felt the cold in her hands travel to her heart. Her teeth chattered and something clotted in her throat like thick mucus.

"Still," Alex continued, "it makes no sense for Dallin to kill them. I mean, was he defending his mother's honor because Anabel was his father's mistress?"

"No, I do not think so," Marta said.

"But you spoke of betrayal and guilt," Alex said.

Brenna trembled and bit her bottom lip.

"I did," Marta said, and again Brenna could feel her gaze.

"None of these things matters," Brenna said. "Knowing who slept with who and why doesn't help us find Pedro. We have to find him. I promised her."

"Sí, you did."

Brenna looked away. It was as if Marta saw into the darkest parts of her. "I keep my promises."

"Do you?" Marta asked.

Alex furrowed her brows. "Brenna? What's wrong?"

Marta answered, "She and Anabel share more than the loss of their only son. They share the guilt of not being able to protect their sons. They both blame themselves for their deaths." She paused and watched Brenna before adding, "And perhaps much more."

Brenna glared at her. She wanted nothing more than to throttle Marta, to slap the wise face and spit in it.

"Brenna?" Alex knelt beside her. "Bella, you're shaking. What is it?"

Angry tears overflowed from Brenna's eyes and her hands formed fists. "I loved my son," she said, gritting her teeth.

"Sí," Marta agreed.

"She told me she loved me."

Alex shook her head. "Who are you talking about?"

But Brenna ignored her. "We were going to be together. She promised me. But she demanded I leave my son."

"Another promise," Marta said, "another broken promise."

Brenna stood and pointed a finger. "How dare you. You just said it. You said we love who we love."

"I did."

"I loved my son," Brenna said. "I wasn't giving up my son no matter how much I loved her."

"What the hell is wrong with you?" Alex stood. "Why are you yelling at my aunt?"

Brenna was aware she was being irrational, but her long-repressed rage, her overwhelming shame and guilt over Edward's and Michaels' deaths, boiled to the surface and she lost control. She turned on Alex and flung her bitter words.

"You fucking pray to your holy mother all you want. Go ahead and pray your guts out. It won't do you any good. Don't you think I prayed? Don't you think I know he's dead because of me?"

Humiliated at her outburst, Brenna covered her mouth and ran from the house, straight for the grove. She made it to the tree line and bent over and held herself as she sobbed. She felt Miguel leave his post and stand behind her and heard footsteps in the gravel as Alex raced to her. How could she explain this? How could she ever expect Alex to understand?

"Brenna, get away from the trees," Alex said.

But Brenna fell to her knees. "It was my fault Michael died."

"It was an accident." Alex tried to get her to her feet.

But Brenna wouldn't stand. She began to scream out her words, yelling them to the sky, to the trees. "I set him down. He was in my arms, and *I set him down.* He wanted Edward, and I set him down because Mrs. Chambers fell, and I set him down to help her, and he ran to his father!" She shook and trembled, snot and spit flying from her as she ranted. "I set my baby down and he's dead. What kind of mother sets her child down in the middle of a tornado? I failed him, don't you see? My baby's dead. Michael's dead because I set him down!" She pulled her hair as she keened, rocking back and forth, wailing.

"You can't blame yourself." Alex tried to stop her hands from their assault.

"I lost my baby! I lost Michael!" She pulled her clothes, her hair, lashed out with her hands, hitting her chest, her stomach, tearing at her heart. "It was my punishment, don't you see? My punishment for cheating on my husband. My punishment for breaking his heart, her heart. My punishment for wanting to die because I couldn't have her."

"No, Brenna, it wasn't punishment. It was an accident." Alex attempted to pin her arms to her sides and to bear-hug her.

But Brenna wouldn't stop her railing. She continued her lament, begging for Michael, condemning herself while shouting until her voice broke like brittle plastic. By now Marta had joined them. She cried out to Alex, something Brenna couldn't comprehend.

"We need to get inside, Brenna," Alex said. "It's not safe this close to the trees." She tried to lift her.

"It isn't fair, it isn't fair!" Brenna wept into Alex's shoulder. "It should've been me. Why take my son from me? Why take my baby? I'm the one that should have died, not my baby, oh God, not my baby."

Marta shouted another warning in Spanish, and Alex struggled to get Brenna to her feet.

"Brenna, please. You need to come away from the trees."

She clung to Alex and stood, taking small steps toward the house. But before she'd gone even a yard, a bellowing snarl howled from the depths of the trees and something snared her by the hair and whipped her backward, landing her on her ass.

"Alex!" she screamed and then grunted as the rough ground tore into her backside. She was being dragged into the trees, into the darkness, into his hell. She screamed again and reached for Alex who lunged and grabbed her by the ankles. Miguel leapt at the unseen force while Marta began shouting commands in Spanish and holding out her hands as if to ward off the attack.

"Alex!" she cried again.

Brenna raked her hands against the ground, then grabbed a tree trunk and dug in her nails. But her grip failed, and she was jerked deeper into the grove. Alex sprang forward and dropped half her body over her. It was enough to stop the momentum of the attack. Miguel tore into someone and raced off into the darkness, and Alex and Marta pulled her to her feet.

"You're bleeding." Alex held her arm, revealing blood along her shirtsleeve.

Marta held a lighter she'd pulled from her pocket, and in the flickering light, they could see the smear of fresh blood on Brenna's shirt. Brenna felt her arm and ribs, noting the bruises, but no torn skin.

"It's not my blood. Not my blood."

Marta pointed to the tree Brenna had clawed. "Ave María Purísima! See here, it bleeds. The grove, it bleeds."

Brenna touched the bark, the place where she'd scraped her fingernails. In the light of the small flame, she could see blood oozing from the tree while maggots writhed in the tender wood, exposed like naked flesh. Then she heard Marta yell and Alex cry out as she felt herself crumple to the ground and her body convulse.

Alex picked her up, carried her, and Brenna wondered at her strength. Inside the bedroom, she felt Alex stripping off her shirt and bra and laying her on the bed. She was spinning, or the bed was, and her head pounded, her body ached. She felt sick to her stomach and shivered violently even though she could feel sweat dripping into her bedsheets. She could smell smoke, too, wood smoke. Were Alex and Marta burning down the grove, she wondered in her daze. She could hear them talking, always in Spanish, but every so often Alex would bend over and whisper something in English. She was also aware of Miguel on the bed. Why wasn't he at his post? But she had no strength to lift her head and scold him. Marta was at her side, holding her head and a cup to her lips. The taste of something hot and flowery flooded her mouth. Liquid was being forced down her throat. Everywhere there were lit candles. And smoke, so much smoke. The smell of sage and tobacco filled her lungs and choked her. She began to cough and the force of it tore at her back and ribs. Something clawed inside her, something fought against her cough.

The church ceiling peeled back like rice paper, the steeple cartwheeled into the air. Edward looked at her one last time, his face both terrified and sad as he clutched their son and dove to protect him from the wooden pew turning summersaults above their heads. She screamed his name, Michael's name. Then, blackness.

She coughed again, but now she realized she couldn't breathe, and she clawed at her throat only to have Alex pin her hands.

Marta held the cup to her lips. "Drink. You must drink and purge it, mija. It will destroy you if you do not."

"Let me die," she managed to say despite the spasms in her chest and throat.

"There are worse things than death," Marta said, and she continued to pour the flowery liquid, a tea, Brenna was certain, down her burning throat.

Something was stuck, something in her chest, fighting the force of her cough. Whatever it was, it had wound its tiny tentacles around her esophagus and refused to budge.

The outline of the trooper's brimmed hat hovered over her as she lay in her bunk. Lights flashed outside the cabin door, and she could hear her friends talking. Jessica cried and held out her arms. There would be no more campfires, no more ghost stories, no more competitions to memorize bible verses. Summer camp was over for her. At her parents' graveside, a minister delivered an empty eulogy. She'd not been able to see them, their bodies, mangled from the car wreck. She was too young, Jessica had told her. She wondered if they were inside the coffins. Maybe they'd simply run away. What was the last thing she'd said to them? I hate you. I don't want to go to church camp. I want to spend the summer on Grandma's farm. She held her angry eyes on the faces of those who watched her with pity. She hated their eyes, wanted to gouge them out.

Miguel paced at the foot of the bed while Alex held her legs and Marta, her shoulders, as she moved something white and spherical over Brenna's body. Then Marta held a cluster of green branches in her hand while she lightly pelted Brenna from head to toe and chanted. Brenna began to cough again, so violently that in her dizziness she could see the spittle of blood landing on a towel draped across her stomach. She was drowning, suffocating, but she didn't mind that. It would be over soon. Alex watched her with tears cascading down her face, and Brenna wanted to tell her she loved her, but the vile plug, which anchored in her throat, prevented her from speaking.

The minister delivered a canned speech about wives submitting to their husbands as she stood at the alter and her wedding dress chaffed under the arms. She glanced at Edward, a good man, a friend in many ways, but she was not in love with him. She turned to face the audience in church. Jessica dabbed her eyes. Was she happy finally to be rid of her troublesome baby sister? She smiled her fake smile. It covered a host of sins—anger, resentment, depression, despair, a death wish.

Her teeth chattered. She was freezing while at the same time burning. She felt something wet and hot on her skin. It was a cloth soaked in some pungent ointment, and Marta was drawing it across her bare chest, down her stomach, and along her neck. She chanted, maybe prayed. Brenna wasn't sure. The candles had burned down, and

Alex sat on the floor with her head bent. Brenna tried to speak, but the tumor in her throat silenced her. She looked at Marta. Her face was as wrinkled at Pedro's grandmother's, her eyes nearly as dark.

"You must forgive yourself," Marta said. "Forgive."

Brenna shook her head and wheezed. She felt tears slide down her face and puddle in her ears. There was no forgiveness for what she'd done, for what she'd wanted to do. She felt something tighten around her windpipe. She tried to take a breath. She tried to squeak out even a bit of air. But her throat had sealed shut. She was dying. She was done.

It was the Saturday night before church. Michael slept, Edward read in bed, and she wept in the bathroom. What had she done to her husband? To her son? She'd fucked up their lives, just as she'd fucked up her sister's, Debra's, and her own. She wondered, as she glared at the prescription bottle in her hand, had she fucked up her parents' lives as well? She calculated how much of the medication she needed to swallow to do the job without making her vomit and alerting Edward. But she was denied her goal when he burst into the bathroom. Now on the bed, he held his head and cried. He'd always known about her, but he'd loved her all the same. He wanted her to be happy, to be the one to make her happy. He'd find a way, he told her, to show her how much he loved her, in spite of everything. He'd get her help, too, find her a good counselor. She'd get over Debra, he was certain. She'd come back to him. He was a good husband, was he not? A good father? For God's sake, didn't he give her everything he could? But she could only weep in his arms. She did not deserve to live. She destroyed the things she loved. She was ungrateful and pampered as her mother had said many times, as her father had confirmed. And didn't Jessica resent her, the burden she'd been? And as Debra had proclaimed, she was a whore, nothing but a dirty cheating whore.

Someone opened her mouth, reached down her throat, and tore away the mass that blocked her breath. In one long retching heave, something came up and landed on her chest. It looked like a cluster of black spiders, their little disjointed legs writhing and twisting. Alex screeched and pulled away, but Marta covered it with a cloth and bundled it away. Brenna fell back, exhausted from the strain, and allowed Marta to wipe blood and sweat from her mouth and face.

"Sleep now, mija. It is out. The darkness is banished."

Brenna closed her eyes, too weak to admit she could still feel a piece of it snaking its way back toward her heart.

Alex and Marta left her to sleep. Agitated, Brenna tossed and turned on her sweat-soaked pillow. She could feel Miguel there with her, the weight of his body pressed against her back. She took some comfort from that. But she worried about Alex. Would Alex still love her, she wondered, still want her? And the feeling of that spidery pulp, which had broken off and remained inside her, made her feel sick even after her fever had broken. When the bed moved, she opened her eyes. Next to her, Anabel sat with her thin shawl drawn around her head and shoulders. She was crying.

"Perdónate a ti misma," Anabel said. "Please, mi hermana, forgive."

Brenna reached out, and Anabel opened her arms and held her, stroked her hair while her ghostly tears fell and mingled with her own. At that moment, Brenna knew, Anabel did not weep for Pedro or the others, but for her and for all she'd lost and suffered.

Chapter Twenty-four

A lex pulled Brenna's Jeep into a parking spot close to the entry of the corporate building where Lanny Poulsen's office was located. "I think I should come in with you."

"This is something I have to do myself." Brenna tucked a file under her arm and felt in her pocket while she looked out the window and shivered. But she wasn't cold. She was burning up, her forehead damp with sweat, the slash along her cheek still oozing even though she'd daubed it with makeup that morning.

Alex held her arm. "Brenna, you don't look well, and I'm worried about you. Last night you were—"

Brenna touched Alex's hand. "Have some of your guys standing by with shovels and the backhoe. And call your father. But tell him not to call the sheriff until we've gotten to Pedro."

Alex opened her mouth to speak.

"No, Alex, you know if he calls now, the entire property will be locked down. It could take days or weeks before investigators find him. I won't keep her waiting any longer."

"And you think Poulsen will tell you where Pedro is? That he'll even remember after all this time?"

Brenna coughed into her hand and wiped her forehead. "He remembers."

Once inside the lobby of the building, she located the office. A private security guard stationed outside Poulsen's door glanced up as she entered, and the woman behind the front desk gave her a guarded look as she approached.

"I'm Brenna Taylor."

The woman continued to watch Brenna as she picked up her phone and mumbled into the receiver. Once she hung up, she led Brenna down a hallway to double oak doors, which she opened to an office with a picture window overlooking a courtyard. Behind the desk a frail prune of a man sat in a wheelchair. His eyes were hidden behind tinted glasses and his face was set in a permanent scowl. Brenna watched him while he studied her and the assistant bowed out of the room.

"You're that woman Marcus said has been living in the house." His feeble voice rasped in his throat. The effort of speaking caused his knobby head to shake with a slight palsy.

"I am."

"I understand you had quite a scare with some illegals tramping through the property."

Brenna glanced out the window to the courtyard where a lawn crew, most appearing to be Latino, trimmed hedges and raked gravel. "I've had a scare, yes, sir."

"They're a degenerate people, you know, most of them criminals." He sneered, deepening the scowl on his face. "Pretty young woman like you out there alone, you're fortunate you weren't harmed."

Brenna swallowed back disgust. "That seems an unjust and unfounded generalization, Mr. Poulsen." Her eyes returned to the men outside the window.

He followed her gaze and scoffed. "The good ones are few. Even then, they stress our infrastructure, demanding free healthcare and education." He turned back to her. "Cost us taxpayers a bundle." He gave her an icy smile. "But Julian, my older grandson, he'll turn it around once he's elected governor."

She shifted her weight and put one hand in her pocket as she took in the rest of the office and the many photographs of Poulsen with various men of some importance.

"I'm a busy man with numbered days, Miss Taylor." He brought his clawlike hands, twisted with age, up under his chin and rested his elbows on the wheelchair's arms. "I only agreed to see you after my lawyer indicated your property broker called to say you're interested in further investments." He tilted his head. "Or perhaps a sizable campaign donation."

She wiped a drop of sweat from her temple. "No, Mr. Poulsen, I'm not here about purchasing more land from you or donating to your grandson's political aspirations."

"Then what do you want?"

Brenna leveled her gaze and withdrew the San Miguel medal from her pocket. "I'd like to discuss this."

He removed his glasses, revealing pale eyes. "That supposed to mean something to me?"

"I believe it belonged to your brother."

A gurgled gasp escaped his mouth, but he kept his eyes on her while he picked up his phone with a shaking hand. "Hold my calls. No one comes in until I've finished." After hanging up the phone, he fiddled with the tubing hooked to his chair and brought a nasal cannula around his head and inserted it in his nostrils. He turned the dial on the oxygen tank, and took a deep breath. "And where did you find that?"

Brenna walked closer and opened the folder under her arm. From it she drew out an old photograph and tossed it across the desk. It was the one of Poulsen as a young boy with his arm around Pedro. She placed the medal on top of it and took a step back.

"In a desk in one of the upstairs rooms," she said. "I suspect your man, Owen Brock, held on to it and this picture as a way of ensuring his employment."

The palsy afflicting his head grew worse as he glared down at the photograph. "Him and that goddamn camera," he muttered to himself. He grew silent, seemed to contemplate something, to weigh his options. Then he looked at Brenna for a long time before speaking.

"My father was a good man, young lady, as good as they come, but he was man, nevertheless. If you think digging up his past transgressions will somehow tarnish my family's name and Julian's future, I'm afraid you've wasted your time. Besides, what do you think this old grainy photograph and that piece of silver proves?"

"I'm not here to blackmail you, Mr. Poulsen. And as I said, I don't care about your grandson's political aspirations."

"No?" He snorted. "Then I don't know what you're hoping to achieve here, but I can tell you, for your own sake, you better prepare that property for development and get back home to Iowa or wherever you're from." He closed his fist over the medal. "We're done here. See yourself out."

Brenna held her position and waited for him to look at her again. When he did, she said, "I saw it happen."

He went still. Even his breathing seemed to a stop. "You saw what happen?"

Brenna watched his pale eyes, as cold and as empty as his grandson's. But she didn't flinch a bit as she said, "I witnessed the night he killed them."

What little color he had drained from his face as his expression shifted from surprise to terror to anger. "Get out of my office," he hissed. He clasped the medal against his chest while it heaved. "Get out now!"

"I found Anabel's body, Mr. Poulsen. I know everything." She waited a beat and added, "Everything but where your brother Pedro is buried."

Poulsen's eyes grew large and his mouth dropped open, giving him the appearance of a skull. He began to shake his head with disbelief as a bundle of contradictory emotions dashed across his face and his eyes roamed the room as if he expected Anabel to materialize in front of him. When he spoke next, his voice had lost its hardness.

"You found her remains?"

"In the garage. Under that slab you had Owen put over her." Brenna sat in a chair in front of the desk.

Poulsen began to wring his gnarled hands and swallow repeatedly, causing the large knot of his Adam's apple to sink and rise in his fragile neck. "You have no idea what forces you're tampering with, my dear," he said, sounding almost tender. "She took Owen, you know." His chin quivered, and his eyes grew moist. "She took my wife and baby daughter, too. Drove my older daughter insane and left my grandsons' daddy dying out in those trees. She took everyone." He looked at her with anguished eyes. "She'll take you, too."

She leaned forward as a swell of pity came over her. Perhaps he wasn't the monster he'd first appeared. Perhaps there was still enough of the sad little boy inside the ruined man that she might reach him.

"She only wants her son, Mr. Poulsen. Tell me where he's buried and you don't need to suffer any longer for Dallin's crime."

Poulsen wheeled backward. "Do not speak that devil's name!" His tortured cry ripped from his chest and shook the room.

Brenna glanced at the office doors, but they remained shut. She turned back to find him sobbing into his hands. He couldn't have committed the crime, but somehow he was implicated, somehow he was tied to Anabel's need for revenge, and it was more than simply hiding their deaths for these many decades.

"Please tell me where Pedro is," she said. "Then this can all end. You can be free of it."

He kept his eyes closed and pressed his fist to his face. "Confessing to you will not absolve me of my guilt." His shoulders shook as another sob gripped him. "Not all the prayers and supplications, not all the suffering my family has endured, not the church or any goddamn force in this universe can do so."

Brenna stiffened with the echo of the very sentiments she held.

He lifted his face. It was distorted with despair. "I'll tell you where those bastards buried him, but it won't save you or me from her wrath."

"Bastards?" Brenna asked. "Who else...?" Her eyes widened. "His war buddies."

"She took them, too," he said, his chin still quivering. "But they deserved what they got." He wiped his eyes and drew in another breath. "And I deserved what I got as well."

She stood, walked around the desk, and knelt in front of him. She felt oddly tender toward him at that moment, and she pried one of his hands into hers.

"But you were only a little boy."

He shook his head as more tears gathered in his eyes.

"Please, Lanny," she said, "tell me where to find Pedro. Let me help him and Anabel and the others find peace. Let me help you."

His mouth twisted with effort as he whispered, "The pump house, down one of the mechanisms. He and his dog."

Brenna's heart thudded. "His dog?"

Poulsen held up the medal. "A big yellow mutt that went with him everywhere. Named him after his favorite saint."

"Miguel."

Poulsen frowned. "How did you—"

"Why did Dallin and his friends kill them?"

He turned toward the window, and she watched the internal struggle play out on his face. She waited a bit before squeezing his hand to prompt him further.

Finally he shrugged. "War has a way of destroying a man's soul, Miss Taylor. The horrors he witnessed, the acts he was forced to commit." He looked at her. "My father told me the guilt had eaten him from the inside out. But I couldn't pity him, and I never loved him. He might have been my mother's firstborn, her darling boy, but he was a monster from the day he returned home. The cruelest man to walk this earth." Poulsen pulled away from her and fingered the medal with both hands as he continued in a strained voice. "It was awful to watch the way he treated that family. But it was a nightmare the way he stalked Anabel."

"But your father?"

"Loved her, yes," Poulsen said. "He tried to marry her after Mother died, to give Pedro his name and birthright, but somehow Dallin stopped it. And not long after, Father became ill with a fever and passed. That's when..." Poulsen bit down on his knuckles and spoke in a hush. "I'd lie in my room at night hearing him downstairs in my father's bed, taking her against her will. He'd banned the rest of the family from the house, especially Pedro. Said if he saw him near the house, he'd shoot him."

Brenna bowed her head and cursed.

"When he'd finish with her, Anabel would drag herself to her room and hold the lamp at the window so Pedro would know to come out of the shadows. Just so she could catch a glimpse of him." Poulsen sputtered and choked on a sob. "But even worse, he'd force her to pleasure those damned friends of his, always threatening her with the death of her son if she didn't do as he asked."

Brenna ground her teeth and fought back a scream.

"Finally, I couldn't take any more, and I asked Owen to help me come up with a plan, some way for the family to escape and get away."

"Wait, you *wanted* to help them?"

Poulsen's face fractured across his deep lines of age. "Pedro was my brother, my real brother. And Anabel was more of a mother to

By the Dark of Her Eyes

me than my own had ever been. I had to save them, don't you see? I couldn't watch any longer the way Dallin abused them."

"But they didn't get away. You didn't save them." Then Brenna remembered what Marta had spoken of the night before. "You betrayed them, didn't you?"

Poulsen's head jerked. "He'd have killed me!" he cried. "You don't understand what he would've done to me. He threatened to flay the skin from my back, to burn me with irons if I didn't tell him what Owen and I had been whispering about. He was the devil. Do you hear me? The man was the devil!"

Brenna's chest caved, and she sank back onto her heels. "Pedro and the others, did they know you'd given them away?"

He shook his head and his eyes looked past her as he forced out his words. "I watched from the trees. Watched her in the window screaming as he beat the life out of her." As he continued, he began to hyperventilate. "Pedro, he ran for his uncles, but I stopped him, begged him to hide with me in pump house." He turned terror-filled eyes on her. "But the guns and the screaming started and"—he reached for her, and she grasped his hand—"his whole family...the women, the babies, his grandmother...everyone."

Brenna locked her eyes on his, and tears started down her cheeks. She could see his fear, feel his helplessness. He'd only been a boy, a sickly, frail boy.

"I couldn't stop Pedro," Poulsen said, still weeping. "He bolted out of the pump house just as those bastards rode up." He looked down at the medal in his hands. "And that damn dog jumped out of nowhere and went right for Dallin's throat. But the son of a bitch took him down with one shot to the head."

Brenna grunted and teetered on her knees.

"And Pedro threw himself over his dog and looked up at me. The look in his eyes, the way he looked at me..." Poulsen kissed the medal to his lips before throwing back his head and wailing. "He was my brother, my friend. Dear God, I loved him. Yes, it was me. I betrayed him. They're dead because of me!" Then he dropped his head to his chest and continued to cry.

Brenna held her throat. She'd wanted to see him as an evil man, but she couldn't help but recognize her own torment in his. When she had the strength, she stood and put a hand on his hunched shoulder. There was nothing she could think to tell him, nothing that might comfort him.

He looked up with a soft and desperate face. "I watched as one brother murdered the other. It was my fault. Do you think there's any power in the entire universe to set it right?"

"I don't know." She squeezed his shoulder and began to step away, but he grabbed her hand.

"I'm sorry, Miss Taylor, that you have now become a part of this tragic conspiracy."

"It's over now, Mr. Poulsen. I'm getting to Pedro today. She'll have her boy, and they'll be at peace finally."

He tightened his grip. "You may uncover Pedro's body. Perhaps it will placate her restlessness, as you say. But you will not go to the authorities. This information will not reach the media. Julian's future will not be compromised."

She tried to pull her hand away. "But the others need to be recovered as well. The medical examiner needs to—"

The softness in his face vanished. "Do you know who I am? The reach I have, the power behind my grandson's badge? I'll have that property seized and have you arrested. It won't be difficult for me to fabricate some reason, and Marcus will be happy to see to it you're taken into custody and secured in a private cell."

She wrenched her hand loose. "But this is your chance to set things right."

Coldness seeped back into his voice. "We cannot unmake the past, Miss Taylor." He put on his glasses. "And I will not let the past destroy my grandson's future."

Rage boiled up in her and she lunged at him. "Maybe it's you that doesn't have any idea what forces you're tampering with."

Before he could react, she snatched the San Miguel medal from his fist and swept the file from the desk. He wheezed and puffed for air as he gripped his chest with both hands and crumpled forward. Right then the doors swung open and the assistant shrieked before running from the room.

Brenna got out the door just as the security guard rounded the corner. She ducked past him and raced across the lobby and through the doors, and jumped into her Jeep. Her face was stained with mascara-tinged tears and her hair was jostled.

"Brenna!" Alex grabbed her arm and watched out the window as the security guard glared from the sidewalk and spoke into his phone. "What the hell?"

"He's in the pump house." Brenna panted with exertion. "Hurry, we need to get to him. We haven't much time."

A fit of coughing seized her as Alex swung the Jeep onto the road.

CHAPTER TWENTY-FIVE

Heavy clouds had built up on the horizon by the time Brenna and Alex reached the property, and a fine mist of cold rain caused a fog to gather along the damp ground.

"Have you dug yet?" Brenna asked, getting out of the Jeep.

Johnny and Hector stood leaning against the backhoe, the remains of the pump house walls splintered about them.

"We were waiting for you," Johnny said.

As Brenna and Alex approached the wreckage, Miguel stood up from where he'd been lying curled against one of two concrete structures, squared and topped with brass covers and standing feet off the ground. He approached Brenna and lowered his head as he came to her side. She knelt and gazed into his golden eyes.

"You'll be leaving me. I know that. You're not of this world."

He licked her face and pressed his forehead against her shoulder. Her heart nearly burst, and she hugged him with all her strength. She saw the others watching and noticed Hector biting his lip, fidgeting with his shovel.

"Alex told you what we're getting ready to do?" she asked him.

"Yes, ma'am."

Brenna looked at each of them again, stopping on Alex. "That one." She pointed to the brass cover over the mechanism where Miguel had been lying. "We need to work quickly. Poulsen will have his goons here in a matter of time."

"My father should call the sheriff now, Brenna," Alex said.

Brenna pointed once more. "No. We get to Pedro first."

Alex sighed, but nodded toward the backhoe and spoke to her men. "Use the bucket to dislodge this concrete block, then dig away four or five feet."

In less than ten minutes, Johnny had the teeth of the backhoe's bucket hooked into the concrete block. The engine growled and the gears creaked until finally there was a sucking sound, a swooshing as the block dislodged from the ground around it and toppled forward. Alex called Johnny off, and they all surrounded the hole as a foul smell swirled up toward them.

"I can't see nothing," Hector said.

"Bring me a flashlight," Alex told him.

Brenna moved next to her and held her hand for support while Miguel stood between them. Hector tossed a flashlight to Alex, and she beamed it into the hole, which was not as deep as it first appeared. It was bottomed out with mud and sludge.

"Thing hasn't been cleared of debris in years, I bet," Johnny said. "Looks like they let this one fill with silt."

"May explain the reason the grove started failing," Alex said. "They probably shut this one down after they dumped him in. And if they only used the one irrigation lock to let in water, the trees weren't getting enough."

Again they stood back while Johnny worked the backhoe and scooped out layers of mud. The sun had set, and Brenna turned on the Jeep's headlights in order to illuminate the area. As they worked, the backhoe and their bodies cast eerie shadows against the fog. After another ten minutes, Alex waved Johnny off, took Hector's flashlight, and dropped down in the hole. Brenna went to the edge and saw Alex on her hands and knees sifting through mud.

"Did you find him?" Brenna asked.

"Not yet. We need to use shovels from here on though. If we go much deeper, we'll need wood supports to keep the walls from collapsing on us." Alex looked up. "Let me find him, Brenna. You don't need to come down here and get dirty."

"I'll be fine. Now help me."

Hector steadied her while she slid into the hole and plopped into Alex's arms.

Alex kissed her forehead. "Okay, hold the flashlight." She went back to pulling away the mud. After a few moments she called for a shovel.

But when Alex stood, the flashlight caught something pale and white.

"Hang on." Brenna shoved the light into Alex's hand. On all fours, she began moving mud, which reeked of mold and decay. Suddenly, she bolted backward. "Pedro!" she gasped, not expecting to see his eye sockets looking at her.

Alex went to her hands and knees to help her pull away clumps of mud, which by now fell away in large patches. In moments, most of the boy's upper skeleton lay exposed.

Alex slowed Brenna's hands. "Let the forensic team do the rest, Brenna. We found him. You kept your promise."

Brenna pulled the San Miguel medal from her pocket and laid it across his chest. When she did, she caught a glimpse of something else. It was white canvas. Part of his clothes? Shoes? She tugged it loose and held it in the flashlight's beam. It was a handmade canvas collar, rotten with decay and wet mud.

"Miguel."

"It can't be." Alex reached out to turn the collar, revealing the stitched lettering. "Oh, Brenna."

"What is it?" Johnny asked.

They looked up. Johnny and Hector were watching along with Miguel who peered at them, his eyes glowing. He leapt into the hole and stood between them while he sniffed Pedro's remains.

"I found your boy, Miguel," Brenna said, her tears flowing. "You'll have the rest of your people soon."

He pressed his head against her leg, and she dropped to her knees and put her arms around his massive neck and kissed the top of his head.

"I never had a dog as a kid. We always had cats. But I love you, Miguel. Thank you for being my friend, for protecting me."

Miguel licked her face, a long wet slurp of his tongue, and then backed away. He sniffed the remains once again before turning and laying himself across the bones, which had once been a dog, which lay across the bones, which had once been a boy—a beautiful boy with green eyes. He looked again at Brenna and smiled his goofy grin. She snickered. He lifted his snout and let loose a soft, humble howl. As he finished, he lowered his head, blinked, and faded away. Brenna leaned into Alex's embrace and sobbed.

"He's with his boy now, Brenna, he's with his boy." Alex comforted her and pulled her phone from her pocket. As she held Brenna to her shoulder she spoke to her father and relayed the news. After she hung up, she lifted Brenna's face. "He's calling right now. It'll be a while. Let's go back to the house and change out of these muddy clothes."

Just then, Johnny bent down. "Alex, there's sirens. Someone's coming."

He and Hector helped them from the grave as an SUV with flashing lights barreled to a stop and Marcus Wilcox, along with two of his loyal deputies, decked out in full riot gear with rifles at hand, emerged and approached.

"Fuck." Alex pulled Brenna behind her.

"He can't hurt us," Brenna said. "Your father...the sheriff..."

"He can do anything he damn well pleases," Alex said.

The group stood together. Johnny and Hector flanked Alex while Brenna gripped Alex's hand and shrank behind her.

The beefy deputy, glaring and smirking, approached them. His men stood on either side and pointed their rifles.

"Granddad's dead," he said and spat on the ground.

Brenna peeked around Alex's shoulder.

"That's right, little bitch, you went and gave him a heart attack."

"Hey!" Alex took a step toward him only to have rifles pointed at her head.

Brenna tugged her back and looked at Wilcox. "I'm sorry for your loss, Chief Deputy."

"Like hell you are." He spit again and noticed the dilapidated pump house. "There a reason you're working into the night, Santana?"

"You know what we're doing, Marcus. Don't play games," Alex said.

He looked around. "Only the four of you, huh? That makes my job easier."

"You're too late," Alex said. "Sheriff Vesik will be here any moment with the medical examiner. My father's calling him right now."

"Is that so? Then I guess I best take care of this quickly." Wilcox put his hand on his weapon and fingered the snap on his holster.

"Too many people know, Marcus," Alex said. "Your family's secret is uncovered."

"And what secret is that, Santana? That my family's business was run into the ground thanks to a bunch of lazy wetbacks? You think anyone cares about some long-dead Mexicans buried in the grove? Huh? Lazy sons of bitches ain't worth the trouble, and nobody will give a damn. They didn't then, and they won't now."

Brenna stepped around Alex. "You can stop covering for your grandfather and your great-uncle. It's over. Let these people be put to rest."

He smiled his oily smile. "No, ma'am, this ain't over, not for me or my brother. He's gonna be governor, you wait and see, and then he'll make a run for president. This country needs a man like Julian. We've sold off our birthright and we're gonna take it back from the illegals and the half-breed mongrels stealing it away."

Brenna shivered as she looked into his eyes. He was frazzled and disheveled and he'd been crying. His shirt was untucked and misbuttoned, and one pant leg was caught in his boot. Worse, though, he continued to finger the pistol that hung on his hip. It was clear he was delusional with hate and prejudice, possessed with the same wickedness that had claimed Dallin Poulsen decades before.

Another SUV arrived and two men climbed out, picking their way toward them. Brenna could see one of them must be Julian Wilcox. He looked like an older, yet smaller, version of Marcus.

"I got 'em, Julian." Marcus turned to his brother.

Julian Wilcox patted his brother's arm. "Okay, Marcus, you let me handle this." He took a step forward and made a face of contempt when his eyes fell on Alex. "Ms. Santana, seems as though whenever there's trouble brewing for me, I find you or your daddy behind it."

Alex sneered.

"And it looks like you and your friends have bungled your way onto some sensitive family business here. I have no choice but to have Marcus bring you in and press charges for some infraction or another. Then we can all sit down and discuss an agreeable outcome for all of us as long as you agree to remain quiet. Otherwise I'm afraid you and the others might meet some unfortunate accident while held in our county jailhouse."

Brenna could see by the way he spoke and his mannerisms that he was through and through a politician, all spit and polish, but no substance.

"My father has already called the sheriff," Alex said. "And we've found Pedro and Anabel. Threaten all you like, but it won't stop the truth from coming out."

Wilcox became rigid, turned, and looked at his brother.

"They found the boy, Julian. Just like Granddad said at the end." He pointed toward the dilapidated pump house.

Julian turned back to the group. "That's unfortunate," he said. "You've left us little time to set the stage. And too bad for your father. I never agreed with his positions, but at least the man had convictions."

"Don't threaten my father." Alex stepped forward.

The deputies raised their rifles once more.

But Wilcox called them off. "No, of course not, Rubén's a good man. It's too bad he'll have his heart broken when he finds out his daughter died in a drug run gone bad, she and her friends double-crossed by coyotes working for one of the cartels. Sounds about right." He looked at Brenna. "Marcus tells me you had a run-in with some of those illegals a week ago, isn't that right, miss?"

"Alex." Brenna gripped her arm. She saw where this conversation was headed.

"Too bad the company you hired to prepare your property was dealing in drugs, Miss... Wilson? Taylor? Which was it?"

"Taylor," she said. "And what you're suggesting is—"

"Yes, too bad you got caught in some nasty business and walked in on a drug exchange, Miss Taylor." He regarded her with callous eyes and turned them once more on Alex. "And too bad your daddy will be so grief-stricken over your murder, Ms. Santana, and the sheriff's department too busy investigating the crime, that the tale of hidden bodies will be forgotten."

"You can't do this, Julian," Alex said. "Right now all you have is the embarrassment of a family secret, something you didn't even do."

"That secret will unravel everything I've worked for. Everything." He turned back to his SUV and said to his brother, "Rebury that boy and his mother before Vesik shows up. Make sure it looks as if the coyotes shot the others execution style."

Marcus Wilcox grinned. "Get the zip ties, boys. We'll make it look like the coyotes had themselves some fun with the ladies before they shot 'em all." He eyed Brenna. "We'll tie up the men first and let 'em watch."

"You touch her and I'll rip your goddamn throat out." Alex lunged for him.

Brenna had anticipated Wilcox's move, had seen him reach for his gun. Her instincts took over, and she threw herself between the deputy and Alex, determined to shield her. It was a move done out of the primal need to protect the one she loved. She had failed Michael, but she would not fail Alex.

While in midair, her arms outreached, she felt the searing cold of the bullet as it entered her side and felt her lungs collapsing. She was deaf momentarily from being in such close range to the gunshot, and her eyes were temporarily blinded by a blur. A lightning bolt, a horizontal streak of gold, raced past her. She heard a growl, deeper than any dog growl she'd ever known. It was wrath and vengeance sweeping out of the remains of the pump house and attacking Marcus Wilcox. In one swift movement, Miguel, or some version of Miguel from her viewpoint, stood over the man as blood spurted from his shredded artery, raining black liquid on his surprised face. She could hear screaming now. Julian shrieked for his brother, commanding the deputies to shoot, while Alex screamed, Johnny and Hector shouted. She felt herself being lowered to the ground, saw the fog part around her as she gazed into the night sky. There were so many stars, more than she'd ever noticed before. Alex was there, she could sense her, but not see her. She could only see the stars like a blanket pulled around her.

She sat in a clearing full of sunshine down which she could see a long, lighted path. The air was laced with the fragrance of citrus blossoms, and behind her the grove lay dark and lifeless. She looked at it, shivered, and turned her attention back to the lighted path while she wondered where Alex had gotten off to.

"Fucking whore." The words hissed from behind.

She turned to face the trees. She could see it hidden in the shadows, its muddy body. She struggled to take a breath and noticed a hot pain in her chest. Someone moved behind her, and she looked back. Edward stood on the path.

"Not yet, Brenna. You need to stay," he said.

She ran to him and hugged him. "Forgive me."

"I already have."

She sobbed in his arms, but her relief was short-lived when she heard the monster taunt her again.

"You let him die," it said.

She whipped around. By now the monster had come out of the shadows, and she could see the disjointed nature of its face, its chin hanging loosely by a strand of bloody flesh while the top of its head gaped open.

"I love you, Mommy." Michael's voice called from behind.

Again she turned. Edward was gone. In his place, Michael smiled at her.

"Baby." She pulled him in her arms and held him to her as she wept into his neck. "I'm sorry, Michael. I set you down. I'm sorry."

"I told you it's okay, Mommy. I'm not scared. Daddy's with me."

Brenna hugged him to her chest, but she heard the trees rustle behind her, and she moved to protect her son from the monster who advanced upon them.

"You don't deserve her," it said. But it stopped at the edge of the trees, unable to step onto the lighted path.

Brenna wheezed and gripped her side and grimaced with each breath, the pain sharper now. She glared at the monster, noticing it no longer resembled Dallin Poulsen, but a face familiar to her nevertheless.

"You deserve to burn, bitch," it snarled.

She whimpered, the pustule of black mass at the base of her throat choking her. She looked at her feet. The shadowy line of trees advanced into the sunny clearing, threatened to overcome her. And just as she saw the darkness reach her toes and felt her lungs turn to fire, she was embraced from behind, steadied and held upright as a thin veil of white linen wrapped around her.

"Forgive," Anabel said. "Forgive and heal, sister."

Brenna winced as the pain intensified in her chest. The wraith in the darkness paced like a ravenous animal and snarled while baring its teeth.

"You must fight the darkness," Anabel urged. "Forgive yourself or you will be lost."

Brenna slumped against her and felt Anabel's hand reach around and hold her heart.

"Take my strength." Anabel lifted her shawl and drew Brenna under its protective mantle.

By now, Brenna could hardly speak, the pain was so intense, but she faced the monster that jeered at her while Anabel held her from behind, supporting her with her arms outstretched and the sunlight beaming through the sheer linen.

She stuttered as she felt the air leaving her lungs for good. "I...I forgive." With that, she vomited the last bit of black tendril, covered in bile.

The demon in front of her shrieked and tugged at its ears, peeling them from its head. It twisted and turned, writhing as tree branches encircled its limbs and began to choke and slash it.

"You whore!" it screamed at her, trying to point a finger, but the trees moved in to rip its hand from its arm. "You goddamn fucking whore!" it managed to yell as it was pulled to the ground. Before it was eviscerated and scattered into bits, its face looked at her, and Brenna saw her own eyes looking back.

When the creature was no longer, the grove spontaneously became illuminated and the grandmother, followed by the rest of the family, emerged. One by one they paraded in front of Brenna, bowing their heads respectfully, saying thanks. The women kissed her cheek, the men tipped their hats, until finally, the grandmother in the faded red skirt stood before her.

"Ay, mija, such courage, such strength." She held Brenna by her face and smiled. Then she passed her hand over Brenna's stomach. "You have done Our Mother's will, and she will reward you greatly."

"But I lost my boy," Brenna said.

"He is not lost. He waits for you. You will be with him again, but today is not the day." She moved to join the others.

Anabel, with Pedro and Miguel, stood before her. Pedro took her hand.

"You are a great lady," he said. "I knew you would be the one to hear us and help. Take this, remember me." He placed his San Miguel medal in her hand, and she bent so he could kiss her cheek.

"He's your dog?" She petted Miguel.

"He looks like him, yes. He knows it gives me comfort, but my dog waits for me." Pedro pointed toward the sunlit road.

Anabel stepped forward and drew her into a hug while wrapping her shawl around her once again. "Until we are together again, my friend, my sister." She placed the silver rosary in Brenna's hand.

Brenna gazed into Anabel's black eyes. She had so much she wanted to say to this woman. This beautiful woman, who'd suffered trying to protect her son, who'd fought beyond the grave for justice, who understood her pain and guilt.

"I feel…" But Brenna shook her head. She had no words for how she felt. Still, she understood she'd been healed. Whether by the light of Alex's love or by the dark of Anabel's eyes, she'd managed to forgive herself and heal. She gripped the rosary in her hands and said, "I love you, Anabel."

Anabel bowed her head and touched her forehead to Brenna's. "Te quiero, mi hermana. Remember, I will always be with you." With that, she kissed Brenna's cheek and stood back. She turned, took Pedro by the hand, and walked with the others down the sunlit path and disappeared, leaving Brenna and Miguel watching after them.

"Are you going as well?" she asked him.

He wagged his tail.

She held up Pedro's medal. "Will you always be with me, too, Miguel?"

He let out a bark and stood on his hindquarters, licking her face before settling on all fours again.

"Phew, you stink." She laughed, kneeling and hugging him, running her hands down his thick fur, inhaling his scent. "It's not any easier saying good-bye the second time, you know. I love you, whoever, whatever you are."

As she held him, she felt him lift his snout, and from his mouth he released a deep, echoing howl, so intense she felt the ground around her tremble, the sky above her crack, and the sound wave ripple from her head to her feet.

The first sensation she felt was the numbing pain in her side and the slick feel of plastic against her chest. She peeked over something covering her mouth and nose and saw a man, then two men leaning over her.

"We got her back!" one of them shouted.

Alex's voice reached her next. "Brenna!"

Alex was there with her, holding her hand. She could feel herself being floated and jostled, and now her ears made out the sounds of radios and men talking. Lights throbbed all around her, and she turned her head and tried to speak through the oxygen mask.

"No, don't talk. Save your strength, bella," Alex said.

Just as the paramedics were about to lift her into the ambulance, she struggled and pulled the mask free. "Miguel. Where's Miguel?"

Alex blinked, shook her head. "He's with Pedro now."

"No, he...I saw him. The chief deputy...he tore his throat out."

"Marcus Wilcox went to fire at us again and tripped. Bastard shot his own damn head off. His deputies refused to fire on us."

"Julian?"

"Dropped dead of a heart attack from all we can gather," Alex said. "They've already loaded him up."

"Her revenge."

"Yes, Brenna. Anabel has her revenge. The nightmare is over."

She managed to slip a hand, although embedded with an IV, into her pocket and drew out both the rosary and medal. One of the paramedics frowned and took them from her, handing them to Alex.

"How?" Alex asked. "We left them with their remains."

But Brenna was too weak to explain. She laid her head back as she was slid inside the ambulance. But before she disappeared into the vehicle, she caught one last look at the stars and the deep purple-blue of the desert sky.

"I love you, Michael," she whispered to the heavens.

Inside the ambulance, Alex continued to hold her hand. Brenna gazed at her over the rim of the oxygen mask the paramedic had returned to her face.

"And I love you, Alex," she said and added in awkward Spanish, "Te amo, Alejandra."

Alex wept. "Te amo, Brenna, para siempre."

EPILOGUE

She felt the soft touch, the fingers in her hair, and opened her eyes to see Alex smiling at her.

"You had a hard night, didn't you, getting comfortable?" Alex asked.

"I'm exhausted," Brenna said. "Your daughter is already practicing her dance moves and is determined to kick me under the ribs every chance she gets."

"I should've let you sleep, but it will be sunrise soon, and I wanted us to watch it together on her special day."

"That'd be wonderful."

"I'll start the coffee," Alex said. "You go out on the patio, and I'll meet you with the twins."

Brenna swung her legs over the edge of the bed and pushed herself up. She pulled flip-flops over her swollen feet and wobbled out to the patio of her custom-built home. She eased herself on a lawn chair, one of the same chairs she'd purchased two years ago for the Poulsen property and had brought with her when she'd moved. She looked at the sky, white and pale blue. The sun was moments away. She closed her eyes and inhaled, smelling mesquite and sage. It'd be a hot summer day, she knew, but the mornings before the sun fully appeared were still slightly cool. Their daughter would be a summer baby, and as many people had pointed out, being pregnant during an Arizona summer was a challenge. But the baby was healthy and so was she. None of the complications she'd experienced in the past plagued her. As a precaution, though, her doctor had arranged to induce labor that morning.

"Here you go, here's your mamá." Alex came out on the patio. She carried two golden puppies. The chubby little pups whimpered as she held them up. Brenna gave each one a hug and kiss before Alex set them in the grassy area off the patio where they stumbled and stretched as they sniffed around. By the size of their paws, they'd grow to be large dogs, a mix of yellow Lab and golden retriever, a sweet but sad reminder of Miguel and his great yellow mane.

"Tell me again your wisdom in getting two puppies just as we're about to give birth to our daughter?" Brenna asked.

"It'll be good for her. I'll speak Spanish, you'll speak English, and Princess and Perrito will speak dog. She'll be trilingual." Alex chuckled and went back inside for coffee.

"Speak dog? You're crazy, you know that?" Brenna called after her.

But getting the puppies had been a mutual decision. And since their arrival last week, the pups had been sleeping in a kennel in the nursery, right next to the crib. Brenna wanted their scent there, their gentle souls impressed upon the furniture and walls. She knew their daughter would bond with them, and they with her, that special bond of child and dog.

The sun began to touch the majestic breast-shape of Red Mountain. It seemed so much bigger from the desert plot where she'd had their home built, an area as close as possible to the mountain and one zoned for horses.

"Hurry, Alex, the sun's almost here."

"Here you go. Decaf, four sugars." Alex held out her cup. "It's all you get until after she's born, so sip it slowly."

Alex sat and put her arm around Brenna's shoulders, and the two watched in the still air of the desert morning as the sun climbed the mountain, illuminated the red sandstone, and emitted a pink hue. Brenna leaned into Alex's embrace while she held her coffee in one hand and patted her stomach with the other. The sun continued to climb, and she remembered that first sunrise, that first moment of intimacy they'd shared the day they'd stood on the porch of the old house, which no longer existed. She'd had the property stripped once the investigation and interment of the remains had concluded. But instead of selling it to a housing developer, she'd donated the land to the county and had it developed into a park, the San Miguel Memorial Park. It, along with this home she'd had built for her and Alex, had taken most of her time and energy in the last years.

"It's beautiful," she said and turned her head to see Alex watching her.

"Yes, you are."

"She's kicking again, feel." She pulled Alex's free hand to her stomach.

Alex leaned and spoke into Brenna's belly. "Today is your day, mija. A special day, just for you."

They sat together a while longer, enjoying the peace and calm before the excitement of the day began. Then Alex went to the stables and fed the horses, and Brenna stayed on the patio and watched her from a distance. Alex loved those horses, caring for and riding them. And before Brenna had gotten pregnant, they'd ridden the horses nearly every day into the desert along dry riverbeds, through little shallow canyons and rocky passes. Now with the baby on the way, Alex suggested one of her cousins come and stay in the guesthouse. That way she'd have help with the horses' care as well as another person to ride with until Brenna was cleared by the doctor. As Brenna thought about which cousin it would be, she saw Alex stop working and turn to look back at her. It was far enough away she couldn't quite make out Alex's expression, but she was sure she was smiling, for the sun, higher now in the sky, was shining from Alex's face and beaming back to her.

As Alex finished her work and came back along the path to the house, Jessica emerged from the guesthouse and joined her. The two hugged good morning and began talking and laughing as they walked together. Brenna smiled. She'd never realized how much her sister resembled their late mother. She was grateful Jessica would be there for the birth of their daughter, that her brother-in-law and nephews would be joining them later in the summer. Her family, Alex's family, had merged.

After her shower, she sat on the bed while Jessica combed her wet hair and chattered about the events of the day.

"You'll have Alex call me as soon as she's born, do you hear me?" Jessica said.

"Yes, we will, but we want to have some time for Marta and Angel to hold her before everyone else arrives. You understand?"

"Of course."

She patted Jessica's hand. "Thank you for all you're doing, Jess. You've been a great help."

"It's my pleasure, Brenna. I can't tell you how excited I am to see the little angel. I can't wait to buy her dresses and ribbons for her hair."

Brenna giggled. "She's going be so spoiled with all the attention. And Marta, oh my goodness, the woman's out of her mind about her first grandchild. I'm glad I'm able to give her this gift."

"Didn't you tell me Alex said her name means gift?"

Brenna rubbed her hands over her stomach. "Yes, Teodora, the Spanish of Theodora, God's gift."

Later, while Alex loaded their two overnight bags into the Jeep, Brenna inspected the baby's room. She stood in front of a shelf where she'd put framed pictures of herself as a little girl as well as one of Alex around age six. She'd also placed a picture of Alex with her parents. It showed Clarita and Rubén holding Alex between them on their laps. In addition, she had one of Alex, Angel, and Marissa together as children. Along with those, Jessica had brought with her one of Brenna with their late parents to add to the shelf. This display was important. Brenna wanted their daughter to know parents and children were special, important and honored, that family gave strength to live and grow. And yet there was one picture she hadn't been able to place on the shelf—a professional portrait of herself with Edward and Michael. Jessica had brought it with her along with the other picture. Alex had seen it, commented Michael had been sweet and cute, but Brenna hadn't placed it on the shelf with the others. Instead, she'd put it in the top drawer of the baby's dresser and left it there along with Michael's music box. Now looking at the spot where it would go, she wondered why she hesitated.

"Brenna?" Alex's voice broke through her concentration.

"I'm sorry. I'm ready. Let's go," she said. This wasn't an important issue, she convinced herself. It didn't need to be discussed.

But Alex came over and touched her face, turned her to look her in the eyes. "I know about the picture. I've seen you looking at it for the last few weeks. That spot on the shelf needs to be filled."

"Alex, this isn't the time, we need to go and—"

"I want you to put it there," Alex interrupted. "Michael is her brother and your son. She should know that. It's important."

"But Edward's in the picture, and—"

"And Edward's his father, yes. He's as much a part of us and this family as Jessica and Bill and their two boys." Alex reached inside the drawer and took the framed picture out, setting it in its place. She looked inside the drawer again and brought out the music box, setting it alongside the picture as well.

Brenna wiped her eyes and nodded.

"My grandfather gave us his blessing, Brenna," Alex said, "and Angel helped us conceive our child. We're a family now. And you know the saying, *Mi casa es tu casa, mi familia es tu familia.*"

Alex brought something out from behind her back. It was one of the old photos from the Poulsen place, the one of Anabel and Pedro alone. Alex had had it rescanned and placed in a silver frame. Brenna wept when she saw it. She hadn't seen an image of Anabel for some time and had forgotten the woman's beauty. Alex placed it on the shelf with the others.

"Anabel and Pedro are part of our family, too. Would it be all right with you if they shared the shelf?" Alex asked.

Brenna wiped her eyes. "Thank you." Now the shelf was complete. She touched the faces of Anabel and Pedro and then the face of her son.

Alex took her by the hand and led her from the room. "Now, let's go bring our rayito de sol into this world."

"Rayito de sol?" Brenna stopped her. She'd learned a great deal of Spanish, but this phrase was new to her.

"Yes, our sunbeam, our little sunshine. If that's okay with you. Or would you rather I didn't call her that?"

For Brenna, the term of endearment was perfect. "I like it. And what's one more name going to hurt anyway? Teodora Clarita María Santana-Taylor. I'm wondering how we'll fit all that on the birth certificate."

They laughed, hugged, and headed to the front door, to the Jeep, down the road to the highway, and to the hospital, where in a matter of hours, they'd welcome their daughter into the world.

The house fell quiet.

But in the baby's room, the lid on the music box lifted, and the instrument tinkled out its tune before closing again. The scent of citrus and roses permeated the air as she stepped forth with her shawl drawn around her head and a golden beast by her side. She gazed about the room with black eyes, the color of onyx, spread her arms over the baby's crib, and gave her blessing before she and the beast dissipated in a shower of fulgent light.

The room now stood sanctified, a sacred space waiting to welcome a new life within its walls, to welcome a baby girl. For she was the gift promised to Brenna that frightful night in the grove, her baby girl, a sunbeam, the sun, a reflection of Alex, who for Brenna was the sun itself. And together, Alex with her warm brown eyes and their dark-haired daughter with shining green ones would illuminate and dispel any lingering shadows in Brenna's soul, giving her the strength to be a mother once again and the courage to live fully once more.

About the Author

Born in Arizona, Cameron prefers the heat and open skies of the desert over any other locale. She earned her PhD in educational psychology with a minor in rhetoric and composition from the University of Arizona in Tucson and has been teaching for nearly three decades. She began reading and writing fan fiction as a creative outlet, and after some encouragement and nudging from family and friends, she committed herself to becoming a published fiction writer. Currently she lives in the Phoenix area with her partner and their daughter and teaches writing and literature at Scottsdale Community College, the only public community college located on Native American Land. She can be contacted at cameronmacelvee@gmail.com.

Books Available from Bold Strokes Books

18 Months by Samantha Boyette. Alissa Reeves has only had two girlfriends and they've both gone missing. Now it's up to her to find out why. (978-1-62639-804-7)

Arrested Hearts by Holly Stratimore. A reckless cop with a secret death wish and a health nut who is afraid to die might be a perfect combination for love. (978-1-62639-809-2)

Capturing Jessica by Jane Hardee. Hyperrealist sculptor Michael tries desperately to conceal the love she holds for best friend, Jess, unaware Jess's feelings for her are changing. (978-1-62639-836-8)

Counting to Zero by AJ Quinn. NSA agent Emma Thorpe and computer hacker Paxton James must learn to trust each other as they work to stop a threat clock that's rapidly counting down to zero. (978-1-62639-783-5)

Courageous Love by KC Richardson. Two women fight a devastating disease, and their own demons, while trying to fall in love. (978-1-62639-797-2)

Pathogen by Jessica L. Webb. Can Dr. Kate Morrison navigate a deadly virus and the threat of bioterrorism, as well as her new relationship with Sergeant Andy Wyles and her own troubled past? (978-1-62639-833-7)

Rainbow Gap by Lee Lynch. Jaudon Vickers and Berry Garland, polar opposites, dream and love in this tale of lesbian lives set in Central Florida against the tapestry of societal change and the Vietnam War. (978-1-62639-799-6)

Steel and Promise by Alexa Black. Lady Nivrai's cruel desires and modified body make most of the galaxy fear her, but courtesan Cailyn Derys soon discovers the real monsters are the ones without the claws. (978-1-62639-805-4)

Swelter by D. Jackson Leigh. Teal Giovanni's mistake shines an unwanted spotlight on a small Texas ranch where August Reese is secluded until she can testify against a powerful drug kingpin. (978-1-62639-795-8)

Without Justice by Carsen Taite. Cade Kelly and Emily Sinclair must battle each other in the pursuit of justice, but can they fight their undeniable attraction outside the walls of the courtroom? (978-1-62639-560-2)

21 Questions by Mason Dixon. To find love, start by asking the right questions. (978-1-62639-724-8)

A Palette for Love by Charlotte Greene. When newly minted Ph.D. Chloé Devereaux returns to New Orleans, she doesn't expect her new job, and her powerful employer—Amelia Winters—to be so appealing. (978-1-62639-758-3)

By the Dark of Her Eyes by Cameron MacElvee. When Brenna Taylor inherits a decrepit property haunted by tormented ghosts, Alejandra Santana must not only restore Brenna's house and property but also save her soul. (978-1-62639-834-4)

Cash Braddock by Ashley Bartlett. Cash Braddock just wants to hang with her cat, fall in love, and deal drugs. What's the problem with that? (978-1-62639-706-4)

Gravity by Juliann Rich. How can Ellie Engebretsen, Olympic ski jumping hopeful with her eye on the gold, soar through the air when all she feels like doing is falling hard for Kate Moreau, her greatest competitor and the girl of her dreams? (978-1-62639-483-4)

Lone Ranger by VK Powell. Reporter Emma Ferguson stirs up a thirty-year-old mystery that threatens Park Ranger Carter West's family and jeopardizes any hope for a relationship between the two women. (978-1-62639-767-5)

Love on Call by Radclyffe. Ex-Army medic Glenn Archer and recent LA transplant Mariana Mateo fight their mutual desire in the face of past losses as they work together in the Rivers Community Hospital ER. (978-1-62639-843-6)

Never Enough by Robyn Nyx. Can two women put aside their pasts to find love before it's too late? (978-1-62639-629-6)

Two Souls by Kathleen Knowles. Can love blossom in the wake of tragedy? (978-1-62639-641-8)

Camp Rewind by Meghan O'Brien. A summer camp for grown-ups becomes the site of an unlikely romance between a shy, introverted divorcee and one of the Internet's most infamous cultural critics—who attends undercover. (978-1-62639-793-4)

Cross Purposes by Gina L. Dartt. In pursuit of a lost Acadian treasure, three women must not only work out the clues, but also the complicated tangle of emotion and attraction developing between them. (978-1-62639-713-2)

Imperfect Truth by C.A. Popovich. Can an imperfect truth stand in the way of love? (978-1-62639-787-3)

Life in Death by M. Ullrich. Sometimes the devastating end is your only chance for a new beginning. (978-1-62639-773-6)

Love on Liberty by MJ Williamz. Hearts collide when politics clash. (978-1-62639-639-5)

Serious Potential by Maggie Cummings. Pro golfer Tracy Allen plans to forget her ex during a visit to Bay West, a lesbian condo community in NYC, but when she meets Dr. Jennifer Betsy, she gets more than she bargained for. (978-1-62639-633-3)

Taste by Kris Bryant. Accomplished chef Taryn has walked away from her promising career in the city's top restaurant to devote her life to her five-year-old daughter and is content until Ki Blake comes along. (978-1-62639-718-7)

The Second Wave by Jean Copeland. Can star-crossed lovers have a second chance after decades apart, or does the love of a lifetime only happen once? (978-1-62639-830-6)

Valley of Fire by Missouri Vaun. Taken captive in a desert outpost after their small aircraft is hijacked, Ava and her captivating passenger discover things about each other and themselves that will change them both forever. (978-1-62639-496-4)

Basic Training of the Heart by Jaycie Morrison. In 1944, socialite Elizabeth Carlton joins the Women's Army Corps to escape family expectations and love's disappointments. Can Sergeant Gale Rains get her through Basic Training with their hearts intact? (978-1-62639-818-4)

Before by KE Payne. When Tally falls in love with her band's new recruit, she has a tough decision to make. What does she want more— Alex or the band? (978-1-62639-677-7)

Believing in Blue by Maggie Morton. Growing up gay in a small town has been hard, but it can't compare to the next challenge Wren—with her new, sky-blue wings—faces: saving two entire worlds. (978-1-62639-691-3)

Coils by Barbara Ann Wright. A modern young woman follows her aunt into the Greek Underworld and makes a pact with Medusa to win her freedom by killing a hero of legend. (978-1-62639-598-5)

Courting the Countess by Jenny Frame. When relationship-phobic Lady Henrietta Knight starts to care about housekeeper Annie Brannigan and her daughter, can she overcome her fears and promise Annie the forever that she demands? (978-1-62639-785-9)

For Money or Love by Heather Blackmore. Jessica Spaulding must choose between ignoring the truth to keep everything she has, and doing the right thing only to lose it all—including the woman she loves. (978-1-62639-756-9)

Hooked by Jaime Maddox. With the help of sexy Detective Mac Calabrese, Dr. Jessica Benson is working hard to overcome her past, but it may not be enough to stop a murderer. (978-1-62639-689-0)

Lands End by Jackie D. Public relations superstar Amy Kline is dealing with a media nightmare, and the last thing she expects is for restaurateur Lena Michaels to change everything, but she will. (978-1-62639-739-2)

Lysistrata Cove by Dena Hankins. Jack and Eve navigate the maelstrom of their darkest desires and find love by transgressing gender, dominance, submission, and the law on the crystal blue Caribbean Sea. (978-1-62639-821-4)

Twisted Screams by Sheri Lewis Wohl. Reluctant psychic Lorna Dutton doesn't want to forgive, but if she doesn't do just that an innocent woman will die. (978-1-62639-647-0)